AWARDS AND ACCOLADES FOR THE
CRITICALLY ACCLAIMED AND BESTSELLING
PASSPORT TO PERIL MYSTERY SERIES

From Bad to Wurst

"Despite the chaos that continually surrounds Emily and
her irrepressible explorers, she remains a constant beacon
of intelligence, practicality, and amiability. The humor is
always spot-on and will surprise readers with its deft wit,
originality, and satire."

—Cynthia Chow, KingsRiverLife.com

Fleur de Lies

"Don't miss the ninth trip in this always entertaining
series."

—*Library Journal*

Bonnie of Evidence

"A delightfully deadly eighth Passport to Peril mystery."

—*Publishers Weekly*

Pasta Imperfect

AN INDEPENDENT MYSTERY BOOKSELLERS
ASSOCIATION BESTSELLER

A BOOKSENSE RECOMMENDED TITLE

"Murder, mayhem, and marinara make for a delightfully funny combination [in *Pasta Imperfect*]…Emily stumbles upon clues, jumps to hilarious conclusions at each turn, and eventually solves the mystery in a showdown with the killer that is as clever as it is funny."

—*Futures Mystery Anthology* Magazine

G'Day to Die

"The easygoing pace [of *G'Day to Die*] leads to a satisfying heroine-in-peril twist ending that should please those in search of a good cozy."

—*Publishers Weekly*

Norway to Hide

"*Norway to Hide* is a fast-paced, page-turning, highly entertaining mystery. Long live the Passport to Peril series!"

—OnceUponARomance.net

Say No Moor

A PASSPORT TO PERIL MYSTERY

maddy
HUNTER

MIDNIGHT INK
WOODBURY, MINNESOTA

FIRST EDITION
First Printing, 2018

Book layout and edit by Rebecca Zins
Cover design by Kevin R. Brown
Cover illustration by Anne Wertheim

Midnight Ink, an imprint of Llewellyn Worldwide Ltd.

Library of Congress Cataloging-in-Publication Data
Names: Hunter, Maddy, author.
Title: Say no moor / Maddy Hunter.
Description: First edition. | Midnight Ink : Woodbury, Minnesota, [2017] |
   Series: A Passport to Peril mystery ; #11
Identifiers: LCCN 2017035772 (print) | LCCN 2017048205 (ebook) | ISBN
   9780738750248 () | ISBN 9780738749617 (alk. paper)
Subjects: LCSH: Andrew, Emily (Fictitious character)—Fiction. | Tour guides
   (Persons)—Fiction. | Tourists—England—Fiction. |
   Murder—Investigation—Fiction. | GSAFD: Mystery fiction
Classification: LCC PS3608.U5944 (ebook) | LCC PS3608.U5944 S37 2017
   (print) | DDC 813/.6—dc23
LC record available at https://lccn.loc.gov/2017035772

This is a work of fiction. Names, characters, places, and incidents are either the product of the author's imagination or are used fictitiously, and any resemblance to actual persons living or dead, business establishments, events, or locales is entirely coincidental.

Midnight Ink
Llewellyn Worldwide Ltd.
2143 Wooddale Drive
Woodbury, MN 55125-2989
www.midnightinkbooks.com

Printed in the United States of America

In Memory of Mum
I miss you

ACKNOWLEDGMENTS

Thank you to friend and fellow author Sean Patrick Little for once again providing the title for the gang's newest adventure. I don't know how he does it, but I'm extremely grateful to be the beneficiary of his genius.

Thank you to Amy Glaser and Becky Zins at Midnight Ink, who bear the distinction of being the most delightful, professional, and encouraging editors I've ever had the good fortune to work with. Love you guys!

Thank you to my fiercely loyal fans who have welcomed Emily, Nana, and the rest of the gang into their families as if they were treasured relatives.

And thank you to my sweetie, Brian, who excels in what he likes to call the "care and feeding of authors." Keep the food coming!

I thank you all…from the bottom of my heart.

mmh

ONE

In that bygone era known as the twentieth century, newspapers hired battle-hardened journalists to write editorials that addressed the critical issues of the day. Cigar-smoking men with suspenders and slicked-back hair published scathing opinion pieces that railed against everything from child labor practices and political graft to Irish immigration and Prohibition.

The new millennium gave rise to the electronic revolution, where faltering print news was replaced by cyber news that can be delivered to a computer device faster than Wile E. Coyote can hit the ground after falling off a cliff. But even though the presses virtually stopped, opinions didn't, so anyone with internet access was afforded an opportunity to editorialize on any topic that he or she was itching to talk, whine, or wax eloquent about.

These posts were first known as Weblogs, which was later shortened to the more diminutive "blog." According to internet statistics, one hundred million bloggers now vie for our attention on a regular basis, voicing their opinions on subjects ranging from the authenticity of catfights on the *Housewives* TV franchise to the best fiction novels featuring a feline in a leading role. Imagine: one hundred million people clogging the telecommunications highway with a nonstop barrage of often inconsequential chitchat.

As a freak Atlantic storm turned the flower garden outside our B&B's window into a pool of mud, I was playing host to six bloggers who'd joined the ranks of our regulars for a tour of southwest England that would include Cornwall, Lyme Regis, Bath, Stonehenge, Chawton, and London. It should have been seven bloggers, but I had received a text from my agency's fill-in secretary that blogger number seven had been involved in a car accident on her way to the airport and would be spending her anticipated holiday in a Newark hospital with a broken pelvis.

Our bed-and-breakfast, dramatically dubbed the Stand and Deliver Inn, sat as isolated as a lost sheep atop a sweeping bluff on Cornwall's north coast—a centuries-old working farm that had been converted into upscale lodgings for the tourist trade. The original farmhouse was a long, rambling one-story dwelling constructed of stone that was whitewashed to igloo brilliance. A half-acre of thatched roof covered the house's many angles and ells, and planters bleeding with summer flowers hugged every window ledge. The interior, dripping with cozy charm and country florals, could have graced the cover of *House Beautiful*, its extensive floor space having been reconfigured into guest suites that bore names as colorful as Cornwall itself: Sixteen String Jack suite, Quick Nick suite, Galloping Dick suite, Blueskin Blake suite.

I'm Emily Andrew-Miceli. With my former Swiss police inspector husband, Etienne, I own and operate Destinations Travel out of Windsor City, Iowa—an agency that caters to intrepid seniors who'd rather be in Paris, taking selfies at the top of the Eiffel Tower, than at home, playing bridge at the senior center that my grandmother helped pay to refurbish. A core group of a dozen hometown regulars keeps our agency in the black. On occasion they even get along with each other in a relationship that I've come to think of as affectionate anarchy. As a bonus for myself, I join the group in an official capacity as chaperone/escort, though on many excursions I've also had to don another hat: reluctant sleuth.

One of the downsides of our international tours has been my discovery of an occasional dead body at some of the major sites we've visited. Unfortunately, most of the victims were members of our tour group, which hasn't enhanced my reputation as an escort among my regulars, but I have high hopes that this trip will be different. And when I say different, I mean corpse-free.

Etienne often accompanies me abroad, but for this trip he's making a side trip to Rome before he meets up with us in Lyme Regis on day six of the tour. Pulling a few strings among the elite in her order of Catholic nuns, his aunt on the Italian side of the family, Sister Mary Giovanna, arranged for all the Miceli men to attend a religious retreat at the Vatican, where they would be enlightened by words of wisdom from none other than Pope Francis himself. It didn't matter that the retreat would interfere with Etienne's travel plans. When Sister Giovanna told the men in the family they were going to do something, they fell in line without daring to voice a complaint.

I was sorry not to have him along on the first leg of our journey, but I could understand his decision not to bump heads with Giovanna. I'd been taught by nuns in school and understood the power wielded by one small woman who wore a crucifix the size of a bludgeon hanging from the belt of her religious habit.

The one thing that bothered me about Etienne's retreat was that he wouldn't be allowed to use any type of electronic device for the duration. No cell phone. No iPad. No laptop. Nothing that would interfere with his temporary spiritual immersion. So if I ran into a problem and needed his advice, I was on my own.

The walls of the Stand and Deliver Inn shook with a thunderous boom as a wave geysered above the two-hundred-foot cliff outside the inn and pounded down on the newly thatched roof, eliciting terrified gasps from the guests who were gawking out the bank of dining room windows.

"The roof's caving in!" cried Helen Teig, tenting her hands above her head to deflect anticipated debris away from her eyebrows. She'd penciled them on with Joan Crawford perfection today, their symmetry a thing of beauty, so I understood why she was being a little overprotective. They hadn't looked this good since her real ones had blown off in the exploding grill incident a couple of decades ago.

"That's codswallop," assured our proprietor as he shooed imaginary dust motes away from the pink-and-white striped dessert plates and matching mugs that he'd arranged on the massively long dining room table. He was a short, square, cuddly Brit named Enyon Gladwish who ran the inn with his partner, Lance, a world-class chef who'd been holed up in the kitchen since our arrival.

"This house has occupied the same spot, undisturbed, for three hundred years," Enyon informed Helen. "What does that tell you?"

"That it's a disaster waiting to happen," Bernice Zwerg shot back. Bernice was a three-pack-a-day ex-smoker whose voice was only slightly less strident than the sound of steel wool being run through a meat grinder.

Enyon sucked in his breath and clapped a hand over his mouth to hide a giggle. "Shame on you for even *thinking* that," he scolded Bernice. "This is what I love about you Yanks. Your senses of humor are so blinding."

"Bernice's sense of humor isn't blinding," corrected Dick Teig. "It's nonexistent."

"Moron," sneered Bernice.

Another wave broke over the house with a roar like a thunder-clap. Windows rattled. Flatware clattered. The floor rumbled beneath my feet, vibrating all the way to my back teeth. Guests reached out for handholds on the windowsills and each other. "Are all your coastal storms this violent?" I asked as a blast of sea spume and brine splattered the outside windows.

"Violent?" Enyon laughed. "This is nothing, luvvie. A mere shower. You should be here when El Niño factors into the mix."

It's moments like this that make me appreciate the fact that Iowa is landlocked.

"Do you mind my asking when we might be able to check in to our rooms?" asked Margi Swanson. Margi was a part-time nurse at the Windsor City Clinic and a full-time activist for instituting a law that would require dispensers of sanitizing gel to be placed inside every building in Iowa, including hog barns, chicken coops, and dog houses.

Enyon's smile froze on his apple-cheeked face. "Did I mention that Lance will be out at any moment with tea, fresh scones, home-made strawberry preserves, and our famous clotted cream? You'll feel much better about your miserably long ride from Heathrow today when you have something in your tummies."

"So we can check in after we eat?" asked Margi.

Enyon bobbed his head, his voice suddenly cracking. "Uhhh…"

Dick Stolee swung his attention away from the scene outside the window to cast a look at him. At a lean six feet tall, Dick Stolee had been playing Mutt to Dick Teig's roly-poly Jeff ever since their grade school days, when getting into mischief had been their main pursuit. Sadly, in the intervening years, the two friends had simply become older versions of the rascals they'd been in kindergarten— and in Dick Stolee's case, significantly taller. "How come we can't check in to our rooms now?"

"Because he's afraid the roof's gonna cave in," said Bernice.

"I'm adopting a cautionary stance at the moment," Enyon explained, his gaze drifting to the low ceiling with its exposed beams. "As I mentioned when you arrived, the new roof is untested in foul weather, so even though this squall is piffling by Cornish standards, should any problems arise, I'd rather have all our guests gathered in one place than scattered about the premises."

"Right," Bernice deadpanned. "It'll be easier for the rescue squad to recover our crushed bodies if we're all heaped in one place."

The kitchen door swung open and a burly hulk of a man in a black chef's jacket emerged rolling a three-tiered food trolley laden with porcelain teapots, trays of pastry, and bowls of what I suspected were the aforementioned jam and clotted cream.

Enyon hailed his appearance with loud clapping and a sigh of relief. "Afternoon tea is served. Don't be shy, my pets. Eat up." He flounced around the dining room, herding us toward the table before he ventured into the adjoining lounge to separate the bloggers from their laptops and earbuds. By the time Enyon had corralled everyone in one area, Lance had poured several mugs of tea and was busily placing fresh-baked scones onto dessert plates in assembly-line fashion.

I eyed Enyon's partner surreptitiously as I plucked silverware off the table, noting that he was seriously intimidating with his shaved head, bulging beefcake muscles, hooked nose, dark eyes, and jagged scar slashed across his cheek. He might have been a chef, but he looked more like a villain in a Disney flick.

"Yo," he boomed without preamble. "This is the dwill for the clotted cweam and jam. Jam first, then cweam. In Devon they do cweam first. But we're not in Devon, so youse do it like I tell youse. Understand?"

The lisp was unexpected, but not half as unexpected as the New Jersey accent.

"I'm only saying this once, so listen up." He'd divided the dessert plates into four groups, and as he spoke he gestured toward each group. "Moving fwom left to wight, we got youse scones with dwied cherwies…with dwied cwanberwies…with bittersweet chocolate…and with gwated citwus zest. Cwispy on the outside, flaky on the inside. Any questions?"

We gulped quietly as we lent him our undivided attention.

"Good. I hate answering questions. Especially iwwitating questions." He ranged a look around the table with his feral eyes. "Amerwican tourwists always ask iwwitating questions. So whaddda youse waiting for? Eat!"

I stepped back as the group snatched whatever plate was in front of them, slopped clotted cream and jam onto their dishes, grabbed mugs and silverware, and raced into the safety of the lounge. "Don't spill nothin'! We just had the upholstery cleaned!"

"Don't let him frighten you," Enyon begged the fleeing masses. "He's just an overgrown pussycat. All mouth and no trousers."

Right. A pussycat who looked as if he'd rip your lungs out through your nostrils if you gave him any lip.

As I waited my turn, I glanced around the dining room, taking note of the spit-polished hardwood floor, the gleaming shine on the spindle-legged sideboard, the floral bouquets sprouting from porcelain vases, the lacy antique picture frames on the wall. A grouping of three hung above the sideboard, and from what I could see, one showed Enyon and Lance toasting each other in front of a wedding cake; one showed a school-age Enyon in a Little Lord Fauntleroy outfit with a man and woman who were probably his parents; and the last one showed a matriarchal-looking woman surrounded by people who bore a strong resemblance to Lance—beefy, bald-headed types with sneers for smiles and names, I suspected, like Frankie Two Fingers and Sammy the Snitch.

"Honestly, Lance," I heard Enyon chide under his breath. "This is *not* your best effort. You can be *such* a knob."

I froze as Lance riveted his gaze on me. "Youse got a pwoblem?" he growled when he caught me staring.

I flashed my most dazzling smile. "You're not from around here, are you?"

"Who wants to know?"

Enyon thwacked him in the chest. "I'm so surprised you can detect his accent, Mrs. Miceli. We've worked so hard to soften his vowels and tone down his consonants."

"Ya," Lance agreed. "Eny said my accent was pwactically gone." His heavy brows collided in a V over his nose as he stared down at his companion. "Was youse lyin' to me?"

Enyon rolled his eyes. "Oh, do stop letting your drama queen tendencies rule your life. Lance hails from Jersey City, Mrs. Miceli, and in case you're wondering, we met at cooking school."

"The Fwench Culinawy Institute. The goombas who run the place changed the name, but that's what it was called when we was there."

"So you're a chef too?" I asked Enyon.

Lance snorted. "*I'm* the chef." He thumped his fist against his chest, gorilla-like. "Eny decided he'd pwefer to awwange flowers and decowate wooms."

Margi crept toward us with her dish extended like a collection plate. "May I have more jam, please…and clotted cream?"

Lance stared at her half-eaten scone. "WHAT HAVE YOUSE DONE?" Storming toward her, he snatched the plate from her hand. "Sacwilege! This is going wight into the wubbish."

Margi swallowed slowly, her eyes growing round and terrified. "But—"

"Jam first, then cweam," he bellowed. "Can't youse follow instwuctions? Look at my scone. You've wecked it!"

Enyon hurried to Margi's side and wrapped an arm around her shoulders to offer support. "There, there. You'll be happy to know that we allow do-overs at the Stand and Deliver Inn." He exchanged an irritated look with Lance. "Don't we, Lance?"

"No!" Lance's nostrils flared like oversized tailpipes as he glanced toward the lounge that opened directly onto the dining room in open-concept style. "The west of them are eating it wong, too, aren't they? That's it. Game over. I'm not making any more scones if youse goombas are gonna eat them all wong."

"He doesn't mean that," countered Enyon in an apologetic tone.

"Yes I do," snarled Lance as he stormed into the lounge. He snatched Osmond Chelsvig's unprotected plate off his lap, then bare-handed the remains of Alice Tjarks's scone onto Osmond's plate.

"But…but I wasn't finished eating that yet," complained ninety-something-year-old Osmond.

"Yes youse were," announced Lance as he put a bead on George Farkas, who, as Lance approached, shoved the remaining portion of his pastry into his mouth and smiled defiantly, his cheeks bulging like overinflated balloons.

"You'll be sorwy youse did that," warned Lance, poking an angry finger at George's nose.

Without warning, George began spewing pastry flakes like Sylvester spewing Tweetie bird feathers. His face turned slightly purple.

"Is George still breathing?" I called out in alarm. "Somebody pound him on the back. Right now!"

"Enough, Lance!" Enyon clapped his hands to restore order. "Private meeting in the kitchen *straightaway*."

Lance swooped Lucille Rasmussen's scone off her plate and onto his growing stack, then strode toward Bernice, who raised her fork as if it were a Bowie knife. "Back off, cupcake," she threatened, "unless you'd like to participate in my free body-piercing clinic."

"Lance!" Enyon persisted.

"All wight!" he roared before stalking back toward the dining room and catching his toe on a scatter rug that sent him skating wildly off-balance. "I told youse to get wid of these damn wugs," he shouted when he'd righted himself.

"And I told you to pick up your feet. You have no qualms about lifting your silly barbells. Why is lifting your feet such a problem?"

"The wugs are a nuisance."

"The rugs are the decorative accent that tie the entire color scheme together. Carry on, my pets," Enyon called back to us as he pushed Lance into the kitchen. "We shan't be long."

The door closed.

The shouting began.

I shot a nervous glance at Margi; she shot a nervous glance back. With a nod from me we tiptoed into the lounge as the shouting in the kitchen increased in volume. "I got ear plugs," offered my grandmother, whose name was Marion Sippel. "But they might not do no good in this situation. What them two fellas need is good soundproofin' material."

Despite Nana's eighth-grade education and regular use of split infinitives and double negatives, she was the smartest and most resourceful person I knew. Not to mention the richest, thanks to a winning lottery ticket. She and George Farkas has been sweet on each other for years but they'd yet to do anything about it, not because they were skeptical about the longevity of a mixed-faith marriage, but because if the announcement appeared in the newspaper, my mom would probably find out.

Nana and Mom had a kind of complicated relationship.

I winced as a volley of colorful epithets floated out from the kitchen, punctuated by the sound of dishware crashing to the floor.

Tilly Hovick raised her walking stick. "According to our itinerary, we're due to eat dinner here tonight. Is that correct?" Tilly was a retired Iowa State anthropology professor whose IQ was probably higher than the combined ages of all our tour guests.

"Yup," I said with more confidence than I felt. "Dinner here tonight."

Another item of dishware crashed and shattered.

"Save your plates, everyone," wisecracked Dick Stolee. "At the rate the china is shattering, we might need 'em later."

"So is this a bed-and-breakfast or an inn?" asked Tilly. "A B&B doesn't normally serve dinner, does it?"

I forced a tentative smile. "I think it's a hybrid. A bed-and-breakfast that also includes dinner. So, would this be a good time to conduct our meet and greet?"

"We're missin' some folks," Nana spoke up.

Which reminded me. "By the way, I haven't had a chance to mention this yet, but I received word from the office a short time ago that Marianne Malec, our garden blogger, won't be joining us at all. She was involved in an auto accident on the way to Newark Airport and broke her pelvis."

"Smart," said Bernice. "She probably looked up the guest reviews on this place and decided a holiday in a Newark city hospital ward would be more relaxing." She cringed as another dish shattered. "Wish I'd thought of it."

"I couldn't find *any* reviews online," puzzled Grace Stolee. "I thought that was a little odd, but I figured Emily and Etienne knew what they were doing. I'm sure I searched the right name."

"I didn't find any reviews either," I admitted, "but their website stood head and shoulders above the rest. There's a music video of the surf crashing against the rocks at the bottom of the cliff. And photos of the newly refurbished suites. And sample breakfast and dinner menus. And a detailed map. Plus, they have the best location of any bed-and-breakfast in the area. They're centrally located to all the good attractions."

"And they have their very own food nazi," sniped Bernice. "Lucky us."

I inhaled a deep breath. "We've probably just caught the guys on a bad day."

The antique picture frames on the dining room wall tilted precariously as another round of dishes exploded against the shared kitchen wall. A nervous hush fell over the room.

"I'm thinkin' paper plates might be on tap for supper," warned Nana.

"Show of hands," announced Osmond, Windsor City's longest serving election official and self-appointed opinion pollster. "How many people think we'll be—"

"Is every person in this room deaf?" cried a latecomer who dashed breathlessly into our midst. "I've spent the last ten minutes *pounding* on the powder room door for someone to let me out." The woman threw her hand toward the interior corridor that housed the Stand and Deliver office, the public loo, and the guest suites. "The door must have swelled because it was stuck tight. Do you have any idea of the trauma a mildly claustrophobic person can suffer from being trapped in a two-piece washroom the size of a gym locker?"

She was stunningly gorgeous, with a flawless complexion, glossy hair, and hourglass figure. Tall as an NBA point guard but infinitely more stylish, she was clothed in black from her sunglasses to her off-the-shoulder tunic to her leggings to her designer boots. Black was the color theme she had chosen for the tour because, sadly, she was in mourning.

Her married name was Jackie Thum and she was a frequent guest on our trips, but in the years before her life-altering gender reassignment surgery and elopement with a high-end hair stylist, she'd been an off-Broadway stage actor named Jack Potter—and I'd been married to him.

TWO

"How come you didn't text no one to come let you out?" asked Nana.

She could have texted any one of the gang because their addiction to their smartphones was so extreme, they were prime candidates for the kind of rehab recommended on A&E's *Intervention* series.

Jackie whipped her oversized celebrity sunglasses off their perch on her head and stuck the bow in her mouth, nibbling the tip. "I didn't think of texting. Obviously I was too traumatized to think clearly." She sighed with exasperation. "Not one of you heard me pounding?"

Heads shook. Shoulders shrugged. Palms lifted skyward.

"Guess we know which room them fellas decided to sound-proof," observed Nana. "That's a real thoughtful touch. 'Specially if the toilet makes a real racket when it flushes."

"You couldn't have been pounding very loudly," challenged one of our male bloggers, "or else I would have heard. I have perfect hearing."

Ignoring the blogger, Jackie fisted her hand on her shapely hip and arched a meticulously waxed eyebrow at Nana. "Well, the *fellas* need to be informed of their malfunctioning door immediately, before someone with fewer coping skills and higher blood pressure gets locked inside. Where are they?"

A chorus of angry male voices rose from the confines of the kitchen, followed by a succession of *BOOMS! Chinks!* And *tinkles.*

"Oh." She snorted daintily as she glanced in that direction, pausing to reassess. "I suppose I can afford to wait until they exhaust their supply of whatever it is they're breaking. Are those scones? And clotted cream and jam?"

"Eat at your own risk," Margi Swanson cautioned her.

"Or all in one bite," advised George Farkas as he dusted pastry flakes off his shirt.

I pulled a face at Jackie. "Could you hold off on the food until we do a quick meet and greet?"

Jackie pursed her highly glossed lips and heaved a long-suffering sigh. "I suppose." When Nana indicated an available space beside her, she flipped her hair over her shoulders and strutted to the loveseat, lowering herself onto the cushion. "Has anyone noticed that I'm dressed completely in black?"

"Nope," said Dick Teig.

"So"—I settled into an occasional chair near the raised hearth and ranged a look around the room—"welcome, one and all, to Destination Travel's Cornish holiday. And a special welcome to our bloggers, who'll be sending out daily reports of our travel adventure to social media forums around the world."

"Who thought of that idea?" asked Alice Tjarks.

"Actually, I did," I said proudly. "It seemed a great way to promote our—"

"Are the bloggers offering you all this free advertising for nothing?" asked Dick Teig.

"We're not that stupid," snorted the man who boasted perfect hearing—a wiry Gen Xer whose thick lips and bulging eyes took up most of his face. Were he the glitterati type, I'd guess he was the victim of cosmetic surgery gone wrong. But he was Spencer Blunt from Pringle Town, South Dakota, population 112, so I suspected his facial peculiarities were genetic hand-me-downs rather than surgical mistakes. "We're getting a huge discount for our efforts. Heck, I couldn't afford *not* to come, even if it means hanging out with duffers twice my age for a couple of weeks."

Frowns. Confused stares. Harrumphs.

Bernice fired a peevish look at me. "How come you didn't offer discounts to the rest of us?"

"Because you're not bloggers."

"Depending on the size of the discount, we could learn to be," said Dick Stolee.

"I don't think so."

"Are any of you familiar with my blog?" Spencer asked the room at large. "It's called Spencer Blunt's Ten-Dollar-a-Day Traveler. I have over a hundred thousand followers."

"Spencer has agreed to blog about the financial issues involved in travel," I explained. "He's going to let his followers know if we're getting the biggest bang for our buck."

"Of course *he* can afford to blog about financial issues," groused Bernice. "*He's* getting a discount."

Oh, God.

I forged ahead. "Articles referencing where amateur genealogical enthusiasts might locate bits of family history in the towns we'll be visiting will be posted by Caroline Goodfriend on her blog, Yours, Mine, Ours, and Theirs. Where are you hiding, Caroline?"

"Over here." She offered a friendly wave from a floral armchair in the corner.

Caroline Goodfriend seemed an island of calm amid our often riotous clientele, boasting a serene disposition, cheerful attitude, and a default setting that began and ended with a smile. Midforties, with short, frosted blond hair, she was a genealogist by trade, which made me wonder if her pleasant nature was due in part to the satisfaction she derived from spending so many years helping people connect the dots to generations of relatives they never knew.

Caroline sat up straighter in her chair. "Could I take a moment to recognize Emily? I've always wanted to travel, even though I have a terrible fear of flying. To come on this trip I actually had to get a prescription for what I've dubbed my 'fear of flying' pill. But maybe it's good that I've been afraid to board a plane because I've never been able to afford it—until now. So thank you for offering your wonderful discount, Emily. I'm thrilled at the opportunity to join all of you, and I promise that my blogs won't disappoint."

"How wonderful a discount was it?" pressed Dick Stolee.

"Fifty percent off the final cost," said Caroline.

"Yeah," interrupted Spencer. "We're probably paying a pittance of what the rest of you are paying."

Yup. That was helpful.

Twelve pairs of unblinking eyes bore into me, demanding an explanation. "In the world of business one must invest money to make money," I defended gently. "The agency probably won't make any money on this trip, but we're hoping that our advertising investment with the bloggers will allow us to make more money in the future. Does that make sense?"

Thoughtful stares. Twitching lips.

"So if you're satisfied that nothing underhanded is going on, could I introduce our next blogger?"

Jackie perked up on the loveseat, letting out the kind of long, agonized sigh that typically signaled how antsy she was getting with the lack of attention she was receiving. "Osmond?" She fluttered her hand. "Would you like to conduct a poll to see how many people have given a fleeting thought as to why I'm dressed in black?"

"Nope," said Osmond.

I flashed her "the look," which caused her to tuck in her lips and flump back into the cushions. "Okay, then," I continued. "Mr. August Lugar is the guest who'll be blogging about our anticipated love affair with British cuisine, and perhaps with his assistance we'll be able to master the art of applying jam and clotted cream to our scones in proper English fashion. His blog is called Knife and Fork, Will Travel."

As I gestured to him by way of introduction, he smiled thinly and bowed his head with a curt nod. He was dead-center of average looking with pale lashless eyes, a complexion that begged for more direct sunlight, ginger-colored hair that was shot through with a premature streak of white, and a chin that was split with a deep Dudley Do-Right cleft. His most noteworthy feature was his Ivy

League clothing, which would be way too preppy for the Windsor City set, but he looked as comfortable in his navy blazer and khakis as Nana was in her pantyhose without the tummy control.

"Would you care to take the floor to impart any words of epicurean wisdom?" I inquired good-naturedly.

"No." He aimed a finger toward the dining area. "If you'll excuse me, I'd like to sample another scone while the coast is clear." Boosting himself to his feet, he made an abrupt departure that felt a little like a snub, but I didn't take offense. He was probably a dyed-in-the-wool introvert who needed a little breathing space away from the crowd to recharge his social batteries.

"I'd like to say a few words." A young man with a scarf draped around his neck popped out of his chair. His hairline was already starting to recede, so he combatted the inevitable by slathering his hair with a vibrantly tinted gel that caused it to stand straight on end like a bed of nails for his skull. "I'll spare Emily the job of introducing me. I'm blogger number four, Mason Chatsworth, and my specialty is hotels and lodging. I've critiqued the best and worst places to stay in the United States, and this trip marks my debut into the European market, so if I look excited to you, it's no illusion. I am. My blog is called Standard Suite, Please, and I just reached eighty thousand followers."

"What do you think of this place so far?" Grace Stolee threw out, a sour note in her voice.

"I'll withhold my opinion until I see our accommodations, but I give the place high marks for interior design and ambiance. Even the storm adds to the atmosphere. It must have cost someone a small fortune to give this place such a posh facelift."

"The hall bathroom still needs work," sniffed Jackie.

Margi stared at him with curiosity. "Why is your hair green?"

"This?" He laughed as he smoothed his hand across the spiked ends. "I'm a millennial. We like to change things up on a regular basis to avoid boredom. And I ask you, isn't green hair a lot less boring than dull brown?"

"My wife had green eyebrows a couple of times," recounted Dick Teig.

Helen crossed her arms over her chest and scowled. "Someone in the cosmetic industry decided that my stubby black eyebrow pencil should look and feel exactly like my green eye shadow crayon. That's fine…until you lose your lights in an electrical storm."

Dick nodded. "No goof-ups since she switched to a more foolproof product. Pressed powder eye shadow has taken all the anxiety out of power outages."

"All right," bawled Jackie. "I know it's killing you, so I won't keep you in suspense any longer. I caught my husband *in flagrante delicto* with a model he hired for a hairstyling event. So I'm divorcing the miserable, no good, two-timing, cradle-robbing cheat." She blinked away tears as she fanned air toward her face. "There. No need to thank me. I knew you were just being polite with your seeming lack of interest."

"What's *fluh-gran-tee di-lik-toh*?" asked Nana.

"I think it's a department store in Canada," said Margi.

Tilly cleared her throat. "*In flagrante delicto* is a term used to describe a situation in which a person is caught in the act of committing an egregious deed. In other words, the person is caught red-handed."

Margi gasped. "So you caught your husband in the act of shopping with another woman?"

"I caught them in bed together," cried Jackie.

Alice looked aghast. "In the department store?"

"There must have been a mattress sale," said Margi.

"Helen and me could use a new mattress," said Dick Teig. "Can you remember what kind of discounts they were offering? 'Course, it might not be worth our while if we have to drive all the way to Canada."

"I caught them in my own house," Jackie wailed. "In my own bed!"

"I'm sorry to hear that, dear," lamented Nana. "That husband of yours seemed like such a nice fella when the two of you was travelin' in Ireland with us. He gave me the most glamorous haircut of my life the night we didn't have no lights. Called it a choppy cut."

He'd given her the worst haircut of her life. She'd ended up looking like a rabbit who'd barely survived a near-death encounter with a weed whacker.

"That was then," Jackie whimpered. "This is now." She swept her hand the length of her body to indicate her attire, her bottom lip quivering. "This is my homage to the death of my marriage. The woman you see before you is a mere shadow of the person she once was—her spirit broken, her iconic sense of style replaced by funereal dullness. You'll never see her wear hot pink or spandex or miniskirts ever again."

Dick Teig's eyes lit up. "Uhh…you remember that corset thingie you wore in Italy? It was like a strapless gown, only without the skirt, and it hiked your software halfway up to your chin?"

Jackie clasped her hands and bowed her head in a prayerful gesture. "My bustier. I loved my bustier."

"Well, if you're getting rid of it, would you throw it Helen's way? She's been on my case about doing something to add a little zing to our—"

Helen's forearm thwacked him in the gut like a metal turnstile.

"Eww." Bernice made a gagging sound. "Would you give us some warning before you decide to creep us out with any more Teig family fantasies? As if the thought of Helen squeezing herself into a bustier isn't disturbing enough."

"In Regency England, a woman referred to her mourning garb as widow's weeds," an officious-sounding female voice informed us.

Heads turned left and right searching out the voice's owner.

"Thank you for that tidbit, Mrs. Crabbe," I said, nodding to the handsome woman with the glorious cap of silver hair who'd commandeered the best seat in the house: the armchair with the ottoman, reading lamp, and candy dish brimming with expensive truffles wrapped in gold cellophane. She was tall and heavy-boned, with broad hips and hockey player thighs, more Clydesdale than racehorse, but she sat in her chair with regal calm, chin elevated and spine straight, like a queen sitting on her throne.

"If we can put aside bustiers and mattress sales for a moment, I'd like to introduce Kathryn Crabbe, who plans to focus her blog on the literary significance of the places we'll be visiting. Kathryn is a Jane Austen aficionado, popularly known as a Janeite, so with our itinerary including a visit to Austen's ancestral home in Chawton, I thought it would be a great idea to have Kathryn serve as our literary guide at some of the actual sites that Austen describes in her books, like the seawall in Lyme Regis and the assembly rooms in Bath."

"Who's Jane Austen?" asked Dick Teig.

Snickers. Snorts. Chuckling.

"Jane Austen happens to be one of the foremost English novelists of the eighteenth and early nineteenth century," Tilly said, aghast. "Surely you've heard of her novels. *Pride and Prejudice? Sense and Sensibility? Persuasion? Emma?*"

Dick crooked his mouth to the side. "They sound like girlie books."

"She wrote about the mannered class," Tilly continued. "Six novels of romantic fiction that are literary classics."

Dick wrinkled his nose. "Girlie books. I don't read girlie books."

"He doesn't read any books," corrected Helen.

"For those of you who haven't lived your entire lives under a rock," Kathryn Crabbe commented with obvious snark, "my blog is entitled Pride, Prejudice, and Beyond, and in it I discuss all things Austen-related. I write it under my nom de plume, Penelope Pemberley."

"Oh my God! *You're* Penelope Pemberley?" The last of our blogger fill-ins leaped to her feet with excitement. She was a twenty-eight-year-old computer expert with a mane of long, spiral-curled blond hair and a rhinestone-studded eyebrow ring. "I've been reading your blog for, like, forever! It's because of you that I discovered the magic of Jane Austen and became a Janeite. You…you changed my whole life. You have to read her blog," she entreated the rest of the room. "It's so inspiring. She draws you into a world where civility is the rule of the day and proper manners are valued more than…than winning the Powerball jackpot!"

"Folks were playing Powerball way back then?" Margi furrowed her brow. "How do you suppose they got those little balls to pop up in the drawing machines before they had electricity?"

"I'm honored beyond words to meet you in person, Mrs. Crabbe," the young woman gushed. "I'm Heather Holloway, last of the six bloggers, and, like you, a Jane Austen devotee." She clasped her hands together and extended them toward Kathryn with unfettered delight. "But to be honest, meeting you is even more exciting than meeting Jane Austen herself. Can you imagine how thrilled I am to be face-to-face with my idol?"

"You're much too kind," Kathryn demurred, seeming rather accustomed to the hero worship.

"I've died and gone to heaven," Heather enthused. "Wait 'til my readership checks out my blog tomorrow. They won't believe it. I'm traveling through Cornwall with *the* Penelope Pemberley."

"For those of you who are interested," I added, "Heather writes an unusual but progressive blog using the pseudonym Austen Zombie Girl, so I'm hoping that between her input and Kathryn's, you'll get a great impression of what Regency England might have looked like and how specific historic sites might have changed drastically or not changed at all."

Kathryn gasped. "Austen Zombie Girl? *You're* Austen Zombie Girl?"

"Omigod." Heather cupped her hands over her mouth in disbelief. "Have you read my blog?"

"Once." Kathryn elevated her chin to an imperious angle. "And once was quite enough."

"Oh." Heather's burst of excitement popped like a too-big bubble. Her voice grew very small. "You didn't like it?"

"No, I didn't like it. No one with an ounce of good taste could ever like the tripe you circulate on the internet and misrepresent as a blog," Kathryn accused. "The word *bilge* is a more accurate description."

Heather stood motionless, seeming to shrink before our eyes. "Well." Her bottom lip quivered as she processed the insult. "That was unexpected."

"Surely I'm not the first person to tell you how appalling your entries are."

"Actually…you are." Heather hardened her jaw and narrowed her eyes. "I have over ten thousand followers who hang on my every word."

"Of course you do. We're witnessing the collapse of western civilization and people like you are in the vanguard, encouraging the disintegration of our literary classics by taking advantage of their public domain status and reworking the stories to include atrocities like…invading armies of otherworldly creatures."

"They're fresh storylines for contemporary readers," Heather said matter-of-factly. "All that literature stuff doesn't play to millennials, but the mashups do. So I'm not going to apologize for including Austenesque pop culture in my opinions and reviews, even though my doing so makes some intolerant members of our society want to light their hair on fire." She arched her brows at Kathryn. "I don't want to be rude, so I won't name names."

"Have you ever bothered to *read* a Jane Austen novel?" Kathryn challenged.

"You mean one of the books Austen actually wrote herself?" Heather lifted a shoulder in a casual shrug. "I tried once, but the style didn't grab me. It was so old-fashioned. Long passages of prose that went nowhere. Vocabulary no one uses anymore. Endless scenes with characters attending balls. But I've read all the mashups: *Emma Versus the Undead. Emma and the Frankenstein Monster. Northanger Abbey and Werewolves. Mansfield Park and Zombies.* And I adore the movies. The language doesn't seem so stilted with actors reciting the dialogue."

"The movies destroy the very soul of Austen and turn her literary masterpieces into romantic drivel," taunted Kathryn. "And as for your taste in novels, you freely admit to having read every modern bastardization of truly great literature. How do you manage to hold your head up at book club meetings? You should be ashamed of yourself."

Heather regarded her, deadpan. "So what's your point?"

"My point is that the Jane Austen Society should revoke your membership immediately. Never call yourself a Janeite in my presence. You're a disgrace—not only to Janeites specifically, but to the blogosphere in general. I wouldn't be surprised if you decided to skip the tour of the elegant assembly rooms in Bath in favor of a zombie pub crawl."

Groaning with impatience, Jackie raised her hands in a gesture of surrender. "When the two of you have finished hogging the spotlight, could we go back to me and my impending divorce again? All those in favor, say—"

"Listen!" ordered Tilly, thumping her walking stick on the floor for quiet. She shushed the room with a finger to her lips. "Do you hear that?"

We listened intently for several seconds before Nana stated the obvious. "I don't hear nuthin'."

"Exactly," said Tilly. "The civil war in the kitchen seems to be over." And as if to press home the point, we heard a muffled clatter that brought to mind images of broken dishware being dumped into rubbish bins.

Enyon swept into the dining room as if he were floating on air, showing no ill effects from the battle that had been raging in the kitchen. "Good news, my pets." He paused to realign the picture frames on the wall before proceeding into the lounge. "Your coach has just pulled into the car park, so you can look forward to being reunited with your luggage shortly."

Our coach had experienced a major windshield wiper problem on our trip from Heathrow, so our longtime tour director, Wally Peppers, had opted to accompany our driver to the local garage to have repairs done immediately rather than off-load the luggage in a torrential downpour. It seems he made a good choice because, from what I could tell, the rain had practically stopped.

"I'll escort you to your suites once your luggage has been delivered," Enyon continued, "and then at promptly seven o'clock this evening we'll serve the first of several exquisite meals in the dining room."

A frisson of unease drifted through the lounge.

"This evening's fare will include a starter of Cornish wild garlic yarg, wrapped in nettle and served bruschetta-style, and for our entrée, Lance's famous stargazy pie. I hope you'll appreciate our efforts to feed you sooner rather than later. I know you Yanks enjoy eating your meals ridiculously early."

"We're having pie as a main course?" trilled Margi, her eyes lighting up.

"I've got a question," asked Dick Stolee. "Can we eat this pie the way we want? Or are there gonna be rules?"

"Oh, my goodness." Enyon fanned his face as if to ward off the vapors. "You're referring to Lance's rather unnatural obsession with clotted cream and jam. No, no. No more rules. And I can assure you he won't start another argy-bargy for the remainder of your stay. You might have noticed that he's a bit shirty, but I've got that all sorted. So"—he folded his hands over his rounded tummy and beamed at us—"look at all you happy people."

"Someone looks happy?" Bernice affected surprise as she glanced around the room. "Who?"

Enyon threw his head back with laughter. "My dear woman, your sense of comic timing is flawless. I should arrange to keep you here after your tour group leaves so you can provide entertainment for future guests."

"All those in favor, say aye," whooped Osmond.

The room exploded with enthusiastic ayes.

"Opposed?"

Silence.

Bernice corkscrewed her mouth into a menacing sneer. "Morons."

Enyon pattered around the room, urging people to their feet. "So, while you're waiting for your luggage to be carried in, why don't you help yourselves to more scones? I've confined Lance to the kitchen to finish up dinner preparations, so it won't matter *how* you eat the things because he won't see you. It'll be our little secret. Up-up!"

As he herded guests toward the dining room for a second helping, I slipped into the foyer to meet Wally at the front door. Enyon might be worried about the roof caving in, but Wally and I had a much bigger problem on our hands.

We'd arranged for Kathryn Crabbe and Heather Holloway to be roommates.

THREE

"TRUST ME." I scurried behind Wally as he rolled Kathryn Crabbe's spinner down the long hallway, my fist secured around my copy of the inn's floor plan and our roommate assignments. "It's not going to work out. She needs another roommate."

Wally stopped outside the Sixteen String Jack suite and spun the suitcase against the wall. "So what's our plan?"

"I'll let Kathryn have the double room all to herself at no extra charge, and then I'll move Heather in with Caroline Goodfriend, who was originally paired with our no-show, Marianne Malec. Heather and Caroline should be fine together, and Kathryn might be better off by herself."

"You're the boss."

I consulted my paper. "So Heather's and Caroline's luggage should be delivered to the Galloping Dick suite down the hall."

"Old Galloping Dick Ferguson." Wally laughed. "I've gotta hand it to the owners, naming the suites after infamous highwaymen was sheer genius. Certainly adds an element of intrigue to the whole operation. And with the inn being so close to Bodmin Moor, you have to wonder if any of these legendary thieves ever walked these very halls in their jackboots and tricorne hats."

"The inn website says this place was a working farm for a few centuries, so I doubt it had any appeal for the criminal element."

"You didn't dig deeply enough. The dwelling started out as an inn in the early 1700s, was converted to a farm in the latter part of that century, then became an inn again. I couldn't pinpoint the year when the most recent conversion took place, but from what I can tell, they did a crackerjack job. Who'd ever guess that the Stand and Deliver Inn had once been a farm? I can hardly wait to check out the hot tub in the outbuilding. That's a recent addition, too."

When the last of the luggage had been delivered, Enyon handed out our room keys so we could unwind, unpack, and freshen up before the evening meal. I was booked into a single room on the cliff side of the inn. It was about the size of a cruise ship cabin but was decorated with far more charm. My bed sported a floral bedspread accented with ruffled throw pillows and a resident teddy bear that was nestled among them. An upholstered cornice with matching drapes dressed the window, although so much sea brine had accumulated on the outside panes, the glass looked as if it were glazed with an impenetrable layer of ice. No way I'd be enjoying my ocean view until someone called a window cleaner. An electric kettle with an auto shut-off feature, a china teacup, and a basket of teabags and biscuits perched atop the dresser. A pedestal sink and mirror occupied a little alcove, and a commode and enclosed shower filled a small compartment opposite the sliding doors of the closet.

I hefted my suitcase onto the luggage jack and put all my clothes away in ten minutes flat. We'd be here for five nights so, happily, I didn't have to live out of my suitcase, where I tended to lose track of everything. After freshening up a bit and changing my clothes, I grabbed the electric kettle and turned on the faucet in the pedestal sink.

ERRRRRRRGG! Water rattled from the spigot in erratic fits and starts, rushing out with a final splat that caused the entire sink to shake. I turned it back off, staring at the graceful high-arc faucet with some trepidation. What the—?

I turned the faucet on more slowly this time, allowing only a trickle to escape.

Errrrrrggg...spishspishspish...errrrrrggg.

My knowledge of plumbing begins and ends with the fact that sometimes air gets caught in the pipes, so to tease it out I turned the faucet on full blast.

BOOMBOOMBOOMBOOMBOOM!

Water jack-hammered through the pipes with such violent force that it sounded as if cannonballs were exploding against the wall. An ear-splitting *creeeeak*, a jarring groan, and then...

Poof!

The water began to flow in a calm, steady stream unaccompanied by sound effects or drama.

I exhaled a sigh of relief as I filled the kettle, hoping that I didn't have to contend with this annoyance every time I turned on the faucet. Had I drawn the short straw—the single room with the dodgy plumbing? Or...a troubling notion crowded my thoughts as I plugged the kettle into the wall socket. Were all the rooms experiencing the same problem?

A shriek rang out from somewhere down the hall.

Guess that answered my question.

I rushed into the hallway to find doors being thrown open and Iowans and bloggers alike crowding the narrow corridor to investigate what the commotion was about.

"It's the roof," Bernice yelled in a triumphant voice. "Told you it was gonna collapse."

"Who screamed?" I called out, but they were too busy stampeding toward the far end of the hall to pay any attention to me.

Another shriek pierced the air.

"Bust the door down," ordered Dick Teig as the troops pulled up outside Kathryn Crabbe's suite, cell phones in hand.

Dick Stolee, George, and Osmond exchanged skeptical looks.

"What are you waiting for?" Dick urged in panic mode. "Knock the thing down. On the count of three. One…two…"

"*You* knock it down," Dick Stolee shot back. He gave his shoulder a gentle rub. "My rotator cuff has been sore ever since that golf pro helped me improve my swing at the driving range last year."

"You want me to unstrap my prosthesis?" George asked helpfully. He'd been sporting an artificial leg for decades, so he'd developed a long list of exciting alternate uses. "It makes a pretty good battering ram."

"Why don't someone try the doorknob?" suggested Nana.

The men stared at her, nonplussed. "That was going to be my next proposal," stammered Dick Teig.

"Sure it was," taunted Dick Stolee, who turned the knob and pushed with such vigor that when the door swung open unexpectedly, he fell into the room on hands and knees.

Water was gushing through the Sixteen String Jack suite like spray from an open hydrant, soaking the rug, the clothes Kathryn had stacked on the bed, the wall, the drapes, and Kathryn herself, turning her crown of silver hair into something that resembled an arrangement of wilted flowers.

"Don't just stand there gawking," she screamed as she swatted hair from her eyes. "Shut the water off!"

Which was going to be a little difficult with Dick Stolee blocking the doorway.

"Let me help Dick," I yelled as I tried to thread my way through the clump of onlookers outside the door. "Can you clear a path, please?"

"Hold that thought," urged Dick Teig, blocking my way as he focused his cell phone on the disaster unfolding in the Sixteen String Jack suite.

"Stop hogging all the space," Bernice snapped, muscling to the front of the pack and standing her ground against the rubbernecking horde. She shoved her cell phone in front of Dick's and began recording the scene.

"Oh, come *on*, guys," I complained as cell phones shot out in front of me from every direction. "You have to do this now?"

Ever since mobile phones had coupled internet access and cameras in a kind of telecommunications *ménage à trois*, my guys had been locked in a heated battle to be the first member of the group to post a YouTube video that would go viral. Unfortunately, from the moment they'd stepped on the plane in Iowa, it had been "game on."

"Who's holding up the show?" Alice asked from the rear of the pack. "We can't see anything back here."

"It's Bernice," accused Margi, her voice wild with frustration. "She's stolen the best spot to record stuff, and she won't move."

"Have not," scoffed Bernice.

"Have so," countered Margi.

"*What* is going on?" Enyon's voice rang out in a high-pitched cry that was frightening enough to scatter the troops. With the doorway cleared, I hurdled over Dick's legs and circled around to his side. He looked up at me with puppy dog eyes.

"I could use a little assistance here," he urged.

"What's the best way to help you to your feet?" I asked, understanding that people with knee replacements might require special care to boost them upright.

"Why are you fussing over *him*?" Kathryn screamed at me. "*I'm* the one who needs help."

"Outta the way," boomed Lance, lumbering into the room in all his muscular glory. He glanced at Kathryn. He glanced at Dick. He glanced at me.

"Mr. Stolee has two artificial knees," I informed him. "So we have to be very careful not to"—

He banded his arms around Dick's waist and in one deft motion hoisted him to his feet with a resounding *thump*.

—"cause injury to his joints." I offered Lance a weak smile. "Great. Thanks."

Enyon fluttered into the room in a breathless dither, sloshing through a half-inch of water. "What has happened to my beautiful room? My dry-clean-only drapes? My dry-clean-only counterpane?" He vised his head between his hands like a nutcracker crushing a nut, his face contorting as if he were posing for Edvard Munch's *Scream*. "Why is my room leaking?"

"You will send my clothes to the nearest dry cleaner," Kathryn demanded. "You will pay the bill. And if any item of my clothing is permanently damaged, you will reimburse me in full. Are we clear on that?"

Lance bellied up to her like a barroom bouncer and thrust his hand toward the open door. "Out!"

"Don't you *dare* presume to give me orders, mister. Do you have any idea who I am?"

His chest swelled to twice its size. Veins the size of ropes popped out on his neck. "*Now!*"

Kathryn stabbed a righteous finger in his face. "You might think you're someone special, but you're nothing more than a lowlife bully. One day soon someone is going to cut you down to size, and it would be the highlight of my trip if I were here to witness the event in person. I might even blog about it."

"I'm twembling in my boots."

"Cretin." Snatching her computer case off the bedside table and several stacks of wet clothing off the bed, she splashed across the room as if she were the proud figurehead on a sailing ship and tromped into the hallway.

"Please don't storm off in high dudgeon," Enyon pleaded, slogging after her. "Silly misunderstandings happen all the time in moments of crisis. Lance didn't mean to raise his voice."

"Yes I did."

Enyon spun around and skewered him with a menacing look. "Apologize to Mrs. Crabbe, Lance."

"No."

"Do you remember *nothing* we sorted out this afternoon?"

"Bite me."

Yup. Lance had sure sorted his anger thing.

"Are we stoppin' this leak or not?" barked Lance, seething with impatience. "I've gotta get pies in the oven."

Nana poked her head in the door. "You fellas might as well quit tryin' to suck up to the Crabbe woman on account of she just ducked into the potty."

"Brilliant," agonized Enyon. "I might as well cross her name off our list of potential return guests."

"Is there anything I can do to help?" I asked as the water level rose around my feet. "Call a plumber maybe?"

Enyon tiptoed across the wet carpet to the wall-mounted sink, dancing left and right to avoid a direct hit from the gushing water. He bobbed his head for a better view of the exposed pipes and pointed a damning finger beneath the sink. "The pipes have pulled apart. How does that happen when the plumbing is all new? Lance, run to the cellar and find a tool that repairs pipes."

"Like what?"

"How should I know? I've never had to deal with exploding pipes before."

"And youse think I have?"

"How about a wrench?" suggested Enyon. "I've seen wrenches at the hardware store. They're like…straight pieces of metal with curvy things on either end."

"How's that supposed to wepair the pipes?"

"We won't know until you find one, will we?" Enyon slatted his eyes. "Sometimes I question my decision to spend the rest of my life with you. On second thought, bring the whole toolbox. There has to be a wrench in there someplace." He arched one eyebrow. "I assume you know what the toolbox looks like? And, for the love of God, hurry before another room gets flooded."

With an unfriendly grunt, Lance bounded out the door, allowing an opportunity for the Iowa contingent to creep into the room with their camera phones and continue recording. I gave them a squinty look. "Really?"

"If this video of mine goes viral, it could be worth a lot of money," defended Dick Teig. He inched closer to the sink, capturing the cascading water from a different angle.

"We need more enticing content," complained Dick Stolee as if he were playing the part of a Hollywood director. "Like…like the force of the water *ripping* the clothes off someone." He eyed me with anticipation. "You wanna volunteer, Emily?"

Like that was going to happen.

"I'll volunteer," offered Bernice. "Where do you want me?"

"Buckets!" cried Enyon, running toward the doorway. "We need buckets."

I chased after him as he raced to the end of the hallway and continued down another corridor to an out-of-the-way room. "I should have thought of this sooner." He led me into a spacious utility closet that was crammed with rollaway cots, shelving, cleaning products, carpet and floor maintenance equipment, brooms, mops, and plastic buckets. "Take as many as you can."

I hesitated. "Uhh…you do realize they're going to fill up as quickly as—"

"I'm doing the best I can!" he squealed. "Why does everyone insist on being so contrary?"

"Okay. Sorry." If he wanted buckets in Kathryn's room, he'd have buckets.

I gathered up as many as I could carry and hustled back to Kathryn's room to find the gang loitering in the hall, their wet shoes squeaking on the hardwood floor as they fidgeted with their phones. The bloggers had apparently grown bored with the spectacle because they'd all disappeared. "Did you get tired of recording the same broken pipe?" I asked as they cleared a path for me.

"Yup," said Osmond. "Show's over."

I crossed the threshold and stopped short, my mouth falling open. Even though the floor had turned into a wading pool, water was no longer spewing from the broken pipe. I wheeled around toward the hallway. "What happened?"

Osmond shrugged. "We cut the water off."

"How?"

"I turned off the valve," said George from his vantage point between Nana and Tilly. "There's always a turn-off valve."

I shot him an exasperated look. "George! If you knew what to do, why didn't you turn it off ten minutes ago?"

"And interrupt the filming? Oh, sure. You can imagine the blowback I woulda gotten for *that* one."

Enyon banged into the room like a burro packed down with mops, rags, and more buckets—all of which fell with a splash when he saw that the faulty dike had been plugged. "Jolly good!" He raised his arms in a celebratory V. "I knew Lance could come through if he put his mind to it. Did he find the wrench?"

I lowered my voice to an undertone. "George Farkas turned the water off." I gestured toward the area below the sink. "There's a valve."

"Really? Wasn't that clever of someone to think of that." He cast a desperate look at the tiny waves rippling over the carpet. "How does one go about drying a flooded bedroom? Oh, dear. I suspect this might involve firing up the furnace at an exorbitant cost." He gnawed his bottom lip. "I can't authorize any financial expenditure without Lance's approval, so I'll need to discuss this with him first. Stay right where you are. I'll be back straightaway."

I wasn't sure what good his talking to Lance would do, other than prick the guy's ire again. Better him than me.

Helen raised her phone in triumph. "Ta-da! My video has been successfully uploaded on YouTube. I'm calling it *Mini Niagara*."

"Major yawn," Bernice wisecracked. "You'll get zero hits with a title like that. You need something with more punch. Something like"—she held her phone close to her face and read the words off her screen—"*Life-or-Death Rescue in Hundred-Year Cornish Flood.* That's what I'm calling mine."

Tilly eyed her with disapproval. "Does it upset your code of moral standards that your video depicts neither a rescue *nor* a hundred-year flood?"

"Nope. I'm practicing a long-standing American tradition. Bait and switch." She smiled smugly. "Bet I'll chalk up more views than Helen."

"Will not," sniped Helen.

"Will so," bragged Bernice.

Margi stood in the doorway, concern in her eyes. "Water damage can lead to life-threatening mold problems. If those two men bungle the cleanup, they could be putting all our lives at risk." Her face grew woeful. "I didn't pack near enough sanitizer to obliterate an infestation of mold."

"Speaking of problems." Bernice nodded toward the two windows facing the inn's parking lot. "Alice and I want to change rooms."

Alice looked stunned. "We do?"

"Yeah. Our room supposedly faces the ocean, but the only thing we can see is the crud that's caked on the window panes. We want a room without the crud."

"Me and Til might not mind switchin' rooms with you," offered Nana.

"Does your room face the ocean?" asked Bernice.

Nana shook her head. "Nope. We got the same view as this one."

Bernice rolled her eyes. "Right. Like I'd be dumb enough to exchange my potentially spectacular view of the ocean for your crummy view of the parking lot."

"Whoever's stuck next door to us might want to change, too," Helen spoke up. "Dick is going to be up all night flushing because he forgot to pack his medication."

"I have a confession, too," Grace apologized. "Dick's CPAP machine has developed some kind of glitch. So whoever is next to us, if you'd prefer not to move to another room, maybe you could just hang in there until he stops breathing."

A hair-raising cry echoed through the house, mimicking the howl of a wounded animal.

"Oh my God," shrieked Helen, clinging to Dick's arm. "What was that?"

I ran into the hallway, trying to gauge the direction from which the sound had come—and whether it was animal, human, or something else.

Nana pointed down the hall toward the lounge. "I think it came from thataway."

I sprinted toward the front of the house. The lounge and dining room were empty, but I heard a suspicious mewling sound coming from somewhere in the vicinity of the kitchen.

I barged through the door.

The mewling grew louder.

I skirted around the butcher block island toward an open door.

"He's dead!" Enyon's gut-wrenching sobs drifted up from the bowels of the house. "Help! Someone, help!"

I stood at the top of a steep flight of stairs and peered downward into a hovel of a space that looked more castle dungeon than basement. Lance lay at the bottom of the staircase, huge and unmoving, sprawled face-down, his neck crooked at an impossible angle. Enyon was collapsed on his knees beside him, wailing uncontrollably.

Oh, no.

Enyon looked up at me. "I warned him," he sobbed, his voice cracking. "But he wouldn't listen. Stupid, stupid man." He bent protectively over Lance's body, awash in tears. "Whatever will I do without him?"

FOUR

"There, there," I soothed, patting Enyon's hand as he rested his head on my shoulder. "Tears are good for the soul."

"But it's so unmanly." He dabbed his eyes with a crumpled tissue. Both sockets had grown so swollen that his entire face looked like a mound of yeast-raised bread dough. "Lance wouldn't have approved."

"I'm sure Lance would be touched that—" I bit off the rest of my sentence, wondering how to complete the thought without refocusing on Lance's recent demise, which would prompt a fresh round of tears.

A fleet of emergency vehicles had arrived at the inn after we'd made the 999 call—rescue squad, ambulance, fire department, and eventually the coroner, who'd performed the sad task of loading Lance's body into his van a little less than an hour ago. I'd been with Enyon ever since, trying my best to console him. The lounge was deserted save for the two of us, the majority of the group having decided to camp out in their rooms to allow Enyon some privacy.

All except practical-minded George Farkas, who'd decided to nose around the place and ended up discovering a couple of emergency exit doors, the cluttered utility closet, a stash of floor fans, and a large capacity wet/dry vacuum that he wheeled directly to the Sixteen String Jack suite. Upon firing up the motor he was joined by the two Dicks, who begged to help him—not so much out of generosity of spirit or a burning desire to quell Margi's fears about an outbreak of deadly mold, but because they didn't want to miss out on a chance to operate a noisy piece of machinery. Between the three of them they managed to suck up all the water and place a half-dozen fans around the room to dry it out, but I figured the carpet would still have to be ripped out and replaced before the suite would be ready for occupancy again.

"What were you saying?" Enyon sniffed.

"I'm sure Lance would be touched that he…that you…that the life you shared affected you so profoundly."

He nodded as he reached for a fresh tissue. "That's nice of you to say. He could be such a wanker, but he was *my* wanker, and I loved him, surly disposition and all. I really did."

"Do you need to call anyone to let them know what's happened? His family? *Your* family? Close friends? Anyone?"

"I don't know," he sobbed, his bottom lip curling outward. "I'm…I'm torn. He's estranged from his family—hasn't spoken to them for years. I doubt they even care whether he's dead or alive."

"They're his family, Enyon. Of course they care."

He shook his head. "They went completely off their trolleys when he took up with me. They're such manly men, you know.

They forced him to choose: them or me. He chose me, so they disowned him on the spot. And that's the last we ever heard from them."

"There's a picture of his family hanging in the dining room, so he must have held out some hope for reconciliation."

"Wishful thinking on his part. It was never going to happen."

"What about your family?"

"My parents died years ago." His voice cracked with emotion. "Lance was my family. And now…I have no one. I'll never be first with anyone ever again." He burst into tears once more, making me wonder if I should fetch him a cold pack for his eyes before they swelled shut.

"I'm so sorry, Enyon." The coroner determined that Lance had probably sustained a broken neck when he fell down the stairs and had died immediately. The upside was that Lance hadn't suffered, but it seemed the height of insensitivity to point that out.

"This didn't have to happen," Enyon bawled. "All he had to do was lift his feet. Was that too much to ask? You saw him trip over the scatter rug in the dining room. He shuffled around like a dotty pensioner. I warned him there could be dire consequences one day." He choked up, his voice escaping in whimpers. "I just didn't think…today would be the day."

The kitchen door creaked open and Wally crept out, looking uncharacteristically self-conscious. He'd been enjoying a leisurely soak in the hot tub when all hell had broken loose, so he was wearing his heart on his shoulder and feeling guilty that he'd been unavailable to lend assistance when I'd needed him. As a form of contrition, he'd banished himself to the kitchen after the coroner had left and had been there ever since, which was a good thing because he was taking over where Lance had left off, which meant we might actually have food on the table tonight.

"About ten more minutes before the pies come out," he said as he crossed the floor toward us. "And I pulled a few things out of the refrigerator that look as if they might have been intended for tonight's dinner."

"Cornish wild garlic yarg wrapped in nettle and served on bruschetta," sniffed Enyon.

"Wild garlic what?" asked Wally.

"Yarg. Cheese from the milk of Friesian cows. You wrap it in a nettle coating that allows the most delicious gray mold to grow all over it. Creamy near the edge, crumbly near the middle." He yanked another tissue out of the box. "It was one of Lance's specialties." The memory spurred another round of tears, after which he blew his nose and inched away from me. "Please don't think me impolite, but would you excuse me? I feel a migraine coming on."

"You bet." I helped him to his feet. "And don't give dinner another thought. Wally and I will see that the troops get fed."

"Splendid. I fear these migraines usually last for three days, though, so the running of the place is officially in your hands now."

I stared at him, gobsmacked. "Excuse me?"

"I can't possibly manage things from my sick bed. In another hour I'll be so knackered I won't be able to lift my head off my pillow, so I'm delegating my duties to the next people in the pecking order: the two of you."

Anxiety gripped my spine like a multi-jaw bench vise. "An inn of this size, and you don't have backup staff?"

"Lance had suggested we enlist a couple of girls from the village to help with the daily slog, but I thought the idea rather absurd at

47

the time. I told him I was perfectly capable of handling everything myself." He let out a forlorn sigh. "In hindsight, I'll admit he was probably right. That might have been the only good idea Lance ever had."

"How have you managed without outside help?" questioned Wally. "How do you have time to do it all? The laundry. The bed-making. Scouring the bathrooms. Mopping the floors. Dusting the furniture. Cutting fresh flowers. Schmoozing with the guests. I live in a six hundred square foot condo, and I have a cleaning lady."

"A strict schedule," said Enyon. "That's the key."

I was suddenly feeling like the world's biggest slacker for giving up care of my hardwood floors to an iRobot vacuum cleaner that glided through the house like a tiny dust-sucking hovercraft. "You and Lance have been doing this for *how* long?"

Enyon peeked at his wristwatch. "Exact amount of time or could I round it off?"

"Whichever."

"Approximately…five hours."

Brits could be so literal. "No, no. Prior to our arrival, how long had you been operating the inn?"

Enyon regarded his watch again before squinting at me, per-plexed. "I told you. Five hours. You Yanks have the distinction of being our very first guests."

"Ever?" Wally's expression hinted that he might lapse into cardiac arrest.

"Ever."

Visions of our blog-worthy Mostly Cornish tour began disappearing like water down a bathtub drain. I suddenly felt so light-headed, I swayed slightly on my feet. "How…how did you have the

48

nerve to accept reservations for twenty-two guests if you've never done this before?"

He considered that momentarily before shrugging. "We had to start somewhere, and everyone in the hospitality business says it's best to start off with Yanks. You people are so laid back that you'll put up with an incredible amount of bother before you ever start complaining." He snatched the tissue box off the sofa and hugged it to his chest. "I have complete confidence that the two of you will keep the ship from foundering while I recover. I shall repair to my bedchamber now, prostrate with grief, so please consider my room off-limits unless the house is burning down…or the roof collapses."

"But—"

He gave my arm a heartfelt squeeze. "To quote a phrase, 'Keep calm and carry on.' Now I must leave you before I'm forced to crawl to my room on all fours."

"But what about Kathryn Crabbe?" I asked as he circled around me. "She doesn't have a room."

He paused long enough to heave a lengthy sigh. "My dear Mrs. Miceli, the man with whom I was to run this establishment is dead. So please don't think me inelegant, but I don't give a toss where Kathryn Crabbe sleeps. Find an empty space and squeeze her in. Whatever you think will work."

He waddled off, head bent and shoulders sagging, leaving me to gape at Wally from across the room.

"It seems our four-star, all-inclusive holiday has turned into a self-catering affair," quipped Wally.

"This isn't funny," I freaked. "Does he expect us to serve break-fast tomorrow morning, then come back from a day of touring and serve dinner as well? I'm not a chef. I'm not good in the kitchen. I can *prepare* meals, but I can't actually cook them."

"I have no idea what that means."

"*Preparing* meals doesn't involve the use of a cookbook or any kind of culinary skills. Its basic requirements are twenty minutes of free time, a can opener, a microwave oven, and a nonstick fry pan. Voilà: dinner."

Wally grinned. "Look, Emily, neither one of us is stupid. We can handle this through breakfast tomorrow, and if Enyon isn't recovered by then, we'll inquire in the village about hiring a cook on a temporary basis. Let's not hit the panic button until we have to."

"Too late. Mine got activated about two minutes ago." I'd confronted crazed killers, marauding sea lions, Irish ghosts, and surly bus drivers, but nothing terrified me more than the thought of cooking a meal for more than two people. My lack of culinary expertise would be on full display, and the result would be humiliating—not to mention either half-cooked, charred, or completely inedible.

I hung my head and groaned. Compulsory KP duty should not be one of my escort duties. Maybe it was time to tweak my job description. "Kitchen drama aside, what are we going to do about Kathryn?"

"Unfortunately, every available suite is being occupied by Destinations Travel guests. There aren't any rooms left. Just think of the straights we'd be in if Freddy wasn't bunking down someplace else."

Freddy was our coach driver. He lived in the area, so he'd leapt at the chance to sleep in his own bed for the next few nights. "So where do we put her?"

"Well, she's already commandeered the half bath. Bernice is reporting telltale sounds of computer keys being clicked frenetically."

I winced as my stomach started to bubble like a caustic stew. "She's probably composing her blog for tomorrow, which, I'm sure, will include some rather choice words about today's debacle. Scathing publicity on our first day out. So much for my blogger idea." I hoped I'd packed enough antacids.

"Should we ask your grandmother and Tilly if they'd be willing to accommodate a third person in their room? Space would be pretty tight, but if Enyon has a rollaway cot, then—"

"I wouldn't do that to Nana and Tilly. Kathryn needs to be in a single. I'm getting the impression that she's way too inflexible to share a room with any of the other guests."

"You want to give her my room?" asked Wally. "I don't know where I'll sleep, but it would certainly solve the problem." He eyed the groupings of loveseats in the lounge and nodded to the nearest one. "I could sleep out here. I might even fit if I sleep in a fetal position."

"You're not going to sleep on half a sofa. You need a good night's rest more than any of us. So there's only one other alternative." I sighed with resignation. "I'll offer her my room."

"Which forces you to relocate where?"

With the only other person besides Wally, Mason Chatsworth, and I who'd booked a single room.

. . . .

"I'd *love* to share my room with you!" Jackie squealed, executing a little pattycake clap before throwing her arms around me and pressing my face into her sternum in a bone-crushing hug. "It'll be

51

like old times in our New York walkup! You, me, ten square feet of living space, and a wonky shower."

"What's wrong with your shower?" I mumbled into her chest.

"The pipes." She led me halfway across the floor and opened the door of a room that made an airplane lavatory look cavernous by comparison. "When I turned on the water, I thought I was being gunned down. And it didn't let up. The pipes *rat-a-tat-tatted* through my whole shower. If the plumbing had been less raucous, I might not have missed out on all the hysteria in Kathryn's room." She glared at the showerhead. "This place should be slapped with a fine for violating the noise pollution ordinance."

"Does Cornwall have a noise pollution ordinance?"

"If they don't, they should. So"—she flashed her most exuberant smile, her eyes twinkling with excitement—"who do you think killed the cook?"

Oh, God. "No one killed him, Jack. According to Enyon, Lance never picked up his feet. He was a serial shuffler. So on his way to the basement to fetch a toolbox, he fell down the stairs, *unassisted*, and broke his neck."

"You actually believe that?"

"It's not my theory. That's what the coroner said. I don't have a theory."

She turned as coy as a cat stalking another cat's dish of warm milk. "Are you telling me you're not the least bit suspicious? Even after those two guys closed off the kitchen this afternoon so they could engage in war games?"

"I'm not suspicious, Jack. There's no killer."

"I've been on your tours before, Emily. There's always a killer."

"Not this time. Lance's death was an accident."

She studied her nails with an air of nonchalance before polishing them on the sleeve of her tunic. "We'll see."

I hung my head and groaned. "You're all jazzed to tail someone, aren't you?"

"Maybe."

The only reason Jackie delighted in tailing possible suspects was because it allowed her the opportunity to wear tacky disguises. I shook my head. "How many wigs did you bring with you?"

She had the decency to look guilty as she lowered her voice to a whisper. "Only one."

"What color this time?"

It was as if I'd flipped a switch to the on position, activating the personality she used to have before she went into enforced mourning. "Red! And it's a beauty. No one will ever be able to tell it's me. You want to see it?"

She needed to work on erasing the delusion that a six-foot transsexual in five-inch stiletto boots could don a red wig and not be recognized as a six-foot transsexual in five-inch stiletto boots.

"Knock, knock." Wally appeared in the doorway. "Are you two all settled here?"

Jackie wrapped her arm around my shoulders and hugged me against her with such might, she nearly collapsed my lung. "Yes! We're gonna be roomies!"

"Great." He smiled at Jackie. "Thanks for offering to be part of the solution. You're really helping us out of a pinch. So the pies are out of the oven and cooling on the counter. Would the two of you see about setting the table while I lure Kathryn out of the loo?"

"Good luck with that," quipped Jackie. "According to my sources, she's been in there so long, it'll be a miracle if the door isn't stuck shut permanently." She tapped her forefinger against her chin as she gazed into space. "I wonder what the going rate for powder room rentals is? This could be a really attractive alternative for tourists who are into that tiny house craze."

"I should probably move my stuff out of my room before Kathryn takes possession."

"I can do that for you," offered Wally. "After I talk to Kathryn."

"Eh!" Jackie held her hand up like a crossing guard raising a stop sign. "No offense to present company, but guys *cannot* be entrusted with such critical duties. I'll move Emily's things. That way she can be sure nothing'll get left behind. You men are so slap-dash. You don't see anything that's not right in front of your nose. But happily, I'm living proof that massive doses of female hormones can eliminate the problem completely."

I handed her my room key. "Sounds like a plan. We can get the cot out of the utility room later."

We scattered like billiards, with Wally pausing outside the loo to address Kathryn while I continued on to the kitchen. The fragrant aroma of fresh-baked piecrust teased my salivary glands as I opened the door, reminding me that I'd failed to sample any of Lance's scones earlier. Six stargazy pies sat cooling on trivets on the island, which seemed far too few considering how hungry I was. Heck, I figured I could eat a whole one by myself.

At least, that's what I thought until I actually stood over one of Lance's famous creations.

Uh-oh. This was definitely going to be a problem.

FIVE

"I SWEAR TO GOD," Helen ranted into her phone the following morning. "There were a bunch of creepy crawly critters climbing out of the middle of the pie, like…like little alien creatures trying to squirm out of quicksand. They had claws for hands, and beady black eyes, and so many antennae that they could probably pick up the local cable channels. And we were expected to *eat* them. I've never been so appalled by anything in all my life." She paused. "No, wait. There was that time your father—" She paused again. "Never mind. This was even more appalling than that."

The Teigs occupied the seat in front of me on the bus, and while the rest of us were suffering shellshock from having our bus whiplashed by overgrown hedgerows on narrow lanes with no shoulders, Helen was completely oblivious, conducting a phone conversation with one of her children in Iowa, complaining about Lance's stargazy pie the night before.

Dick snatched the phone away from her. "And that wasn't the worst of it. For an appetizer they tried serving us moldy cheese on toast, so no one ate anything last night, except for one blogger guy who probably has a stomach made of cast iron. And Emily. Man, she really packed it away."

Of course I'd packed it away. I was starving. Besides, the stargazy pie—with its cluster of mini lobsters baked into a sauce of bacon, eggs, onions, and mustard—was absolutely delicious. Lance might not have been blessed with charm and charisma, but he'd obviously made up for the deficit with extraordinary culinary skills. None of which we'd be sampling for the rest of our stay.

"Breakfast?" Dick boomed into the phone. "Breakfast was great. Dry cereal and toast. But we're not paying top dollar to eat corn flakes. Hell, we can get that at home."

My eyes rolled around in their sockets like misdirected pinballs. The locals ate stargazy pie and Cornish yarg, both of which had been served last night, but neither of which he would sample. *That's* what he was paying top dollar for, but it wouldn't do me any good to point it out because I doubted he'd see the connection.

We were on our way to the Bedruthan Steps, a secluded beach near St. Eval that was famous for the great chunks of cliff that had broken away from the headland to form a Jurassic-like series of columns that resembled gargantuan elephant legs. The surf was unsuitable for swimming because of the strong currents, and visitors ran the twofold risk of either being cut off by the tide or crushed by falling rock, but photos of the beach had looked so amazing that I insisted we give it a try. So with the tide schedule in our favor, sunshine overhead, and some newly rented equipment stowed in our baggage compartment, we were planning to spend a couple of hours at the beach metal detecting.

The owner of the hardware store where we'd rented the detectors had congratulated us on scheduling our adventure the day after a squall because local beaches apparently became a beachcomber's paradise in the aftermath, exposing treasures that might have been buried beneath the ocean floor for centuries. When Wally passed this information along, the gang seemed excited about the prospect of finding authentic buried treasure, but they seemed even more excited about having the opportunity to eat lunch somewhere other than the Stand and Deliver Inn—at a place where they'd be able to order American fare with only a *hint* of Cornish flair. Like maybe having the meal served on pink-and-white striped plates.

The view out the coach windows was more claustrophobic than enchanting. Towering hedgerows on both sides of the road. Ramshackle sheds. Tidy stone fences. Grassy fields. Rolling hills. One red phone booth at the edge of someone's driveway. And every so often a break in the hedgerows to allow banks of pink flowers to overhang the road. In Porthcothan Bay we passed a community of homes as pale as seashells that were nestled on a hillock overlooking a white sand beach. The beach stretched between a deep split in the headland and was bisected by a series of flowing tidal streams, but at high tide I suspected that, like the Bedruthan Steps beach, the Porthcothan beach would disappear completely.

The bus's sound system rasped into life as Wally activated the mike. "Only a few more kilometers until we reach our destination, folks, but before we arrive, I want to turn the microphone over to Caroline Goodfriend, who has an exciting offer for you. Caroline?" He handed her the mike.

"This is just a suggestion," she said in her usual cheery voice, "but it could be fun. As Emily mentioned yesterday, my expertise is in the area of genealogy and family history, and one courtesy I love to offer groups like this one is to do a quick computer search to see if I can discover never-before-known facts about ancestors you didn't even know you had. The results can be quite thrilling. So if any of you are game, I'll be more than happy to fire up my iPad and see what I can find. Have any of you ever researched your family tree?"

"I'm gonna pass on the family tree thing," Nana piped up. "Been there, done that."

Caroline swiveled in her seat to face the back of the bus. "Who said that?"

Nana raised her hand.

"Were you pleasantly surprised with the results?" asked Caroline.

"Nope. The whole dang tree's got blight, so I don't wanna find out no more about 'em."

"Oh." Caroline looked crestfallen. "I'm sorry to hear that."

"Not half as sorry as me. I'm related to the dang buggers."

"I wouldn't mind having you add a few leaves to my family tree," George spoke up. "I don't know diddly about my Farkas ancestors. Maybe you'll discover my tree is more like a shrub."

"The Tjarks emigrated from Norway sometime in the 1800s," Alice revealed, unable to hide her excitement. "But I don't have any specifics. I'd love to know more."

"Dick's ancestors are Norwegian, too," Helen Teig reminded everyone, "but if his ancestors are anything like him, you might hit a lot of brick walls."

"Why is that?" asked Caroline.

"Because I'm shallow," Dick said glumly. "I got the diagnosis last year from some psychic. And shallow people don't leave much of a blip on the radar. I don't know if I'm the only one affected or if the condition runs through the whole clan, but I'm looking at it as a hereditary defect rather than something I have to take responsibility for."

"I don't require your services," Kathryn Crabbe remarked with a dismissive air. Her clothing had apparently dried overnight, so she'd been spared the misery of having to don soggy clothes this morning. "My pedigree is impeccable."

"You're related to dogs?" asked Margi.

"I belong to a long and impressive line of English aristocrats who date back to the days of King Henry VIII," Kathryn boasted. "I imagine the Anglophiles among you might have seen my ancestor's name listed in the book of English peerages? Crispin Truscott-Tallon? Known affectionately in my family as the Baron Penwithick? He was the first baron, actually. We're up to number twenty-two now."

Stiff smiles. Vacuous stares.

"Have any of your relatives ever been in that Westminster Dog Show?" Osmond inquired.

Before Kathryn had a chance to respond to that, Caroline jumped in. "I have a clipboard and paper here. I'll pass it around while we're still in transit, and for those of you who'd like to participate, just jot down the name you'd like me to plug into my software program, in legible handwriting please, and I'll get started as soon as possible. And if you know of any applicable dates, like births or deaths, feel free to write those down, too. Every detail helps."

As a trill of excitement rippled through the bus, I pulled my cell phone out of my shoulder bag and sat staring at it, mired in indecision. After about a half minute, Jackie leaned toward me. "If your phone's dead, you can borrow mine." She angled it toward me.

"It's not dead. I'm just too chicken to read what our bloggers wrote about the first day of our trip. I'm not sure how much ridicule I can handle this early in the morning."

"You want me to look for you? Ridicule doesn't bother me one bit...as long as it's directed at someone else. Whose blog do you want to start with?"

I crooked my mouth and shrugged, her idea seeming like the perfect solution. "Okay, but if any of the blogs are really scathing, I don't want you to tell me. At least, not this very minute. Deal?"

"You've come to the right girl, Em. You know, looking back at my life, I think I've always excelled at enabling other people to make really stupid decisions. So. Who do you want me to read first?"

Not Kathryn. "August Lugar. He scarfed down a second helping of pie last night, so I'm going to interpret that as a good sign."

Her thumbs flew over her screen. "Here it is. And it's dated today. Give me a sec to scan what he has to—oh, my."

My stomach dropped to my knees. "What?"

She silenced me with a raised forefinger as she continued to read.

"He hated it, didn't he?" I buried my face in my hands. "*Why* did I decide to put the agency's reputation on the line like this? I should never push the envelope. If nothing is broken, *why* do I insist on trying to fix—"

"'The evening's main entrée was not only a Cornish specialty but a perfect marriage of savory taste and visual appeal. I have never eaten finer fare.'"

I snatched my hands away from my face and gaped at Jackie. "He liked it?"

"'The chef at the Stand and Deliver Inn should receive a medal of excellence for his dish, but unfortunately, it will have to be presented posthumously because he died in a tragic accident not long after our arrival. I have no idea what today's dinner will have in store for us, but I mourn the fact that we will no longer be able to sample the epicurean delicacies of Chef Lance Tori. Stay tuned.'"

"Oh my God," I squeaked. "That's sensational! Will you send the link to Etienne so he can read it after his retreat? This is the kind of attention that'll really boost our standing in the group travel world."

Jackie's thumbs went into overdrive again. "Who should we try next?"

"Caroline." I regarded the clipboard as it made its way toward the back of the bus. "If she didn't have anything nice to say, I bet she might have made something up."

She accessed the site as our bus driver downshifted to a crawl and made a sharp turn into a graveled parking lot with a building about the size of an extinct Fotomat kiosk guarding the entrance. We were on a wide, grassy plateau high above the shore, but exactly how high, I couldn't tell. While Wally hopped off to pay the admission fee, Jackie demonstrated her ability to speed-read a blog page in one long breath. "'My pre-trip reading…blah, blah, blah…tales of highwaymen on Bodmin Moor…blah, blah…the outlaws have long disappeared but legends of their misdeeds live on in the literature…blah, blah, blah…charming names for our suites that capture the spirit of Cornwall three centuries ago…' and so on and so forth. Nothing bad, just researchy-type stuff. Who's next?"

But before I could answer, Wally hopped back on the bus and began to announce instructions. "Your metal detectors are in the luggage bay, so that should be your first stop when you step off the bus. *Do not* head to the beach without your detector in hand. Operation is simple: just flip the switch to the on position and you're good to go. If the equipment starts beeping, that's a good sign. Start digging."

"With what?" George threw out.

"Your digging tools are included. Small garden spades are attached to each detector. Don't lose sight of your detectors or your spades because we'll have to reimburse the hardware store for all lost or damaged equipment. We'll have a show-and-tell at the inn later today to see if anyone really did unearth a buried treasure. Questions?"

Margi raised her hand. "Are these detectors fresh out of the box?"

"I'd guess they've been used hundreds of times, Margi. But they're top of the line and in really good shape."

"Wonderful." Her voice dropped like the tone on a slide whistle.

"One more thing before you head out. The stairs down to the beach are extremely steep and can be slippery if standing water has pooled on them, so climb down slowly, don't crowd each other, use the handrail, and exercise caution at all times. And I probably don't have to tell you this, but do not—I repeat, *do not*—venture into the water. The currents are strong and unpredictable and could drag you out to sea before you knew what hit you. I don't even want to see you getting your toes wet. Understood?"

Heads bobbing. Murmurs of assent.

"We'll be here for two hours, so make note of the time so you can make your way back to the bus promptly. Good luck, everyone."

This admonition was mainly for the bloggers because the only viable excuse my ever-punctual Iowans will accept for tardiness is if a person drops dead unexpectedly.

As the bus's rear door whooshed open, everyone crowded into the aisles and began streaming down the stepwell. Jackie, however, remained planted on the seat beside me, looking like a sports car that had just suffered a major breakdown on the way to Vegas.

"What should I do, Emily?" She dropped her head to her chest. "I'm going to need a permanent job once my divorce goes through, but I'm so bummed, I don't even know where to begin." She dashed a stray tear from the corner of her eye and sniffed pathetically. "You know all the confidence I used to have? My soaring self-esteem? It's gone. Vanished. Poof!" She fluttered her fingers to simulate an imaginary burst of fireworks. "I'm a mere shell of the man I used to be. I mean, the woman I was. Or am. Whichever."

"C'mon, Jack, chin up. You can always revisit one of the professions you've already test driven." She boasted an eclectic list that included actor, master caulker, romance novelist, life coach, and cosmetics sales representative. "You were good at all of them."

"I know. The younger me really knew how to kick butt. But that was then; this is now. For my own emotional health, I need a powder-puff job that's stress-free and pays lots of money."

I laughed. "When you find a job like that, let me know. We can apply together."

She paused. "Well, I was thinking you already have a job like that."

I stared at her, dumbfounded. "What?"

Suddenly energized, she sat up steeple-straight in her seat. "What would you think about hiring me as a travel escort at your agency so I can do the same stuff you do? Travel to exotic locales, have all my expenses paid, hang out with the group, smooth the occasional ruffled feather, schmooze with the tour director. It's the kind of job that was made for someone with my considerable talents."

I didn't know what made the louder noise, my jaw hitting my chest or my eyes ballooning out of their sockets. "We don't have job openings, Jack. We're a two-person operation—except when we have to hire the occasional temp secretary."

"Right *now* you're a two-person agency, but you'll have to expand once your good publicity starts flooding the internet. You could hire me now to get ahead of the game. I'd be up and running to escort your next tour!"

Oh, God.

"Will you ladies be here much longer?" Freddy called out from the front of the bus. "I'm getting ready to lock up."

"Sorry." I shot out of my seat and pulled Jackie up with me. "We're leaving now."

"What about the job?" Jackie persisted as I herded her toward the exit and down the stairs.

"Can we talk about this later, Jack? You know I can't give you an answer without crunching the numbers, and Etienne is in charge of numbers crunching."

"I have him on speed dial. You want me to call him?"

"No."

"Text?"

"No! He's with the Pope. Look, you can discuss this with him face-to-face when he meets us in Lyme Regis. Okay?" Etienne could brainstorm with her about future job opportunities without being weighed down by emotional baggage or guilt. In part because he was Swiss, but mostly because he hadn't been married to her. Him. Her.

Jackie's mouth slid into a resigned pout. "I suppose. You just better hope no one hires me before you can make an offer. Losing me could be a terrible blow to your company."

"Last one!" As we neared the luggage bay, Wally hefted the remaining metal detector into the air and extended it toward us—a long metal rod capped off at the base by a disc that resembled a miniature flying saucer. "You want to flip a coin for it?"

"Jackie can have it." Maybe she'd unearth a cache of buried treasure that would leave her so filthy rich, she wouldn't have to find a job. "I need to keep an eye on the gang while they're on the beach. You know how freaked out they get when they hear the words 'incoming tide.'" Living in a state where there are no tides, the average Iowan has a deeper understanding of the derivatives of trigonometric functions than he does of daily tidal charts.

Wally handed the detector to Jackie, who cooed with excitement over its readout screen and switches before propping it against her shoulder as if it were a military rifle. The rest of the troops were already hot-footing it toward the stairs, all except Margi, who was scouring the handle of her detector with the entire contents of her mini sanitizer bottle.

"I have to make a few phone calls," Wally commented as he closed the luggage bay, "so I'll join you when I'm done. Save a place on the beach for me."

We sauntered toward Margi, who'd just completed her decontamination process and looked quite tickled with herself. "I'm letting it air dry," she explained while fanning her hand over the rubberized grip. "Much more hygienic than a total wipe down."

The entrance to the stairs sat wedged between two walls of rock that could be closed off to the public by a barred metal gate that looked like a relic from a prison cell. As I descended the staircase, stepping cautiously onto blocks of chiseled granite, I gripped the metal handrail on either side of me and eyed the steel mesh fencing that clung to the cliff face like a lady's hairnet, preventing loose rock from spilling onto the stairway. A ragged carpet of flora crept over rocks and crannies in an outbreak of greenery that poked through the hexagonal openings in the steel fencing. I turned my face into my shoulder as the wind howled upward from the beach like a gale in a wind tunnel, whistling past my ears, stinging my eyes, and lifting my hair off my head in wild streamers. The stairs zigzagged through a narrow fissure in the headland at an angle too steep for anyone with height phobias to negotiate, but even for those of us not affected by acrophobia, the steepness caused a bit of tingling in my feet and toes.

Rounding a sharp bend, I shivered involuntarily as I passed a life preserver encased in an orange storage unit and couldn't help wondering when someone had last needed it. Hopefully, it wouldn't be needed today. On the final landing I noted a battered sign attached to the railing that read Do Not Enter Water At Any Time. I hoped everyone had taken the time to read it, as it reinforced what

Wally had already cautioned us about. I just hoped they heeded the warning. As many years as I'd accompanied the gang on coastal tours, seeing them anywhere near the water still gave me heartburn.

As I descended the final section of risers, I noticed an angular gash in the headland to my left—a narrow maw that looked to be the geological equivalent of a black hole. A cavern that looked so eerie, I vowed to stay as far away from it as humanly possible. After dancing around a series of puddles on the last steps, I hopped onto the sand and beheld the vista before me.

It was as if I'd stepped through a portal into Jules Verne's *Journey to the Center of the Earth.*

"Holy cow," said Jackie as she hopped onto the sand beside me.

The view was breathtaking in a primordial kind of way. Fractured rock from landslips strewn about the base of jagged cliffs. Shallow caves that looked to be lairs for winged creatures with lizard's skin and sharpened claws. Rock formations slick with algae. Cataracts of water streaming down the cliff face, the wind blowing spray into the air in a soaking drizzle. The massive chimney stacks of rock that squatted like broken molars at the water's edge, dwarfing the metal detectorists who looked as tiny as ants standing beneath them.

"What are the chances there's treasure buried here someplace?" Jackie asked with some skepticism as she switched her device to the on position.

I shrugged. "Like the guy at the hardware store said, this part of the coast was apparently a graveyard for sailing vessels over the centuries, so who knows what you might find?"

"Okay." She ranged a look around the beach, looking a little creeped out. "I just hope I don't dig up any dinosaur bones or anything because it looks to me as if this is the place they came to die."

I hoped she didn't dig up any dinosaur bones either because they'd be way too big to fit on the bus.

As she headed off in the direction of the chimney stacks, I found a sun-drenched rock to sit on where, amid the haunting whoosh of pounding surf and the caw of gulls soaring overhead, I could keep a close eye on my detectorists. They seemed to have mastered the "sweeping the ground" part of the activity pretty well, but the digging component looked to need a little tweaking because sand was flying everywhere. I figured that was the one potentially good thing about a high tide. The incoming waves would automatically fill in all the divots so the group wouldn't have to.

After about twenty minutes of watching everyone walk in mindless circles, sweeping, digging, and cussing, I took out my phone again, feeling a little more confident about scanning the rest of the blogs.

Mason Chatsworth had nice things to say about our accommodations in his blog. He mentioned the inn's country charm, exquisite interior design, and well-appointed rooms complete with "en suite bathrooms, a riotous tumble of throw pillows, and proper English teddy bears." He did mention a bit of difficulty with the plumbing in one suite but didn't go into detail, which eased my nerves even more.

Spencer Blunt was equally complimentary, citing the substantial financial savings a traveler would enjoy by having both his breakfast and dinner included at the Stand and Deliver Inn. "Even though not every traveler will appreciate the authentic Cornish cuisine served at the inn, if you're watching your pennies, it's a win-win situation."

I was a bit hesitant to access Heather Holloway's blog, so I scanned the text one-eyed for most of its length, cringing when Austen Zombie Girl came out swinging. "My regular readers know what a fan I've been of Penelope Pemberley's blog throughout the years. It was because of Penelope's influence that I became a die-hard Janeite. Imagine my excitement when I learned that Penelope herself was a guest on this tour. My idol! Traveling with me to Jane Austen's Chawton! You can also imagine my disappointment when the woman hiding behind the name Penelope Pemberley suggested that my membership in the Jane Austen Society be revoked simply because she thinks my blog entries don't pass her personal literary purity test. Why, you might ask, would she suggest something like that? Because she's a narrow-minded snob with no appreciation for the beauty of modern literature. Rise up, zombie sisters! Join me in online shaming Penelope Pemberley on worldwide social media!"

Oh, God. Had Heather just cast the first stone in a literary cyber war?

"Would you like to use my metal detector?" Caroline Good-friend trudged toward me, ruffling sand from her hair. "I can't seem to stay upwind of the digging enthusiasts and I'm paying the price, so I'm hanging it up."

"Thanks anyway, but I want to stay alert in case someone decides the No Swimming sign doesn't apply to them."

She laughed as she sat down beside me. "They seem to be enjoying themselves. I guess treasure hunting is like catnip to the masses, playing on people's fantasies of riches. Good call."

"For now. I'm sure I'll get a few complaints about what a waste of time it was."

She peered over my shoulder. "You're getting cell service down here?"

"Yup. Unbelievably." I held up my phone. "I'm catching up on my online reading."

She removed her phone from her shoulder bag. "Good idea."

I peeked at her screen. "Getting a head start on your genealogical research?"

"Nope." She flicked through a couple of screens before angling her phone toward me.

"Solitaire?" I asked, eyeing the stacks of virtual playing cards.

"Twenty-One. My favorite guilty pleasure. That and Sudoku. They satisfy my inexplicable love affair with numbers."

"The gang's favorite guilty pleasure is Farmville. I think it reinforces their relationship with seed corn and swine."

"Do you play anything?"

"Candy Crush. It reinforces my relationship with sweets."

"I found something!" Dick Teig's voice echoed off the surrounding cliffs. I shot a look toward the far end of the beach, watching as the gang and a handful of bloggers made a beeline toward the outcropping of rock where he stood, their metal detectors clunking into each other as they swarmed around him. After receiving a minute's worth of congratulatory backslaps, Dick pelted toward me, his entourage following behind like a gaggle of hyperactive geese.

"I've really hit the jackpot this time!" whooped Dick as the rest of the gang scampered toward him. "Easy street, here we come."

"What'd you find?" I asked as he and his band of rubberneckers crowded around me.

He extended his palm, revealing a baseball-sized sphere whose sand-coated exterior was a conglomeration of mussels, tiny seashells, barnacles, and sea gunk. "Ta-da!"

"This is your jackpot?" accused Helen, lips pursed with distaste. "How absolutely underwhelming."

I stared at the hideous lump, struggling to match Dick's boyish enthusiasm. "Well, would you look at that. It's a"—I tilted my head left, then right—"...a..."

"It's a hot mess," droned Bernice.

"Maybe it just needs to be cleaned," suggested Margi, squirting a stream of hand sanitizer toward it.

We watched the sanitizing gel spread over the blob like spilled honey, adding another layer of goop to the mess.

"Dang," said Nana. "That didn't do no good at all. We need somethin' with more teeth in it."

Helen gasped. "Dick is *not* using his teeth. You hear that, Dick? I forbid you to bite into that thing." Then, to the crowd, "We just cashed in an IRA to have all his old amalgam fillings replaced with resin composite."

Nana gave her a squinty look behind her wirerims. "I was thinkin' more like one of them ball-peen hammers. They probably sell 'em at the hardware store what rented Emily the metal detectors."

"Why don't we just cut to the chase and call up the big guns?" suggested Dick Stolee. His eyes twinkled with resolve. "Low-impact explosives."

"No explosives!" I warned.

"Crack it open with a rock," urged Kathryn, sweeping her hand to indicate the breadth of the beach. "I'm sure you can find a suitable one, considering all the many different sizes you have to choose from. And when you're done smashing it open, you can use it to smash Heather's computer. It might be the only way to prevent her from spreading any more of her libelous vitriol over the internet. Don't be fooled by the girl's wide-eyed innocence, my good people. She's nothing more than a bottle-blond cyber bully."

Uh-oh. Sounded as if Kathryn had discovered Heather's blog post this morning.

"You started it," accused Heather.

"I did not. But I'll take great pleasure in finishing it." Kathryn's mouth slid into a stiff smile that caused alarm bells to go off in my head. Much to my horror, she suddenly looked like the movie franchise Chucky doll before he slashed his first victim, prompting me to wonder if the two women would even be speaking to each other when we reached our first Austen site.

"Why are you so sure there's something of value inside that thing?" Spencer Blunt asked Dick. He opened his fist. "All I've found so far is a couple of beer bottle caps. Just what I need to take home with me. Limey litter, compliments of some Cornish sot too pie-eyed to find a rubbish barrel."

"This metal-detecting crap is embarrassing," snarled Bernice. "Grown adults digging in the sand like two-year-olds." She held up her find. "Here's my reward for wasting fifteen minutes of my life with Emily's dopey metal detector."

"Oh, wow," enthused Margi. "A nail. Looks really old."

Bernice's lips curled into her signature sneer. "Yeah. Rust can have that effect on stuff. I should charge the prime minister a fee for removing litter from his public beach."

"But…what if it was part of a famous ship that wrecked off the coast here?" speculated Helen Teig. "Like a Viking ship or one of the ships in the Spanish Armada."

"Or the Good Ship Lollipop," mocked Bernice.

Helen fixed her with a piercing look. "What if it's worth a whole lot of money to someone who collects shipwreck memorabilia?"

Bernice regarded the nail with slightly less impatience. "Who'd be dumb enough to fork over good money for a rusty nail?"

"Perhaps someone wise enough to know that a rusty nail could turn out to be the find of the century," theorized Tilly.

Spencer skirted the perimeter of the group, eying the gang in the same way he might study artifacts in a museum. "Out of curiosity, what would you folks be doing right now if you weren't metal detecting? Snoozing? Massaging your joints with arthritis cream? Playing an exciting round of charades? I bet your demographic kills at charades. I mean, before the invention of TV, what else was there for old duffers like you to do at get-togethers?"

The gang stared at him, deadpan.

"I don't understand," puzzled Margi. "Is he talking about *us*?"

My cell phone chimed as an incoming call came through. Wally. "While I take this call, why don't you go back to your beachcombing? You still have a large area to explore, and don't forget the caves."

Dick Teig set his sphere of sea gunk down on the rock where Caroline was still sitting. "You don't mind watching this for me, do you, Emily? And I don't need to tell you to guard it with your life."

73

In the next instant a half-dozen of the gang shouted out the same instructions as they dumped their bottle caps, shards of sea glass, and metal pull tabs on the same rock. Bernice lifted the flap of her shoulder bag and dropped her rusty nail inside, seemingly afraid that if I were to guard her treasure, I'd be tempted to auction it off on eBay.

"I thought you were going to join me in a few minutes," I said to Wally as the troops dispersed across the beach. I ranged a look toward the cliff. "Where are you?"

"Near the coach. But I wanted to share the latest with you. Just received a call from Enyon. He's being escorted to the police station for questioning, so he wanted to tell me where to find the master key so we can let ourselves in."

"The police are questioning Enyon?"

"There's evidence suggesting that Lance might not have fallen accidentally. The postmortem revealed both bruising and a fractured vertebrae in his spine, which means someone may have literally drop-kicked him as he was heading down the staircase."

"And the police think it was Enyon?"

"They're not throwing the book at him, Emily. They're only holding him for questioning."

"But why would Enyon murder Lance on day one of their new venture? Who murders the chef on the same day the overseas guests arrive?"

"Well, someone apparently killed him. If Enyon didn't do it, who did?"

"You're not suggesting that one of the guests had a hand in it, are you?"

"They were the only other people in the house at the time, Emily. You do the math."

Not what I wanted to hear on the second day of our Cornish adventure.

In my mind's eye I could see the gang and the bloggers gathered in the hallway outside Kathryn's suite, all part of the frenzy. But the bloggers hadn't hung around for the duration. Was it possible one of them had snuck off to the kitchen to confront Lance?

My stomach executed a double flip at the implication.

Oh, God. Not again.

SIX

THE TOWN OF PORT JACOB was situated on a hill so steep, a sign warned travelers to check their brakes before venturing down High Street, which dead-ended directly into the harbor without benefit of a sea wall or guard rails. I wondered how many rental cars had careened into the drink before the town had decided to place a car park at the top of the hill, which is where our bus had let us out.

Port Jacob exuded quaint coastal charm with its whitewashed buildings tumbling higgledy-piggledy down High Street hill, leaning into each other like drunken soldiers. Flowering shrubs drooped over picket fences, their boughs dangling above cobblestone walkways that looked more menacing than a bed of nails. Pots of flowers cheered every door stoop, while hanging baskets swung from every portico, spilling out blossoms in pink, red, and purple. The hardware store where we'd rented our metal detectors—Kneebone Hardware and Museum—sat at the very top of High Street, so while Wally escorted the rest of the group down to the harbor with its galleries, craft shops, tearooms, pottery shops, restaurants, and pubs, Jackie and I returned the detectors to a man who was only slightly taller than he was wide, the proprietor of the store himself, Treeve Kneebone, who steadied himself on a walker behind the counter.

"Did you ladies have a spawny outcome?" he asked as we stacked the devices in front of him. He wore a knit cap that was pulled all the way down to his eyebrows, a knitted vest that strained to cover his expansive chest and belly, and a friendly smile that caused the loose flesh in his face to jiggle like a turkey wattle. "You should have been here for the brouhaha a few years back. The deep-sea explorers had a bit of a knees-up. Struck it rich, they did. Two hundred fifty million pounds sterling in gold and silver coins from Mexico, salvaged from the wreck of the *Merchant Royal* that went down off the coast here in 1641. And there's jewels that's still washing ashore."

"No jewels for us." I sighed. "Our discoveries fell more into the rusty nail, bottle cap, and sea gunk category."

Treeve grinned, revealing a missing canine tooth. "You found all our duff."

I gave him a blank look. "Excuse me?"

"Our junk. Our rubbish."

Jackie rolled her eyes. "Oh, yeah. We found plenty of other people's rubbish."

"Bully for you for tidying up." He slammed his fist on the counter and broke out in a bark of laughter. "Bill the government! Tell them it's for litter removal. Maybe you'll provoke an international incident. Always warms me heart to have someone throw a spanner at those bleedin' tossers in London."

"Funny you should say that," I confided. "One of our more opinionated female guests threatened to charge your prime minister for her waste-disposal services."

Treeve flattened his hand over his breast and bowed his head. "A woman after me own heart." Then back to business. "If you give me a minute, I'll dig out your paperwork and send you on your way, but since you're staying at the Stand and Deliver, I'd recommend you visit our highwayman museum before you leave." He gestured toward the far corner of the store. "It's me hobby: collecting highwaymen curiosities. You'd be surprised what people sell at flea markets and jumble sales thinking it's worthless. And to give me little display an air of authenticity, I even have a couple of exhibits on loan from the library in Truro. Me boy Jory's an accomplished artist, so he's added his own touch. And we're planning to expand from one aisle to three once we sort through everything I've collected. It's right over there in aisle five—at the end of four-wheel rollators and forearm crutches. Mornin', Nigel!" he called out as the bell above the front door jangled.

The man who entered the store wore an aircast boot strapped to his leg and was maneuvering on a set of aluminum crutches that were snugged beneath his armpits.

"I heard about your spill. Nasty break, eh?"

"Not the first time, Treeve. Won't be the last. You know how it goes."

"We'll give the museum a look-see," I agreed, unsure if Jackie gave a flip about British bandits. "Do you want to wander over to aisle five while I sign off on the paperwork?" I asked her as Treeve riffled through his receipts.

She rolled one shoulder in a half shrug and sighed with a hint of ongoing malaise. "I'll wait for you."

"Here we are." Treeve plucked our receipt from the pile and slapped it onto the counter in front of me. He handed me a pen. "Signature and date, if you please."

"Would you happen to know of any villagers who'd be willing to cook dinner at the Stand and Deliver for a night or two?" I asked as I signed on the dotted line. No time like the present to get an honest opinion from one of the locals. "For a small party of, say, twenty-one people?"

Treeve's eyes lengthened as he pulled his cap lower over his eyebrows. "Your troubles at the inn are all over the Twittersphere. It's trending number one. Me hat goes off to Gladwish. I don't know what the bloke will do without his chef, but I can tell you that all the cooks for miles around are employed elsewhere. It's summer, luv. Demand is high."

"Do you think we could lure someone away from their current position by offering them a ridiculously high wage?"

Jackie snapped to immediate attention, dollar signs registering in her eyes. "How ridiculous?"

I stared her square in the face. "Can you cook?"

A pause. "Is that a trick question?"

"No. It's the kind of question you ask a person who's applying for a position as a cook."

She fisted her hand on her hip. "I happen to be a fabulous cook. In fact, I could spit when I think of how many precious hours I wasted preparing meals for that two-timing snake I married."

Jack had learned his way around the kitchen? I fought off a twinge of jealousy that my transgender ex-husband, who couldn't even operate the electric can opener when we were married, had evolved into a decent cook while I hadn't. Obviously I needed to spend some serious face time with Betty Crocker. "Do you have any specialties?"

"Sure." She ticked the list off on her manicured fingertips. "Toast. Toast n' serve waffles. Toast n' serve breakfast tarts. Toast n' serve—"

"What about food that doesn't require a toaster? Anything from scratch?"

She regarded me, befuddled. "I thought breakfast tarts *were* from scratch."

"So tell me, ladies, what do you think really happened over there at the Stand and Deliver?" Treeve Kneebone leaned toward us, his voice a conspiratorial whisper. "Do you know the last time a murder occurred in Port Jacob? Never. Not even during the war when enemy spies were crawling out from under every rock."

"See there?" Jackie shot me a smug look as she bobbed her head at Treeve. "I'm not the only one who's suspicious of the 'Lance accidentally fell down the stairs' narrative."

"I'll not be pointing me finger at anyone, mind you," Treeve confided. "But our local DC must be suspecting a certain inn proprietor of something suspicious. Why else would he give him a personal escort to the nick for questioning this morning? Our DC is planning to retire his badge in a fortnight, so you know he'll be wanting to wrap up this case before he leaves. Me mates on High Street are taking odds that he'll be willing to pin Tori's death on anyone just to be rid of it, and Gladwish is the most likely candidate. Scuttlebutt has it we're talking murder. Port Jacob's first.

Could be good for business, though. Might even attract a film crew to do the documentary."

Jackie fired a look at me, her mouth falling open. "Did you know about this?"

Busted. "Uh…Wally might have mentioned it in a phone call to me earlier."

"And you didn't tell me?"

"If I told you, I'd have to tell everyone else, and the whole group would have hypered themselves into a frenzy."

"What's wrong with that?"

"Because just before they completely imploded, Enyon would be cleared, and all that emotional upheaval would have ended up being a total waste of energy. So no, I didn't tell you."

She twitched her lips, looking offended. "*I* would have told *you*."

"The thing is," Treeve continued, "Lance Tori was a damp squib. He didn't fit in. And I think he enjoyed not fitting in. No one understood how Gladwish tolerated the bugger's foul moods or vile temper."

"I never met Lance personally," shared Jackie, suddenly sounding like a witness for the prosecution, "but I'm pretty sure no one in our tour group liked him either. He apparently picked a fight with everyone he came in contact with, including some of the most patient and tolerant members of our group. Between you, me, and the bedpost, I think everyone had it in for him."

"Is this a good time to browse through the museum?" I asked Jackie, hoping to pry her away from Treeve before she could implicate the tour group any more than she already had. Even I knew it wasn't a good idea to admit to a complete stranger that everyone in your tour group despised the dead guy.

The store phone rang, interrupting our conversation, so while Treeve answered it, I pulled Jackie away from the counter and herded her toward aisle five. "For future reference, Jack, I'm not sure it's wise to spread the word that every guest on our tour despised Lance."

"You think I should be more accurate? Like...nineteen out of twenty-one guests despised him? What would that work out to on the percentage chart?"

"It doesn't matter. You've basically given the police a viable reason to question and detain all twenty-one of us."

"Oh." She pondered this as we passed shelves of furniture polish, feather dusters, and household cleaning products. "How are the police going to find out what I said to Treeve? Is the store bugged?"

"What if the constable is a personal friend of his? They could even be related for all we know. Do you know how easily your comment could be passed along the grapevine to someone who might decide your observation warrants further investigation? You could become the number-one trending item on Twitter."

"Really?" She gave a little shimmy of excitement. "I've never trended on Twitter before."

"Do you have any idea what this could do to our time schedule?"

"If the police release Enyon, don't you want the whole group interrogated just in case one of the guests *did* kill Lance? Or would you rather have the killer strike again after we *leave* Cornwall?

Look, Emily, if Lance's death wasn't an accident, none of us are safe, are we?"

I sometimes longed for the good old days before Jack had undergone gender reassignment surgery. She made such common-sense arguments now. She'd never been this astute when she'd been a guy.

"Okay, point well taken." As much as I'd want to find a killer, if there was one, I felt as if I was stuck between a rock and a hard place. I found Enyon so likable that I didn't want him to be the perpetrator. But if he was released from custody, that would suggest someone else at the inn had killed Lance—realistically, someone in our group—and I didn't want that to happen either.

Not this time.

We strolled past floor space jammed with four-wheel rollators and three-wheel roller walkers, aluminum crutches, wooden crutches, and walking sticks. Beyond the pegboard displays of canes in every form imaginable—folding, comfort grip, quadpod, round handle wooden—and shelving stocked with forearm and underarm crutches, we arrived at Treeve's highwayman museum.

"Have you ever seen a business that sold hardware and high-wayman lore?" asked Jackie as we scanned the orderly arrangement of glass cases.

"Nope. Night crawlers and cold beer. Fresh corn and fireworks. But never anything like this."

The display cases sat against the wall and were overhung with an exquisite hand-drawn map of Bodmin Moor that showed the moorland's proximity to Port Jacob. Squiggly lines that resembled mountain peaks illustrated the area's geologic anomalies, their names spelled out in spidery calligraphic lettering—Showery Tor,

Tolborough Tor, Brown Willy Tor. A dozen photographs flanked the map, showing panoramic views of barren wasteland, gray sky, marshy bogs, and stark isolation. And as we perused the moor with its bleak terrain and eerie rock formations, I grew aware of just how inhospitable a place could be without LED streetlights or a single PDQ.

"Brown Willy Tor," said Jackie, reading the label beneath a picture that depicted a massive tumble of rocks at the summit of a rise. "I bet there's something creepy buried under that rock pile. Look at these photos. The whole place is creepy. Cheesewring Tor." We studied a column of enormous granite slabs that were piled one atop the other like children's blocks to the height of a two-story building. "I don't think this place is in danger of turning into a golf resort any time soon. Not unless some developer can make it look a lot more tourist friendly."

"It was probably even more forbidding three hundred years ago when the highwaymen were plying their trade." I noted an antique carriage in one photo, fully restored and polished, probably sitting in a museum somewhere, and I wondered at the terror its occupants might have felt when chased across the moor in the dead of night by a masked horseman wielding pistols and knives.

As I continued to study the photographs, Jackie wended her way down the row of display cases. "Hey, the name on these charcoal sketches is Jory Kneebone. You think this is the touch Treeve's kid added? A portrait gallery of eighteenth-century criminals? They're really good."

I joined her at the display case and read the name on the identifying label beneath the drawing. "Sixteen String Jack. So that's what he looked like." He sported a straight patrician nose, overly large ears, and a mop of curly hair that peeped out from beneath the floppy brim of his hat. "He looks more like a teenage heartthrob than an infamous highwayman."

"He wasn't much more than a teenager when he died—1750–1774. He was only twenty-four years old." She scanned the biographical information that was typed on a placard below the sketch. "'Yada, yada, yada. Acquired the name Sixteen String Jack from the sixteen colorful ribbons he wore to lace the knees of his silk breeches. Yada, yada, yada. Hanged at Tyburn Tree wearing a pea-green suit with a nosegay in the buttonhole and blue ribbons tied around his leg shackles.' Ooo. A man with unfaltering fashion sense. I would've liked this guy."

"Not if he shoved a pistol in your face and demanded your valuables, you wouldn't."

As small as it was, the exhibit was intriguing. Not only had Treeve's son sketched portraits of the most notorious highwaymen of the era, he and his father had provided examples of much of the plunder the thieves had filched and showcased them amid yards of flowing satin. There was a porcelain box the size of a cosmetic compact that held breath sweeteners, porcelain eggs with enameled motifs that were used as hand-coolers for young ladies who were attending balls, and flintlock pistols, powder flasks, and hair ornaments studded with what looked like precious gems.

Treeve must have spent a fortune at flea markets in an attempt to add to his collection, but in his haste to share his hobby with the public, I wondered if he'd allowed security concerns to slip through the cracks. Upon closer examination, the display cases were more rickety than they'd first appeared, with wobbly legs and protective glass that was both chipped and loose at the corners.

"Hey, Em, look at this." Jackie lingered over one of the better-built cases. "This is a handwritten ledger kept by the constable of Port Jacob in 1749, and the ink hasn't faded—you can still read the entries. It lists all the valuables that highwaymen stole from peers of the realm on Bodmin Moor. First item on the list is a gold egg-shaped etui with ivory and agate inlay. What's an etui?"

"Isn't that like a little case that holds sewing materials or manicure sets?"

She eyed me skeptically. "How do you know that?"

"Etienne. He's developed an addiction for crossword puzzles."

"Well, this etui thing was apparently lifted from Lord and Lady Rosemurgy, along with an emerald necklace and a gold timepiece. And listen to some of the other stuff: gold snuff box with agate emblem of crossed swords inscribed with initials AT. Porcelain scent bottle painted with initials MR. Gentleman's personal fob-seal with trumpet-shaped amethyst fob, gold base, and inscribed with initials BP. Double-earred silver porringer engraved with initials SD." She turned toward me. "Sounds like these guys didn't own anything that wasn't monogrammed. Do you suppose they were all related to Donald Trump?" She snickered. "So the thieves basically stole tobacco, air freshener, a stamp, and a bowl, but the only items of value were the containers. Man, if the highwayman craze hadn't died out on its own, recyclable plastic would have killed it."

She craned her neck, giving the surrounding shelves the once-over. "Would you mind if I take a quick spin around the store? I might spot something that could come in handy for our investigation."

"*We* aren't investigating anything, Jack."

She smiled coyly as she flounced off. "We'll see."

The fact that she felt motivated enough to do a little shopping was encouraging, though. Maybe this would be her first step on the long road to emotional recovery.

I made my way back to the sales counter where Treeve was concluding a transaction with a customer in a closed-toed fracture boot who'd just purchased a plastic pail and shovel for his toddler. "At low tide, the harbor beach at the bottom of the hill will be perfect for mud pies and fairy princess castles." He gave a little peek-a-boo wave to the toddler as she raced away toward the door, pail in hand. "Mind the cobbles," he cautioned as the bell jangled their exit.

"A little late for that," the man called over his shoulder with forced humor.

"So." Treeve turned to me. "What did you think of my little museum?"

"It's awesome. Your son's drawings look like they should be hanging in an art gallery. The whole display is fascinating. But it's stuck way over there in the corner." I lowered my voice. "Aren't you afraid someone might steal something?"

"In Port Jacob? Bollocks. We don't have much problem with theft, and the tourists tend to be a good sort."

"But some of the hair ornaments look as if they're embedded with real gemstones."

"That's because they are, and I have documentation from an independent appraiser in Exeter to prove it."

"Back in the States, a thief with the right tools could rob you blind in a few minutes flat—and in broad daylight. You're not at all worried about that?"

He peered left and right before hooking his forefinger in the air to beckon me closer. "Surveillance cameras. Just in case. We've hidden them all over the store in places that don't even look like places. If a bloke so much as nicks a pack of chewing gum, we'll have his face on so many videos, it'll be plastered over the telly from here to the Orkneys. Me boy's idea." He smiled his gap-toothed smile. "When he's not working on his art, he's full-bore with his computer toys. And with the price of his toys, he'll turn me into a bloody pauper one day."

Jackie emerged from a nearby aisle with a lilt in her step and an armful of items that she dumped onto the counter. She'd obviously hit the processed food aisle, buying up a dozen packages of cookies and potato chips, or as the English would say, biscuits and crisps. Maybe her investigative plan entailed forcing potential suspects to eat excessive amounts of carbohydrates until they confessed. Like enhanced interrogation, only with sugar.

She flashed a satisfied smile. "All stocked up."

I eyed her stash. Dark chocolate digestives. Milk chocolate digestives. Shortbread rounds. Custard creams. Bourbon cream biscuits. Fruit shortcakes. *Uh-oh.* I hoped she wasn't planning to binge-eat her purchases to fill the emotional vacuum left by her husband. She'd end up hating Thom *and* herself.

"Did you find everything you were looking for?" asked Treeve as he started ringing up her items.

"Not everything." She smiled hopefully. "Do you carry ladies' wigs?"

SEVEN

ONE OF THE UNINTENDED consequences of touring a town built on a hill is that at the end of the day you have to climb back up the hill to board your bus. Since we weren't on a strict time schedule, I encouraged everyone to make the ascent in stages, with plenty of rest stops in between. I was heartened when the group followed my instructions without complaint as they made strategic stops at the tearoom for cream tea and sandwiches, the nut shop for snacks, and the ice cream shop for cones. No one suffered a heart attack from the stress of the climb, but I feared that the liberal ingestion of saturated fats during the ascent had clogged so many arteries, I'd be dealing with a slew of medical emergencies in the days to come.

Of course, the best part of the group's slow ascent to the bus was that they'd scarfed down so much food, they'd probably be too full to eat later, which was a relief since I had no clue what to do about dinner. In a perfect world Enyon would be cleared of suspicion, return to the inn, blow the dust off his cookbooks, don his old chef's hat, and prepare a meal that would knock our socks off. But the world was fueled by imperfection, so as I descended into a slow panic, I surprised myself by wondering if the local market sold toast n' serve breakfast tarts and waffles.

When we pulled into the parking lot of the inn, I was greeted by another surprise.

A neon yellow and blue checkered Port Jacob police cruiser.

I got so excited, I nearly broke into handstands, but lacking the adequate space to perform even limited acrobatics, I grabbed Jackie's arm instead. "The police. They must have finished questioning Enyon and driven him back."

She peeked out the window at the uniformed officer who was leaning against the back end of the squad car. "Oh, *pul-leese*. Do you see the look on the guy's face? Trust me. He's not here to deliver good news." She grunted with frustration. "I so need to buy more wigs. How is it that Kneebone Hardware carries every walking aid known to man but not one stinkin' wig?" She frowned. "Do you recall passing a costume shop any time in our travels today?"

A frisson of unease rippled through the bus as guests noticed the police car.

"What's up with the fuzz?" questioned Dick Teig, whose tone grew alarmed as he tacked on, "Are they going to arrest us for digging stuff up on the beach?"

"They can't arrest us if we didn't know it was illegal," assured Dick Stolee.

"They should arrest Emily," railed Bernice. "It was her idea."

Wally grabbed the microphone. "I can guarantee you that no one is going to be arrested for exercising your right to metal detect. But I do have some recent information to share, and now seems as good a time as any. Lance Tori's postmortem indicated that his death might have been deliberate rather than accidental, so earlier today, the police took Enyon in for questioning."

Gasps. Murmurs. Shock.

"If Enyon is still being questioned, I'll need to retrieve the key from its hiding place before I can open up the inn, so I'd like you to remain on the bus until I find out what's going on."

"The authorities think Enyon killed Lance?" Heather Holloway called out. "Why would he murder his only chef?"

"Maybe so he wouldn't have to eat no more stargazy pie," suggested Nana.

"Heather's right," offered August Lugar. "Without a chef, the Stand and Deliver is doomed."

"I couldn't disagree more," argued Spencer. "The inn was doomed with Tori. How long do you think their doors would have remained open if Lance had been allowed to interact with future guests like he interacted with us? The way I see it, Enyon had a choice. Run the business into the ground with Lance or run a successful business with a new chef. It seems perfectly clear which option he chose."

"Maybe a stint in a rehab facility would've helped that fella," Margi commented.

"Do they got places to rehab folks what got no manners?" asked Nana.

"Charm school," suggested Caroline Goodfriend.

"Charm school is a thing of the past," asserted Kathryn Crabbe. "People don't cough up money to learn manners anymore. They'd much rather be obnoxious."

"You oughta know," taunted Heather Holloway.

"I need to clarify my statement," Wally spoke up. "No one has accused Enyon of Lance's murder. He's only being questioned. So let's remember he's innocent until proven otherwise."

Snickers. Guffaws. Snorts.

I glanced toward the police car to find the officer limping his way across the parking lot toward us. That he walked with a pronounced limp and needed the assistance of a cane came as no surprise. From what I'd observed, everyone in Port Jacob was suffering with an ambulatory disorder that required the use of a cane, crutches, or a rolling walker. The place was probably a goldmine for orthopedic surgeons.

Wally hurried down the stairs to greet him, returning a few minutes later to deliver the news.

"Unfortunately, your afternoon and early evening schedule is about to change. The Port Jacob police have received credible information that Chef Lance Tori didn't exactly endear himself to certain members of our tour group, so Constable Tredinnick would like to document those encounters."

"How many folks does he wanna talk to?" asked Nana.

Wally hesitated. "All of us. No one gets a pass."

As a symphony of groans erupted throughout the bus, Jackie slid down in her seat as if it were a freshly waxed slide. I arched a brow. "So the police had no way of learning what you said to Treeve, huh? How's that working out?"

"We don't know it was Treeve who blabbed, Emily. I mean, maybe Enyon tried to divert suspicion away from himself by telling the police that everyone in the group had a reason to hate Lance, which is the truth—except for me." She boosted herself back up to a sitting position. "In retrospect, I'm glad I was stuck in the powder room and never got to meet him. My interview should go really quickly."

I gave her a withering look before cupping my hands around my mouth and calling out to Wally, "Is Enyon back?"

"The constable hinted that he'll probably be released late this afternoon."

Oh, thank God. I'd be off the hook for dinner, and Enyon would be in the driver's seat again…even though he was still sure to be numb from the shock of Lance's death, and suffering from another migraine, and severely depressed, and maybe unresponsive.

I flinched at the likelihood of my prediction.

Okay, so maybe Enyon would be in the back seat rather than the driver's seat, but at least he'd be here to give us some guidance.

"Constable Tredinnick will be conducting your interviews in the spa." Wally gestured toward the outbuilding at the far end of the parking lot. "I'm going to open up the inn so you can stow your things and use the facilities, but when you're done, he wants you to form a queue outside the spa. First come, first serve, so the quicker you get in line, the sooner you'll be interviewed."

"Can I go first?" Jackie leaped to her feet. "I never met Lance, so I'll be in and out of there in a minute. And that'll give the constable a lot more time to interrogate those of you who had it in for him."

I shook my head, knowing what would happen next. For the gang, queuing up for restrooms, meals, or unassigned seats was a competitive sport, so they never allowed *anyone* to get ahead of them.

Ever.

Like a silent film being played at warp speed, they were out of their seats, down the stairs, and racing toward the outbuilding beyond the parking lot. Tote bags swinging, elbows set defensively, they cut each other off like a herd of camels at the children's zoo, turning their footrace into more of a death match than an athletic contest. One of these days they were going to get their feet tangled and crash to the ground in a Gordian knot of twisted limbs and broken bones, and then there'd be hell to pay.

On the upside, at least I knew where to find the world's largest selection of ambulatory aids.

I directed Jackie's attention to the mob scene outside. "I think that was a no."

"Sorry about the chaotic exit." Wally exhaled a breath as he addressed the six bloggers who remained on the bus. "The Iowa contingent is a little obsessive about punctuality and being first in line. They're not being rude. It's just the way they're wired. I've made appeals to slow them down, but nothing seems to work."

"How about a stun gun?" suggested Spencer Blunt. "They're available commercially. And you can use them on anyone as long as the person doesn't have cardiac issues. Stun someone with a heart condition and you could be looking at fifteen years to life."

Seriously? I was beginning to think that two weeks with the gang might not be long enough for Spencer Blunt to realize that seniors could do everything he could do, but with orthopedic shoes and trifocals.

"Sprinting is probably good exercise for them," said Caroline Goodfriend, laughing. "Gets their heart rate up."

"Someone's going to get killed," Heather Holloway predicted as she stared out the window.

"Throw in a vampire and a couple of zombies and you'd have tomorrow's blog," needled Kathryn.

"How about you lay off Heather?" Mason Chatsworth scolded Kathryn. "If you have a sarcastic comment, keep it to yourself. It'll improve everyone's day."

Kathryn rose in slow motion, like an uncoiling snake, and turned around to stare at Mason. "You're young and callow. I'm going to pretend you didn't say that." She stepped into the aisle and headed toward Wally. "If the inn is locked, I'd encourage you to open it up. My readership is clamoring for my next installment."

Which reminded me: I still hadn't read her post for today.

"I'm on it," said Wally as he hurried down the steps. "Walk slowly," he called back to us.

Constable Tredinnick was limping his way toward the spa as we exited the bus, his first wave of interviewees already lined up outside the door in zigzag formation, collapsing against each other as they gasped for breath. Jackie and I trailed behind the bloggers, who were meandering toward the inn in a convivial clique light years behind Kathryn, who was already standing on the front stoop.

"I worked on the group's genealogies this afternoon in the tearoom," Caroline enthused. "I managed to dig up some fascinating information on a few people. I can hardly wait to share. Your name isn't on my list, August. Did the signup sheet pass you by without your seeing it?"

"I saw it."

"I could add your name if you like."

"I don't," he said curtly. "But I appreciate the offer."

He sure didn't sound as if he did. I couldn't read August Lugar. He was quite chatty on his food blog, but I hadn't heard him utter more than a dozen words since yesterday's meet and greet. He was sharing a room with Spencer. Did the two men talk or was August so preoccupied with his computer and online presence that he shunned any attempt at conversation? Maybe this had been going on for so long that he'd forgotten *how* to converse—plugged in electronically but out to lunch socially. Kinda made me want to throw my smartphone over the cliff.

The moment Wally opened the front door, Kathryn barged through to the interior, hot-footing it out of sight before the rest of us could even reach the lounge. The unfortunate state of affairs at the inn was on full display once Jackie opened the door to our room because everything remained as we'd left it—beds unmade, teacups unwashed, throw pillows stacked high on our one armchair with the room's teddy balanced precariously on top. I guessed Enyon's migraine had been too intense for him to perform house-keeping duties before he'd been hauled off for questioning. *I* didn't mind the oversight, but I worried that our more nitpicky guests might complain about the lack of maid service.

I sighed. I should have thought to buy more antacids at the hardware store.

Jackie dumped her bag of cookies and chips on her rumpled sheets, then hurried to the window to see how fast the line was moving at the spa.

"I wonder how much of a stickler for protocol this Tredinnick is? Someone should tell him he's wasting his time talking to those guys. None of them killed Lance."

"*I* know that, and *you* know that, but I suspect the constable is going to have to find it out for himself."

Jackie wheeled away from the window. "Would you like to see the wig I brought from home with me?" She hurried toward the mirrored dresser. "It's right here."

She opened the top drawer and riffled through the contents, pausing with consternation before slamming the drawer shut and pulling open the one below. "Did you move my stuff?"

"I haven't touched your stuff. I haven't even touched *my* stuff." I pointed to the luggage jack in the corner. "Everything is still in my suitcase."

"Well"—she opened a third drawer—"how come I can't find my wig? I put it in the first drawer. I know I did. How is this happening? I never misplace anything anymore. Oh my God. Do you think my emotional distress is causing my hormone levels to fall off the cliff? Am I going to lose my memory?"

"We all misplace stuff, Jack. Even women with perfectly balanced hormone levels, so stop stressing."

She shoved the final drawer shut and screwed her face into an unflattering contortion. "Where did I hide it?"

"It'll show up. It has to. The room isn't that big." I craned my neck to check out the interrogation line. "Now that the grass has dried out from yesterday's rain, I think I'll take a spin around the grounds. You feel like joining me?"

She shook her head as she opened the dresser drawer once again. "Not until I find my wig."

"Okay, but don't get so distracted that you forget your date with the constable."

She was already so distracted that she didn't even bother to answer me.

I meandered down the corridor, bypassing the inn's many offshooting nooks, all which ended in short hallways with upholstered window seats and oversized throw pillows. Arriving at the exit that George had discovered yesterday, I read the sign on the door that indicated this exit was for emergency use only, but I figured my exploring the premises could be categorized as an emergency since I wanted to do it before we got hit with more rain.

I didn't see evidence of an alarm system anywhere. The door appeared to be locked by a solitary deadbolt, so I shot the bolt, cracked the door slightly, exhaled a breath when no alarm sounded, and made my way down three granite stairs that were so uneven with wear, I suspected they might have been part of the original house. I also suspected there were few emergencies at the Stand and Deliver, else the stairs might have warranted better upkeep. As it was, the narrow opening where they stood was being enveloped by the boughs of a broad hedge in the same way that Sleeping Beauty's castle had been enveloped by the witch's forest.

The coastal plateau opened before me, flat as an Iowa grain farm, with grass sweeping toward the lip of a precipice that dropped off into nothingness. As I hiked toward the cliff's edge I could hear the surf rumbling below, its hollow booms vibrating through the soles of my feet. I paused a short distance from the edge and with added caution inched toward the lip.

I wasn't sure if the tide was in or out, but I could see a crescent of beach below, strewn with boulders and scree, that looked completely inaccessible except by a rappelling rope. Powerful waves broke over the rocks, leaving a froth of sea foam that lingered until the next swell whooshed over the beach, coughing up clumps of seaweed and kelp. I was looking down from such a dizzying height that the arches of my feet prickled with sensation, so I slowly backpedaled away from the edge, letting out a cry when the small patch of earth on which I'd been standing gave way like a Florida sinkhole and avalanched down the length of the cliff, sending soil and grass tumbling into the sea.

Holy crap!

Hands shaking with fright, legs wobbly, and heart lodged in my throat, I ran toward the safety of the inn as fast as my feet would take me, suddenly questioning whether the inn was as safe as Enyon had led us to believe. It might have been perched on the same spot for three hundred years, but time was catching up to it. Time…and plain old erosion.

I re-entered the inn through the emergency exit and reset the deadbolt, then navigated the corridor back toward my room, running into Nana and Tilly on the way. I cupped my hands around Nana's shoulders in a protective grip. "Listen to me. Do not go anywhere near the edge of that cliff. It's not safe. It's falling into the ocean bit by bit, and it could easily take one of you with it. It almost took me."

"No kiddin'?" said Nana. "I guess that's why them fellas warned us ahead of time."

I blinked stupidly. "They warned us?"

"It's in the informational folder in our rooms," said Tilly. "First sheet of paper in the packet. In big red capital letters: WARNING TO ALL INN GUESTS. It really grabs your attention."

"And it says the ground what's near the edge of the cliff is real unstable," Nana recapped, "so we're s'posed to stay at least ten feet back."

"Oh." *Note to self: in future, read all informational material offered by hotel, no matter how boring it looks.* "I—uh…I guess I changed rooms before I had a chance to open the folder."

Nana patted my hand in the same soothing way she used to do when I'd been a kid whimpering about a skinned knee. "You want a cup of tea, dear? We got clean teacups."

"That's good to hear. Enyon never got around to tidying our room this morning, so ours are still dirty."

"Enyon didn't wash 'em. I done it myself," she said as she and Tilly ushered me to their room. "I been doin' my own cleanin' ever since I seen them TV reports about housekeepin' shortcuts in hotels. I'm not takin' no chances no more. Everything gets cleaned even *before* I use it."

"How long have you been doing this?" I asked as Tilly unlocked their door.

"Since last night." She followed me inside. "I'm doin' what you'd call a trial run."

"Oh! How did your interview go?"

Nana flicked her hand as if swatting a fly. "Aced it."

By the time I finished my first cup of tea, I'd calmed down enough to enjoy a second cup. Tilly posted herself at the window to give me updates on the length of the interrogation line, and when it had dwindled down to one, I hightailed it out the door.

Caroline Goodfriend passed me in the parking lot on her way back from her session. "I think you're the last one, Emily. Mason is in there now."

"How'd it go?"

She grinned. "I don't want to give anything away. I'll let you find out for yourself."

The outbuilding was a rectangular structure the size of a Holly-wood bungalow. Like the main inn, the exterior was constructed of whitewashed stone, but unlike the inn, the roof was covered with shingles rather than thatching. A thicket of thorny hedges hugged the building, serving as a deterrent to would-be peeping Toms who might be tempted to spy on guests who were availing themselves of the facilities. Rose vines climbed trellises on either side of the door. Pots of flowers clustered on the front stoop. I suspected it might have served as a tool or machine shed before its renovation, but you'd never know that from looking at it now. It had undergone quite the spectacular facelift.

After waiting my turn for an exceedingly long fifteen minutes, I was delighted to have Mason Chatsworth finally exit the building, looking positively giddy rather than ruffled or beaten down. He held the door open for me. "Next."

"Went that well, did it?" I asked as I stepped onto the stoop.

"What can I say? He's a big fan of my blog and plans on visiting the states after he retires, so I gave him a list of hotels that offer the best deals during the weeks he'll be visiting. Sorry my interview took so long. It was a long list. And get this, he even complimented my 'do." He grazed his fingers over the top of his gel-spiked hair. "Said his grandson's hair is the same color green. Kid plays guitar for some heavy metal band in London, and he promised that if the band has a gig while we're in London, he'd send me an electronic ticket. The police in Cornwall are all right."

I stepped inside the building and shot a quick look around, thinking I'd accidentally stepped into a Finnish sauna, except for the floor, which was fancy poured concrete. Wood ceiling with dimmable recessed lighting. Wood-paneled walls with bench seating. Tables stacked with thirsty terrycloth towels outside the changing-room doors. A low wooden platform skirting the perimeter of the overly large spa with its battery of souped-up jets. It sat in the middle of the floor and looked big enough to accommodate at least a dozen people. The fiberglass was painted an exotic blue, a color so inviting that it conjured images of a Caribbean sea, though the faint smell of chlorine that wafted through the air reminded me more of a hospital than an exotic beach.

"Come in, come in." Constable Tredinnick motioned me forward from his perch on a bench near the changing rooms. "Step around the puddle on the floor there, if you would. Looks like the tub has sprung a leak. Enyon will have to address that when he gets back. How many after you?"

"I'm the last one."

He thwacked his cane on the bench, indicating where I should sit. "Brilliant. I'm running out of room in my notebook." He waved a pocket-sized spiral pad at me and let out what could only be described as an exhausted breath. "I feel as if I've just been introduced to every character from *The Canterbury Tales*."

With leathery skin, a shock of white hair, and a bulbous nose cobwebbed with broken veins, Constable Tredinnick looked ready to enjoy the rewards of retirement. He narrowed his gaze as I sat down next to a window that extended all the way to the ceiling. "I know you."

"You do?"

"Your face. I've seen it on the videos the guests shot when they were filming the broken pipe in the Sixteen String Jack suite. You're the tour escort. Emily Miceli."

"Afraid so."

"I've been asking everyone to verify their whereabouts from the time Mr. Tori left Mrs. Crabbe's suite until the time his body was discovered, but I've seen a dozen different camera views of where you were for the time in question, so I suspect this could be a blessedly short interview."

"I disappeared for a short time to fetch buckets with Enyon, but I carried them right back to the room, so I wasn't really alone but for a couple of minutes. And Enyon followed right behind me with more buckets, so he was in the middle of the commotion until he went to ask Lance about firing up the furnace to dry the carpet."

Tredinnick thumbed through his notepad. "The guests from Iowa were all in agreement that Mrs. Crabbe had a rather ugly kerfuffle with Mr. Tori after the water pipe burst."

"She listed her dry cleaning demands in no uncertain terms and Lance was too irritated to offer any sympathy, so he kind of kicked her out of the room. She didn't take too kindly to that."

"Did she threaten him?"

"Not officially. She called him a few unflattering names, said she hoped she was around to witness someone cut him down to size, and then she ran out of the room and isolated herself in the powder room."

"Which Lance had to pass by on his way to the kitchen," he commented, reading from his notepad.

I visualized the layout of the inn. "Uhh…yes. Kind of. It's located in an ell off the main hallway, opposite the office, fairly close to the guest lounge."

"How many minutes would you say elapsed from the time Mr. Tori left the Sixteen String Jack suite until the time you heard Enyon cry out?"

"Umm…" I did a quick calculation. "I ran down to the storage room. Ran back. Chitchatted with Enyon when he showed up.

Chitchatted with the gang after Enyon left." I bobbed my head. "Fifteen minutes?"

"Do you know where your bloggers were during this time?"

"I know they were outside Kathryn's door when the commotion first began, but they didn't hang around very long after they found out what the fuss was about. Probably wasn't blogworthy. So, except for Kathryn, I assume they all went back to their rooms."

"So they tell me. To work on their computers. Your blokes Spencer Blunt and August Lugar vouched for each other. Caroline Goodfriend and Heather Holloway vouched for each other. The only person unable to provide an alibi was Mason Chatsworth, who, although booked into a single room, had no motive to attack Mr. Tori, and Kathryn Crabbe, who, as you've already pointed out, made a great show of locking herself in the loo for a space of time that no one can verify."

The tone of his voice sent up a red flag. Had Treeve Kneebone's instincts been correct? Was Tredinnick angling to pin Lance's murder on the first viable suspect he could find? Namely Kathryn? "Are you questioning Kathryn's powder room stunt?"

"Perhaps. If the bloggers were in their rooms when Mr. Tori departed for the kitchen, and all the Iowa guests were still shoe-horned into the flooded suite in full view of each other, Mrs. Crabbe could have easily followed Mr. Tori into the kitchen without anyone seeing her and run back to the loo without being spotted."

"But…getting in and out of the powder room is a bit tricky. The door has a tendency to stick, so if she had to wrestle with it to get it open, wouldn't someone have heard the racket?"

"Mrs. Crabbe is a woman of impressive physical stature, Mrs. Miceli. I doubt she'd find a door—any door—an impediment. But please don't misinterpret. I'm not accusing her of anything. I'm simply not discounting the fact that she had a window of opportunity and a motive, however anemic." His bushy brows winged upward. "I've discovered that some people are extremely thin-skinned and get brassed off at the tiniest slight. I think of it as verbal road rage."

"Have you found any physical evidence that places Kathryn in the basement?" I was having a hard time wrapping my head around Tredinnick's scenario. Was she sufficiently fleet-footed to pull it off? Did she possess the physical dexterity to dispatch someone as muscular as Lance, even with her height and rugged frame?

"The crime scene unit was here this morning, but the only full prints they could lift off the cellar railing belonged to Enyon and Mr. Tori. There were too many officials here yesterday contaminating the area before they realized it was a crime scene. The railing turned into an alphabet soup of smeared prints. And as for hair, they found Enyon's, but, as you're well aware, Mr. Tori was rather lacking in that area."

"Are you going to arrest Kathryn?"

"I never said anything about arresting the woman. At least, not yet. But you can be sure that your tour group hasn't seen the last of me. You'll be at the inn for how long?"

"Until Friday." I grimaced inwardly. As critical as I knew it was to track down Lance's killer, I bemoaned the fact that we'd probably have to face more hours of grilling by the Port Jacob constabulary, which meant substantial changes to our day tours. I was not looking forward to breaking the news to Wally.

"In the meantime, Mrs. Miceli, I'll ride back to the nick and fetch Enyon for you. The bloke has had quite the long day of it. I'm sure he'll be glad to return home."

Yes! "So he's no longer a suspect?"

Tredinnick offered me a broad grin. "There are times, Mrs. Miceli, when a copper has to rely on good old-fashioned logic to eliminate a suspect, and this was one of those times."

I waited for him to finish, noting a flash of movement on the edge of my peripheral vision.

"We subjected Enyon to a brief psychological evaluation at the nick today, and it indicated that he's as sane as any bloke can be. And no sane bloke is going to destroy his fledgling business by killing his cook the first day out. That would be financial suicide. He and Mr. Tori had their differences, but nothing that generated animosity strong enough to commit murder. So we're releasing him—and you." He nodded toward the door in a kind of dismissal. "Thank you for speaking with me, Mrs. Miceli. But trust me, we'll be seeing much more of each other in the days to—"

The door banged open. August Lugar stormed into the room, his cool, unflappable facade disintegrating before our eyes. "Someone burglarized my room and made off with every bit of cash I brought with me. All of it!" He stabbed a finger at Tredinnick. "And you know damn well who took it. There was only one person left in the house after we took off this morning. Only one person had personal access to all our rooms."

Oh, no. He was talking about—

"Enyon Gladwish might not be a murderer," August raged, "but he *is* a thief, and I want him arrested!"

My oasis of momentary relief blew up in my face like a wad of exploded bubble gum.

Great. This was just great.

106

EIGHT

"Enyon isn't coming back tonight," I said in a rush of words, struggling not to sound panicked as I delivered the news to Wally.

He set the plates he'd just removed from the dishwasher on the counter and grew very still as he regarded me, his complexion fading from ruddy to ashen. "Why not?"

"August has accused him of going into his room and stealing all the money he'd tucked away in his suitcase, so Constable Tredinnick has decided to hold Enyon overnight for more questioning."

Wally stared at me, looking as if his whole life had just flashed before his eyes in a brief but painful heartbeat. "You gotta be kidding me."

My voice rose to Alvin the Chipmunk pitch. "Do I look like I'm kidding?"

"When was this supposed to have happened?"

"After we left the inn this morning. Enyon was the only person in the house before the police arrived, and the only person with access to the guest suites, so all fingers are pointing at him."

"How much money are we talking about?"

"Over a thousand pounds British sterling. August told Tredinnick that he and Spencer tore the room apart, but they couldn't find any trace of it."

"Was Spencer burglarized, too?"

I shook my head. "He's carrying his cash in a neck wallet."

Wally shook his head as he leaned against the sink to steady himself. "A killer isn't bad enough? Now we're dealing with a thief? And it's only day two. I can hardly wait to see what's in store for us tomorrow." He fanned his fingers through his thinning hair before holding up his forefinger as if to activate a non-electronic version of a pause button. "Give me a minute to think."

The door to the dining room swung open. Dick Stolee stepped inside, looking surprised to see us. "Oh, good. You're both here. Say, I've been elected in a landslide vote to ask what time we eat because we're all famished. We thought the battered sausage and cheesy chips we had for lunch would stick to our ribs, but nosiree. And the ice cream sundaes on our way back up to the bus were so dinky, I can hardly remember eating mine. So we're hungry again. Bernice says it's because of that lousy pie none of us could eat last night. We're all suffering from starvation accompanied by low blood sugar, dehydration, and possible kidney failure. So when do we eat, and what's on the menu?"

"Uhhh…" I lasered a look at Wally.

The door creaked open again. Margi poked her head inside. "Here you are." She retreated a step to call "They're in here!" over her shoulder before hustling across the threshold to stand beside Dick. "Caroline Goodfriend wants to know if this would be a good time for her to share the results of her genealogical search with the folks whose names she investigated." She shot a wary look around the kitchen. "Doesn't look like any food's in the works yet." She eyed the stove suspiciously. "You're not going to serve any more of those pies, are you?"

"I promise you. No more pies."

She smiled blissfully at my response, but I wondered how happy she'd be if she understood that an absence of pies meant an increase in the one food I knew I couldn't ruin.

Dry cereal.

The door banged open and Dick Teig scudded into the room at the head of a human stampede. "Are we gonna have that show-and-tell thing anytime soon, Emily?" The gang crowded in around him like sticky buns in a bundt pan. "I cleaned up my ball of sea gunk and you'll never guess what I found inside."

"Jimmy Hoffa," jeered Bernice.

Boos. Hisses. Razzberries.

"A chewy chocolate center?" I volunteered.

"I'm not telling you!" crowed Dick, letting loose a comically evil laugh. "I'm making everyone wait until the show-and-tell. But lemme tell you, it's gonna wow your shorts off."

"It better wow someone's shorts off for the mess you left in our sink," sniped Helen. "I'm not touching that faucet until housekeeping thoroughly scours and disinfects the basin. Speaking of which, no one cleaned our room today, Emily. The bed's still unmade, the towels need replacing, the mugs are dirty, and there's no mint on our pillows. For the price we're paying to stay here, I should think we deserve at least a couple of crummy mints."

"Our room wasn't made up either," confided Alice. "Is there some kind of maid's strike going on?"

"Was anyone's room cleaned?" asked Lucille.

"Ours was," said Osmond. "At least, I'm pretty sure it was." He scratched his head as he exchanged a confused look with George. "Was it?"

"Don't look at me," protested George. "I don't notice stuff like that."

"Well, I refuse to sleep in an unmade bed," crabbed Bernice, "so if housekeeping doesn't snap to it before I turn in this evening, someone is going to be giving me a big fat discount." She waggled her eyebrows in my direction.

"Is there something wrong with your physical stamina that you can't make your own bed?" quizzed Tilly.

"Yeah, there's something wrong," Bernice fired back. "I'm on vacation."

"Quiet!" Dick Stolee's voice echoed through the room. "Why did you delegate me to track Emily down if you were planning to crowd into my space and talk over me? This is supposed to be *my* gig."

Tilly sighed. "Hand a man a little power and it goes right to his head. It's rampant in every culture."

"I'm officially withdrawing my previous vote," said Bernice.

"Show of hands," Osmond called out. "All those in favor of recalling Dick Stolee, raise your—"

"I'm not gonna stand here and let you conduct a recall," griped Dick. "I quit." Elbowing his way out of the scrum, he charged through the door, shouting behind him, "Count me out of any of your future elections. The whole system's rigged!"

"Oh, dear," fretted Margi. "What do we do now? Should we nominate someone else to take his place?"

George waved his hand above his head. "Someone needs to refresh my memory. What did we elect him to do?"

Shifting stares. Blank expressions. Silence.

"Dang it," groused Osmond. "I hate when that happens."

"Maybe we didn't elect him to do nuthin'," chimed Nana. "Kinda like them folks what we send to Congress."

"Show of hands," said Osmond. "How many people think—"

"No more voting!" I snapped. It was time to cough up a schedule, sketchy as it might be. "Okay, here's the plan. Tell Caroline Goodfriend this would be a perfect time for her to go over your genealogies with you." The interlude would give Wally and me time to scrounge up something for dinner. "We'll serve dinner when she's done, and the minute you're through eating, we'll have our show-and-tell. Then tomorrow it's on to—" I fluttered my fingers, blanking out. I canted my head toward Wally. "Where are we going tomorrow?"

"To the most iconic destination in Cornwall: St. Michael's Mount."

Oohs. Ahhs. Nods of approval.

"So off you go." I made a shooing motion, but they remained anchored to the spot. I rolled my eyes. "Something else?"

"Have we seen the last of the police constable," Tilly inquired, "or will he be coming back to badger us about our whereabouts when the crime occurred?"

"I'm afraid he'll probably be popping by on a regular basis until he solves Lance's murder. But the good news is, you've all been cleared, so I'm pretty sure he won't need to question any of you again."

"Why not?" protested Dick Teig. "Does he think Iowans are too spineless to commit murder? Excuse me, but I take that as a personal insult."

"Try not to be too offended," I soothed. "You made terrible suspects. You backed up all your alibis with rather lengthy video footage."

"That shouldn't make a difference," fussed Margi. "What if we lied about our alibis? What if the video was doctored? I'm with Dick. What makes the constable think that Iowans can't be just as two-faced, deceitful, and untrustworthy as other people?"

"Yeah," Bernice enthused.

Head bobbing. Fist bumps.

I guess it was an indication of how topsy-turvy the world had become when people would take offense that they weren't deemed malicious enough to be included on the deadly suspects list.

I fixed my gaze on the group. "Did you lie about your alibis?"

"No," they responded in unison, heads shaking.

"Did you doctor your videos?"

"Of course not," Tilly spoke up. "That would be the height of dishonesty."

"Then I hate to burst your bubbles, but before you can make a name for yourselves as deplorable human beings, you're going to have to undergo some major behavioral modifications, so you better get cracking."

Faces fell. Shoulders slumped. The room filled with the murmured sounds of disappointment.

"Emily, dear," Nana tossed out, "if the constable don't think none of us killed Lance, who's he thinkin' done it?"

"Well—"

"It has to be one of the bloggers," Grace theorized. "They were the only other people in the house."

I shook my head. "They have alibis."

"All of them have alibis?" asked Lucille.

"All except Mason Chatsworth, but Constable Tredinnick is convinced that our amiable green-haired millennial had no motive to commit murder."

"He must have spread his clotted cream and jam in the right order," George reflected. "Didn't give Lance any reason to terrorize him."

"What if the bloggers lied about their alibis?" asked Margi.

"Then the constable will have to sniff out who was lying and why. But none of our bloggers knew each other before the trip, so I'm not sure what would compel them to lie for each other."

"What makes you so sure they didn't know each other?" pressed Helen.

I met her gaze, feeling slightly unsettled. "They appeared to be meeting each other for the first time at the meet and greet, so what reason would I have to think otherwise?"

"What if they were lying about not knowing each other?" suggested Margi, milking her "liar, liar, pants on fire" theme for all it was worth.

I stared at her, stunned into speechlessness. Oh. My. God. What if two of them *did* know each other? What if they were working as a team? Why hadn't I considered that angle? "I...you could be right, Margi. I have no way of knowing if any of the bloggers knew each other or not."

"Why is everyone supposing the killer was a guest at the inn?" asked George. "Is it too far-fetched to think that someone could have entered the kitchen from the outside? A neighbor? A delivery-man? Someone from the village that Lance had rubbed the wrong way one too many times?"

All eyes flew to the mudroom door as if it had just morphed into a malevolent portal through which all evil passed.

Someone from the outside? I hadn't thought of that either. Treeve Kneebone had implied that Lance hadn't fit in with the residents of Port Jacob. Had he created more enemies than friends while he was here? Mortal enemies? People who'd stop at nothing to get rid of him?

Uff-da. A minute ago there were no viable suspects other than Kathryn. Now I had so many potential bad guys to choose from that I felt as if my head was going to explode with the possibilities. "George raises a good point. In fact, you've all raised good points."

"It's like performing anthropological field research," Tilly said proudly.

I offered them a thin smile. "Look, all I can tell you at the moment is that I haven't had a chance to make an exhaustive survey of our bloggers' posts, but should any of you feel the urge to examine their archived content for material that might link them to any of their fellow bloggers, have at it. You could uncover a clue that Constable Tredinnick might overlook. Or if you access the local newspaper online, maybe something will leap out at you about the kind of relationship Lance had with the villagers and why one of them might feel impelled to arrive here in the middle of the day to kill him."

Nods. Excitement. Foot shuffling.

"One more thing before you go." I held up my hand to stop them from bounding out the door. "There's been a theft. August

Lugar has had all his money stolen from his suitcase, so until we discover the culprit, I caution you to keep your cash, passports, and valuables close to your body at all times. I packed extra neck wallets if you need another."

"Did he report the theft to the police?" asked George.

"Yup…which is the reason why Enyon won't be rejoining us this evening. He's no longer a suspect in the murder, but he's being questioned about the theft. The money didn't walk away on its own, and Enyon was the only person with access to all the rooms, so he's having to deal with the new allegations."

Nana shook her head, tsking her sympathy. "Seems to me if that young fella didn't have bad luck, he wouldn't have no luck at all."

The kitchen door inched open to reveal Caroline Goodfriend looking a bit awkward as she stood in the doorway. "I don't want to interfere with your meeting, but I'm all hooked up and ready to go if any of you want to hear the results of your ancestry searches."

"Go ahead," I encouraged. "Don't keep Caroline waiting any longer than you already have."

They maneuvered around each other like human bumper cars in their haste to be out the door first. When the room had cleared I turned back to Wally, who was still propped against the sink, looking more down-in-the-mouth than I'd ever seen him.

"I should have listened to my mother," he philosophized in a faraway voice. "I should have married the girl next door, had a dog, two-and-a-half kids, bought a station wagon, and sold women's shoes for the rest of my life."

I circled my arm around his shoulder. "Aw, c'mon, it's not that bad," I lied, wishing I'd opted for the career in shoe sales myself. "We've been through worse."

He peered at me with one eye. "When?"

The kitchen door banged open again and Nana shuffled in. "Don't know what I was thinkin'. If that young fella is stuck in the pokey tonight, he won't be here to cook us no meal."

"Nope," I admitted. "Tonight you get potluck. Wally and I will throw food into a pot, and with any luck, you'll be able to eat it."

Nana gave a loud suck on her uppers. "Get outta here, the two of you. I'll do the cookin'. Won't be much. Sandwiches maybe. But at least folks'll get fed."

Her pronouncement seemed to rouse Wally from his earlier stupor. "Can't let you do that, Mrs. Sippel. We're not going to assign guests to kitchen duty."

"You're not assignin' me. I'm volunteerin'." She scurried around the room, throwing open the doors of the kitchen's two industrial-size refrigerators to check out the inventory before disappearing into the pantry. "Plenty of fresh fruits and vegetables stockpiled," she announced when she reappeared. "Them fellas believed in surplus. Bread. Canned goods. You name it, they got it."

"And there's a massive freezer in the basement," said Wally.

"You got any menus around here what shows what we was s'posed to be served tonight?"

"Absolutely not, Nana." I twirled my forefinger in the air as an indication that she should turn around and march back through the door. "We appreciate your offer, but this is not your problem."

"No offense, dear, but if we gotta eat your cookin', it's *everyone's* problem."

My mouth dropped open at the slur. I would have feigned indignation if it hadn't been the truth. "I assume you're referring to my recent rhubarb pie?" I said in a small voice.

"You bet." She raised an eyebrow at Wally. "Worst concoction I ever ate in my life. My mouth stayed puckered for so long, the folks at the senior center thought I'd had one of them facelifts what went bad."

"What was the problem with the pie?" he asked.

"I left out the sugar," I confessed. "I kinda got distracted."

"And there's plenty in this place what can cause more distractions, so if you leave me alone, I'll see about gettin' some food on the table."

No, no, no. She had more enjoyable things to do than whip up dinner for the masses. Besides which, I'd have a guilty conscience forever. Not to mention that Mom would kill me if she found out I'd let her elderly mother engage in unnecessary physical labor. Nana hadn't cooked a full meal since Grampa Sippel had died. Her kitchen skills could be so rusty, her meal might taste even worse than my dry cereal option. And everyone would have an opinion. Would she be able to deal with the brutal aftermath? The mockery? The incivilities? The scathing review on August Lugar's food blog?

I pinned her with my gaze, steel in my eyes, my decision unwavering. "Okay."

She had this.

I'd nearly forgotten.

She spent most Sundays binge-watching the Food Network.

NINE

"I saved the best for last," Caroline Goodfriend announced, fairly giggling with excitement. She adjusted her reading glasses, her gaze ping-ponging between her computer and her notebook. "The name I researched was Baker, which is the surname Jackie Thum asked me to investigate. Baker is her mother's maiden name."

For nearly an hour now, we'd occupied the squidgy chairs in the lounge, a captive audience to Caroline's entertaining presentation that was informative, often surprising, and, in many cases, unexpectedly humorous. Even the bloggers had set aside their computers and ear buds long enough to join us, which allowed Wally the opportunity to get them up to speed with the details surrounding Enyon's continued incarceration, our recent theft, and the unwelcome news that until Enyon returned, all guests would have to tough it out with the same bed linens and towels.

Through Caroline's efforts we learned that although Alice Tjarks's family tree had first sprouted in Norway, a branch had settled in Switzerland, where they served as town criers and made quite a name for themselves as first-class yodelers. I imagined their vocal talent would have been as popular on early morning radio as Alice's crop reports, if radio had existed back then.

Dick Teig's family had its origins in Norway, too, and although the more daring Teigs immigrated to Iowa in the early 1800s, a less adventurous spur moved to Austria, becoming involved in philosophical studies at the University of Vienna, where their academic writings were seen to have influenced such notable scholars as Sigmund Freud. Dick was bummed to learn that his ancestors might have rubbed shoulders with the father of psychoanalysis because it shattered the fiction he'd built up to explain away one of his most obvious character flaws, which meant he'd no longer be able to blame his shallowness on a defective gene pool.

Caroline resumed her final genealogical narrative while Jackie sat beside me, leaning forward over her knees and clicking her fingernails against her teeth, breathless with anticipation.

"The name Baker has undergone many iterations in its journey through the centuries," she began. "In Jackie's family I found evidence of variations that include Bakewell, Bagwell, Backhouse, and Bakehouse."

"Backhouse?" squealed Margi. "Oh my goodness. Do you suppose her relatives and mine knew each other? Maybe even worked together?" Margi had been shocked to learn that her English ancestors had toiled as nightsoil men in the neighborhoods of London during the Victorian era—hearty souls who collected human waste in their little carts and disposed of it in outlying areas until the flushable toilet made its way onto the scene. London's first sanitation workers. Margi was over the moon, relieved that her fixation on hand sanitizer was less a crazed obsession than it was a subconscious nod to family genetics.

"Backhouse isn't the same as outhouse or privy," Caroline explained to Margi with a hint of amusement. "I think you might be confusing the two."

"Of course she's confusing them," Jackie sputtered, aghast. "My mother's ancestors didn't shovel poo. I'm sure you found they were an extremely tall and highly skilled bunch—artists, craftsmen, guildsmen." She made a panoramic sweep of her hand as if lighting up all the letters on *Wheel of Fortune*'s big board. "Stage actors. Playwrights. Wig makers. Famous makeup artists. Acclaimed athletes."

"They baked bread," said Caroline.

Jackie's hand fell to her lap. "Excuse me?"

"Bread. They were in the business of baking bread—for a very long time, actually. In fact, during the reign of Edward IV one of your ancestors was pilloried for selling loaves of bread that were underweight. Bakery bread used to be sold by weight, so if the weight was found lacking, the baker was in violation of the law and could be fined, flogged, or pilloried."

Jackie clutched her throat. "That is *so* inhumane."

"Life stinks, doesn't it?" sniped Bernice.

Bernice was disappointed because her genealogy hadn't wowed her. It indicated that her paternal ancestors had fled Europe because they didn't like the politics, fled the American plains because they didn't like rampaging buffalo, fled the American West because they didn't like dust storms and drought, and settled in Iowa because they didn't like having to move around so much. The revelations were more than historically informative; they were proof positive that Bernice wasn't adopted.

"Happily," Caroline continued, "the violation of underweight bread appeared to be a onetime offense, so your ancestors continued baking bread loaves throughout the early 1500s, when they began experimenting with other types of pastry and confections. Henry Tudor took note and issued a royal decree that their bakery should be closed and all your relatives should have their—"

"Oh, God!" Jackie agonized. She clapped her hands over her ears and pinched her eyes shut. "They should have their heads lopped off?"

"They should have their belongings sent to Hampton Court Palace," said Caroline.

Jackie looked even more horrified. "So they could be burned at the stake?"

Caroline laughed. "So they could be installed in the kitchen as the king's own pastry and confection cooks. Monarchs might have come and gone, but your family attained such high acclaim for their culinary innovations that they remained in the palace for generations. They were the premiere bakers for the Tudors, the Stuarts, and most of the Hanovers. In the annals of baking history, your ancestors were absolutely unparalleled."

Jackie straightened up so quickly, I heard her spine crack. "They were famous?"

"On a grand scale," Caroline assured.

Bernice snorted. "If they were so famous, how come no one's ever heard of them?"

"A lot of people have heard of them," Caroline acknowledged, "but you probably don't run in the same circles. I bet Lance would have known who they were. I suspect culinary institutes around the world still teach some of the techniques Jackie's ancestors perfected."

"Imagine," cooed Jackie, clasping her hands beneath her chin with delight. "My relatives schmoozed with Henry Tudor and Elizabeth the First and—"

"Don't delude yourself," Kathryn Crabbe spoke up. "Kings didn't schmooze with the riffraff in the kitchen. Your relatives were servants of the crown; nothing more. *My* relatives, on the other hand, have been consorting with royalty on an equal footing for centuries."

Caroline was quick to respond. "I think even you might agree, Kathryn, that none of us can know with any certainty who schmoozed with whom."

"*I* know," Kathryn huffed.

"Is there anything you *don't* know?" challenged Spencer Blunt.

Kathryn eyed him with the same regard she might give a food stain on wash-and-wear fabric. "Perhaps we should compare academic degrees, if you dare."

Before the dialogue could escalate into an insult-laced free-for-all, I hopped off the settee. "I'm sure everyone would like to join me in thanking Caroline for taking the time to research so many of our family histories. How about treating our genealogist to a well-deserved round of applause?" I clapped enthusiastically, gratified when the entire room filled with applause that lasted so long, I missed the cue from the kitchen until Nana marched into the dining room with a handbell in her fist, ringing it as if she were soliciting charitable donations for the iconic red kettle.

"Dinner's ready! Come and get it. We're doin' this cafeteria-style on account of I'm not no waitress, so you can all file into the kitchen to pick up your food and silverware."

The clapping stopped, but no one moved as they regarded Nana in some confusion.

"We were thinking you were going to surprise us with takeout pizza," said Dick Teig.

"Sorry," I apologized. "No pizza. Since Enyon is still at the police station, Nana has graciously volunteered to prepare our dinner this evening."

Mumbling. Frowns. Arm crossing.

"Your brochure said a world-class chef would be cooking our meals in this hellhole," grumbled Bernice.

A smile froze on my lips. "As well he would…if he weren't so inconveniently *dead*."

"So now we're stuck eating Marion's homestyle slop?" Bernice contorted her mouth with distaste. "You should have found a substitute. That's your job, isn't it? To deliver what you promised? I can tell you one thing: you'll never convince me to eat Marion Sippel's version of Cornish cuisine."

"I second what she just said," Kathryn agreed. "I didn't pay top dollar to eat cut-rate food served cafeteria-style by a woman who doesn't have official cooking credentials."

Bernice raised an eyebrow at Kathryn. "*You* didn't *pay* top dollar. You got a discount, so your opinion doesn't count."

"Yes it does," snapped Kathryn.

"No it doesn't," countered Bernice.

"Yes it—"

Nana gave her handbell a furious ring again. "No skin off my teeth if some of you folks don't want no supper, but if the rest of you are fixin' to eat tonight, the line starts at the kitchen door."

Her message delivered, she marched back toward the kitchen. Kathryn folded her arms beneath her bosom, smug in her dissention. "I'm planning to boycott the event. Should any of you decide to join me, you're certainly welcome to sit here with—"

The lounge emptied in five seconds flat, with Bernice sprinting to the front of the pack to be first in line.

I had to hand it to her, if there had been any fast-talking politicians among her immigrant ancestors—the kind who said one thing to your face but did another behind your back—she would have done them proud.

"Look at them," Kathryn mocked. "Lemmings. Lining up for a meal that has all the earmarks of tasting even worse than the one last night."

· · · · · · · · · ·

The meal was magnificent.

Nana had raided the pantry and refrigerator until she'd found the perfect ingredients to concoct a Marion Sippel original—an open-faced sandwich on sourdough bread with turkey, green apple, fig jam, and melted brie cheese. So many people requested a second serving that Nana ended up slaving away in the kitchen until she announced that there wasn't any more fuel in the little gizmo she was using to melt the cheese.

"If we pick up more fuel on our way back from St. Michael's Mount, will you cook the same thing tomorrow night?" pleaded Dick Teig.

We were still seated around the dining table, feeling fat and happy.

"What about breakfast?" asked Margi. "Do you take requests? Because my favorite is pancakes with fresh strawberries, brown sugar, chocolate chips, a sprinkle of confectioner's sugar, and lots of low-cal whipped cream." She smiled benignly. "Have to watch those calories."

I pushed my chair away from the table and stood up. "I hate to disrupt your breakfast plans, but Nana isn't our official cook."

"Well, she should be," declared Lucille. "Marion can cook rings around that Lance fella."

"All those in favor of making Marion our official cook, say aye," instructed Osmond.

The response came in a collectively shouted "aye," which prompted Dick Stolee to explain, "The only reason I'm voting is because being hungry gives me indigestion. But I still think the system's rigged."

"That settles it, then," enthused Dick Teig. "Marion's our new cook. So what have you whipped up for dessert?"

"I didn't have no time to whip up no fancy dessert, so you're gettin' storebought ice cream."

"With chocolate sauce, sprinkles, whipped cream, and maraschino cherries?" asked Margi.

"With a bowl and a spoon," said Nana.

"I'll dish it out." Wally hopped out of his chair. "And I'm volunteering for clean-up, so as of now your duties have ended, Marion. Here. You can have my seat."

"I hope you're not planning to serve ice cream every night," crabbed Bernice. "You're really pushing the envelope with the lactose-intolerant set."

"Nana is *not* our official cook," I reiterated.

"Yes she is," corrected Dick Teig. "We voted on it."

"Contrary to the results of your vote," I clarified, "she's a guest on this tour, not an employee."

"But the vote was unanimous," said Margi, puzzled.

Lucille looked apoplectic. "If you discount our vote on the small things, what'll stop you from taking it to the next level? Birth certificates to prove we were born. Photo IDs to prove we're not impersonating each other. Shortened time periods for shouting out our vote. You might as well ship us off to a third-world country."

"Or Wisconsin," said Tilly.

"We don't need to ship no one off to Wisconsin," said Nana as she removed her apron and took a seat at the table. "I don't mind feedin' you folks until that Enyon fella comes back, but I'm not caterin' to no picky eaters. You eat what I put in front of you, no bellyachin', else every one of you can hightail it into the kitchen and fix your own grub."

A dozen pairs of unblinking eyes riveted on Bernice.

"What?" Bernice barked.

"Did you hear what Marion said?" questioned Grace. "No complaining. From *anyone*."

Dick Teig made a gun of his forefinger and aimed it at her. "If my wife has to walk into that kitchen and cook my meal, I'm gonna be one unhappy camper because Marion's cooking is a helluva lot better than Helen's, so you better keep your negative comments to yourself."

"Excuse me?" snapped Helen.

"You'll be persona non grata in this tour group," warned Lucille.

Margi nodded agreement. "Not only that, but you won't be welcome."

"We could decide to ban you from all future trips," boomed Dick Stolee.

Bernice raised an eyebrow. "Says who?"

"Osmond could bring it to referendum," suggested George. "Secret ballot. Everyone votes."

Margi's face contorted in confusion. "But Emily said our votes don't count anymore."

"I did not. I was merely pointing out that your collective approval to make Nana your cook wouldn't hold water if she wasn't on board with the idea."

Margi squinted behind her glasses. "Right. So our votes don't count anymore. Dick's right. The system's rigged."

"Morons," spat Bernice. She slid her chair away from the table and stood up. "Maybe I won't want to sign up for any more of your stupid trips. Maybe I'd rather be around people who think the same way I do."

"Are you sure the isolation won't be too depressing?" asked Alice.

"You people would wander off a cliff if it wasn't for me feeding you a constant dose of reality. You need someone like me to help you break out of your dopey liberal bubbles, but you're just too stupid to realize it. So someone else can have my ice cream. I'm not hanging around for dessert."

"Wait, Bernice," I urged as she crab-walked toward the lounge. "They were just pulling your leg. They didn't mean any of the things they said."

"Yes we did," said Dick Teig.

I glared at him. "They love traveling with you!"

"No we don't," said Dick Stolee.

She disappeared down the corridor without a backward glance. I fisted my hands on the table, ranging an irritated look left and right. "I trust you'll do the right thing and apologize to Bernice *in person* tomorrow morning."

Groans. Grumbles. Razzberries.

"As contrary as she can sometimes be, she's a longstanding member of this group and deserves to be treated with your respect. And furthermore, I'll hear no more talk about banning anyone from anything, Dick Stolee. That's not your call to make."

He shrugged. "It works for presidential candidates."

"You're not running for president."

"What if we don't see her in the morning?" asked Dick Teig.

I regarded him oddly. "Why wouldn't you see her?"

"What if we're already on the bus before she drags herself out to join us? Can we send her a text message instead?"

"No."

"How about a Tweet with the hashtag #sorrybernice?" suggested Dick Stolee.

"Or a 'We're Sorry, Bernice' Facebook page," enthused Dick Teig.

"Or a Snapchat photo of all of us saying we're sorry at the same time," persisted Dick Stolee.

Oh, God.

"I've got vanilla and vanilla," announced Wally as he swept into the room carrying two sherbet glasses. "Who wants them?"

. . . .

After scarfing down our ice cream with only Heather Holloway and George complaining of brain freezes, we retired to the lounge for our show-and-tell, joining Kathryn, who had stuck by her boycott and remained in the room for the entire meal, working on her laptop.

"You might want to think about ending your boycott," August Lugar commented as he found a chair near Kathryn. "Mrs. Sippel's cooking is sensational. Mouth-watering, even. A tempting treat for the taste buds."

Kathryn stuck her nose in the air like a pampered pooch. "Huh."

"Does everyone have their treasure?" I asked as the group spread throughout the room, staking out the most comfortable seats.

"If this gets really boring, we can leave, right?" asked Spencer Blunt.

I gave him an indulgent look. "Show-and-tell isn't mandatory, Spencer. You can leave at any time."

"Good. Because the whole exercise sounds pretty lame to me."

"Well I'll be," said Nana, smiling. "Who does that sound like?"

Spencer reached inside his shirt pocket and handed me a round metal object. "This is the best thing I found on the beach today. Looks like a button. Woohoo. That's my contribution, so I'm outta here. I need to work on my blog." With a half salute to the room, he was loping toward the hallway before everyone had even found a seat.

"I didn't find any buttons," said August Lugar, rising to his feet. "In fact, I didn't find anything, so I'm going to borrow a page from Spencer's book and retire for the evening."

"Me, too," Mason Chatsworth spoke up. "I struck out at the beach and I've got a lot more work to do on my blog before I can post it tomorrow, so duty calls. But I hope the rest of you had better luck than I did."

That three of our bloggers were returning to their rooms shouldn't have bothered me, but considering the recent incidents of criminality at the inn, it did.

"What did Spencer find?" asked Tilly when the men had left.

I held it up between my thumb and forefinger for the room to see. "A metal button. It's pretty beaten up, but there's an anchor on it, so maybe it's some kind of Royal Navy button."

"Looks to me as if it belongs in the dustbin," said Kathryn.

"I'll take it," said Nana. "My great-grandson has a button collection, so he'll think it's nifty. Won't matter that it's beat up. I've seen his collection. He's not into pretty."

I flipped it through the air to her. "Okay, who wants to go next?"

At the end of ten minutes we'd accumulated an unimpressive stash of junk to show for our metal-detecting stint at the Bedruthan Steps. Chief among the non-metal throwaways was a piece of yellow sea glass that Alice swore resembled an ear of Iowa sweet corn and a rock that Osmond swore was shaped like Elvis's guitar...or anyone's guitar, for that matter. Dick Stolee had found enough beer bottle caps to rival my nephew David's button collection, and Jackie had dug up a political campaign pin from 1984, but the majority of finds was an assortment of bolts, nails, corroded hinges, metal badges, and other miscellaneous scraps of hardware.

"Well," I lamented as I regarded the pathetic display on the coffee table, "I wonder if we would have had better luck on dry land?"

"And then there's me," said Dick Teig, bouncing out of his chair to join me center stage. "The morning wasn't a total failure." He opened his fist to reveal an object that was neither rusted, rotted, nor junky.

It was a coin about the size of a half dollar.

He'd scraped away all the gunk so that the impressions were visible: the bust of a man wearing a periwig and cravat on one side with a heraldic shield stamped on the other. The date beneath the bust read 1798. The lettering over his head was more cryptic. "H-I-S-P," I said aloud, trying to dredge up grade-school history lessons. "Would that be shorthand for Hispaniola?" I flipped the coin over to study the reverse side. "I don't know what any of the lettering on this side means." But I was fairly certain about one thing.

The coin was neither silver nor copper nor bronze. It sat heavily in the palm of my hand and glinted like the teeth in Captain Jack Sparrow's mouth.

"Oh my God, Dick." I stared at the coin, transfixed. "Is this gold?"

"You betcha!" he whooped. "Told you I hit the jackpot." He raised his arms above his head in celebration and rotated his hips in a gyrating motion that sparked images of the hula hoop craze... minus the hoop. "Pack your bags for easy street, Helen. We've got it made now, baby!"

She offered him a bland smile, her eyes filled with skepticism. "You'll understand if I wait for a professional appraisal before I pop the champagne cork."

"May I see that coin, Emily?" Tilly extended her hand in my direction. "While I have no expertise in numismatics, I do have a slight familiarity with the history of coins throughout the ages."

I didn't want to question Tilly's humble assessment of her own knowledge, but her definition of "slight familiarity" usually entailed enough information to fill up every available gigabyte on a thumb drive.

Dick Teig snatched it out of my hand and hurried it over to Tilly himself. "It's the real McCoy, right? It's not something a college kid would have ordered online for a Pirates of the Caribbean frat party, is it?"

While Dick hovered bedside Tilly in breathless anticipation, I addressed the rest of the room. "Anyone else have something to share?"

"I do." Heather threaded her way through the maze of furniture with a lot more enthusiasm than Spencer had shown.

"This should be priceless," Kathryn scoffed in a voice that carried throughout the lounge. "Let me guess what you found: scrap metal in the shape of a zombie?"

Heather ignored the slur as she held her treasure up for the room's scrutiny.

Oohs. Ahhs. Scattered head scratching.

"That's a real nice find," commented Nana. "What is it?"

"I think it's some kind of stamp like you buy at scrapbooking stores for making impressions in sealing wax."

Only a stamp like this wasn't purchased in any scrapbooking store. It was shaped like an Easter lily, about two inches long, and was made of lavender glass with a metal ring attached to the top.

"At first I thought the thing was made of some type of synthetic material, but I'm pretty sure now that it's made of amethyst because it looks exactly like my birthstone. And I'm willing to bet that the base it's mounted on and the ring at the top are made of solid gold because my detector went nuts when I got close."

"What's the ring at the top for?" asked Margi.

"I wondered about that, too," admitted Heather. "That's so the owner could wear it on a chain around her neck like a piece of jewelry and have it handy in case she needed to personalize letters and stuff."

Kathryn snorted. "In addition to zombies, you're an expert on fob-seals, are you?"

"No." Heather's voice was cool and controlled. "I merely consulted the experts online. Their websites were quite informative and explained everything there was to know about fob-seals. Based on their documentation, I have reason to believe that my seal may date back to the 1700s."

"Which part of the beach were you exploring when you found it?" asked Grace.

"I was in that gnarly looking cave by the stairs. At least, I thought it was a cave—it turned out to be a tunnel that led to a really rocky beach on the other side of the headland. My detector started pinging like crazy near the entrance to the other beach. That's where I dug it up."

"Based on aesthetic appeal, Heather wins the prize," declared George.

"There's a prize?" asked Heather.

"No prize," I spoke up. "That's just wishful thinking on George's part."

"As far as I can tell," Tilly interrupted, adopting her professor's voice, "Dick's coin is authentic."

"Wha'd I tell you!" cried Dick.

"It's most probably of Spanish origin," she continued. "In fact, I'd guess that the bust on the obverse side is none other than King Ferdinand himself—of Ferdinand and Isabella fame—and the coat of arms is the Hapsburg Shield, which denotes the royal lineage of the couple." She held the coin high in the air. "Can you see that the edges have a manufactured finish? This lends authenticity to its 1798 mint date because prior to 1733 coins were produced by simply slicing them off the end of a gold bar, giving them an irregular shape that was easy to counterfeit." She elicited a girlish laugh. "I believe what Dick has found is a gold doubloon."

"Pirate's gold?" whooped Dick. "A real gold dubloon?"

"Can we back up a minute?" Jackie asked, waving her arm above her head. "I still have questions about Heather's fob-seal. Are there initials at the bottom?"

"Sure are." She studied the base. "They're engraved in the amethyst."

"Can you tell what they are?"

Heather shook her head. "There's so many curlicues, I'm really not sure."

"Shall I give it a try?" asked Tilly as she handed Dick's doubloon back to him. "I'm quite convinced that if I can decipher my doctor's handwriting, I can decipher anything."

"Knock yourself out," said Heather.

"Does anyone know what the going rate for a gold doubloon is?" asked Dick. "It's gotta be gazillions, right?"

The gang fired up their smartphones.

"You're spot-on about the curlicues," said Tilly. "But if I eliminate all the swirls and fussiness, I believe I can make out two distinct letters."

"Geez Louise," hooted Dick Stolee. "It says here that depending on the physical condition and date of issue, that coin in your hand could be worth as much as ten thousand dollars."

"Ten thousand?" marveled Helen in disbelief. She launched herself out of her chair and ran open-armed to Dick, smothering him in kisses. "You wonderful man! Ten grand would be enough to replace the appliances in the kitchen or the furniture in the den or—"

"My website says two thousand," countered Lucille. "That might be enough to replace your toilet."

"The first letter is an extremely stylized B followed by an equally stylized P," announced Tilly.

"BP?" questioned Jackie with excitement. "You're sure?"

"Well, I'll be," said Nana. "You s'pose some fella from British Petroleum lost it when he was cleanin' up an oil spill?"

"I think it belonged to an aristocrat who was robbed of an amethyst fob-seal on Bodmin Moor," regaled Jackie. "Emily and I browsed through the highwayman museum in the hardware store in Port Jacob today and read an official ledger that listed the personal items reported stolen on the moor. The fob-seal listed on the museum ledger was supposedly trumpet-shaped, like Heather's, made of amethyst, and inscribed with the initials BP. This might be the wildest coincidence in history, but I wonder if Heather found the seal that was stolen from some squire or lord three hundred years ago? His name is probably in the ledger. You think we should phone the proprietor to see if he'll tell us the exact name?"

"No need to bother the proprietor." Kathryn executed a few keystrokes on her laptop. "I know exactly who BP is." She turned her laptop around so that the screen was visible to the rest of the room. She'd accessed a site with a coat of arms prominently displayed in a banner that flowed across the top of the page. "Baron Penwithick. The tenth baron, to be precise. It's all documented here in the family history. You all know how meticulous the British are about writing down all the minutiae in their lives." She scrolled through the document until she found what she was looking for. "And I quote, 'The tenth baron was relieved of an amethyst fob-seal when beset by highwaymen on the moor—13 August 1742. He commissioned another to replace it in a similar trumpet shape, but made of cornelian, with the same gold fittings. Report was made to the constabulary of Port Jacob for entry in their ledger.'

"So as you can see, that fob-seal rightfully belongs to me." Kathryn skewered Heather with a fierce look. "And I want it back."

TEN

Heather burst into peals of laughter. "Like *that's* going to happen."

"If it *doesn't* happen, I'll give you fair warning." Kathryn's voice dripped with self-righteousness. "You can expect consequences."

Heather scrutinized the seal, rotating it in her hand like a rotisserie chicken. "I don't see your name engraved anywhere on it. Gee, I guess that means finders keepers."

Kathryn narrowed her eyes, her face morphing to stone. "I would encourage you to realize the seriousness of this matter. My family is very influential. We have lawyers who will delight in crushing you in court."

Heather bobbed her head with casual indifference. "If you were a nicer person, I might be tempted to hand it over. But you're not. So I'm keeping it."

Kathryn paused for a long, tension-filled moment. "That's the worst decision you'll ever make."

Heather smiled. "Whatever. You want some free advice from a fellow blogger? Work on a kinder, gentler you. This pretentious, self-important act you're peddling gets really old, and it's not winning you any friends." With an exaggerated flourish, she bowed to the audience. "That's all I have to say, so I guess I'm done."

"You most certainly are," Kathryn muttered in an undertone loud enough for me to hear.

"Okay, this concludes the evening's entertainment," I announced as people started shifting in their seats. "Thanks for participating. I hope you had fun, and I hope all your treasures turn out to be valuable."

Dick Stolee heaved himself to his feet. "If Bernice was here, this is the point where she'd say, 'Another evening wasted on one of Emily's screwball ideas.'"

"Or 'I'da had a better time watching the test pattern on TV,'" said George.

"Or 'This show-and-tell baloney is for losers,'" added Margi.

Osmond nodded. "Aren't we lucky she's not here so we don't have to listen to any of her negative comments?"

"One more thing before you go." I made a megaphone of my hands so I could be heard above the chatter. "We should try to get a fairly early start tomorrow for St. Michael's Mount, so I'm going to suggest breakfast at eight o'clock." I glanced at Nana. "Can you manage eight o'clock?"

"There's nuthin' I can't manage once, but I don't wanna make no steady habit of it."

She was such a trooper. Her stint in the kitchen had seemed to energize her tonight, but I feared what would happen if she overdid it. "Okay, then. Tomorrow morning at eight o'clock it is."

"Anyone want a closer look at my doubloon?" asked Dick Teig as the gang started to break up. "Private viewings begin in my room in five minutes."

It was so like Dick to want to show off his coin. I just hoped he had sense enough to secure it in a safe place afterward.

· · · · · · · · · ·

"My wig has to be here someplace," reasoned Jackie as she checked the dresser drawers yet again in the improbable hope that she'd missed seeing it the previous six times she'd looked. "How does a wig just disappear into thin air?"

"You're absolutely sure you packed it?" I said, yawning. I was in my cot, my forearm braced across my eyes to block the glare from the overhead light.

"I don't remember packing it as much as I remember unpacking it. I shook it out and put it right here in this drawer." Her tone grew anxious as she crossed the room to the closet. "This is a disaster, Emily. I haven't even paid the charge on my credit card for it yet." She hauled her suitcase out of the closet and threw it open. I turned my head on my pillow and squinted at her through one eye.

"Any luck?"

"Not here." She shoved the suitcase back in the closet before slumping onto the bed, shoulders bent, head hanging down to her chest, her voice laced with self-recrimination. "I never should have bought it in the first place, but I was so angry at Thom that I decided I needed to treat myself to something expensive." A slight lilt returned to her voice. "It actually made me feel much better at the time. I wonder why doctors pooh-pooh the curative powers of shopping, especially since the side effects don't include things like nausea, constipation, diarrhea, dizziness, internal bleeding, or death?"

"Maybe they'll give it more attention when debt and bankruptcy get relabeled as medical conditions."

She let out a groan that conjured an image of an animal whose paw was caught in a trap. "I really stepped in it this time, Emily. I'll never be able to pay that bill. I am so screwed." She sniffed pathetically, on the verge of tears. "Do you know what a 'non-payment of bill' notice will do to my credit rating? It'll send it nosediving into the toilet. I loved my credit rating. It was almost perfect: eight hundred thirty-three. Did you know some institute conducted a study recently that suggested a high credit score was a better predictor of a successful marriage than a compatible astrological sign?" Her voice grew small and wistful. "Except, of course, in my case."

Even though she'd left me high and dry for another man, upended my acting career, and turned my life into an American telenovela, seeing her this miserable tugged at my heartstrings. I boosted myself onto my elbows. "Do you need a hug?"

She nodded, teary-eyed. "Okay."

She shuffled over to my cot and sat down on the edge, crumpling against me, her head nuzzled into the crook of my neck. "Things will get better, Jack. You'll see. They always get better." I patted her back in a soothing rhythmic motion.

"No they won't. They're only going to get worse. I can picture the outcome now. I'm going to end up homeless and alone, like some sixties cult-film antihero."

"You are not. You're made of stronger stuff than that. Look at your ancestors. Did they throw in the towel after they were convicted of selling underweight bread? No. They improved their effi-

140

ciency, expanded their product line, and became the premiere bakers to three of the most famous royal houses in England."

Jackie sighed. "A lot of good that does me."

"But Jack, you have their genes! They weren't quitters and neither are you." I paused as I recalled her work history. "So what if you resign from positions on a regular basis? That usually happens only *after* you've achieved success, so you're not really quitting. You're...you're moving on to greater challenges."

She chewed on that for a moment. "What you're saying is, I have a short attention span and get bored really easily."

I bobbed my head. "In so many words."

She eased away from my hug as she knuckled tears from her cheeks. "Is my mascara smearing?"

"Nope."

"It's a new kind." She blinked rapidly, sniffling. "Guaranteed not to smear even after exposure to torrential rain, jet spray shower heads, or Oprah book club novels."

I studied her lashes. "Wow. So how do you take it off?"

"I haven't figured that out yet."

She executed a little shimmy-shake that appeared to reboot her emotional state to a less melancholy setting, at least momentarily. "Okay, so I have noteworthy genes. *Famous* genes. What I don't have is a job."

"I'm getting to that." I'd probably end up kicking myself in the morning, but it suddenly occurred to me that I could address two immediate problems with one simple solution. "I've given your request for a job at Destinations Travel further consideration, and I'm willing to make an offer."

"Omigod! You are?"

"Employment starts immediately."

"How immediately?"

"Tomorrow morning immediately. Are you up for it?"

"Yes!" She threw her arms around me in a crushing hug. "Thank you, Emily! You won't be sorry. I'll be the best travel escort ever. I'll make you so proud. Guests will be lining up to sign onto my tours. Where am I going? Someplace really exotic? I'd love to do the South Pacific islands before the ocean swallows them up. Tahiti. Fiji. Bora Bora. Or maybe Antarctica, but I'd have to buy warmer boots with a fur lining and maybe two-inch heels instead of five. So don't keep me in suspense." She pushed away from me, her eyes bright with excitement, her hands effecting little pattycake claps. "Where's it going to be?"

"The kitchen."

She froze up like a plaster body cast. "Did you say kitchen? Or did you mean Ketchikan? Because I could certainly conduct a tour in Alaska. I'd just have to buy more boots."

"I did say kitchen—the kitchen here at the inn. I think Nana's workload might wear her out more than she realizes, so as a probationary assignment, I'd like you to act as her sous chef."

"But…I thought you were hiring me as a tour escort."

"This is one of those responsibilities that falls under the umbrella of 'other duties as specified by the employer.' If you knock it out of the ball park, I'm sure you'll earn enough rewards points to be in line for other assignments."

"But…it involves cooking. I can't do what Mrs. S did at dinner, Emily." A nervous tremor distorted her voice. "Now that I think about it, I really can't do anything more complicated than toast n' serve."

"If your ancestors could do it, you can do it. All you have to do is tap into those dormant genes and you'll be golden. It's in you, sweetie. Where's that famous confidence of yours?"

"It went into hiding when I found Thom in bed with his bleached-blond bimbo."

"C'mon, Jack. This could be the start of a whole new future for you. Are you going to let Thom's behavior stand in the way of that? Because if you do, he wins. Is that what you want?"

She gnawed her bottom lip like a squirrel gnawing nuts. "You really think I can do it?"

"I know you can." At least, I was pretty sure she could…as long as she followed Nana's directions, was okay with being out of the spotlight, and didn't get bored in the middle of meal preparation and flounce off. That was possible, wasn't it?

My stomach fluttered with a legion of hyperactive butterflies.

Oh, God. What have I done?

She gave her head a single decisive nod. "Okay. I'll do it." She gave another pattycake clap. "Should we discuss salary?"

"We should, but I'll need to finalize the numbers with Etienne before I present them to you."

"How long is that going to take?"

"I'm sure he'll contact me as soon as he gets his cell phone back." And I wasn't looking forward to the call because I had no idea how he was going to react.

But we *had* to feed the guests, so if Jackie was willing to help Nana out, wasn't it my moral obligation to hire her whether we could afford the expense or not? Besides, Jackie's having a job might prevent her from suffering an immediate nervous break-down, so that was a bonus, wasn't it?

Etienne couldn't fault me for my motives, could he?

The butterflies treated me to a repeat performance.

"The next thing we should discuss is my wardrobe allowance," Jackie said matter-of-factly. "Is footwear normally included in that or are shoes covered under a separate allowance?"

. . . .

By the time the alarm on my cell phone went off in the morning, Jackie's bed was already empty, but she'd propped pillows behind Teddy and written a note that she'd placed between his paws. "Thanks, Em," it read, followed by the happiest smiley face ever drawn.

I was tickled that my job offer had buoyed her spirits so much. I just hoped that Nana would find her assistance to be more help than hindrance and that her enthusiasm would last for more than a minute.

Cradling my phone in my hand, I stared at the screen, wondering if this would be a good time for me to compose a message to Etienne, explaining why I'd found it necessary to hire a new employee without consulting him first.

Knock, knock, knock.

Darn. Guess I'd have to put it off until later.

"Just a sec!" Giddy with my reprieve, I threw my robe over my shoulders and opened the door to find Alice Tjarks looking nervously apologetic.

"I'm sorry to bother you so early in the morning, Emily."

"That's okay, Alice. What's up?"

"It's Bernice."

A frisson of alarm slithered down my spine. "Is she all right?"

"I have no way of knowing. She's not in our room."

"Is she in the dining room?"

"Nope. The thing is…she's been gone all night."

ELEVEN

"SHE WASN'T IN THE ROOM when I got back from the show-and-tell last night, but I figured she might have sneaked out the back way to the spa, so I got ready for bed without thinking too much about it. You know Bernice. As much as she enjoys acting like a drama queen and getting all upset, she doesn't stay upset for long."

After throwing on some clothes, I'd scurried Alice off to Wally's room, so she was obliging us by giving us the blow-by-blow of the night before.

"What was she upset about?" asked Wally.

"You were in the kitchen when the melodrama erupted," I explained. "Long story short, the gang was trying to rein in Bernice's negativity, and she reacted with a rant that ended when she left the dining table in a snit."

"So she was mad at her friends," concluded Wally.

Alice nodded. "And vice versa."

"So…you called it a night despite Bernice's being absent from the room," Wally reiterated. "What happened next?"

"Well, I washed my face and brushed my teeth and flossed, of course. Then I crawled into bed and fell asleep. When I woke up this morning, I was still alone in the room and Bernice's bed hadn't been slept in, so I figured there was no help but to ruin your day by telling one of you."

"We appreciate your alerting us first thing, Alice. Thanks." Wally stared at me, befuddled. "You have any ideas where she might be?"

"She could still be in the spa."

"I'll check it out."

"Did you find a note anywhere?" I asked. I mean, even Jackie had taken the time to write a note.

Alice shook her head. "I didn't see one."

"What about her belongings?" questioned Wally. "Is her stuff still in the room? Pocketbook? Cell phone?"

"Her suitcase is still in the closet. I didn't look for anything else. But if she spent the night in the spa, she's probably wearing her bikini. She was keeping it in the top drawer of her dresser with her underwear."

That stopped me cold. "Bernice packed a bikini?"

"Sure did. Ordered it from Frederick's of Hollywood online. It has a strapless top and one of those bottoms that's got less fabric than a headband."

"A thong?" asked Wally, trying unsuccessfully to mask his disbelief.

She snapped her fingers. "That's what it's called. A thong." She pursed her lips in thought. "These high-fashion suits might be fine for Bernice, but I'm a full-coverage kind of girl myself." Eyeing her watch with some anxiety, she stood up. "I've told you all I know.

Would you mind if I head out to the dining room? Breakfast starts in a half hour and if I wait much longer, all the good seats will be gone."

"Go right ahead," said Wally as he ushered her to the door. "But would *you* mind if we gave your room a once-over to make sure there's no note hiding in an obscure place?"

She reached into her pocket and retrieved her key, dropping it into his palm. "Bernice's dresser is the one closest to the window."

Wally exchanged an apprehensive look with me when she'd gone. "I'll run out to the spa. You check their room."

"What if we come up empty?"

"I'll contact the Port Jacob police."

"Will we have to wait forty-eight hours before we can report her as officially missing?"

"Not in England. The authorities want to be notified as soon as possible." He handed me Alice's room key. "Let's hope it doesn't come to that."

Their room was neat as a pin. For all Bernice's complaining about lack of maid service, both beds were made up with military precision with throw pillows and stuffed bears arranged almost playfully. I searched the closet, the bathroom, and every horizontal surface for a note but found nothing obvious. Moving on to her dresser, I found her pink and black polka-dot bikini right where Alice said it would be—in the top drawer with her lacy push-up bras and thong panties. As eye-poppingly risqué as the swimsuit was, it *did* symbolize a milestone for Bernice.

At least she'd discarded the idea of going *au naturel*.

I finished searching the dresser just as Wally arrived back from the spa. "She's not there. Did you find anything here?"

"Way too much; none of it good. Her pocketbook was in the bottom drawer with her wallet, driver's license, and credit cards still in it. She might have been angry enough to leave the tour, but not without taking her pocketbook with her. She wouldn't get very far without her credit cards."

"What about her cell phone and passport?"

"Not in her pocketbook. She usually kept her passport and extra cash in her neck wallet. I haven't found that yet. Her cell phone isn't here either, but—" I looked across the room, suddenly enlightened. "Missed a drawer."

I walked around the bed to the nightstand, opened the top drawer, and removed the lone item that was tucked inside. "One cell phone. So she'd stowed her phone for the night, but she still must have been wearing her neck wallet, else I imagine that might be here, too. It's too far for her to walk into town to find other accommodations. She might have called a taxi, but I didn't hear a car drive up last night. Did you?"

He shook his head. "Could she have taken a walk along the coastal path?"

"I hope not. A chunk of the bluff disintegrated beneath my feet yesterday, so if she went anywhere near that spot..." My mouth went dry. "It's a sheer drop-off to the rocks below."

He stared at me, his silence causing the hair on my arms to stand on end.

"I think I'll just have a run outside to see if there's anything suspicious going on near the cliff."

"You want me to go with you?"

"Nope."

"But what if—"

"Let's not panic until we have good reason."

I demonstrated my tentative assent by nodding like a bobble-head doll. "I'd take the back exit if I were you. That way you can avoid having to explain to the breakfast crowd why you decided to explore the coastal path before having your first cup of coffee."

By the time I changed into some decent daywear and applied a little makeup, Wally was knocking on my door with his report.

"I located the landslip you told me about, but I didn't see any further erosion along the bluff, so I hope that's good news."

"You and me both."

"I also took the liberty of calling Constable Tredinnick. He was pretty reassuring that missing persons usually show up within twenty-four to forty-eight hours of their disappearance, but in deference to our schedule, he allowed me to file a report over the phone. I passed along every detail I could think of, including Bernice's emotional state at the time of her disappearance, where we've searched, and what she left behind. He asked for a physical description, so I sent him the photo I have of her in my current guest photo file. How did we ever function without smartphones? I couldn't tell him what she was wearing yesterday, but maybe Alice will remember. He said he'd show her photo around at the local hotels and B&Bs, and he'd stop by the inn sometime today to look around the premises, but he didn't sound overly concerned."

"Does he need to question anyone?"

"Only if she doesn't reappear within forty-eight hours."

"But she could be dead by then. Can't we do something more proactive? Like…like form a search party or hire a pack of blood-hounds?"

"I don't make the rules, Em."

As nerve-wracking as it was to be told to take a deep breath and let the law handle it, it occurred to me then that Constable Tredinnick wouldn't have to question the entire group because everyone had been gathered in one room when Bernice went missing.

Well, almost everyone.

Unlike Constable Tredinnick, I knew three bloggers I'd very much like to question.

· · · · · · · · · ·

Wally and I arrived in the dining room just as the breakfast crowd was breaking up.

"Awful good breakfast," Dick Stolee announced to me as he gave his stomach a satisfied rub. "Too bad you missed it."

I noted the time. "Missed it? But it's only 8:10."

Helen Teig pushed away from the table. "Since we were all seated by 7:30—well, everyone except Alice, who got here late and ended up in the chair that's obstructed by the table leg—your grandmother decided to serve early. Family style. Pass the platter and dig in." She gestured to the empty serving dishes strung out along the table. "Pancakes with real whipped cream and fresh fruit. Waffles. Sourdough French toast. Hardboiled eggs that were easier to peel than a ripe banana. Vegetable omelets. Sausage links and patties. Bacon. Cinnamon toast. Raisin toast. Plain toast with marmalade for fussy eaters. Plus coffee, tea, and a variety of cafe lattes, mochas, cappuccinos, and caramel macchiatos."

I stared at her, dumbstruck. "Nana knows how to make lattes?"

"I think Jackie made them," said Dick Teig. "She found a machine. They're working in one well-equipped kitchen. That was the best breakfast I've ever eaten in my entire life, I kid you not."

Osmond waxed philosophical. "It's a darn shame Marion's a millionaire. She could make a fortune as a cook."

"When that Crabbe woman saw the spread your grandmother laid out, she even decided to end her hunger strike," Margi said in an undertone. "Not that she offered a single compliment about the food, but I was keeping track. She downed five pancakes, an omelet, two waffles, and what looked like a whole pound of bacon in the space of ten minutes. I started setting the serving platters out of her reach so there'd be enough food left for the rest of us."

I scanned the length of the table to find wadded-up napkins, empty plates, and two puny sausage links on a meat platter as big as a cookie sheet. I motioned to the platter. "That's all that's left? Two shriveled-up sausages?"

"Whoa! How'd I miss those?" Dick Stolee snatched the links off the platter and nibbled away at them as if they were logs going through a wood chipper. "These babies are too good to waste," he mumbled around a mouthful of sausage.

Grace slatted her eyes at him. "Good move, Dick. Did it ever occur to you to save the leftovers for Emily and Wally?"

He swallowed dramatically, looking suddenly chagrined. "Oops. Sorry. I couldn't help myself. They looked so forlorn lying there all by themselves that I felt morally obligated to give them a home."

"What a crock," scoffed Lucille, smiling at her own comment. "That's not me talking. That's what Bernice would say if she were here."

"Speaking of Bernice," George piped up, "where do you think she is? Alice gave us the lowdown at breakfast."

"We don't know where she is," replied Wally, "but we're doing everything we can to find out. I suspect she might be nursing her bruised feelings in a safe and comfortable place somewhere nearby. We just have to figure out where. Constable Tredinnick is working on that, which reminds me—does anyone recall what Bernice was wearing yesterday?"

They looked from one to the other, shrugging.

"I'm pretty sure she was wearing slacks," Alice ventured. "And a top."

Nods of agreement. "I remember that, too!" enthused Margi.

That information might have had greater impact if the preferred uniform for all the ladies on the tour had been something *other* than slacks and a top. "Do you recall the color?" I asked.

"Green," said Dick Teig. "I remember thinking her outfit matched that gross slime on the rocks at the beach."

Helen thwacked his arm, glaring. "That wasn't Bernice's outfit. It was mine. Bernice was wearing hot pink."

"She was wearing pink the day we arrived," corrected Tilly. "If I'm not mistaken, she was wearing aubergine yesterday."

"What color is that?" asked Dick Teig.

"Purple," I spoke up.

Dick angled a frustrated look at Tilly. "If it's purple, how come you just can't say purple?"

Tilly looked down the length of her nose at him. "Because it's not purple. It's aubergine."

"You could have said eggplant," chided Dick Stolee. "I bet he knows what color eggplant is."

Margi made a face. "I don't like eggplant." She backed up her assertion with a revulsive curl of her tongue, followed by a moment of reflection. "No, wait. Maybe I'm thinking of zucchini."

"Does anyone besides me remember her wearing red yesterday?" asked Osmond. "I recall thinking at the time that the only folks who should ever wear fire-engine-red pants are golfers and clowns."

I sighed. Yup. You couldn't beat the accuracy of an eyewitness report.

Wally held up his hands to stop the barrage. "Thanks for your input, everyone. Her photo is probably more important than a description of what she was wearing anyway."

"Not if she was dressed like a clown," objected Osmond.

"Kitchen's closed," announced Nana as she and Jackie entered the dining room, greeted by spontaneous cheers and riotous applause.

"Will you give us a hint about what'll be on tomorrow's breakfast menu?" Dick Stolee shouted above the ovation.

Nana responded with a two-shouldered shrug. "Don't know yet. I'm waitin' on inspiration." When the clapping died down, she began issuing orders. "How about you folks make yourselves useful by clearin' off the table and stackin' the dishes next to the sink so's Wally can get 'em into the dishwasher? That'd be real helpful. We're gonna need clean dishes for dinner."

Motivated by the prospect of another mouth-watering meal, the troops did what Nana asked without a hint of complaint or chaos, though it helped that Jackie appointed herself field marshal and took charge of establishing traffic patterns. Off came the dishes and platters. Off came the napkins and tablecloth. Into the kitchen went everything that Enyon would need to launder. I motioned to Nana as the activity died down.

"If I scrounged around in the kitchen, would I find any leftover hardboiled eggs or waffles?"

"Didn't you get no breakfast?"

"Wally and I were otherwise engaged."

"That's a real shame, dear, on account of all we got left is corn flakes."

"Okay, then. Jackie has cookies. Maybe I can mooch something off her to tide me over."

Nana glanced across the room to where Jackie had assumed the role of human doorstop to keep the kitchen door propped open and the troops moving. "You coulda knocked me over with a feather when that girl showed up to help me this mornin', Emily. I never thought she'd be one to roll up them sleeves of hers and pitch in like she done, but I couldn't of done it without her. Me and her make a crackerjack team, especially seein' as how she can reach stuff that's too high up for me to fetch. That was a real good idea you had, dear. Thanks."

"I'm tickled it's working out."

With my worries about the Nana/Jackie working relationship being put to rest, I was freed up to address the next item on my to-do list, which would involve a bit more finesse than a friendly chat with my grandmother.

"Hey," said Mason Chatsworth when he answered my knock on his door. He took a quick peek at his watch. "Am I late or something? I thought we were leaving at nine."

"You're not late. I just wanted to ask you a few questions about last night."

"What about last night?"

"You heard that Bernice is missing?"

155

He held the door wider and motioned for me to step inside the room. "Yeah. We all heard the news at breakfast. How weird is that, huh? You have any clues about where she went?"

"Not yet, but that's where you can help. Did you hear any strange noises in the corridor after you returned to your room last night?"

"I heard the fans blowing when I passed the Sixteen String Jack suite. Man, someone's wasting a lot of electricity on a lost cause. That carpet's not salvageable."

"You didn't hear, like, screams or footsteps or dragging sounds or any kind of commotion?"

"Dragging sounds?" He cracked a smile. "You mean, like the sound of someone's body being dragged down the corridor?"

"Uhh...okay." If Bernice hadn't left under her own power, then she'd left under duress, which might have precipitated a whole host of unusual sounds that someone should have heard.

"Boy, Emily, you have quite an imagination. So I didn't hear a body being dragged past my door last night, but I did hear some commotion from the lounge every so often. Voices. You guys were really loud. I eventually popped in my ear buds to drown you out so I could finish my blog."

I predicted that millennials would live long enough to regret their unremitting use of ear buds. It boggled the mind over the potential sounds they were preventing themselves from hearing. The musical calling card of the Good Humor man's ice cream truck. The symphonic chorus of Sunday morning church bells. The earsplitting whistle of a freight train speeding straight at them.

"Did you see either Spencer or August after you returned to your room?"

"Nope. They had blogs to write, too." He drew his brows together. "You non-bloggers don't get it. Blogging eats up a ton of time, especially for conscientious bloggers like myself. I don't know about the rest of them—Heather and Spencer and August—but I'm having a heck of a time knocking out a daily blog with the tour schedule you've set up. I'm earning every penny of that discount you offered me. So you can tell that to Bernice…if she ever shows up again."

I regretted she wasn't around to hear Mason's comment. Knowing that even one of the bloggers felt burdened by the discount would please her to no end.

I received pretty much the same story when I stopped by August and Spencer's room.

"Unusual noises?" Spencer asked me. "Like what? Screeching? Gun shots?"

"All of the above?" I said.

He shook his head. "I was working on my blog, which puts me in a kind of meditative zone, so I didn't hear a thing other than that annoying hum from the fans that are still blowing in the flooded room. Is it really necessary to run those things 24/7? It's maddening. Listen to the racket they're making."

I listened, hearing nothing.

"You have to agree that it's way beyond an acceptable decibel level."

I cocked my head, straining to pick up a whirring sound. "Sorry. I can't hear a thing."

He regarded me, wide-eyed. "Geez, for someone as young as you are, your hearing sucks."

"Don't be cowed by Spencer's superhuman hearing," advised August from the room's lone armchair. Computer balanced on his lap, he stared at his screen as he clicked away on his keyboard. "I can't hear it either."

I was impressed by August Lugar's ability to talk and type while focused on the data on his computer screen. He'd probably never have to worry about walking and chewing gum at the same time. "So...did you hear *anything* last night that was out of the ordinary?" I asked him.

"Spencer snored. Loudly. But that seems to be a normal occurrence. Quiet would have been out of the ordinary." He continued typing.

"You didn't happen to see Bernice in the hallway when you returned to your room last night?"

"The last time either one of us saw Bernice was when she stormed out of the dining room," said Spencer. He directed a look at August for confirmation. "Right?"

"Exactly." August finally looked up, his eyes snapping with exasperation. "Not to be a bore, but I'd like to post this before we leave, and I've yet to put the finishing touches on it. So, do you mind?" He lasered a look at the door that was coupled by an expression indicating I should open it. Immediately.

"Don't mind at all. Sorry to take up your time. Thanks for your help."

But they'd been no help at all. Their room was located two doors down from Bernice's and they'd heard nothing? Spencer, with his superhuman hearing, had failed to hear anything but the whirr of blowing fans? Mason's room was at the opposite end of the hall, so he'd been more insulated from general activity. But Spencer and

August were claiming that they'd heard no door close? No footsteps? No inkling of a disturbance or departure?

Gimme a break.

No one had had a window of opportunity to do anything nefarious last night except the two of them.

But maybe I'd asked the wrong question. Maybe instead of asking if they'd seen Bernice, I should have asked if Bernice had seen *them*.

Was it possible she'd caught them in the act of committing a crime? Picking the lock of someone else's suite while the rest of us had still been in the lounge? Or sneaking out of another guest's room, loaded down with cash and other people's valuables? If that had been the scenario, would Bernice have been able to run away from them or would they have overpowered her before she'd had time to cry for help? Overpowered her and...

In my mind's eye I saw the razor-sharp rocks jammed together at the foot of the cliff and heard the violent pounding of the surf.

I inhaled a deep breath, swallowing slowly.

Oh. My. God.

Had they killed Bernice? Killed her because she happened to be in the wrong place at the wrong time?

Who *were* these guys? Killers posing as tour guests? Thieves posing as bloggers? Scammers who made their living by stealing from unsuspecting seniors? Had August Lugar even been the target of a crime or had he made the whole story up in an effort to pose as victim rather than perpetrator? Could he find any better way to deflect suspicion away from himself than to pretend to be the injured party?

So maybe they'd been more help than I realized.

My gut was telling me that August and Spencer were in cahoots with each other, just like Helen and Margi had suggested last night. All I needed to do was find the thread that linked them together.

As I hurried back to my room, I forced myself to ignore the little voice in my head that taunted, *"Good luck with that."*

TWELVE

No one reported any valuables missing when they boarded the bus a short time later, which forced me to question my own assumption about the blogging burglars. I hung onto the possibility, however, that things might have gone missing without anyone noticing yet. Of course, people's concept of what was valuable was probably all over the board. For Grace Stolee, it might have been the lovely diamond studs Dick had bought her on their last milestone wedding anniversary. For Nana, it might be her new denture case with the sparkly finish.

As we got underway to St. Michael's Mount, I sat down next to Jackie, fully intent on occupying myself by scouring the internet for tidbits to back up my theory. I might have succeeded, too, if cell service hadn't been so impossibly spotty.

"Doggonit." Jackie gave her phone a two-handed shake. "How's a girl supposed to find recipes with the service cutting out every five seconds?"

"You're really jazzed about this cooking thing, aren't you?"

"Yes!" She beamed like a lighted snow globe. "Just think, Emily, if Caroline hadn't told me about my Bakewell/Backhouse/Bagwell/ Bakehouse ancestors, I never would have realized that I'm a walking repository for centuries of culinary expertise."

"Nana implied that you're a natural."

"She did?" She squeaked like a chew toy in the jaws of a playful Rottweiler.

"Yup. She said the two of you make a crackerjack team and that she couldn't have done breakfast without you."

"She couldn't, Em. She really couldn't. She actually needed me. Isn't that the bomb?" She hugged her arms to herself and gazed heavenward, a beatific look on her face. "Someone needs me!"

Her phone chimed. She riveted her attention on her screen. "Out of the dead zone and back into civilization again. Hallelujah." She began swiping her screen with trigger-finger quickness. "Mrs. S put me on dessert detail tonight, so I'm looking for a delectable confection that I can prepare in under an hour. Ahhh. How does this grab you? English trifle. Sugar, cornstarch, eggs, blah, blah, blah, and two packages of ladyfingers. I could whip this up tonight." She studied the screen. "No I can't. This thing has to chill for three hours. Shoot."

While she continued her recipe search, I googled Spencer Blunt, only to have my service shut down again when we rounded a bend in the road. "Nuts. Are you getting service?"

"I was up until two seconds ago." Leaning forward, she shouted toward the front of the bus, "Anyone's phone still working?"

Groans. Shaking heads.

"Mine works," Mason Chatsworth called out.

"Can you find out how long tiramisu needs to chill before it can be served?"

"Seven hours," responded August Lugar. "Minimum."

"Great." She sank back into her seat. "All the impressive desserts take forever to be table-ready. How am I supposed to dazzle everyone with an exotic creation in under an hour?"

"Maybe you're aiming too high for your initial outing. Maybe you need to simplify."

"And serve what?"

"How about instant pudding? If you serve it in a pretty dessert glass with a lot of whipped cream and a maraschino cherry, people might mistake it for Baked Alaska."

She regarded me without blinking. "You do realize that Baked Alaska is only served after someone *sets it on fire*?"

I shrugged. "Enyon probably has matches." He might even show her where they were once he was released from custody, which needed to happen really soon in order for me to be able to stop hyperventilating.

Snorting at my suggestion, Jackie began flipping through screens again, only to shake her phone and let out an aargh of frustration ten seconds later. "Doggonit!"

And so it went throughout the entire trip. I wasn't connected to service long enough to dig up anything on my bloggers, and Jackie was connected just long enough to discover that even "instant" desserts took much longer than an instant to prepare. So I occupied myself by peering out the window, desperately searching for a wiry-haired woman who might be wearing red clown pants.

As we hit the Newtown roundabout and headed east on a narrow-shouldered road flanked by an impenetrable sweep of trees, Wally fired up his mike to do his tour director's thing.

"I'm sure you've all seen pictures of St. Michael's Mount—the towering rock formation that sits in the middle of Mount's Bay. It's basically a smaller version of Normandy's Mont Saint-Michel, but both places were originally founded as Benedictine monasteries, with St. Michael's Mount being dependent on the larger priory in France for three hundred years. As a result of war and attrition, the bond was eventually severed, and in 1424 St. Michael's Mount was handed over to another monastic order that oversaw the construction of both the harbor and the causeway that connects the island to the mainland. This is the same causeway you'll be walking on today, so I hope you'll grasp its historic significance."

Helen Teig waved her hand in the air. "Which one did you say we're visiting? Mont Saint-Michel or St. Michael's Mount?"

"The latter," said Wally.

Nervous silence.

"Which one's the latter?" asked Dick Teig.

Tilly raised her walking stick, volunteering an answer. "In American grammar the term *latter* refers to the second of two options. In the British lexicon it's the opposite: latter refers to the first choice."

"So which one are we going to see?" reiterated Helen. "The first one or the second one?"

"Can someone remind me what the first one was?" asked Osmond.

I hung my head and heaved a sigh.

"St. Michael's Mount!" yelled Spencer Blunt. "If you look outside, you might realize there are a few clues indicating we're in England, not France."

"Like what?" asked Lucille.

"This is way too confusing," fussed Helen. "They should have named this place something different because it sounds too much like the other place."

Wally grinned. "I believe that was intentional. Both monasteries were named in honor of St. Michael. Anyone want to take a guess what the French word for Michael is?"

Dick Teig shot his hand into the air. "Francois?"

Oh, God.

"Those poor monks," fretted Helen. "Can you imagine? St. Michael's in England. St. Michael's in France. I bet they spent half their time trying to figure out which country they were in."

"It's too bad they didn't have GPS," offered Margi. "That might've helped."

"Wouldn't have done 'em any good," argued Dick Stolee. "Six hundred years later and the cell service still sucks."

If there was a smidgen of logic in their thinking, I was too mentally fatigued by the discussion to figure out what it was.

"After Henry VIII broke ties with the Roman Papacy and disbanded the monasteries," Wally continued, "the mount was turned into a military fortress, and for nearly a hundred years it protected the coast from would-be invaders, including the Spaniards of Armada fame."

Jackie waved her hand desperately over her head. "Did Henry have his spat with the Papacy before or after he installed my family at Hampton Court?"

Wally regarded her, bemused. "Don't know. Unfortunately, information about your family isn't included in the official *St. Michael's Mount History and Guidebook*."

"I'll wager *my* family receives more than one encomium in the official history," boasted Kathryn. "The Truscott-Tallons left an impressive thumbprint wherever the aristocracy gathered."

"What's an encomium?" asked Nana.

"Praise," said Tilly. "It's like the positive spin political hacks spew about their candidate after he's revealed his lack of insight, knowledge, and intelligence in an electoral debate."

"Oh, I get it," said Nana. "Bull."

"You can learn if your family is mentioned in the guidebook when we arrive on the island," Wally assured Kathryn. "The National Trust gift shop is located a stone's throw away from the causeway."

"If there's mention of even *one* Truscott-Tallon in that guide-book," Jackie whispered to me, "I'll eat the page."

"Why does it matter to you?"

"Really? You have to ask?" She shook her head. "Because I'm establishing an historical timeline between my ancestors and the British monarchy. I can't very well sell myself as 'the Pastry Chef to Kings' if I can't fill in all the blanks now, can I? You know what the media is like, Emily. One wrong detail or dubious fact and they'll tear me apart."

She hadn't prepared one dessert, yet she was already planning her strategy to market herself. While my pep talk last night had apparently worked miracles, it also might have blinded her to her blatant lack of training and unproven skill—a circumstance which made me think that maybe she should ditch the culinary gigs and,

166

like other highly unqualified people in recent years, run for public office.

As we reached the city limits of Marazion, where hedgerows gave way to stone walls and chimney pots sat atop whitewashed houses like tins on a shooting range fence, Wally took up the thread of his narrative again. "In 1659 the monastery-turned-fortress was purchased by a Colonel John St. Aubyn, who'd been appointed by Parliament to serve as Captain of the Mount. And long story short, the St. Aubyn family has been in continuous residence at the castle ever since."

"How'd a military guy earn enough money to buy an island with a castle on it?" Dick Teig called out.

"Maybe he won the lottery," said Nana. "That's what I done."

After getting a few peek-a-boo glimpses of the coastline between hedges and houses, we let out a collective *oooooh* when we passed by a clearing and caught an unobstructed view of the bay.

The mount rose like some horny beast in the middle of the harbor, all spiny rock and jagged pinnacles. The sea had receded beyond my vision, isolating the island amid tidal flats that stretched out like the heaths of Bodmin Moor. I spied the outline of a short causeway and was surprised by how close to shore the mount actually sat but happy that the gang would have less distance to walk than I'd originally thought. The tide might be out, but that didn't preclude the possibility of twisted ankles and unintended falls on a walkway that had been constructed before Columbus set sail for America.

"How long is the causeway out to that place?" Lucille questioned.

"I can't quote you an exact length," said Wally, "but timewise you should be able to navigate it in a matter of minutes. As you might have noticed, the tide is out, so we'll plan to hoof it out and catch a launch back."

"Anyplace to eat out there?" asked Osmond.

"Two great eateries," said Wally. "Both serve light lunches, but the Island Café boasts the added attraction of having great sea views from its garden. And there's also two terrific shops that sell items ranging from fudge and Italian leather bags to artisan gifts and handmade jewelry. Any other questions?"

"You bet," said Nana. "I wanna ask that green-haired fella what kind of phone he's got what lets him stay connected when the rest of us don't got no service at all."

"Mason?" asked Wally. "Would you like to oblige?"

"Show of hands," announced Osmond. "How many people—"

"Why do we have to vote?" complained Dick Stolee. "Can't he just tell us?"

"I second the motion," said Dick Teig.

"Whose motion?" asked Margi. "Osmond's or Dick's?"

"Dick didn't raise a motion," said Alice. "He asked a question."

"So what are we voting on?" demanded Helen.

Yup. The more things changed, the more they stayed the same.

After passing a public square where pensioners squeezed together on wooden benches to watch the cars go by, we encountered an unexpected display of palm trees and other desert vegetation outside a gallery and tea garden, then slowed to a crawl past the stately cream-colored Godolphin Arms. At a fish-and-chips shop we banged a left onto a short street that was flanked by stone walls, provided access to public parking, and dead-ended at a boat ramp that was probably submerged at high tide.

Before us the waterfront opened up in a grand vista, with the castle dominating the background, the beach seeming to stretch to infinity, and the official car park posting prices for every kind of vehicle except tour busses.

"Coaches aren't allowed in the car park," Wally informed us, "but Freddy's going to idle at the entrance just long enough for us to hop off. So when the bus comes to a stop, get ready to move."

When the doors whooshed open, we piled out onto the pavement, then followed Wally onto the beach, where he provided us with final instructions. "Synchronize your watches or cell phones or whatever. We're scheduled to be here for four hours. That should allow everyone adequate time to make the crossing, complete their tour of the castle, have a leisurely lunch, browse through the shops, and prepare to take a launch back to the mainland."

As the wind whipped up, billowing jackets and sending our hair flying around our faces, Wally's voice grew louder. "We're not under a tight time crunch today, so if you find the island so interesting that you'd like to spend more time exploring, we can probably arrange for that to happen. But in four hours I want you to gather at the sheltered benches at the island's entrance so I can conduct a head count, and then we can discuss any change of plans. I'm going to run ahead of the pack to pick up our tickets, and I'll hand them out when you arrive. I'll caution you to watch your step on the causeway. Take your time and enjoy a stroll you'll never experience in Iowa or anywhere else."

As he headed out across the beach, the gang remained anchored in place, heads bent, hands clutching their phones. "Hot damn," yelled George. "I've got service!"

"Me, too!" rang out a chorus of jubilant voices.

"'Bout time." Jackie thumbed through a flurry of screens until she found one that caused her breath to catch in her throat. "This is it. Omigod, Emily: chocolate seduction cake. Listen to the description: chocolate cake, chocolate Bavarian cream and ganache, topped with fudge-dipped brownies and chocolate chips." She squinted at the screen as she read further. "Bugger. It only serves eight."

While the gang splintered into groups of two and four, the bloggers forged ahead in a loosely formed clump save for Kathryn, who played the role of outcast by walking nowhere near them. Buffeted by a fierce wind whose howls screamed past our ears, we followed in the bloggers' footsteps across the rippled sand, past the seawall that fronted the sailing club, and onto the famed causeway that lay camouflaged beneath a layer of beach sand.

It was cobbled together from stones of every size and shape, like a medieval version of the yellow brick road, only it wasn't yellow or brick or flat. It was the gray of a battleship—an uneven plane with shallow dips and rises, each irregular stone worn smooth from centuries of footfalls. Much of the mortar between stones had disintegrated, creating deep cavities that isolated the cobbles like molars whose gums had worn away. Fractures. Fissures. Cracks and clefts. *Uff-da*. Picking our way through a Bosnian minefield might prove to be less challenging.

"Watch your step, everyone," I called into the wind. "Seriously, watch where you're walking. Baby steps if you have to. Hold onto each other." Then again, was advising them to hold onto each other wise? If one of them fell, they'd topple like a row of dominoes.

"I think I'm onto something," Jackie said, waving her cell phone, "so I'm gonna hang out at that Godolphin Arms place until I lock down a dessert for tonight. I'll catch up to you when I'm done."

"But what about the castle tour? Lunch? Shopping?"

She angled her chin in the air and placed her phone over her heart. "As a woman who takes her job probation very seriously, I'll ask you to please refrain from asking me to choose between my present position or an opportunity to spend several carefree hours frolicking about on an island retreat. It's simply too cruel."

"But the carefree hours thing is part of the tour."

"Even so. I'm not going to give you an excuse to fire me."

"I'm not going to fire you, Jack. I *need* you."

She batted her eyelashes and smiled with every professionally whitened tooth in her head. "In that case, how do I go about submitting a formal request for a raise?"

"This way!" shouted Dick Teig, acting like a traffic cop as he rerouted the group onto an alternate walkway that angled toward a massive rock formation made tourist friendly by the addition of an inviting set of engineered stairs. "Good spot for a photo op."

"I gotta go," I said as I watched them hotfoot it toward a geologic anomaly that could double as the petrified hull of an ancient shipwreck. "Detours aren't on the itinerary."

Jackie followed my gaze. "Apparently, they are now. Off you go. I'll catch up."

The alternate causeway was obviously less than six hundred years old because the cobbles were perfectly positioned, dead level, and showed no signs of erosion. Around us the tidal flats were littered with rocks that were scattered like ribs in a bone yard. Green algae crawled over every moist surface. Water pooled amid the fractured debris, home to gleaming rocks and broken shells. By the time I caught up to Dick and the gang, they were already up the stairs with phones in hand, staking out the best spots to pose for selfies.

"Take your money shot right here," declared Dick Stolee, indicating his choice for best photographic site in an optional setting. A manmade path composed of a hardened substance that resembled pebbled concrete cut through the formation, but the space was impossibly narrow, forcing the gang to walk in single file. "I give you the quintessential flat rock where you can park your keister and take a selfie with the mount in the background." With his toupee standing on end from wind shear, he plopped himself down, smiled into his phone, and tapped the screen. "Like this." He assessed the results. "I might have to photoshop the hair, but it looks good otherwise. Who's next?"

While they went through their typical deliberations of whether they should line up by age or height, I seated myself on a slab of rock near the stairs where I could continue my internet search while I waited for them.

I accessed Spencer Blunt's Ten-Dollar-a-Day Traveler website and, out of curiosity, scanned the blog he'd posted for day three of the tour, thrilled that his comments were so positive. He complimented the inn's amenities, raving about the luxurious spa whose hot tub he was hoping to enjoy, and mentioned that the absence of housekeeping staff not only allowed guests to save money on tips but prevented them from being ousted from their suites at inopportune times. He then devoted the rest of his blog to the cuisine, employing such adjectives as "spectacular" and "unparalleled." "The grandmother from Iowa has turned simple meals into such exciting feasts that many guests, myself included, would prefer to do nothing more on this tour than remain at the inn and eat. I'll regret having to leave the Stand and Deliver Inn with nothing better to look forward to than merely excellent fare prepared by professional chefs. Marion Sippel makes the title of chef seem highly overrated. However, as a sidebar, we're dealing with Agatha Christie intrigue at the Stand and Deliver because it appears our original chef, who purportedly died in a tragic accident the day we arrived, didn't die accidentally: he was murdered. Cue the organ music."

Even though Spencer's revelation about Lance seemed both insensitive and cavalier to me, I couldn't help but be wowed by the rest of his post. With press like this, Nana could become as well known as some of the competing chefs on the Food Network's reality TV challenges.

I read the tabs on Spencer's website and saw that they were divided into numerous geographical labels from New England and the Pacific Northwest to Tornado Alley and the Southwest Desert. The Sunshine State, the Lone Star State, and the Golden State were all big enough to boast individual tabs. Clicking on the Farmbelt tab, I arrived at a page that allowed me to access his archived blogs by either city, town, lake, zip code, oldest, or newest. I hit oldest, which shunted me to a blog Spencer had written five years ago with recommendations about how to get the most bang for your buck in the Swiss village of New Glarus, Wisconsin. *Five years ago?*

I got a sinking feeling in my stomach as I scrolled through his posts. He'd written a blog about some travel location on a daily basis for five years. That meant 365 posts a year for five years, for a grand total of—I made a mental calculation and rounded off a few numbers—over 1,800 blog posts. So if I hoped to prove that Spencer and August had known each other before the tour, I was going to have to view all 1,800 of Spencer's venues and cross-reference them with August's blogs to see if both men might have had occasion to visit the same town on the same date. *Ugh.*

I left Spencer's website to access August's Knife and Fork, Will Travel blog, horrified to learn that the only way to retrieve posts in his archived material was by year, month, and word search, which meant I was going to have to type each location Spencer had written about into August's search field to find a match.

The voice inside my head groaned.

The voice was right. There had to be a better way.

And then it struck me.

Maybe I could do it in reverse, especially if August blogged with less frequency than Spencer. I could skim August's posts, categorize them into a few regions, and cross-check them against Spencer's lists. It'd be pretty labor intensive, but it could work, couldn't it?

With ever-increasing excitement I retrieved the oldest post on August's website and continued scrolling down, noting the frequency of his blog activity.

Well, it might have worked…if August hadn't been outpacing Spencer by producing *two* blogs a day for *ten freaking years*! That was more than 7,000 posts. How was I supposed to skim 7,000 posts with spotty cell service?

"Are you waiting to take a selfie or have you planted yourself here to count heads when we're done?" Tilly appeared before me, feet apart and head bent, anchoring herself against the wind. She waggled her cane in the direction of the queue. "We went with tallest first, so I'm the first one done."

I held my phone up. "I'm performing clandestine research."

"On whom?"

"Our bloggers."

"Excellent." Her eyes twinkled as she lowered herself onto the rock beside me. "I'll have you know I haven't been idle while Marion's been in the kitchen." She dropped her voice to a stage whisper. "I have information for you on our recently departed chef."

She removed her phone from the pocket of her blazer, swiped the screen, then tapped it a couple of times. "I just sent the link to your email, but the upshot is that Chef Lance Tori was universally despised by the residents of Port Jacob. According to a scathing article in the *Port Jacob Crier* that appeared a few weeks ago, Lance was conducting an ongoing feud with the green grocer about produce that Lance claimed was inferior. Their last disagreement actually ended with Lance throwing a cantaloupe through the storefront window, so the constable had to be called in to restore order. But the incident left a sour taste in the mouths of many of the locals, most of whom are related to the green grocer. So public opinion was definitely not in Lance's favor. There was even mention of a restraining order to prevent further run-ins between Lance and the grocer, but Enyon stepped in to assure Constable Tredinnick that such a measure was unnecessary because he would be making all future purchases at the store in Lance's place."

"Oh, wow." I accessed Tilly's link through my email and began skimming. "The owner of the hardware store told Jackie and me that Lance was kind of a square peg in a round hole, and proud of it, but he failed to mention that the situation had required police intervention."

Tilly fluttered her finger at my screen. "Scroll down to the op-eds at the end if you'd like a taste of how bad things really were."

I began reading the letters to the editor, puzzled by the local slang but pretty sure none of it was complimentary. Lance was accused of being "a gormless twat," a "whiny sod who delighted in throwing never-ending wobblers," a "cranky wanker who was always in a nark," and the ever-popular "bloviating Yankee arse." Several letters concluded with the suggestion that Lance should either "get stuffed," "naff off," or "get off our island." I suspected a couple of these suggestions were the height of obscenity, but if you ignored the intended translations, the words themselves were actually quite melodic.

"Kudos to George for his theory," Tilly spoke up when I'd finished reading. "With the level of animosity Lance roused in the village, one of the locals could very well have sneaked into the inn to kill him. They were making no bones about their feelings in their letters to the editor. They wanted him gone."

"It must be terribly hurtful being hated by everyone."

Tilly nodded. "If Bernice were here, we could ask her."

Bernice. *Ugh.* I could feel myself start to hyperventilate again.

"Chop-chop, everyone." Grace Stolee executed a couple of hasty claps as she came up behind Tilly. "We're through here, so let's move on to the next attraction."

"How can you be through?" questioned Tilly. "There are people in line behind you."

"Well, when it was Margi's turn she refused to sit on the rock because of the crusty mold that's crawling all over it, so she sani-

176

tized the area, but the goo wouldn't dry, so no one wanted to sit down. Dick tried blowing on it, but that didn't work, so we cut to the chase: turned our backs to the castle and snapped our selfies right where we stood. Dick's a little put out about our taking matters into our own hands, but he'll get over it."

Nine individual selfies—in Iowa parlance also known as a group photo.

We walked the rest of the way to the island using the buddy system, picking our way along the causeway like animals making their way to the ark. Thankfully, no one incurred the injuries I'd anticipated. Once beyond a massive wall whose arms formed a protected harbor for the island's small fleet of boats, I spied Wally with our tickets and herded the group in his direction.

"The bloggers have gone on ahead of you," he announced as he handed out tickets, "but you'll probably run into them inside the castle. If you want to avoid having to stumble over more cobblestones on the harbor front, follow the gravel path to the end of the hedges"—he pointed straight ahead—"and take a right. It's a cobble-free lane that leads to the entrance gate of the castle, and that's where you'll be asked to present your ticket."

"Where's the little boys' room?" asked Dick Teig in a pinched voice. He gave a frantic glance left and right. "Nearby?"

Wally gestured to the stucco building with green shutters to our left. "Just around the corner."

All four guys rocketed toward the building, with Dick Stolee taking the lead as they rounded the corner. "I warned Dick to quit after his third cup of coffee this morning," tsked Helen as we watched them disappear. "But nooo. The only reason he quit after six was because they ran out."

"Do they got a potty for us girls down there, too?" Nana inquired.

Wally nodded. "It's even closer than the men's room."

"Oh, thank God," said Lucille in a relieved gasp. "I drank seven cups." Breaking from the group, she raced across the gravel path, only to be overtaken by the rest of the girls, who were obviously unwilling to take a chance that the ladies' comfort station might turn out to be the dreaded one-seater.

With the entire Iowa contingent addressing internal plumbing issues, I regarded Wally and exhaled a deep breath. "Are you absolutely positive that the bay will be sufficiently flooded to allow us to take a launch back to the mainland? Because I have a very bad feeling that if we have to pick our way back over those cobblestones again, someone is going to—"

"Come quick!"

We looked toward the harbor front to find our green-haired millennial pounding over the cobblestones toward us.

"We have injuries!"

THIRTEEN

"She pushed me."

"I did not."

"Then how do you explain these?" Kathryn Crabbe held up her hands to show off her skinned palms. "And these?" Her capris were bunched high on her legs, exposing her bloodied kneecaps.

We were being administered to in a back room behind the ticket sales counter at the far end of the harbor, surrounded by an exhaustive supply of wound wipes, bandages, rolls of sterile gauze, and surgical tape.

"I lost my footing and stumbled into you," defended Heather. "There was nothing deliberate about it. It was an accident. You can ask Mason. He was walking beside me and saw the whole thing."

"Birds of a feather." Kathryn's voice became a hiss. "It was probably a coordinated effort."

"Where *is* Mason?" I asked, realizing he'd disappeared as soon as he'd dropped us off.

"He said he was heading up to the castle," said Wally. "He apologized for cutting out, but touring the castle is a big deal for a hotel blogger, and he wasn't sure how long all this"—he panned his hand from left to right to indicate our present surroundings—"would take."

"Turning tail and running to avoid being questioned, more likely," huffed Kathryn.

Heather made a pointer of her forefinger and aimed it straight at Kathryn's face. "If this is the thanks Mason and I get for peeling you off the ground and trying to find a first-aid station, the next time you fall, *I*, for one, won't be volunteering to put you back together again."

One of the clerks at the ticket counter, a gray-haired lady named Fiona, had revealed herself to be a retired nurse, serving a dual role in sales and first aid, so she'd offered to dress Kathryn's battle wounds in the privacy of their makeshift infirmary, which, she confessed, overflowed with visitors during the summer tourist season. "It's the cobbles," she fretted as she ripped open a hygienic packet that looked like the moist towelettes Blimpies provided with an order of buffalo wings. "There's some days when we have more guests queued up here than in the castle. I blame the bloody footwear industry. How do they convince women they can walk in shoes that have heels like stilts?"

I sucked my lips into my mouth, trying not to look guilty. *Because some styles make your feet look really small?*

"You should tar over every one of those cobblestones," sniped Kathryn as Fiona doctored her injured knees. "They're a public health hazard."

"In case you weren't aware," Heather wisecracked while gathering up her belongings, "one of the main reasons tourists visit England is to see those cobblestones. I should think the woman posing as the penultimate authority on Jane Austen would know that." She turned to Wally and me. "I'm heading up to the castle now. I expect my services are no longer required here. What's that quote? 'No good deed ever goes unpunished'?"

I squeezed her arm. "Wally and I can't thank you enough, Heather. We're in your debt."

Kathryn snorted. "Don't think your phony Good Samaritan act changes anything. It doesn't. I still want my fob-seal back."

Heather shot a look at Wally and me, her eyes spitting fire. "Can you believe her? Man, has she ever pulled the wool over everyone's eyes. The world of Jane Austen is so mannered. So proper. Penelope Pemberley claims to be a part of that world, but she's not mannered and proper. She's mean-spirited and vindictive, so I'm taking great pleasure in pulling the curtain aside and letting my fellow Janeites sneak a peek at the real person behind the blog. Penelope Pemberley is a hoax perpetrated by Kathryn Crabbe…who, in the time-honored Austen tradition of revealing characters' personality traits through their surnames, is exactly what her name implies—a crab."

At the doorway she turned back to Kathryn to deliver a parting shot. "I am *so* taking you down."

"I survived the first takedown. Where will you choose for your next attempt?" Kathryn glared at her retreating back. "The basement stairs at the inn? That venue is a bit overused, don't you think? Ow! That stings." She shot an irritated look at Fiona.

"There, there," Fiona quipped as she disposed of the wound wipes. "I'd give you a spoonful of sugar if I had it, but all I've got is that artificial rot, and you certainly don't want to take that straight. Crushed cardboard would taste better. Don't fret, now, pet. I'm almost done."

Kathryn stabbed her finger at the doorway where Heather had exited. "I demand you provide me with protection from that girl. She's dangerous."

I looked at Wally. Wally looked at me. We both looked at Kathryn. "Protection as in a bodyguard?" I asked.

"Of course a bodyguard. You see what she's done to me. If you don't do something, it'll happen again. And next time, the outcome might be far less benign than cut knees and skinned palms."

"She claims your fall was an accident," Wally pointed out.

"And you believe her?"

He opened his mouth to reply, then snapped it shut again. "Look, the reality is that until we talk to Mason, we're dealing with one of those he said/she said situations."

"And you're choosing her side."

"I'm not choosing anyone's side."

"But after you talk to Mason and he parrots her version of the incident, you will choose a side, and I can guarantee it won't be mine. Throw me to the wolves, then. And when my personal safety is compromised, you can bid farewell to your career as a tour director because once people learn what you're allowing to happen, you'll never work again."

"Hands, please," instructed Fiona, making a gimme motion.

Cupping my palm around Wally's elbow, I urged him toward the door. "Why don't I stay here with Kathryn while you check to see if the other guests found their way to the castle? Don't want any of them getting lost."

"Take the stairs at the far end of the courtyard," Fiona piped up. "They'll lead you straight to the entrance gate."

Wally gave a tug back on his arm. "I don't think that's necessary, Emily."

"Yeah, it is." I shuffled him toward the exit. "Make sure that the Dicks abide by the rules on the castle tour, and I'll see you when I see you."

I could tell he wasn't happy about leaving, but I wasn't about to allow Kathryn to subject my employee to more of her intimidating behavior.

"There you go." Fiona assessed her handiwork as she peeled off her disposable gloves. "All done. Your knees will probably stiffen up like an old barn board, so the best thing you can do is to keep moving. If they lock up to the point where you can't walk, try an over-the-counter anti-inflammatory."

"Delightful." Kathryn grimaced as she rolled down the legs of her capris.

"Not to rain on your parade any more than I have to, pet, but I'm not so sure you'll be wanting to tour the castle on those knees. It's not the interior of the castle that's the problem; it's the access *to* the castle. The stairs are a bit wonky. And I don't dare mention the hill beyond the stairs." She gave her head a woeful shake. "All cobblestones. Much like Port Jacob, if you've been there."

After offering profuse thanks to Fiona for her services, I escorted Kathryn into the courtyard outside the ticket office, where we were confronted by yet more cobblestones. To our left was the protected harbor where boats lay grounded in the tidal muck like a pod of beached whales. To our right were two finely crafted wooden benches bedecked with pillows that advertised the Courtyard Shop. A sign for the Sail Loft Restaurant was attached to a rock wall behind one bench. "Where to?" I asked Kathryn.

"Are you my self-appointed bodyguard?"

"Until we can come up with a better solution, I guess I am."

She arched an eyebrow. "Have you seen the security detail hired by celebrities? Muscle-bound body builder types stuffing two-hundred-fifty pounds of rippling sinew into slim-fit suits. What do I end up with?" She fixed me with a sour look. "A fun-size bodyguard. My right thigh weighs more than you do."

"Unfortunately, our agency has to fill emergency needs with the employees we have, not the employees we'd like."

"Oh, whatever. At least you'll be around to witness the next attempt that girl makes on my life."

"Would you like to browse through the Courtyard Shop? Pick up a few gifts to take home to the family?"

"I loathe shopping. Besides"—her voice bristled with a defensive edge—"I don't have family to take anything home to."

I blinked in confusion. "But…didn't you tell Heather that your family—the Crispy Triscuit-somethings—would crush her in court if she didn't hand over the fob-seal?"

"The Crispin Truscott-Tallons," she corrected. "Permit me to amend my statement. I have no *immediate* family. The Truscott-Tallons are scattered about and wield global influence, but we're not what you'd call close."

"Christmas card relations?"

Her eyes grew hollow as she paused to reflect, but the emotion evaporated as quickly as it had appeared. "I don't see where it's any of your business knowing how close we are. But you can be sure that if I have to drag that girl to court, I'll have their complete backing. The family is quite adamant about protecting their interests in matters that require litigation."

Or so she'd like me to believe. I wondered if the Truscott-Tallons even knew Kathryn existed. I was beginning to wonder if her boastful rants revolved around the family she *imagined* she had rather than the one she actually had. "Have you decided to take Fiona's advice and skip the castle tour?"

"Of course I'm skipping the castle tour. Do I look like a complete dolt? I'm not even sure why you booked this tour. Senior citizens? Wonky stairs? Cobblestone hills? What detail about this venture *didn't* spell disaster?"

"My regulars aren't afraid of a challenge," I replied in a measured tone, looking her square in the eye. "They might have a lot of birthdays under their belts, but they're not daunted by stairs or hills or physical activities geared toward the younger generation." In fact, the only two things that truly terrified my guys were cell phone dead zones and pay-to-use Wi-Fi.

And maybe the occasional spider.

"Paragons of virtue one and all," she gibed.

I gestured to the sign for the Sail Loft. "The restaurant is on the next level. Would you like an early lunch?"

"I'm not hungry."

"There was a sign advertising the Island Café at the other end of the island. That's the one with the ocean views. Do you want to try there instead?"

"What part of 'I'm not hungry' don't you understand?"

"The walk might prevent your knees from getting stiff."

"My knees are already stiff. I'm old. It goes with the territory."

"Would you like an anti-inflammatory?" I began riffling through my shoulder bag. "I have some ibuprofen with me."

"Do you know what I'd really like?" Her voice exploded from her throat in an angry bark. "I'd like you to go away. Good God, you're worse than my ex. Where are you going? Who are you going with? Why do you have to go? When will you be back? I felt as if I had a leash strapped around my neck. And you want to know the irony of it all? The entire time he was keeping tabs on me, smothering me, peppering me with endless questions, he was having an affair with my best friend's daughter. He even set her up in her own luxury apartment and paid the rent. His love nest."

I winced. That had to have hurt. "I'm so sorry, Kathryn."

"Why are you sorry? My life is much better without him. I don't even hold a grudge. In fact, when the two lovebirds got hitched, I sent them a wedding gift."

My eyebrows winged upward in astonishment. "You sent them a gift? That was generous of you. I'm not sure I could be so forgiving."

"A lovely set of carving knives." Her lips curved in a malicious grin. "You do realize that it's considered bad luck to be gifted with something sharp for your wedding?"

"Hadn't heard that." I obviously needed to spend some time brushing up on current superstitions.

"And these beauties were the sharpest I could find. I even included a sharpener for good measure."

I nodded half-hearted approval. "What newlywed household doesn't need a knife sharpener?"

"Kingsley didn't need one. He always insisted on having his knives sharpened by professionals. It was a business expense, of course, along with all the high-end appliances and cookware and dinnerware and wait staff and linens and on and on."

"Your husband worked in a restaurant?"

She let out a harsh guffaw. "He *owns* the restaurant. King Crabbe's—on the Jersey shore. I don't imagine you've ever heard of it. You Iowans probably have no need to read the Michelin Guide. Why would you? You don't find a lot of starred restaurants popping up in the boonies."

The twinge of sympathy I'd begun to muster faded like an image on an Etch A Sketch. "So, no castle tour, no lunch, no walking, no ibuprofen, and no shopping. Anything else you don't want to do?"

She spent a moment in quiet reflection. "I don't want to waste an entire afternoon being bombarded by your inane questions, so I'm releasing you from your bodyguard duties." She waved me away. "Shoo."

"You're sure about that? Because less than ten minutes ago you were demanding protection."

"I wouldn't have *said* it if I hadn't *meant* it. I'm going to find an out-of-the-way bench to sit on somewhere on this godforsaken rock, and then I'm going to work on my blog." She peered down at her capris. "After I treat the bloodstains on my pants."

"The blood isn't noticeable, if that's what you're worried about." She'd been fortunate to wear black capris for the trip today, so the stains were invisible to the naked eye.

"When the blood dries, it's going to leave the material stiff and scratchy. Does that offer you a clue as to why I want to rinse the stains out?"

"You bet." I swept my hand toward the roofed shelter directly opposite us where visitors could sit on a shaded bench while waiting to use the comfort station. Ladies to the right. Gents to the left. "You're in the right place then."

"Ah. Good." She hobbled toward the facility without another word. I guess she didn't think saying thank you was very Austenesque. At the ladies' room door she turned. "Have you read my blogs yet?"

The contents of my stomach began to churn like veggies in a Bullet blender. "I'm afraid I haven't had the opportunity."

"Really?" She lifted her brows ever so slightly, her expression hovering somewhere between surprise and disdain. "I would have thought you'd be anxious to read my opinion of your tour thus far."

Yup. About as anxious as I was to chew carpet tacks. "I'll play catch-up when I find a little downtime. Some things are just too important to be rushed."

"Indeed." She opened the door to the ladies' room and disappeared inside, leaving me to wrestle with the question of when I should allow the venom in her blog posts to ruin my trip—now or later?

Marshalling my courage, I plucked my cell phone from my shoulder bag, intent on getting it over with, when I noticed a group of women exiting the Courtyard Shop with countless shopping bags dangling from their arms, their laughter echoing off the stone walls, their eyes alight with the kind of giddy excitement that accompanies multiple credit card purchases.

I looked from my cell phone to the door of the shop, then back again. *Misery or shopping? Misery or shopping?*

Dropping my phone back into my bag, I headed across the cobblestones.

The shop was a treasure trove of items that had been selected with maximum appeal to the hardcore shopper. Beautifully illustrated coffee-table books. Jams and jellies in adorable jars. Italian leather handbags in luscious pastels, displayed on illuminated glass shelving that was meant to dazzle. Sheets of chocolate fudge waiting to be cut. Jewelry set out on velvet trays in sparkling glass cases. Perfumes in bottles shaped like seashells and starfish.

As I wandered around the shop, breathing in the hunger-inducing aroma of fudge, I felt the tension in my muscles start to recede. *Ahhh.* Full-body massage might help other people relax, but for me, browsing aisles filled with merchandise I could ooh and ahh over had the same effect. And as a bonus, they were offering free samples of the fudge!

Having sampled my way through an array of creamy chunks, I was in the process of making a purchase when I heard a familiar voice at the far end of the shop.

"I feel like a hypocrite for admitting this, but does anyone besides me miss hearing Bernice whine about everything?" asked Lucille.

"I kinda miss her gripin'," confessed Nana. "It just don't seem natural startin' the day without no one callin' us morons. What'll we do if she don't ever come back?"

"She'll be back," asserted Helen. "She's like a bad penny."

"But what if she don't?"

As I walked toward them, I could see their expressions grow somber as they contemplated Nana's question.

"Do you think we should appoint someone to impersonate her?" suggested Alice.

"But what if the appointee isn't as caustic or mean-spirited as Bernice?" said Grace. "Do any of us have the acting chops to portray her?"

"We could hold auditions," floated Nana.

I wandered into their midst with my purchase.

"You heard any news about Bernice yet?" Nana asked me.

I shook my head. "But on a more positive note, Wally did give me the police station's phone number." I yanked my cell out once again and punched in the number. "Hi, this is Emily Miceli, the tour escort whose guest disappeared from the Stand and Deliver Inn this morning. The missing guest's name is Bernice Zwerg, and I was wondering if you could tell me if she's been located yet? Uh-huh...uh-huh...Oh, really? Okay, then. Yes. I'll look forward to that. Thank you."

I let out an excited breath. "There's news. The dispatcher said Constable Tredinnick would be contacting us shortly. It sounds promising, ladies, so keep your fingers crossed. Maybe we can all start breathing a little easier." *Please let her be okay. Please let her be okay.* As they exchanged nods and smiles, I regarded them anew.

"How come you're not touring the castle? Tour now, shop later. You don't want to be weighted down with packages while you explore the castle, do you?"

"We're opting out of the castle tour," Helen spoke up.

I paused a half second to digest her comment. "But why? This is why you're here—to walk the same paths where Benedictine monks walked over nine hundred years ago. To soak in history. To...to view the seascape from the top of the castle parapets. To post your pictures on Facebook to see who gets the most likes. This is a once in a lifetime opportunity. You're already here. What's the problem?"

"We was okay until we seen them stairs," said Nana.

"They were just a bunch of rocks with handrails attached," complained Helen.

"And they were all catawampus," disclosed Alice, elevating her hands up and down to demonstrate their unevenness.

"And had lots of gaps between them," added Margi.

"And were *reeeally* steep," said Grace, sounding winded from the simple act of having seen them.

Considering how fretful I'd been about their walking across the causeway, I couldn't fault them for declining to climb stairs that were apparently even more of a challenge. But I'd have to brace myself for more derision when Kathryn discovered that the entire tour group, with the exception of our bloggers, had nixed the castle tour. I wondered if she'd make a point of mentioning that in her blog. Although—I eyed the group—we were missing several people besides bloggers. "Where are the boys?" My spirits rose as I imagined telling Kathryn that while the ladies had decided that shopping was more appealing than a castle tour, the guys had been gung-ho to tackle the wonky stairs and cobblestone hill.

Helen pointed toward the courtyard. "They're eating ice cream cones at the al fresco dining tables on the next level."

"They said they already had their fill of exercise walking across the beach and causeway, so they weren't keen on climbing the stairs either," said Grace.

So much for my argument about my guys not being daunted by stairs or hills or activities geared toward the younger generation. I peeked at my watch. "So what do you plan on doing for the rest of the afternoon? You have a lot of time to kill now. And even though this shop is lovely, it's one shop, not a strip mall."

"I think we should discuss our plans over ice cream cones," proposed Alice.

"We'll be too full to eat lunch if we have ice cream now," warned Lucille.

"The guys are eating ice cream," objected Margi.

"But they won't get full," explained Helen. "They're pretending their cones are appetizers."

Quiet nods. A frisson of excitement.

"So if we pretend our cones are appetizers, we won't get full either?" asked Margi.

"That's genius," said Lucille.

"I shouldn't give the boys so much grief," confided Helen. "They're obviously smarter than I give them credit for."

"I'll run ahead and put dibs on a table," offered Alice as she rushed toward the door.

They chased after her en masse, all except Nana and Tilly, who continued to linger despite everyone's rapid exit. "You're not joining in the footrace?" I teased.

"Don't matter who arrives first. Them girls still gotta decide what order they're gonna line up in, so Til and me are just gonna wait 'em out. We already done height once today already, so this time it'll probably be age, which is gonna take forever on account some of the girls are gettin' a little testy about tellin' their age."

I held out my purchase to Nana. "I bought you a little something."

She read the label on the box. "Opera cream fudge." She opened the box, her eyes rounding with delight. "Well, would you lookit that." She stuffed a chunk into her mouth before offering the box to Tilly.

"Oh, my." Tilly closed her eyes in ecstasy as she savored a piece. "Vanilla cream infused with maraschino cherries. They must have known you were coming, Marion."

I smiled as Nana popped another chunk into her mouth. "So how does it taste?"

She let out an orgasmic sigh. "It tastes like one box won't be enough." She craned her neck to locate the fudge counter. "You got any idea how much they got left?"

I laughed. "Why? Are you planning to buy them out?"

"You bet. C'mon, Til. I don't know how many boxes I can carry by myself."

As I loitered by the perfume display, spraying a variety of tester scents into the air and sniffing, I was surprised to see Margi charge back through the shop door and make a beeline toward me. "What? The ice cream place doesn't have a flavor you like?"

She responded with an eye roll and a flip of her wrist. "I wanted to line up by age, youngest to oldest, because that puts me first, but Lucille charged elder discrimination and Helen said that disclosing our age might violate privacy laws, so they decided to go with the last four digits of our social security numbers, lowest number first."

"And?"

"I'm having a senior moment. I can't remember mine. So…no ice cream for me."

"Well, we can't have that, can we? Here's an idea. How about you wait until they're done and buy your cone when there's no line?"

She regarded me as if she were struggling to withstand the seismic shift I'd just created in the ground beneath her. "But that's cheating."

"No, it's not. It's a loophole."

Her mouth slid from a skeptical twitch into a slow, satisfied grin. "There's no downside, is there? I skip the waiting-in-line part and get my ice cream anyway. How come I didn't think of that?"

"Years of indoctrination?"

With a spurt of newfound enthusiasm, she unzipped the front pocket of her handbag and removed a sheet of paper. "I was hoping you'd still be here, Emily, because I have something for you. Remember when I suggested that the bloggers might be lying about not knowing each other? Well, I accessed their blogs and did a whole lot of cross-checking using keyword searches, and I was right. The evidence is right there in plain sight for anyone who cares to find it."

"You cross-checked their blogs? But there were thousands of them, and they weren't even formatted in a way that was cross-check friendly. How did you even know which words to search?"

She offered me an indulgent look, making me feel as if I had rocks for brains. "*Pfft*. I do stuff like this all the time at the clinic. It's a piece of cake for anyone with even baseline knowledge of a computer."

The woman who didn't realize that standing in line with her fellow Iowans was not a state law had cracked a problem that I couldn't even begin to wrap my head around. Go figure.

"Spencer Blunt and August Lugar were both in Bayfield, Wisconsin, *at the same time* four years ago," she said with breathy excitement. "August wrote a review about the food in that famous Bayfield Inn, and Spencer rated a new tourist rooming house. Quite a coincidence, huh? Two bloggers together in the same tiny town at the same time? What are the chances they didn't run into each other? And coincidentally, they *both* mention taking the lighthouse tour of the Apostle Islands, so I'm betting that's where the original meet and greet took place."

"A meet and greet that developed into something more sinister," I theorized, taking the ball and running with it. "Two criminal minds who combined forces to relieve unsuspecting tourists of their cash and whatever valuables they left lying around. They're a tag team, maybe working together on certain occasions and alone on others. I knew they were in cahoots. They probably began by targeting domestic tours, and I made it possible for them to go international. And they've upped the ante from simple grand theft larceny to murder." I threw my arms around Margi in a huge hug. "You're brilliant! Would you be willing to take your search a step further to document how many of the same tours they've—"

"I'm not done yet." She shuffled back a few inches to give herself space. "I found another incidence where August was in Burlington, Vermont, for a restaurant review, Mason Chatsworth arrived on the same date to review a new economy motel, and Spencer was in a nearby town rating a popular diner."

Whoa. All *three* guys in the same place at the same time? My tag team was turning into a polo team. "How long ago was that?"

"Two years ago."

Was Mason being used as backup? A substitute player should something go awry? Or was he engaged in an apprenticeship of sorts, observing the pros in action before venturing out on his own? Either way, their clandestine alliance was pretty unsettling.

"And then there's Heather Holloway."

"Heather?" I pulled a face at Margi. "You can't be serious."

"Mason reviewed a hotel in Heather's hometown about a year ago. I don't have any proof that they met when he was there, but I think it's highly suspicious. Heather hasn't traveled around like the guys. She just watches a lot of movies about Jane Austen, reads creepy books where Jane appears with zombie armies and vampires, and then blogs about them from the comfort of her apartment."

"But if they *did* meet," I said with growing excitement, "he might have baited the hook with expectations of travel and reeled her in with promises of an uptick in her monthly cash flow. That might have looked pretty appealing to a hometown girl with limited financial prospects." Had Heather and Mason formed a team, too? An expansion team that was in direct competition with August and Spencer? Or were they more like a franchise, pooling their ill-gotten gains for the benefit of both teams?

"From what I could tell, no one visited Caroline Goodfriend's town, so she might be the only blogger with no ties to the others. She doesn't need to move around to write her blog. I guess she gets all the information she needs from internet websites."

"She lives in South Carolina, doesn't she?"

"A tiny little town in the sticks. She doesn't mention her hometown on her blog, so I had to check the white pages for an address.

The place is so small, it doesn't have a hotel or a restaurant. She probably has to drive forever to get a burger and fries."

"What about Kathryn?"

"Penelope Pemberley doesn't reveal a location on her website, but according to the white pages again, Kathryn Crabbe lives in DC, which all the male bloggers have visited at one time or another."

"Any indication that she met up with them?"

Margi shook her head. "Kathryn and the fellas don't live on the same planet. She's all literary, symbolism, figurative language, and historical context. And the fellas are like, show me the cheapest hotel in this or that location and I'll tell you if the food in the dive next door is any good. DC is so big, it kinda cancels out coincidence."

"So, in essence, four of our bloggers could be putting on a big act for us."

"Yup. But they're honest-to-goodness bloggers because I've been reading what they've said about our trip so far, and they've nailed it."

I screwed my face into a painful wince, head bent, nose scrunched, eyes pinched shut. "*Oh, God.* How damning have Kathryn's blogs been?"

"Well, other than the one she wrote about having the misfortune to be on the same tour as a Janeite traitor, they've been pretty complimentary."

I raised my head and eased one eyelid open. "You're kidding."

"Nope. She spent a lot of time saying what an improvement your grandmother's cooking was over the previous chef, and she gave you high marks for finding a substitute so quickly."

"Really?"

"Yup. Her last blog didn't mention Jane Austen at all. All she did was applaud Marion's culinary skills and post a mini menu of the food served since Marion took over the kitchen. In fact, that's what all the bloggers have been posting about: Marion's cooking and how delicious it is. Trust me, we could be touring Mars and these folks wouldn't want to write about the scenery. They'd want to write about Marion's out-of-this-world cuisine. Hope the attention doesn't go to your grandmother's head. These bloggers are pretty generous with their praise."

"Gee." I suddenly felt taller, lighter, and less likely to swallow an entire bottle of antacids in one sitting. "That's unbelievable."

"Yeah. I thought Kathryn was like Bernice two-point-oh. But her blog actually makes her sound like a pretty decent person." Margi lifted her brows in reflection. "If Bernice ever comes back, we should encourage her to write a blog. If she digs deep enough, maybe she'll discover her inner nice." She wriggled her nose in the air as she ranged a look around the shop. "Is that fudge I'm smelling?"

I spun her around in the direction of the confection counter. "Just follow your nose. And as an added bonus, they're giving out free samples."

"Appetizers! I like this place."

As she headed off, I turned toward the door to find Wally standing on the threshold, searching. When I waved, he wasted no time hotfooting his way toward me. "The very person I was looking for."

"You can't be through touring the castle already."

"I got turned around before I hit the entrance. I just fielded a call from Constable Tredinnick, who's found no trace of Bernice anywhere. She's not registered at any of the local B&Bs, inns, hotels, motels, or rooming houses. The cab company has no record of picking her up. None of the local eateries have served her. No one fitting her description boarded the train at the nearest rail station. The authorities at Heathrow say she hasn't checked in to board a flight to the US."

The bottom seemed to fall out of my stomach as my earlier elation whiplashed into full-blown despair. I heaved a dejected sigh. "Guess I jumped the gun expecting good news. I don't know what our next move should be. Do we tell her family? Do we adopt a wait-and-see attitude? Dammit, Wally, she has to be someplace. She can't have vanished into thin air."

"That's exactly what Tredinnick said, which is why he wants us to head back to the inn as soon as possible for questioning. I'm afraid he suspects foul play."

FOURTEEN

"Blokes don't disappear into thin air." Voice stern and eyes steely, Constable Tredinnick probed each of our faces as he addressed us back at the inn. "Ms. Zwerg doesn't even appear on any of our CCTV footage, so wherever she is, it's not Port Jacob. So where does that leave us?"

We'd managed to round up everyone in record time and escort them across the causeway before it flooded on the incoming tide. Wally had texted the bloggers, asking them to speed up their tour of the castle, and I'd texted Jackie, telling her to wait for us at the Godolphin Arms rather than venture to the mount. The bloggers had been annoyed that they couldn't enjoy their tour at a leisurely pace, and Jackie had been peeved that she wasn't even being allowed to set foot on the island, but no one else seemed to mind our early departure. As Dick Teig commented, "The faster we get back to the inn, the faster we get to sample more of Marion's cooking."

Since there'd been no time to eat lunch, we'd gotten takeout from a Cornish pasty shop in Marazion and been granted permission by our driver to eat on the bus, which violated the cardinal rule that passengers not be allowed to carry open containers of food onto the coach. For this breach in protocol, Nana had presented Freddy with a pound of her opera cream fudge, which calmed his nerves about the errant bits of steak, potatoes, rutabaga, and onion that might escape onto the upholstery from our pasties.

"It leads me to conclude that a second party might be involved in Ms. Zwerg's disappearance," Tredinnick continued. "And if a second party is involved, there's a good possibility that we might be looking at foul play."

Gasps. Eye-widening. An involuntary hiccup.

"What kind of foul play?" asked George.

Tredinnick paused. "She might have suffered the same fate as Lance Tori."

"But her body isn't at the bottom of the cellar stairs," Grace pointed out.

"No, mum. But depending upon how her killer dispatched her and where, her remains could be just about anywhere—in the boot of a car, down a well, in the middle of a pond..."

"Why would anyone want to kill Bernice?" asked Alice. "She was well-meaning in spite of her political leanings, even though anyone who spent any time around her ended up wanting to strangle her because of her insults, and negativity, and—"

"Whining," called out Dick Stolee.

"And constant complaining," added Dick Teig.

Helen elbowed her husband in the belly. "That's the same as whining. Try pretentiousness or braggadocio."

"What Helen just said," quipped Dick.

"And pessimism," continued George.

201

"And cantankerousness," Osmond threw out.

"And—"

"Excuse me," Alice interrupted. "Could I retract my question? Now that I think about it, it's probably a miracle that someone didn't take her out long before this."

Tredinnick narrowed his eyes at the bunch of us. "She was universally disliked by everyone? None of you can find anything good to say about the woman?"

Vacuous looks. Shoulder-shrugging. Margi raised her hand. "After she had her bunion surgery, she wore some very nice shoes that coordinated quite well with her outfits."

Tredinnick regarded her, deadpan, before pacing across the floor of the lounge, relying heavily on his cane. "A woman who is detested by her entire tour group goes missing. Tell me why I shouldn't suspect that the whole bleedin' lot of you had a hand in her disappearance?"

"They all have alibis," I spoke up. "We were all together eating supper in the dining room when she stormed off, and we remained together for more than an hour while we did show-and-tell from our metal-detecting excursion at the Bedruthan Steps. When Alice, her roommate, went back to their room"—I gestured to Alice, who gave a finger wave in response—"Bernice was already gone and never returned all night."

"Is this accurate, Alice?" questioned Tredinnick.

"You bet. All except the part where all of us were together for more than an hour. Three of the fellas skipped out before the show-and-tell got started because they said they had to write their blogs."

I hadn't gotten around to that part yet.

Tredinnick raised one eyebrow. "Which fellas?"

"She's talking about us," Spencer Blunt volunteered. "August, and Mason, and I." They identified themselves with a casual flutter of their hands, like competitors raising bidding paddles at an auction. "The only thing I found at the beach was a beaten-up button, so since I didn't have anything for folks to ogle over, I left. August and Mason didn't find anything either, so we left at about the same time. We all had blog posts to write."

Tredinnick limped across the floor to stand in front of Spencer. "So what happened when you returned to your room?"

He gave Tredinnick the same spiel he'd given me earlier this morning. He'd worked on his blog. Slipped into a meditative state. Been annoyed by the noise from the blowing fans. Hadn't heard any other unusual sounds.

"I can vouch for my roommate," August spoke up.

Of course he could. They were always going to vouch for each other. It was their shtick.

"We were up past midnight tweaking our posts," alleged August. "End of story. It was a rather uneventful evening, Constable. One that did not include our taking time out to harm a woman neither one of us knew."

"A man doesn't need the excuse of knowing a victim to do them harm," Tredinnick fired back. "There are instances when a victim is simply in the wrong place at the wrong time, and suffers because of it."

"Not in this case," August replied glibly. "I'll be magnanimous and take no offense at what you're implying because, like it or not, our alibis are airtight."

Tredinnick offered a half smile. "For now."

"What's that supposed to mean?" asked Spencer.

"My investigation isn't over yet. I'll let you know when I'm done."

Yes! Tredinnick was on to them. And when I told him what I'd found out about the duo, I suspected their airtight alibis might spring a few leaks.

"You." Tredinnick stabbed a finger at Mason. "You're the one in the single room."

Mason nodded, giving him a palms up. "Right. The green-haired guy has no alibi again. No witness to how I spent my evening. I can show you my blog. Does that count?"

"Your single room has proven to be a very convenient excuse," Tredinnick observed.

"Hey, don't punish me for enjoying my privacy. Last time I looked, my preferring not to share personal space with a stranger wasn't a crime."

"It's *her* you should be locking up," bellowed Kathryn, rising to her feet and pointing an accusatory finger at Heather. "She tried to kill me today."

"I did not!"

"She shoved me to the ground in the hopes that I'd hit my head on the cobblestone walk and suffer a traumatic brain injury that would kill me."

"That is *so* bogus!" Heather shot off her chair, all bluster and indignation. She threw a pleading look at Tredinnick. "I tripped on the cobblestones and accidentally knocked her down. It was an accident. Ask Mason. He was walking with me."

"He's not going to tell you the truth," warned Kathryn. "The two of them are buddy-buddy. He's going to back up every lie she tells you. Meanwhile, I'm risking my life every time I'm within a foot of them. And while I'm on the subject, that girl has stolen something that belongs to—"

The shrill blare of a whistle echoed through the room. Hands flew to ears to blunt the sound, but Tredinnick didn't stop blowing until both Kathryn and Heather sat back down. He removed the whistle from his mouth but kept it at the ready, palmed in his fist. "The floor is mine. Remember that before you allow yourselves to indulge in future outbursts." He eyed Mason once again. "I'd like to hear your version, please."

"It's like Heather said. She and I were walking along the waterfront at St. Michael's Mount when she lost her balance on the cobblestones and went crashing into Kathryn, who was walking in front of us. Heather got up pretty quickly, but Kathryn stayed down, so I ran off to find help while Heather stayed with her. It was an accident, plain and simple."

"I told you he'd back up her lie," shouted Kathryn.

Tredinnick brandished his whistle in the air, his tone growing strained. "I'd prefer not to use this again, but should you persist…" He settled a meaningful look on Kathryn. He twiddled a finger at Heather. "Your shoe, please."

"My shoe? Why do you want my—"

"Show me the sole, if you would."

She slid one foot out of her elastic strap wedge sandal and held the sole up for his inspection.

"Brilliant," he said after a moment. "Thank you. With your slippery sole and elevated heel, you're lucky your fall was a one-off. The majority of tourists who navigate our cobblestones in fancy footwear like yours usually end up at the hardware store having to purchase mobility aids. Gum rubber soles work the best on our walkways, which is why the proprietor of Kneebone Hardware doesn't sell any. There's a much higher profit margin for mobility products. So"—he put a bead on Kathryn—"I have no reason to doubt the young woman's version of what happened. But I'll be giving you a word of advice: avoid walking near her if she ever wears those shoes again."

Kathryn was stone-faced as she raised her hand like an obedient schoolchild. "What about the other matter? The theft of my personal property?"

"Do you have an abridged version?" he asked.

She made her case for why Heather's unearthed bobble belonged to the Truscott-Tallon family and why *not* returning it constituted theft, but Tredinnick seemed unconvinced. "This isn't a matter for a local constable," he concluded. "If you can't sort out a solution between you, I suggest you bring your grievance to a solicitor."

"You can be sure I will," Kathryn replied in an oily voice.

He looked out over the lounge again, his expression hovering somewhere between seriousness and exasperation. "It's not uncommon for pensioners to just wander off. Sometimes their disappearance is triggered by emotional trauma. At other times they wander off because of undiagnosed mental health issues. Please be thoughtful when you answer. Did Ms. Zwerg show signs of suffering from senility or dementia?"

"You mean, is she certifiable?" asked Dick Teig.

"She's not batshit crazy," offered Dick Stolee. "She's just a little nuts."

"Is that better or worse than being certifiable?" asked Lucille.

I rolled my eyes, catching Tredinnick's gaze when he looked my way. "Are you toying with the idea that Bernice might have been so traumatized by her emotional upset at the dinner table last night that it could have disturbed her mental health enough to cause her to wander off on her own?"

"It's a possibility I'm considering. Unfortunately, if she exited by the rear door, she may have meandered onto the coastal path. And if she strayed too far off the path, she could very well have taken a tumble over the cliff, hit the rocks below, and been carried out to sea. It wouldn't be the first time something like this has happened."

A hush fell over the room.

"So...Bernice could really be dead?" asked Dick Teig.

"I won't conclude that right now, but should all my other avenues of investigation collapse, I may find myself resorting to that theory. She was elderly. It was dark. The two can be a deadly combination."

She wasn't dead. She couldn't be. I refused to go there.

"Poor Bernice," lamented Tilly. "When all is said and done, she really wasn't such a bad sort."

"She bought Emily's bouquet for her weddin'," said Nana. "That was a real big deal considerin' how penny pinchin' she is."

"She paid me a compliment once," admitted Osmond. "I'll never forget. She said I got around pretty well for a spindle-legged geezer with one foot already in the grave."

"That Bernice." Dick Teig chuckled. "She sure had a way of personalizing her insults."

"She was the master," Helen reminisced. "Remember how quick she was with her nasty comebacks? No sooner were the words out of your mouth than *zing!* She'd make you feel like a pile of poop in no time at all. That takes talent."

Sniffs. A few tears.

Jackie waved at Tredinnick. "Excuse me, but from what I'm hearing, there's a slight chance that Bernice is still alive, so with that in mind, would you excuse Mrs. S and me so we can get dinner started? If Bernice shows up, she's going to be hungry, and I'm planning to make an incredible treat to welcome her back. But even if she doesn't show up tonight, the other guests will still be gung ho for a dessert that's going to knock their socks off. I got the recipe from the pastry chef at the Godolphin Arms, who said it's his biggest seller. I guarantee you, it's going to be"—she raised her voice an octave and sang out in a prolonged vibrato—"a-*maaaaaa*-zing."

Nana boosted herself to her feet. "The girl's right. If you don't got no problem with us leavin', we'd like to head to the kitchen, else there won't be no supper at all. So can we go or are you aimin' to turn the thumbscrews until one of us cries uncle?"

Tredinnick eyed Nana. He eyed Jackie. Mouth wrenched askew, he bobbed his head toward the kitchen. "Go." But when everyone else started boosting themselves to their feet, he raised his hand to halt them. "That was not a signal for the rest of you to leave."

Grunts. Groans. Impatient snorts.

"What are your plans for tomorrow?" he asked.

"We're heading for Mawnan Smith to visit the maze at Glendurgan," said Wally.

Tredinnick looked perplexed. "Why would you want to go there?"

"Because it was planted a hundred and seventy years ago and looks like a fascinating place to explore?"

Tredinnick flashed a googly-eyed expression that mirrored doubt. "If you say so."

"Have you ever been there?"

"No. And I'm afraid you'll not be getting there either—at least, not tomorrow."

Mouths opened. Jaws dropped.

Wally regarded him in confusion. "Why not?"

"Because tomorrow you'll be spending the day with me. And there won't be any more fannying around. *All* of you will be here with me until we discover who's behind the trouble at the Stand and Deliver Inn."

Wally looked apoplectic. "But we have reservations."

"Cancel them."

"You're confining us to our quarters?" Spencer objected. "How do you propose we occupy ourselves all day tomorrow? There's nothing to do here."

A smile lifted the corners of Tredinnick's mouth. "With what I have planned, I guarantee you won't be bored." He elevated his palms in a gesture of dismissal. "Now you may leave."

He left amid the gripes and grumbles of a lounge full of unhappy tourists. I followed him to the front door. "Excuse me, Constable, could I speak to you for a minute?" I looked over my shoulder to check for eavesdroppers. "Outside?"

"You can walk with me to my car."

I launched into my theory once we hit the front path. "I think there's a good reason why the bloggers heard nothing suspicious last night. I think Spencer Blunt, August Lugar, and Mason Chatsworth have formed some kind of criminal cabal where they prey on tourists, so naturally they're going to vouch for each other's whereabouts. They're in this together."

"You have evidence to back up what you're telling me?"

"Well, the evidence is kind of circumstantial, but one of my Iowa guests discovered instances where all three men were visiting the same place at the same time back in the States. So it's quite likely they all knew each other before they signed up for this trip, even though they're not admitting anything."

"Kind of circumstantial?" He guffawed. "You mean *highly* circumstantial."

"And then Mason visited Heather Holloway's hometown only last year. So she could be in on the caper, too."

"I'm not aware it's a criminal offense to visit the town where another blogger resides, Mrs. Miceli."

"So you're not going to look into this more closely?"

He withdrew his pen and notebook from his breast pocket and jotted something down. "I've made a note."

"Okay. Thanks. Because I really think they had something to do with Bernice's disappearance."

He leaned against the door of his squad car. "Why?"

"Because I can't see any other explanation. I think Bernice caught August and Spencer in the act of burglarizing another guest's room, so they were unexpectedly forced to deal with her in a way that...that didn't go well for Bernice."

"Your Mr. Lugar himself was the victim of a theft, was he not?"

"So he says. Personally, I think he faked it to throw you off the scent."

"Have any of your other guests reported their valuables being nicked?"

"No, but that doesn't mean they weren't. It could boil down to the fact that they just haven't noticed yet. We've been keeping the group pretty busy."

"Are you also placing blame for Mr. Tori's death on their heads?"

I hadn't quite figured that out yet. "I'm not saying they're to blame, but I'm also not saying that the two incidents aren't connected. And once again, if the bloggers are using each other to confirm their alibis, who's to know?"

That gave Tredinnick pause and me an opening to pose another question. "Are you planning to release Enyon anytime soon? My troops have rallied to keep up with meal preparation, but it would sure be a lot easier if Enyon could take charge again. It's not much of a holiday for my grandmother and my roommate. We're doing the best we can to keep the place running, but with the added stress about Bernice, we're running out of gas."

"I'll be releasing Mr. Gladwish when I return to the nick, Mrs. Miceli."

"You will? Oh my God! That's the best news I've had since we arrived."

"Questioning him is turning out to be less productive than beating a dead horse. He claims to know nothing, and I have no evidence that would allow me to hold him any longer, so you may soon look forward to order being restored at the inn."

I raised my arms in a V over my head. "Yes."

"Besides, my wife tells me I need to exercise Christian charity by allowing him to make funeral arrangements for Mr. Tori, and he can't very well do that from jail."

Mention of Lance's funeral triggered another thought. "I'm not sure how relevant this is, but when I spoke with Kathryn Crabbe today she informed me that her ex-husband was a famous chef and that their marriage had ended quite badly because of an adulterous affair he'd been conducting with her best friend's daughter."

"Not bloomin' likely, is it?"

"What? That her husband was having an affair?"

"No. That she had a friend."

"Please don't go yet!" Caroline Goodfriend waved her arm over her head as she sprinted down the front path toward us, her usual calm replaced by visible distress. "He's struck again!"

"Who's struck again?" asked Tredinnick when she'd skidded to a stop in front of us.

"The thief." She gasped to catch her breath. "The wad of cash I hid in my jar of night moisturizer—it's gone."

FIFTEEN

I GROANED. "You didn't keep your cash in a neck wallet?"

"I bought one for the trip, but it felt itchy and made my clothes look lumpy, so I left it at home. Besides, who's going to know to look for anything in a night moisturizer jar?"

"An accomplished thief," said Tredinnick.

She pressed the heels of her palms against her forehead as if trying to squeeze an image out of her brain. "I removed some money from it yesterday evening, before we gathered in the lounge for my presentation, but when I went to put money back just a few minutes ago, it was empty."

"Are you quite sure you haven't mixed up your jars?" asked Tredinnick.

"Yes, I'm sure. I only packed two—an empty one for my cash and a full jar of daytime cream that I planned to apply both day and night." She touched her fingertips to her cheek. "I didn't think that using only one product for a few days would make that much of a difference in my complexion."

Tredinnick regarded her blandly. "Where was the jar?"

"In my toiletry bag on the dresser, along with my toothpaste, facial scrubs, and everything else."

"So to the best of your knowledge, the theft occurred in the time period between yesterday evening and a few minutes ago?"

The same time period when Bernice had disappeared. The same time period when August, Spencer, and Mason had enjoyed sole access to the rooms and hallway. Was it Caroline and Heather's room that the bloggers had been sneaking out of when Bernice had interrupted them?

Which led me to a more insidious thought.

Had it been Heather who'd alerted her fellow bloggers to the stash in Caroline's jar of beauty cream?

"Yes," said Caroline, responding to Tredinnick's question. "Twenty-four hours ago I was flush with cash; now all I have left are my credit cards. But my door was locked! How did someone get into my room without a key?"

"Wally is carrying the only master key," I confirmed.

Tredinnick massaged the thigh of his bad leg. "There's those who've made a handsome living breaking into locked rooms, Ms. Goodfriend. I'd guess that picking locks was the specialty of a few score of blighters who called Her Majesty's prison in Dartmoor home."

"Are you sure the door was locked?" I asked Caroline. "They don't lock automatically. You have to use your key to lock it. So unless you did that, you might have accidentally left it op—"

"Yes, the door was locked. Heather locked it after we left the room."

Or tricked you into thinking she'd locked it. I arched my eyebrows at Tredinnick, giving him a look that screamed *Do you believe me now?*

Catching my drift, he pushed himself off the car, his eyes narrowed as he focused on the inn. "It's just occurred to me that I may have a few more questions to ask before I leave."

The police radio inside his car squawked to life. " Consta…*zzt*… *zzt*…*zzzzzt*…in please," said a woman's voice amid a background of static.

Leaning through his open window, he picked up the car microphone. "Come again, Bess?" After a brief interlude where the connection thrummed with more static, he returned the microphone to its cradle and pulled out his cell phone. "System needs updating," he griped as he punched in a number. "Bess. The car radio's dodgy. What can I do for you?"

His breathing changed as he listened, his body language indicating that he was preparing to kick into high gear. "Call the ambulance. Keep him comfortable until I get there."

"What's happened?" I asked as he piled into his car.

"It's Enyon. He's doubled over with pain. Bess says he needs to get to hospital."

He gunned his engine and peeled out of the parking lot as if he were participating in time trials for the Indy 500.

"I'm sorry about Enyon," Caroline allowed, "but in the meantime, what am I supposed to do about my missing money?"

She was sorry about Enyon? My blood pressure had just shot through the top of my head and would probably trigger a brain aneurysm that would kill me, but immediate death was not an acceptable reason to shirk my professional responsibilities.

"Two things," I said when I could breathe again. "First, we have an emergency cash fund to float you a loan, and second, you need to stop by my room to pick up a neck wallet. I brought extra."

· · · · · · · · · ·

"This being our second substantial theft of cash since we arrived, I'd like to encourage all of you, *again*, to keep your valuables on your person at all times in a neck wallet, a fanny pack, or a money belt."

After braving the cooking frenzy in the kitchen to give Nana and Jackie a heads-up about the situation, I enlisted Wally's assistance to help me gather everyone back in the lounge so I could advise them of our latest setback. Tilly raised her hand.

"When you say we should keep our valuables close at all times, are you suggesting that we take our possessions to bed with us?"

"I'm not sleeping with my blasted wallet around my neck," declared Dick Stolee. "I tried that once."

"He did," Grace attested in a grave tone. "He had a horrible nightmare and thrashed around so violently, he got the cord all tangled up in his CPAP machine and would've choked to death if I hadn't cut him free."

"What were you dreaming about?" George asked him.

Dick shivered at the memory. "Medicare vouchers."

"Say, Emily, let's pretend a fella was hiding money in the heel of his wingtips," Dick Teig piped up. "Would you advise him to wear his shoes to bed?"

"He wouldn't have to wear both, would he?" asked Margi. "If it were me, I'd only wear the shoe with the money in it."

Alice frowned. "Wouldn't a thief be curious about why a fella is wearing a shoe to bed?"

"Not if he sees how old the fella is," retorted Osmond. "He'd probably figure Dick was suffering from dementia and just forgot to put the other one on."

Helen thwacked Dick's arm. "Why don't you announce to the immediate world that you're hiding money in your shoe?"

"I never said it was *me*," protested Dick.

I raised my hand for quiet. "I'm not recommending that you take your valuables to bed with you. I'm just saying that during the day, please carry them on your person in a secure pouch or wallet. If you lock your door at night, your valuables should be safe."

"Please don't take this as a criticism," Caroline demurred, "but my money was stolen despite my door being locked. I don't know how it happened, but it has me pretty rattled."

I sidled a look at Heather, knowing exactly how it had happened, but I couldn't divulge anything until Tredinnick verified my suspicions.

"So tonight, I'm planning to wedge a chair under my doorknob to make sure no one can sneak in and steal anything else," Caroline continued. "And if the rest of you were smart, you'd do the same thing."

Nods. Grumbles. A few deer-in-the-headlights stares.

"My cash was stolen despite my door being locked, too," August Lugar reminded us.

I regarded him stiffly. Right. And I was the reigning Miss Brazil.

"It might not be my place to comment on this," he went on, "but I think somebody should because it's become the elephant in the room." He looked left and right to make eye contact with every guest in the lounge. "Somebody on this tour is one hell of a thief."

I rolled my eyes. Right on cue. Deflecting suspicion away from himself again to imply that the thievery should be blamed on someone else. He was as predictable as a vindictive politician with a Twitter account. But his words had hit their mark because everyone was quite suddenly exchanging distrustful looks with their neighbors, which was, I suspected, the very reaction he'd been hoping for.

"Please stop looking at each other like that," I urged them. "It's painful to watch."

"But that fella's right, isn't he?" asked Osmond. "Someone in this room is a thief." He cast a slow look around him. "Show of hands. How many folks—"

"As of this minute, all voting is suspended," I announced in a forceful voice. "Instead of sitting here, pointing fingers at each other, I'd like you to go back to your rooms to make sure all your valuables are still where they should be. And if you're missing anything, come down to my room and let me know so I can pass the information along to Constable Tredinnick. Okay?"

Pouting. Grudging nods.

"And one more thing. Enyon suffered some kind of medical emergency while he was being held for questioning, so he's been taken to the hospital and I don't know when we should expect to see him again. Please keep him in your thoughts and prayers."

"So Marion gets stuck with KP until we leave?" lamented George.

"Sorry, George. I'm afraid it's looking more that way."

"Gee," said Dick Teig, looking as gleeful as a kid with an Xbox capable of both Blu-ray and video streaming, "that's a shame Marion can't hang up her apron. Isn't it a shame, Dick?"

"You bet." Dick Stolee rubbed his hands together with such vigor, I expected flames to shoot out of his palms. "So how much longer before we can sit down to eat?"

Wally sprang out of his chair and popped his head into the kitchen to ask the cooks. "Couple of hours," he called back.

Apprehension morphed into anticipation. Frowns turned to smiles. All was right with the world again. Music might have charms to soothe a savage breast, but the thing that apparently worked best with my guys was the continued promise of Nana's home cooking.

I regarded them fondly. Iowans were so basic.

As they began to ease out of their chairs, Kathryn Crabbe went out of her way to hobble directly in front of Heather. "I hope you're storing my fob-seal in a safe place."

Heather didn't skip a beat. She plastered a smile on her face and addressed her as if she were a favorite aunt. "Thanks so much for your concern, Kathryn. How are you doing after your spill today? Anything I can do for you? If there is, you just let me know and I'll be happy to oblige. No need for you to suffer in solitude when I'd be more than willing to keep you company. Can't you just feel it? I think we could become the best of friends."

Kathryn fell into silence as Heather brushed past her, her expression signaling that she was both confounded and thrown off-kilter by the girl's unexpected response.

I guess no one in Jane Austen's novels had made a habit of spouting one of Nana's favorite proverbs: What can the enemy do when the friend is cordial?

Figuring that what was good for the goose was good for the gander, when I went back to my room I took inventory of my own stuff to make sure that our phantom thief hadn't paid me a visit. I didn't have to worry about my cash, credit cards, or passport. I always carried those with me, unless the room was outfitted with a personal safe, which this one wasn't. I went through my dresser drawers and jewelry pouch, finding all in order, but when I checked the closet I stopped short.

I'd brought five pairs of shoes with me. I was wearing one pair, which left four pairs in the closet.

So how come I was only seeing three?

I rummaged around in the closet, removing our suitcases for a better look. I checked under my cot and Jackie's bed. I searched the bathroom, under the nightstand, and went through Jackie's drawers, thinking she might have accidentally grabbed my shoes and stashed them in with her stuff. But I found no missing pair of ankle-tie flats in canary yellow.

I slumped down on my cot, confused. They were so stunning... and brand-new! I could swear I remembered bringing them, but was it a false memory? Had I actually left them at home? Or—I perked up a bit—had Jackie simply overlooked packing them when she'd volunteered to move my belongings our first night here?

Of course! They must still be in my original room—the suite Kathryn now occupied.

Anxious to find out, I hurried across the room and opened the door to find Dick Teig in the corridor, preparing to knock. I paused on the threshold. "Oh, no. You found something missing?" I hoped it wasn't his gold doubloon.

"I'll say. My Fruit of the Loons. I've been cleaned out of a whole bunch."

"Fruit of the *Looms*," I corrected with some relief. "I'm pretty sure the brand refers to the bounty from the textile looms rather than the plumage from a flock of aquatic birds."

He offered me a blank stare. "What?"

"Never mind. So what are you missing? Boxers or briefs?"

He hitched up his trousers, clearing gravel from his throat. "Getting kind of personal, aren't you, Emily?"

"Not if you want your skivvies back."

He shrugged one shoulder in a sign of submission and after glancing both ways, lowered his voice to a whisper. "Boxers. The kind they sell in the economy five-pack. Helen buys the tartan plaid ones because she says they're more slimming than the solid stretch knits. Do you need the size?"

"Uhhh…"

"Four XL. But they look a lot smaller when I'm wearing them." He clutched his rounded belly with both hands. "Helen says my pot looks more like a six-pack when I step into my tapered Burberry checks." He let out a bawdy chuckle. "Don't tell Helen I told you, but you wouldn't believe how frisky she gets when she sees me wearing—"

"Too much information," I cried as I clapped my hands over my ears. I was already getting heartburn thinking about having to strip-search August and Spencer to see if they were wearing Dick's shorts.

"*DICK!*" I heard Helen's voice explode through the hallway despite my attempt to render myself deaf. She brandished a white plastic garbage bag in the air at him. "I found your underwear! They're in your dirty clothes bag."

"No kidding?" He rewarded her with a thumbs-up before turning back to me with a sheepish look. "Say, Emily, would you have a problem forgetting everything I just told—"

"Already forgotten. Anything else you want to report stolen?"

"Nope. Helen's eyebrow pencils are all accounted for, so we're good."

I peeked at my watch. "If you're all done with your inventory, why don't the two of you head out to the spa? You have loads of time before dinner."

"Leave the room when there's a burglar on the loose? *Pffft*. I don't think so. Helen's laid down the law. She's not letting her makeup out of her sight. That'd be like asking the president to ditch the briefcase with the nuclear codes for the evening."

I headed down to Kathryn's room and knocked on the door.

"Who is it?"

"Emily."

"How do I know it's Emily and not the burglar?"

"Because I have her voice?"

"You could be a voice impersonator."

"I'm not that gifted." I could hear her shuffle closer to the door.

"I want to see three forms of identification. You can slide them under the door."

"I just want to ask you a question."

"Three forms of ID."

"I'm not giving you three forms of ID, Kathryn. Look, I seem to be missing a pair of shoes. Canary-yellow flats. I think they might have gotten left behind when I moved out of this room the other

222

night. Would you check around your bed and closet to see if they're there?"

"What if they are? I suppose you'd want me to open the door."

"That's the idea. I'd like them back."

"Sorry. I'm a bit too smart to fall for a ruse like that."

Air streamed from my nose like fire from a blow torch. "Then would you at least look around your room, and if you find them, give them to me at dinner?"

"I'm not planning to leave my suite," she announced through the locked door. "So this evening I'm ordering room service. You can relay the message to Emily."

"I *am* Emily, and room service is *not* available."

"Well, if the real Emily has any hope of continuing this tour, she might want to rethink that option."

Why, when I tell people that their best defense against the thief would be to secure their valuables and lock their doors behind them, do they take that to mean they should burrow in their rooms like Old Testament hermits? Is it my choice of words? My inflection? My tendency to smile when I make suggestions?

As I headed back to my room, Dick Stolee ran out of his. "You're not going to believe what the thief stole."

"Lay it on me."

He lowered his voice. "My underwear."

"Check your laundry bag."

He stared at me, a ray of hope in his eyes. "I didn't think of that."

"*DICK!*" Grace called out through their open door. "They're in your dirty clothes. I told you that no one would be desperate enough to steal your undies."

"Thanks, Emily. You're a lifesaver. I was worried I'd have to go shopping to replace them."

As he turned back toward his room, I called after him, "You've got time to kill before dinner. Why don't you and Grace have a soak in the hot tub?"

"No can do. Not with this burglar striking at will. We're sheltering in place."

Of course they were.

He paused at his threshold. "By the way, Grace wanted me to ask you. What would we have to do to get room service tonight?"

Feeling as if the whole tour were unraveling before my eyes, I struck out for the dining room to investigate the tray situation. It galled me to give in to frivolous demands, but I could see the handwriting on the wall, so I wanted to be prepared.

As I passed through the lounge, I heard a knock on the front door, so I made a quick detour through the foyer to answer it.

"Hi. Can I help you?"

Two thirty-something couples stood on the front stoop, dressed in polo shirts and walking shorts, their finely gauged sweaters tied loosely around their necks like magicians' capes. They looked as if they'd just stepped off a golf course in Palm Beach. "Is this the right Stand and Deliver Inn?" asked one of the men, giving away his American roots with his accent.

I offered my best welcoming smile. "The right Stand and Deliver Inn for what?"

"The food," he replied. "We were touring in the area—we're from Boston—so we thought we'd stop by to see if we could make last-minute dinner reservations for this evening."

"Uhhh..."

The shorter of the two women held up her smartphone. "It's on August Lugar's blog. He's been raving about the food so much that we didn't want to miss out. No one can whet your appetite for fine cuisine more convincingly than Mr. Lugar."

"August's blog," I hedged. "Right."

"We never miss reading his posts," attested the other man, who was painfully red-faced with sunburn. "He's made some tremendous recommendations over the years. We've tried just about every restaurant he's deemed a must visit, and we haven't been disappointed yet."

I sucked in a breath, releasing it in slow motion. "So here's the thing. We're not accepting reservations."

"Can you put our names on your cancellation list?" asked the guy with the sunburn.

"We don't have a cancellation list. We don't have any list. The proprietor is off the premises at the moment, so the tour group I'm escorting is kind of running the show, and we don't have the wherewithal to open the dining room up to the public. We barely have the capacity to feed ourselves."

The lady with the smartphone slipped into dog-with-bone mode. "What about takeout? Could we make a selection from your menu and have your chef prepare it to go?"

I sighed. "We don't actually have a menu. Every meal is what you'd call a surprise."

"That's a pretty radical way to conduct business," said the first man.

"Radical?" said Mr. Sunburn. "I'd say it's pretty damn stupid. No dinner reservations? No menu? No takeout?" He looked me in

225

the eye. "You should consider yourself lucky if you're not out of business by the end of the week."

I smiled stiffly. "With the way things are going, that's a real possibility. But thanks for the vote of confidence."

Heads shaking, they retreated back down the path to their car. "Maybe you'd like to come back when there's a real staff!" I called after them. "The rooms are quite lovely!"

I was pretty sure I was wasting my breath, but it'd been worth a try. The unfortunate truth was that if Enyon didn't take over the operations of his inn soon, his dream of being a premiere player in the travel accommodation industry was doomed to go bust.

Quite spectacularly.

. . . .

Supper in the dining room turned out to be a quiet affair.

Since the Iowa contingent had talked themselves into self-enforced lockdowns in their suites, Wally and I grudgingly capitulated and served their meals to them on trays, just like authentic hotel room service. The only guests who ventured out to sit at the table were the bloggers minus Kathryn, who received room service like the rest of the gang. I was too busy delivering meals to either engage in or overhear the conversation around the dinner table, but I suspected that with Caroline present, the one thing the other four bloggers wouldn't be discussing was their next hit.

Nana knocked the ball out of the park with the meal she whipped up, serving individual pastry tarts filled with baby asparagus and garlic, and smothered in ricotta, gruyere, and parmesan cheeses. As a courtesy to those who detest asparagus, she also provided several variations with broccoli and spiffed up both vegetable selections by including bacon, ham, and prosciutto. She added color with a lettuce, orange, pecan, and crumbled goat cheese salad, then rounded off the presentation by heating up yummy store-bought rolls. Jackie wowed the troops with homemade apple pudding that combined fresh apples and cobbler batter with touches of cinnamon and lemon and was served warm with a scoop of ice cream.

I ate my meal on the run, shoveling forkfuls into my mouth in between responding to text requests for additional condiments, drink refills, and seconds on dessert. In fact, I had to pop up from my chair so much that I sent out a text blast to the gang informing them that there would be no repeat room service at breakfast, so they had two choices: either show up at the dining table as usual or stay in their rooms and not eat at all, which started a war of words on their Twitter feeds.

From Helen: *Even TV game shows offer THREE choices. Door number one, door number two, or door number three.*

From Dick Stolee: *We deserve another choice.*

From Lucille: *We should stage a hunger strike if our demands aren't met.*

From Margi: *I must have missed a Tweet. What have we demanded?*

From Grace: *Ask Lucille. She's the one who brought it up.*

From Lucille: *Don't blame me. Helen started it.*

From Helen: *Did not.*

From Lucille: *Did so.*

From Dick Teig: *Hey, is anyone carrying an extra eyebrow pencil that Helen can borrow in case hers gets stolen while we're sleeping?*

227

From Osmond: *Who would want to steal Helen's eyebrow pencil?*

From Dick Teig: *The thief, you lunkhead. Why do you think we're locked in our rooms?*

From Osmond: *Beats me. I was just going along with what the rest of you were doing.*

And so it went.

By the time Wally and I collected all the trays, cleared the plates, and stacked the dishes in the dishwasher, I was so worn out from the emotional stress of the day that I didn't even bother to take my shoes off when I flopped face-first onto my cot. I saved just enough energy to phone the police station one last time, only to be told that there was nothing new to report with either Bernice or Enyon.

Jackie found me in the same prone position when she pirouetted through the door sometime later. "Ta-daaa! Before I forget, Mrs. S sent out a text blast. Breakfast at 7:30 tomorrow morning. We want to get it out of the way early so we can have first dibs on the spa."

"That shouldn't be a problem," I mumbled. I angled my head on my pillow to stare at her through one eye. "You're not tired? If you're on something, would you please shoot me up with an extra-large dose?"

"It's called a natural high, Emily." She danced over to my cot, twirling and stomping with moves that landed somewhere between boogie and ballet. "Did my apple pudding rock tonight or what?"

"It rocked."

"I'm queen of the world!" She struck a pose with head high and arms thrown back, as if she were standing on the prow of the *Titanic*.

"Yes, you are."

"I've found my true calling, Emily. All because of you."

As tired as my brain was, it perked up enough to register the fact that this might be the first time in her life that Jackie Thum credited another person for aiding in her success. "Aww, that's sweet, Jack, but I can't really take credit."

"I know. It's actually because of my superlative DNA. But you look so pathetic, I thought I should say something to make you feel better."

"Thanks. It's not working." Okay, a little premature on the kudos. She was still a work-in-progress.

"I'm already thinking about tomorrow's dessert, Em. And since we're confined to quarters, I'll have all day to prepare. I can create a real gourmet masterpiece—my day four at the Stand and Deliver extravaganza. The pastry chef at the Godolphin Arms offered a few suggestions about recipes today. Wasn't that upstanding? The restaurant had an extensive dessert menu, so I said to myself, Jackie, I bet this pastry chef would be thrilled to meet a descendant of the family who once cooked for kings, so…"

Jackie's voice was the last thing I remember hearing before an insistent pounding on the door woke me from a sound sleep.

"Hold on!" I rolled out of bed fully dressed and squinted into the daylight. Jackie was gone. It couldn't be time to cook breakfast already, could it? I darted a look at my wristwatch. Seven o'clock? *Zowie!* I'd been conked out all night.

More pounding.

I threw the door open.

"I just found Heather in the hot tub," Caroline cried hysterically. "She's dead!"

SIXTEEN

"So I called 999 immediately, and when I hung up I ran out to the spa and found Heather facedown in the hot tub with her hair feathering outward like"—I made a wavy motion with my fingers to mimic the way her long strands of hair had undulated in the water—"like seaweed." I shivered involuntarily. "I'm sorry. I've never seen a drowning victim before."

"May you have the good fortune never to see one again, Mrs. Miceli."

I sat opposite Constable Tredinnick in Enyon's office, recounting my actions as best as I could remember.

A steady stream of police and emergency vehicles had pulled into the parking lot throughout the morning. Fire truck. Ambulance. Official-looking SUV carrying men with cases that resembled tool boxes. Coroner's van. The fire truck and ambulance had left within a half hour of their arrival, and three hours later the coroner's van had departed with Heather's body. But the SUV remained in the parking lot, which was a good indication that the scene was still being processed.

When Tredinnick arrived he had warned us that he'd be taking statements from all the guests, so he'd cautioned us to remain in the inn and not wander off. When he began the interview process he questioned Caroline first, but she remained so visibly shaken by her discovery that he offered to have the paramedics return to administer a sedative. She'd declined medical treatment in favor of returning to her room to take one of her "fear of flying" pills, but I doubted that any anti-anxiety drug would be powerful enough to erase the image of Heather's lifeless body from her memory.

Tredinnick tapped the point of his pen on his mini notepad. "What did you do after you verified that Ms. Holloway was dead?"

"I called Wally to tell him that Heather had drowned, that help was on the way, and that he should keep everyone away from the spa. And then I sat down on the bench along the wall and just kinda stared at the hot tub. I wasn't sure what else to do, but I…I didn't feel as if I should leave her alone." I blinked to clear away the moisture that was glazing my vision.

"How long did you remain in the spa?"

"Until the ambulance arrived. I met them in the parking lot and let them take over from there."

He made a notation on the page. "Did you notice anything out of place in the immediate vicinity of the spa while you were waiting for the ambulance? Anything overturned or broken? Any signs that would indicate a struggle?"

I shook my head. "I…everything looked pretty much in order to me…other than Heather's body."

"She apparently suffered a nasty gash on her forehead, Mrs. Miceli, so we're thinking her injury might have contributed to her death."

"When would she have sustained a head injury? When she was climbing out of the tub?"

"There was no trace of blood on the decking, no wet footprints anywhere to indicate she'd actually emerged from the tub. There *was* a puddle of water on the floor, but it was from the same leak I noticed two days ago. And she was expecting Ms. Goodfriend to join her, so I doubt she would have entertained leaving before her friend even arrived. You ladies are rather courteous about such things. And yet another curiosity: she'd set no towel on the decking for herself. Do you find it curious that a woman would have no towel available to dry herself off?"

"I'd probably have one, but if she was waiting for Caroline to arrive, maybe she figured Caroline could grab one off the pile for her."

"There was no pile, Mrs. Miceli. There were no towels in the building at all."

"None? But there was a whole stack on the bench by the dressing rooms when you interviewed us the other day."

"Have your guests been indulging themselves in the spa experience?"

I shook my head. "Our tour director used it once, but as far as I know, Heather was the first actual guest to try it out."

"The first, and the last. Per my official order, the spa will remain closed until further notice."

I searched his face, clinging onto one last glimmer of hope. "This could simply be a freak accident, right?"

Tredinnick drew his brows together over his nose. "Port Jacob recorded its very first murder the day your tour group arrived, Mrs. Miceli, and three days later we're recording what is possibly our second. My instincts tell me her death was no accident, but I'll be having to wait for the postmortem to confirm it."

So. No spa. No optional tours. No wandering. No nothing.

On the upside, at least there was no way this trip could get any worse.

"I want to interview your bloggers on an individual basis, but seeing as how the members of your Iowa contingent were together when the crime was perpetrated, I'd like to interview them as a group."

I heaved a hopeless sigh.

Wrong again.

· · · · · · · · · ·

"I've established a tentative timeline," Tredinnick announced from the front of the room, "but I'd appreciate your helping me fill in the blanks. Mrs. Miceli rang up 999 at 7:02 this morning according to the emergency services log. I'll be needing to know what happened before then."

Wally and I had knocked on every door, requesting the gang's immediate presence in the lounge, and, true to form, they'd arrived promptly, rolling their suitcases with them and snugging them by their legs like they did in the airport.

"Before we begin," said Tredinnick, looking confounded, "is there a reason why you went through the trouble of dragging your luggage out here with you?"

"Anti-theft protection," volunteered Margi. "A new policy we started implementing at breakfast. If we carry all our valuables

233

around with us, the thief won't have anything to steal if he breaks into our rooms." She rested a loving hand on the top of her spinner. "No way is he going to get his paws on my hand sanitizer."

"Emily forced our hand," accused Dick Teig. "She told us there'd be no more room service, so we had to find another way to protect our stuff."

I hung my head. *Oh, God.*

Tredinnick's tone turned sardonic. "You don't find your solution a trifle…inconvenient?"

"It's not bad," confessed George, "unless you've got a suitcase with a screwy wheel. Which reminds me, did anyone bring a travel-size can of WD-40 with them?"

"Returning to the matter at hand," said Tredinnick, clicking his pen with a slight show of attitude, "where are the cooks?"

Nana and Jackie raised their hands.

"What time did you start serving breakfast this morning?"

"When folks was at the table."

"What time was that?"

Nana shrugged. "I dunno. I was so busy I didn't pay no attention." She caught Jackie's eye. "You know what time we begun?"

"It was right after I suffered my injury." She stuck her forefinger in the air to display the foreshortened stump of her nail to Tredinnick. "I might have to lop them all off now to make them all the same length. And I didn't bring any polish with me for touchups because the bottles always leak in transit."

"What time was that?" Tredinnick repeated.

"I don't know! How would you expect me to glance at a clock when I'm dealing with a level-one trauma?"

He scribbled something on his pad before nodding toward the gathered crowd. "What time did you eat breakfast?"

"Awhile after we showed up," said Osmond.

"Specific time, please?"

Shrugs. Lip twisting. Googly eyes.

Tredinnick frowned. "Are you telling me that not one of you bothered to look at your watch or cell phone to check the time?"

"They were in our suitcases," explained Helen.

"For their own protection," reiterated Margi.

I gazed heavenward. *Seriously, Lord?*

"Does the inn provide nightstand clocks in your suites?" persisted Tredinnick.

"You bet," said Dick Stolee. "Digital models that light up the whole room."

"Did any of you check your room clocks to see what time you came out to breakfast this morning?"

"I did," enthused Alice. "It was precisely six o'clock. I was the first one to arrive."

"Thank you. Was breakfast scheduled to be served at six?"

"It was scheduled for seven thirty," Alice continued, "but I wanted to get there before all the good seats were taken. I didn't want to get stuck with the obstructed spot again."

"The good seats disappear fast," asserted George, "so you gotta get there early."

Tredinnick scratched his jaw. "What is your definition of a good seat?"

They sidled slow, bewildered glances at each other, as if they'd never bothered to think about that before.

He made a doodle on the page. "I'll note your response as a question mark. How soon after the lady claimed the good seat this morning did the rest of you arrive?"

"A couple of minutes," said Dick Teig.

"More like a couple of seconds," argued Dick Stolee. "The rest of us were neck-and-neck in the hallway and gaining fast, but our suitcases slowed us down a bit."

Tredinnick made another notation. "So all of you arrived within a few minutes of each other?"

"More like seconds," grumbled Dick Stolee.

"For the purposes of my timeline, I have you sitting down at approximately six o'clock. How soon after you sat down did you see Ms. Holloway exit through the lounge on her way to the spa?"

"Couple of minutes," said Dick Teig.

"It was not," argued Helen. "You were going on about websites that buy gold doubloons for a good fifteen minutes before we ever saw that girl."

George rubbed his forehead. "You sure it wasn't longer than that?"

"Seemed a lot longer," droned Grace.

Dick folded his arms across his chest. "Well, it only felt like a couple of minutes to me."

"That's because the only time you find conversation worthwhile is when you're doing the talking and everyone else is doing the listening," chided Helen.

"Show of hands," Osmond piped up. "How many people—no, wait. Emily says we can't vote anymore. Forget I said that."

Tredinnick's pen suddenly snapped in two, shooting out from between his fingers and flying off in different directions like tiny missiles. He looked as if he might be counting to ten as he watched the pieces land on the floor. "Let's try this again, shall we? Did any of you see Ms. Holloway leave the inn this morning?"

"Everyone at the table saw her," affirmed Tilly, "except Osmond. He forgot his eyeglasses back in the room."

"She waved to us," recalled Lucille.

"And she told us not to eat all the food before she got back," added George.

Tredinnick actually smiled. "Brilliant. So you saw Ms. Holloway enter the lounge sometime after six o'clock. Did any of you see Caroline Goodfriend trek through the lounge on her way to join Ms. Holloway in the spa?"

Eyes shifted. Brows lowered.

"I don't remember seeing her at all," admitted Dick Stolee.

"Me neither," said Dick Teig.

"I saw a flash of something in the corner of my eye," Lucille revealed, "but I figured it was the tail end of an optical migraine."

"Did she come through before or after the second helping of bacon arrived?" Grace asked Tredinnick. "Because when Jackie set that platter on the table, it was a free-for-all. The fellas wouldn't have noticed if a bomb had gone off in their shorts."

I didn't want to quibble about the guys' level of unawareness, but even they might have noticed that.

"I saw Caroline," Tilly affirmed with ironclad conviction. "I believe she left a good thirty to forty minutes after Heather, just as we were finishing up our meal. And a few minutes later, she ran back through the lounge as if the hounds of hell were nipping at her heels."

"To my room," I spoke up. "To tell me about Heather. And that was precisely seven o'clock because I checked my wristwatch."

"Surprising it was on your wrist and not in your suitcase," Tredinnick quipped.

"Yeah. I didn't get that memo."

He scanned his notes. "So most of you can verify that Ms. Holloway left the inn sometime after six o'clock. One of you saw Ms. Goodfriend leave thirty to forty minutes later. The majority of you were too preoccupied with bacon to notice anything. One of you thought Ms. Goodfriend's jaunt through the lounge was a visual anomaly. And you haven't a clue what time you actually ate breakfast because you finished eating at least a full half hour before you were scheduled to begin. Does that cover everything?"

Heads bobbing. Satisfied smiles.

"Mrs. Sippel," Tredinnick's gaze riveted on Nana, "none of your bloggers were at the table when you started serving much earlier than you'd indicated, were they?"

"Nope. And I can't say's I blame 'em. They probably got wind that all the good seats was gone."

"So how did you plan to deal with that?"

"I set vittles aside and stuck 'em in that oven what stays warm all the time. I wasn't gonna let them folks starve. Emily wouldn't abide that."

"Constable?" Caroline wandered into the lounge, looking wobbly-legged, dazed, and in need of an arm to lean on. I hopped out of my chair and hurried to her side.

"Are you okay?" I circled my hand around her forearm.

"It's the pill. I took more than the recommended dosage, so I've got spaghetti legs." She gestured toward Tredinnick. "Before I conk out, I wanted to ask you about Heather's belongings. Did you find her neck wallet in the spa?"

"If it's there, the evidence team will collect it."

"Okay, but...just to let you know. The fob-seal that she and Kathryn Crabbe have been haggling over? Heather stashed it inside her neck wallet before she left the room this morning, so you should probably have your people double-check to make sure it's still there. It's probably worth something."

"Thank you for that. Excuse me for a moment." While Tredinnick limped into the dining room to make a call, I ushered Caroline back to her room and helped her into bed, taking note of the straight-back chair she was probably using to secure her door.

"Be sure to lock up when I leave. Okay?" I didn't want to make things any easier for Spencer and August than they already were.

She nodded groggily, offering scant proof that she'd follow through.

"Are you going to be alert enough to wedge your chair under the doorknob, Caroline?"

She responded with a sublime facial twitch that might have developed into a smile if her eyes hadn't fluttered shut first.

"Caroline?"

Her pills had obviously kicked in big-time because she was dead to the world.

Reluctant to remove her key from her room, I nonetheless grabbed it off the nightstand and exited into the hall, locking the door behind me. Wally could slip into her room with his master key and replace it on her nightstand before she even realized it was gone.

I hurried back to the lounge to find that Constable Tredinnick's phone call had set off another alarm bell in his investigation.

"The fob-seal that was purportedly in Ms. Holloway's neck wallet is missing," he announced as I walked into the room. He lasered a look at me. "Where do I find Kathryn Crabbe?"

SEVENTEEN

TO KATHRYN'S UTTER INDIGNATION, he turned her room inside out and upside down looking for the fob-seal but came up empty-handed. "I told you I don't have it," she railed as he marched her into the office for her interview. "This is police brutality. The entire world is going to hear about this deliberate miscarriage of justice in my blog. And the full force of global opinion will come raining down on your he—"

He closed the door behind them.

So he hadn't found the fob-seal, but I wondered if he might have run into a pair of yellow ankle-tie flats.

Thirty minutes later Kathryn exited the office a supposedly free woman, storming back to her room minus handcuffs or leg irons. However, the fact that she slammed her door hard enough to rattle the china hinted that she was infuriated. I'd have to deal with the fallout from her latest snit later, but I'm not sure why she thought she deserved a pass in the investigation. She'd been at odds with Heather from the beginning—from wanting to have her stripped of her Janeite status, to claiming ownership of the fob-seal, to accusing her of trying to kill her at St. Michael's Mount. With the fob-seal missing, what made her think she'd be immune to scrutiny?

Was it possible she'd committed murder to take possession of the artifact? Could she have followed Heather out to the spa without anyone seeing her? But how could a woman of Kathryn's impressive physical stature skulk from place to place without being noticed? Lance's killer had escaped detection so far, but—

A red flag popped up in my brain as I made a detour into barely charted territory, noting a gruesome pattern.

Kathryn suffers humiliation at the hands of her husband, a chef, and lo and behold, another chef who humiliates her suddenly ends up dead.

Kathryn suffers the humiliation of being online shamed by Heather's Austen devotees, and lo and behold, Heather ends up dead.

Was that a coincidence? Did it seem that everyone who humiliated Kathryn ended up dead? Or was the pattern so blatant that even Tredinnick would disregard it as being too obvious to be believed?

Had he even remembered to ask her about her husband during her interview?

I ambushed him on his way to his car after he'd completed his amazingly brief interrogation of Mason, Spencer, and August. The SUV had finally departed after cordoning off the spa with blue and white police tape, so his squad car was the only vehicle parked in the lot. "You've decided against hauling any of my guests off to jail?"

"There's nothing that places them at the scene of the crime, Mrs. Miceli, at least not yet. But I took their fingerprints, so we'll see if that changes anything."

"Did you happen to question Kathryn about her husband?"

"I did remember to do that. There's no love lost there, but loathing one's ex-husband isn't a crime."

"It could be a motive for committing one."

He leaned wearily on his cane. "I suspect that any solicitor hoping to prove that Mrs. Crabbe killed Lance Tori because she transferred her repugnance of her husband to the chef would find the feat next to impossible." He sighed, bobbing his head toward the inn. "Your bloggers were unable to shine any light on what transpired this morning. Mr. Chatsworth claimed to have slept through the entire incident, and Mr. Blunt and Mr. Lugar vouched for each other's whereabouts once again, although Mr. Blunt did mention that he thought he heard a scream while Mr. Lugar was in the shower, but later attributed it to air in the pipes."

"He claims to have bionic hearing, so maybe he did hear something. Did he give you a time?"

"Of course not. For all the fuss that's made about you Yanks being workaholics, none of you ever bother to notice the time. What kind of workaholic doesn't look at his watch? And at your request I did inquire if they'd established friendships with each other back in the states, and they gawked at me as if I were a daft cow. All three swear that the first time they laid eyes on each other was when they boarded the tour coach at Heathrow."

"And if they're not telling the truth?"

"I've no way to gauge that right now, do I?"

I sighed. "So…what do we do now?"

He lifted his brows and smiled as if he were about to reveal something good for a change. "With all the chaos this morning, I neglected to tell you. Enyon's medical emergency turned out to be appendicitis, so he's in hospital and might be released as early as tomorrow. They don't keep surgical patients as long as they used to in the old days. It's more like catch and release. I'll drive him back here myself. So by tomorrow, with Enyon back in charge, you should be able to resume your normal schedule." His smile deepened. "And with Ms. Zwerg accompanying you once again."

"Bernice? Omigod! You found her?"

"Our CCTV in Exeter showed an image of a woman fitting her description exiting a passenger vehicle last night. The police haven't located her yet, but they're quite confident it's your Ms. Zwerg."

"She's safe? Omigod! Thank you!" I threw my arms around him in a moment of unrestrained glee, my heart beating out a tattoo that nearly took my breath away. "She's in Exeter? How far away is that?"

"It's near the M3—where it intersects with the A3052. On the way to Newton Poppleford? Branscombe? Seaton? Lyme Regis?"

"It's on the way to Lyme Regis?" The puzzle tumbled together in my head like the pieces in a kaleidoscope. "That little stinker. Wait 'til I get my hands on her. Do you know why she might be heading to Lyme Regis? Because that's our next destination. She's probably planning to greet us on the seawall to surprise us. How in the world did she get to Exeter?"

"It appears she may have hitched a ride. We don't recommend hitchhiking because of security concerns, but travelers still try it and drivers still pick them up."

"I can't believe she did that to us. The worry…the police involvement…the disrupted schedule. I should leave her suitcase behind to show her just how irritated I am that she'd pull a stunt like that. You should probably accompany us to Lyme Regis to restrain me, Constable, because when I see her, I might decide to kill her myself."

"I'm sure the police will have a long discussion with her before you arrive, Mrs. Miceli. They might even convince her to offer you an apology."

"I seriously doubt that. Bernice is into shoes, not apologies."

"I'll make a note to give you a bell with the results of Ms. Holloway's postmortem when I receive them. I imagine you'll want to share the information with her family."

Heather's family. Wally had called her parents earlier, but I wanted to contact them, too. I couldn't say for sure if she was part of the bloggers' thievery ring, but that didn't matter now. Two parents had lost a daughter, so I needed to offer them as much sympathy as I possibly could.

Despite the happy revelation that Bernice was alive and well and would be rejoining us in Lyme Regis to make our lives a living hell again, the day dragged on interminably, the only relief from full-scale boredom being the appetizers that Nana and Jackie served throughout the afternoon. Baked brie with crackers and jam. Bacon-wrapped water chestnuts with teriyaki sauce. Smoked salmon triangles. Olive cheese balls. Mini grilled cheese sandwiches with chutney. Pears with blue cheese and prosciutto.

Nana had announced her decision to skip a formal lunch rather simply. "We're not doin' no sit-down meal for lunch on account of we're gonna whip up a few things and just let you graze all afternoon."

The gang really got into the whole grazing thing, but in between snacking, they'd flop down in the lounge with their suitcases by their side and simply stare at each other.

"Who's bored?" asked Dick Teig.

Ten hands flew into the air.

"We wouldn't be bored if we had our cell phones," lamented Alice.

They cast forlorn looks at their suitcases.

George scratched his head. "What did we do for excitement before cell phones?"

"I never did anything exciting before cell phones," said Alice.

Helen pulled a face. "Hold on. I'm remembering something. Didn't we used to…talk?"

"You mean…to each other?" questioned Osmond.

"I believe our most exciting pursuit was watching the Dicks act like buffoons," recalled Tilly.

"Yeah," Dick Teig agreed. "Those were the glory days."

"Anyone know what time it is?" asked Dick Stolee.

They cast more forlorn looks at their suitcases.

"I could dig my Timex out of my grip," offered Lucille as she massaged her naked wrist. "It only cost twenty bucks, so if it gets stolen, it won't be that big a loss."

Spencer strode into the lounge looking both curious and annoyed. "The racket in this place is never-ending. Did you hear that noise just now?"

Shrugs. Vacant stares.

"What did it sound like?" asked Tilly.

"I don't know. But I've never heard anything like it before."

"Gurgling?" asked Helen. "Swashing? Bubbling?"

"Maybe a little."

Helen rolled her eyes. "Does anyone have a gas relief tablet for Dick?"

"It was more than that, though," urged Spencer. "It was more like...like what a dragon would sound like if he had bronchitis."

The room went quiet as questioning glances were exchanged.

"What kind of dragon are you talking about, son?" needled Dick Teig. "The kind you see in the movie theater or a real one?"

Helen thwacked her husband's shoulder. "Don't encourage him. If he's one of those loonies, he could go after you."

Margi threw Dick a terrified look. "What do you mean, real one?"

A sudden pounding on the front door sent me to my feet, but before I could cross the floor, three unexpected guests emerged from the foyer to stand in sullen silence before us. Two men were dressed in cat burglar black with physiques like Russian nesting dolls—squat and hefty, with shaved heads, dark eyes, four o'clock shadows, and mysterious lumps in their sports coats. The woman who stood between them was white-haired and pear-shaped, with an enormous fanny pack sitting at her waist below bosoms that were big as punching bags. She had a puffy face, eyes like black buttons, and a forbidding aura that hung over her like a thundercloud. She looked like the kind of person who might enjoy cracking walnuts open with her teeth.

And, for some reason, she looked vaguely familiar.

"I'm Maria Cacciatore," she announced without introduction. "Which one of you killed my boy?"

EIGHTEEN

OMIGOD. IT WAS LANCE'S FAMILY from the wall photo—the ones I'd facetiously nicknamed Frankie Two Fingers and Sammy the Snitch.

"What'd you say your name was?" asked Dick Teig.

"Maria Cacciatore," she repeated, the hard vowels of her New Jersey accent piercing the air like darts.

"Like the chicken?" Margi called out. "Chicken cacciatore was one of my mother's favorite Sunday dinner standbys, although I wasn't too fond of the tomatoes, onions, peppers, or potatoes that went with it."

"There are no potatoes in chicken cacciatore," challenged Helen.

"Are so," said Margi.

"Are not," said Helen.

Acting on a subtle nod from Maria, Two Fingers and the Snitch removed the lumps from their pockets and aimed the barrels in the general vicinity of the cushy chairs and loveseats.

"Are those real guns?" questioned Alice.

"They can't be," insisted Osmond. "Handguns are outlawed in England."

"Manufacturers certainly make authentic-looking toys these days," said Lucille.

Maria nodded to the Snitch.

BANG! He shot a hole in the floor an inch away from his feet.

"I bet that wasn't a real bullet," scoffed Grace.

Osmond sprang out of his chair. "Show of hands. How many— dang." He slumped back down. "I keep forgetting."

"Was that real ammo or a blank?" George called out.

Maria nodded to Two Fingers, who trained his gun on George.

"No!" I cried, sprinting in front of the furniture grouping with my arms spread wide like a human shield. "They're real bullets. We believe you. Just...just no more shooting, okay?"

Nana raced out of the kitchen to the lounge, her tone scolding. "Keep it down in here, would ya? Jackie's got a mousse in the oven." She glanced at me. She glanced at the newcomers. She gave a little suck on her uppers. "Are them guns real?"

"*YES!*" I yelled before the boys took aim again. "They're real, and they're loaded."

She fisted her hands on her hips. "Didn't no one tell you fellas that guns what look like them are illegal over here?"

"Rules don't apply to us," Maria allowed. "We make our own."

"Hey, Ma," Two Fingers enthused. "She's got a moose in the oven. I've never tasted moose. Can we stay 'til it's done?"

"Yoohoo!" Helen waved her hand over her head. "Excuse me. I think there's been a misunderstanding. Mousse is never baked in the oven. It's always chilled in the refrigerator."

"So the old broad lied?" said Two Fingers, sneering.

Maria smacked the back of his head with her open palm. "What'd I teach you? You never *ever* disrespect your elders. Now apologize to the lady."

Two Fingers lowered his gaze in repentance. "Sorry."

"This question is for Marion," Margi jumped in. "If moose is on the menu for tonight, can we make substitutions?"

"No substitutions," huffed Dick Stolee. "Remember? Marion said if we started complaining, she'd stop cooking, so you'd better well eat what she puts in front of you."

Nana let out a disdainful snort. "Just so's you know, the mousse what Jackie's got in the oven isn't no hunk of meat. It's a chocolate mousse cake that don't need no chillin'."

"Oh, thank God," choked Margi. "I was worried what the antlers might do to my dental work."

"Chocolate *cake*, Ma," Two Fingers pleaded. "That's even better. Can we stay now?"

My ears perked up at the sound of footsteps running down the hallway, but before I could think of a way to send up a warning flare, Wally appeared with August, Spencer, Mason, and Kathryn bunched up behind him. "Did I just hear a gunshot?" He ground to a sudden stop when he spied the guns. "Holy hell. Are those—"

"They're real!" I cried, cutting him off.

Up went his hands. "I surrender." Up went the bloggers' hands. "They surrender, too."

"It might be too late to ask now," said Margi, "but when the two boys flashed their weapons, were we supposed to put our hands up?"

"Will you put a lid on it?" growled Dick Teig.

Maria extended a hand toward Wally and the bloggers. "Please. I invite you to take a seat. Including you," she said to Nana. "There. Is everyone here?"

"What about the one cooking the moose?" asked the Snitch.

Maria snapped her fingers, which sent him galumphing toward the kitchen. "Hey, Ma," he said, pausing as he passed the sideboard. "There's a picture of us hanging up on the wall here. A real nice one. Youse oughta see it."

"Am I in it?" asked Two Fingers as he lumbered off for an apparent look-see.

Maria grabbed his arm. "One more step and I'll take that gun away and use it on you myself. Get back where you were."

"Geez, Ma," he whined, slinking back to her side. "Youse know what a picture buff I am."

Jackie marched into the lounge at gunpoint, with her hands up and a horrified expression on her face. "I'm well aware that you're holding me at gunpoint," she railed at the Snitch, "but when my timer goes off, will you at least let me check my cake for doneness? It's my first ever and I'll die if it's overcooked."

Given the situation, I wondered if another idiom might have been more appropriate.

Jackie and I got hustled into a loveseat together while Maria assumed center stage. "For the newcomers in the group, I'm Maria Cacciatore, and I want to know which one of you killed my boy Anthony."

"Who's Anthony?" asked Helen.

"Anthony Cacciatore."

"Like the chicken?" questioned Dick Stolee.

I hung my head and slapped my hands over my face.

251

"He changed his name," wisecracked the Snitch. "He was gonna be a big-shot chef, so he wanted a name with more star power."

Two Fingers screwed his mouth into a sour contortion. "Somethin' that would look good trending on the frickin' Twittersphere."

"He ripped his mother's heart out of her chest," Maria wailed, clutching her hands over her bosom as if to hide the wound. "Trashing the name his own father gave him the day he was baptized. Sacrilege!" She paused in counterpoint. "Of course, that no-good SOB father of his didn't care that I already *had* a name for the baby. Why should he ask *me*? Me—who blew up like an air mattress the minute his sperm landed. Me—who had to wear flipflops all winter because I couldn't squeeze my fat sausage feet and ankles into my shoes. But according to him, *he* was the one who suffered for nine long months because *he* had to share *his* bed with the Goodyear Blimp."

"Right on, sister! Men are such pigs," Jackie blurted, amending her outburst when Two Fingers and the Snitch redirected the barrels of their guns at her. "I hope you know I mean that in a general sense. Not specifically…or literally."

Two Fingers wrinkled his brow as he riveted his gaze on her. "What?"

Maria cuffed the side of his head. "Quiet. I'm talking. So when we get to the church for the christening, Mr. I've Had To Suffer For So Many Months says, 'We're namin' the kid Anthony, after me.' No negotiation. No back and forth. Whatever Anthony said was law. The no-good SOB." Her voice oozed bitterness.

"What name had you picked out for him?" I asked in a feeble attempt at hostage cordiality.

Her face brightened. "I was going to call him Caesar."

"Like the salad?" asked Dick Stolee.

"Like the conqueror," she fired back. "I imagined him taking his place as the head of *all* the families one day. Just like the Roman emperor. Caesar Cacciatore." She smiled beatifically. "Besides, I liked the alliteration."

All the families? Holy crap. I was getting a very bad feeling about this—even worse than I'd had before.

"But my firstborn, my Anthony, does he want to become head of the families? No. He wants to cook. Wants to be like his idol, Julia Child. So he needs to change his name. He likes Lance, he tells me. Lance Tori. It's more streamlined, he says. More efficient. Three syllables instead of seven, just like Julia Child. He rips my heart out of my chest again."

"*And* starts batting for the other team," sniggered the Snitch.

Maria whacked his head. "You don't ever laugh at your brother."

"Excuse me?" Margi waved her hand. "Have you read any of the recent medical reports on concussions?"

"My Anthony was a good son. Smart. Focused. Articulate, if you could get past the lisp. I didn't do right by him when he told me he switched teams. I reacted like that no-good SOB father of his would have acted instead of behaving like the mother who loved him. I never should have done that." Her eyes screamed regret. "I've been paying for it ever since." She wagged a cautionary finger at the gang. "A mother should never turn her back on a son because, in the end, she's the one who suffers the most. And now, because of someone in this room, I can't even tell him I'm sorry. I have to spend the rest of my life living in guilt. So…which one of you killed him?"

I inched my hand into the air.

"You?" Maria bellowed, snapping her fingers at the boys to take action.

"No! I only want to ask a question."

Snitch scuffed his foot on the floor in disappointment. "Mother#!&*#!" he spat.

Maria whacked him harder. "You're not too old to have your mouth washed out with soap, mister."

"I'd really make a point of reading those concussion reports if I were you," advised Margi.

I took a chance and stood up, hoping to ease the chaos. "Enyon mentioned that since Lance had been disowned by his family, he didn't feel obligated to notify you of his death. Did he change his mind and call you?"

"I read it in the blogs," said Two Fingers. "It was in all my favorites: Knife and Fork, Will Travel; the Ten-Dollar-a-Day Traveler; Standard Suite, Please. And he didn't just die, he got whacked. Hey." He jerked to attention as if he'd just been electrocuted by the light bulb that went on over his head. "I just thoughta somethin'. They're here in this room—all the famous bloggers. Where are youse hiding?"

August, Spencer, and Mason elevated their hands with the enthusiasm of volunteers being asked to serve as targets for live-round firing squad practice.

"Look, Ma. It's my bloggers!" Two Fingers thrust his hand inside his jacket, pulling out not a bigger gun, but what looked like a wrinkled merchandise receipt. "Can I have youse autographs? I love youse guys."

"I have a pen," offered Helen, reaching into her pocket. "Anyone need it?" She flashed the implement into the air.

"That's not a pen," rasped Dick. "It's your eyebrow pencil."

"No autographs," Maria snapped at Fingers. "Not until the guilty party fesses up."

Sidelong glances. Quiet gulps.

Wally joined the discourse. "The constable in charge of the investigation hasn't found any evidence linking anyone in this room to Lance's death, Mrs. Cacciatore. No motive. No fingerprints. No opportunity. Nothing."

Had I told Wally about Kathryn's no-good SOB ex-husband, the chef? Maybe not.

"So if you're planning to hold us at gunpoint until someone confesses, you could be in for a very long wait."

Maria lifted her brows nonchalantly. "Do we look like we're in a hurry?"

"How'd you get those guns into the country anyway?" razzed Dick Teig.

"We didn't have to get them into the country," said Maria. "They were already here. You think we don't have associates in the UK? We have a whole network in place that's part of our global initiative."

"Did your associates tell you about the reputation Lance had earned for himself in the village?" asked Tilly in her professor's voice. "He feuded with everyone: the merchants, the fishermen, complete strangers. He was possessed of a violent temper that apparently erupted like Old Faithful on a daily basis."

"He got that from his father," defended Maria. "The no-good SOB."

"It's quite obvious he didn't inherit the trait from you," flattered Tilly. "So might I suggest you may be barking up the wrong tree by accusing someone in this room of your son's murder? Because there's an entire village a few miles away from here whose residents shed no tears when he passed away."

"How do you know that?" challenged Maria.

Tilly sighed. "Google search. Shall I send you a link?"

"Would anyone mind terribly if I dashed into the kitchen to see how my cake is doing?" asked Jackie.

"No one leaves the room," warned Maria.

"Ever?" croaked Margi.

"What if we gotta use the potty?" asked Nana. "We're old. We got plumbin' issues."

"Quiet!" Maria rubbed her temples as if she were suffering from sensory overload with a migraine chaser.

"What if they got cell phones, Ma?" fretted Snitch. "They could call the police while they're in the can."

Maria cast a suspicious look at us. "Yes. They. Could." She punched Two Fingers in the arm. "You leaving everything to your brother now? How come you didn't think of that?"

"Much better," commended Margi, bursting into applause.

"Lemme see your cell phones," Maria demanded. "And don't pull any funny business and try to hide 'em. My boys don't take kindly to cheats."

I raised my phone over my head with reluctance, unsure of how we'd message anyone for help now. With a nod from their mother, Fingers and Snitch collected my phone as well as Jackie's, Wally's, and the bloggers' and piled them on the dining table.

"What about the rest of you?" Maria eyed the gang. "You expect me to believe that not one of you has a cell phone?"

"They're in our bags," Helen offered helpfully. "Technically, we have them, but we're not using them, so that's pretty much the same as *not* having them, isn't it?"

The boys methodically unzipped every suitcase and removed every phone, adding them to the stack on the dining table. "Hey, Ma, shouldn't we stow these things someplace to keep 'em safe?" asked Snitch.

"That's why we had them in our luggage," deadpanned Helen.

"Empty out one of their suitcases and dump 'em all inside," instructed Maria. "Then lock it up tight." She regarded the suitcases scattered about the room. "Do you people schlep those things around with you everywhere you go? Even on day trips?"

"We do now," said Dick Teig.

Maria shook her head. "And here I was complaining about a fanny pack. Geesh."

The boys emptied the contents of Osmond's small suitcase onto a chair and refilled it with our phones. "Where's the key to lock it?" Fingers asked him.

"Back home on my bureau dresser," said Osmond. "In my coin dish."

"This one's lyin', Ma." Finger's mouth began to twitch with barely suppressed excitement. "Can I break his little finger?"

"No!" I sprang from my seat, but Jackie yanked me back down. "He's not lying. None of us use keys anymore. The TSA wants luggage accessible for random inspection, so we simply don't lock them. It saves a lot of hassle."

Nana threw a long look at the boys. "You young fellas don't get out much, do you?"

"Take your belts off," barked Maria, gesturing to the entire room. She nodded to the boys. "Wrap the belts around the suitcase. Every single one of them. That'll work better than locking it."

She heaved a sigh as Fingers and Snitch whipped their belts out of their pant loops. "Not *your* belts, you morons. *Their* belts."

I regretted that Bernice wasn't here. She and Maria probably would have gotten along famously.

After Osmond's suitcase had been wrapped tighter than a ball of rubber bands and placed on the dining table like a Christmas ham, Jackie stood up. "May I please be excused to check my cake *now*? If not, I hope you'll be willing to accept blame when my masterpiece hardens into an inedible charcoal briquette."

Maria looked her up and down. "There's something about you I can't quite put my finger on." She canted her head. "You're very tall, aren't you?" Then, gesturing to Fingers: "Go with her."

At the sound of car engines, Snitch darted to the window overlooking the parking lot. "It's cars, Ma. Like a whole convoy of 'em. One, two, three, four cars and a big passenger van. Five vehicles."

He'd go far with math skills like that.

"Whadda youse want me to do?"

"See what they want, then get rid of them."

"You mean, waste 'em?"

"I *mean* see why they're here, then make up an excuse to turn them away. Do you have an excuse ready?" she questioned as he turned away from the window.

"Yeah. I'm gonna tell 'em they can't come in because we're holding a bunch of old people hostage until one of 'em fesses up to killin' my brother and we put a bullet in his brain."

Maria inhaled a deep breath. "That's the *truth*," she explained patiently. "You don't want to tell them the *truth*. You want to *make up* a reason why they can't come in. Understand?"

"Ohhh. I get it now."

"I'm not sure you do," she said, sighing.

"Try this, junior," suggested Dick Stolee. "Tell them all the guests have come down with measles, so the place is in quarantine."

"That won't work," objected Margi. "Most people have been vaccinated against measles. Tell them we've had an isolated outbreak of super deadly tuberculosis."

"Or an infestation of rats," said Dick Teig. "Everyone hates rats."

I rolled my eyes in disbelief. Yup. Feeding excuses to the Snitch was really helpful.

"What about mold?" asked George. "The black kind is toxic and can wreak havoc on your lungs."

"Or fleas," Lucille added. "Once they're in your carpet, your life can become an itching, scratching hell."

"Okay, okay." Snitch headed for the door.

"Hide your gun!" ordered Maria.

"There it goes again." Spencer cocked his head. "Don't tell me you can't hear it. You *have* to be able to hear it. God Almighty, it's really loud."

Maria lowered her brows, regarding him with suspicion. "What's he hearing?"

"Dragons," said Nana.

Snitch returned from his assignment without firing a single bullet. As car engines revved and faded from earshot, Snitch grinned at his mother. "How'd I do, Ma? Good, huh?"

259

"What did you tell them?"

"I told 'em the walls were crawling with mold so the place was in quarantine until we could all be vaccinated."

He'd only been around the gang for a half hour and already he was suffering the effects.

"Why were they here? What did they want?"

"They were here because of the food they've been reading about on the blogs. They wanted dinner reservations, Ma. But here's the best part: since I turned 'em away, there'll be more food for us. When do we eat, anyway? I'm starvin'."

Due to the rave reviews of her culinary skills, Nana was allowed to return to her cooking. The rest of us settled into an unspoken truce as seconds turned into minutes and minutes turned into quarter hours. Maria dragged a chair into the center of the floor where she could watch us with an eagle eye while resting her feet. Fingers remained in the kitchen, keeping an eye on Jackie and Nana as they provided more appetizers for the group and proceeded with dinner prep. Snitch's role became twofold: turning away more carloads of people who'd read the blogs and hoped to eat at the inn, and accompanying guests to the loo. And even though the ladies needed to use the facilities on a regular basis, I noticed that the guys' usage seemed to drop to an historic low. Probably because without their belts, their pants fell to their ankles every time they stood up.

With no cell phones to divert their attention, the gang was forced to invent other ways to entertain themselves. Dick Stolee and Grace engaged the masses by conducting a sing-along that included Hollywood musicals, folk songs, Christmas carols, and classic songs like "Row, Row, Row Your Boat" that are sung in three-group rounds. Unfortunately, the activity came to an abrupt end when Osmond's screechy flat notes caused so many people to cover their ears, he ended up singing all three staggered rounds of "Three Blind Mice" by himself.

Tilly started the memory game of "I Put Something in My Suitcase Starting with an A," but that game came to a grinding halt when the gang refused to put anything in their suitcases other than their cell phones.

Helen asked if anyone recalled the first trip they'd taken as a group to Switzerland, which sparked a nostalgic walk down memory lane. Dick Stolee remembered my clunking him on the bridge of his nose with room deodorizer when he ran into the corridor of the Grand Palais Hotel with his CPAP paraphernalia still attached to his face. "I've still got a bump," he said, removing his wire rims to flaunt it like a war wound. George recalled my diving into Lake Lucerne fully clothed in the fog to save him when he fell off the sightseeing boat. I remembered breaking my tooth on vegetable lasagna on top of Mount Pilatus and ending up with a funny lisp. Dick Teig recalled the nudies he'd seen on the spa beach in Titisee-Neustadt in Germany. Lucille recalled the angry words she'd exchanged with her husband, Dick number three, before he died near that very spa.

"I miss old Dick," admitted Dick Teig in a moment devoid of self-absorption.

"I miss him, too," sniffed Dick Stolee, struggling not to choke up.

"I don't miss his practical jokes," said Grace.

"Or his cockiness," said Helen.

"Or his stinky cigar," added Lucille. "Dead all these years and I still can't get the smell out of the drapes."

A smile split Osmond's face. "How come we don't talk about the good times we've had together anymore?"

They cast looks back and forth amongst themselves, completely stumped.

"I'll tell you why you don't talk anymore," I piped up. "Because you don't look up from your cell phones long enough *to* talk!"

"Emily?" Caroline crept into the lounge, still looking half-asleep. "Have I missed dinner?"

"Who's this?" demanded Maria in an ominous tone. "Where'd she come from? Have you been holding out on me?" She motioned to Snitch. "Search the rooms. See if they're hiding anyone else. And get your brother and those women in here on the double."

But Snitch didn't move. He stood anchored in place, staring at Caroline. "I know who she is, Ma. She's the dame on the video."

"What video?"

"The one where she's taking all our money. I swear it. It's her."

"It can't be her." Maria speared Caroline with a piercing look. "She's dead."

NINETEEN

"*VINNIE!*" THE SNITCH ANGLED HIS HEAD toward the dining room. "Get in here! And bring the broads with you." He motioned Caroline farther into the lounge with the barrel of his gun. "So I got a question. If youse are dead, what are youse doin' here?"

Vinnie bounded into the dining room with his gun at the ready, herding Nana and Jackie in front of him. "What?" he shouted at his brother. "Youse can't step into the kitchen and ask me something in a nice tone of voice?"

"Get in here!" barked the Snitch. "Look whose come to visit."

"We *can't* be out here greeting guests," Jackie argued as she and Nana marched into the lounge at the point of Vinnie's gun. "My cake needs me."

"Screw your cake," snapped the Snitch.

"And I got pots on the stove," protested Nana.

"Tough!" He tossed his head in Caroline's direction. "Take a look at what the cat dragged in, Vin. She look familiar?"

After plopping Nana and Jackie into available seats, Vinnie gave Caroline a leisurely look up, down, then up again. "Never seen her before. Who is she?"

"*How* can youse not recognize her?" squealed the Snitch. "The dame from the surveillance video? The one who took all the money? The one we had the come-to-Jesus talk with?"

"That dame?" Vinnie scrutinized her more carefully. "Can't be her. She's dead."

"She's *not* dead. She's standing right in front of us."

Vinnie shook his head. "It's not her. The other dame had black hair and glasses and was real...blubbery."

"That is *sooo* politically incorrect," chided Jackie. "To avoid hurting a person's feelings, you should use terms like plus-sized or horizontally challenged or—"

"Zip it!" Snitch warned her before gritting his teeth at his brother. "Youse ever heard of hair dye, contact lenses, and a diet plan?"

"I like Weight Watchers myself," Lucille volunteered. "It's so user friendly. If you haven't reached your goal for the weekly weigh-in session, no one wags a finger at you or makes nasty comments on your Facebook page about your epic fail."

"I been thinkin' about tryin' that 360 diet myself," said Nana. "I seen on TV where it's the one all them cavemen used."

"The Paleolithic diet," Tilly clarified.

"Are you sure that'd be the best plan for you, Marion?" asked Dick Teig. "It didn't work out real well for the cavemen. I mean, where are they now?"

"I've seen some of them on those insurance commercials on TV," said Margi, "so it worked out pretty well for the ones who had acting ability."

The Snitch panned his gun toward the gang. "The next one of youse who says somethin'...*anythin'*...is gonna get a bullet between the eyes. Youse understand?"

Heads nodded. Eyes rounded. Lips got sucked into mouths.

"Who are youse?" he bellowed at Caroline. "What's your name?"

Paralyzed into statue stillness, Caroline stared at Maria and her sons wide-eyed. "C-Caroline Goodfriend."

"*Bzzzzz.* Wrong answer. I want the name youse was usin' when youse walked outta our joint with three hundred Gs."

I shot up steeple-straight in my chair. *Oh. My. God.* This wasn't right. Caroline couldn't possibly be a thief. Could she?

"My n-name has always been Caroline G-Goodfriend."

"I don't think so," snarled Snitch. He snapped his fingers at his brother. "What was her name? Youse remember?"

"Evelyn Friday," said Maria, dropping her voice to a sinister whisper. "Her name was Evelyn Friday."

"That's not my name," swore Caroline.

"You got the video on you?" Maria asked Snitch.

"I got it, Ma," Vinnie preempted, whipping his cell phone out of his pocket before his brother could reach his. "Hang on. It's in the Cloud."

"What? You gotta check the weather report before you can—"

"Here you go, Ma." He slapped the phone into her palm. "Tap the triangle."

Maria studied the screen for a full minute before reaching into her fanny pack for her reading glasses. Tapping the screen again, she studied the image even more intently before glancing from Caroline to the screen to Caroline again. "You." She jabbed her finger at Caroline. "Over here." She indicated a spot directly in front of her.

Caroline inched forward.

"You have any idea what video I'm playing back?" asked Maria.

Caroline shook her head.

"It's showing me a blubb—a plus-size woman with black hair and glasses sitting at a blackjack table in my casino, and she's got a whole mountain of chips stacked in front of her. Three hundred thousand dollars' worth. And you know what she does with them?"

Caroline was so unnerved, her knees were knocking. "She goes all in on a sure bet and loses them?"

"No. She cashes them in and waltzes out the door...*with my money*. That's not supposed to happen, understand? *I'm* supposed to be the one who comes out ahead. Not the nickel and dimers playing the slots or the whales around the roulette table or the hopefuls playing blackjack. *Me*. It's my organization, so I get to keep the profits. Except when someone cheats me."

"I...I don't know what you're t-talking about," stammered Caroline.

"Let me see if I can help," said Maria in a chirpy tone. "Do you wear glasses?"

"Contact lenses."

"Uh-huh. Natural blond? And don't think about lying. I know where to look to find out the truth."

Caroline shook her head. "It's d-dyed. And frosted."

"Uh-huh. Lost any weight recently?"

She hesitated. "How recently? I'm up and down a lot. You know how it g-goes. Gain weight over the holidays and lose it over the s-summer. I'm the thinnest I've ever b-been right now."

Maria made a *tsking* sound. "Evelyn, Evelyn. And you were doing so well." She returned her attention to Vinnie's phone. "The woman in this video is wearing a very attractive tunic with a scoop neck. And the nice thing about the neckline is, it's low enough to expose a funny mark on the woman's collarbone. I don't know what the mark is, but if Vinnie zooms in on it for me, I bet I'll be able to tell."

She handed the phone to Vinnie, who expanded the image. "Hey, it looks like a funny-colored wart growing on her skin, Ma."

"Lemme see," insisted Snitch, crooking his mouth in mocking disgust. "It's not a wart, doofus. It's one of those gross skin tag things like youse see growing on old people. This one looks like a raisin—more specifically, a golden raisin, like Ma puts in her Christmas fruitcakes."

Maria nodded her satisfaction. "So, Evelyn, do you have a golden raisin growing on your collarbone? No need to trouble yourself. Elmo won't mind looking."

Dick Stolee exploded with laughter. "Elmo? You mean, like the Tickle Me Muppet character?"

BANG! Vinnie blasted a hole in Dick's suitcase.

I leaped a foot off my seat. Holy crap! They weren't bluffing!

Elmo pulled the jewel neckline of Caroline's top askew and grinned. "Look, Ma. A golden raisin. Youse want I should whack her now?"

"Have you heard her confess to killing your brother?" Maria asked calmly.

"Not yet."

"THEN YOU CAN'T KILL HER."

"I can explain," whimpered Caroline.

Maria drilled her with a hostile look. "Why aren't you dead? We read your name in the newspaper. You died in that commuter train wreck going into the city."

Caroline bobbed her head convulsively. "I missed my train that morning because I was rattled. And maybe you can understand why since your two offspring paid me a late-night visit the evening before and gave me twenty-four hours to hand over my blackjack money."

"Or *boom*," boasted Vinnie, making a bull's-eye of her head.

"It wasn't your money anymore," defended Caroline. "It was mine. I won it fair and square."

"Did not," said Elmo.

"Did so," countered Caroline. "I used finesse and memory and excellent math skills."

"To count the cards and cheat me out of my money," accused Maria. "You're a card counter! You broke the law."

"I did not! Card counting is not illegal in New Jersey or anywhere else in the United States. It's not illegal to use your brain."

"Well, it's illegal in my casino, and you broke *my* law."

"Like you didn't violate *my* rights when you sent Beavis and Butthead to my apartment to threaten me?"

"I'M KILLIN' HER NOW, MA," announced Elmo, trigger finger poised.

"You'll kill her when I *tell* you to kill her. So tell me this, Evelyn. If you didn't die in the wreck, why did the newspaper say you were one of the casualties?"

"Because in the aftermath, there were a number of passengers whose bodies were never identified. They were crushed beneath tons of twisted steel, and when the fire started, their remains were charred beyond recognition. I had no way of knowing the devastation would be so extreme, but it worked in my favor in the end. After the derailment the whole railway system shut down, so I was stranded at the station with no rail access to get me to the office. And that started me thinking about your goons and my newly acquired nest egg."

"Are youse gonna let her talk about us like that, Ma?" huffed Vinnie.

"Quiet!"

"I thought about contacting the police, but what were they supposed to do? Slap a restraining order on you people? I could be dead before the ink dried. Give me my own security detail? Like *that* was going to happen." Caroline sucked in a breath, on the verge of hyperventilating. "As awful as the accident was, I felt like I'd just been handed a Get Out of Jail Free card. Could I disappear in all the confusion? Could I escape with my nest egg that very minute, before your goons tracked me down again? My car was parked in the commuter lot. If I left it there, the authorities might think I'd been on the train that derailed. I always took the early train. My officemates knew that. If I didn't show up at work, they'd think I'd been involved in the wreck. That'd give me time to get out of Dodge."

"Shame on you," scolded Maria. "You'd do that to your mother? Let her think you'd been in a train wreck and not let her know you were still alive?"

Tsking from the assembled guests.

"Look, my mom and dad died a few years ago. Cancer. Both of them. So there was no one to wring their hands over my death. I left my car where it was parked, hoofed it home on side streets, crammed my money into a backpack, and boarded the next regional bus leaving town. I didn't even stop long enough to pack a toothbrush."

More *tsking* from the crowd, who, at their age, understood the ramifications of poor dental hygiene.

"And ended up where?" asked Maria.

"A little Podunk town in South Carolina, and that's where I've been ever since."

"Back up," ordered Maria. "You just left out a whole slew of chapters."

"Yeah," agreed Vinnie. "Youse can't just become someone else unless youse go into that witness protection program."

"Yes, you can. Especially if you know the ropes. That was my job in New York. I worked for an organization called the Woman's Domestic Care Network, so I knew the ropes. I checked into a woman's shelter once I got into town, told them I feared for my life—which was the absolute truth, by the way—and they helped with everything else. They found me a job as a live-in companion to an elderly woman, and they gave me all the information I needed to establish a new identity. And once I settled in, I learned that New Jersey was just too far away for anyone in rural South Carolina to notice what happened there, including train derailments where bodies had been too mangled to be identified. So I became Caroline Goodfriend, home companion and budding genealogist, which is something I'd always wanted to pursue. And here I am."

Maria nodded. "Here you are in Cornwall at my boy's inn. How'd you know he was my Anthony?"

"The photo, Ma!" Vinnie ran into the dining room and ripped the photo off the wall, delivering it to his mother. "It was hangin' right there in the open. She must of recognized me and Elmo." He smiled at the image. "See? Youse can tell in this picture that I'm way taller than the rest of the family."

Maria blessed herself with a quick sign of the cross. "I remember the day this was taken. Your Uncle Carmine had just poured concrete for the new stadium and told us that Fat Joey Bananas wouldn't be skimming any more money from our accounts. Such a happy day." She glared at Caroline, steely-eyed. "And you take my happy day and use it against me. You use it to kill my son!"

Oh my God. *Caroline* killed Lance?

"I—" Caroline stirred the air with her hands in what looked like a futile attempt to provide an explanation. "This wasn't an easy choice, okay?" she said, voice trembling as she gave in to the inevitable. "His family—*you guys*—wanted to kill me. What if he recognized me?"

"Ma never showed him the video," taunted Vinnie.

"Well, I didn't know that, did I? What if he told you I was here? Are you going to tell me you wouldn't have told him to take me out?"

Elmo frowned. "Youse mean like a date?"

"No! I mean like knocking me off."

"Oh, okay, because in case youse missed it the first time, Anthony batted for the other team."

"I'm not a crazed killer," defended Caroline, "but I'm not a victim either. What was I supposed to do? Wait around until he ambushed me with a carving knife in my back? I was petrified. Can you understand that?"

"How did you kill my son?" Maria asked in a near sob.

"I pushed him down the basement stairs."

271

"No one heard you? No one saw you?"

"I…everyone was distracted. A pipe burst in one of the rooms, so most of the guests were gathered down there trying to record the chaos. My roommate and I went back to our room to work on our blogs, but she said my keyboard was too noisy so she decided to work in the bathroom with the fan on—kinda like creating her own white noise. So while she was in there, I sneaked out the back door and ran around the side of the inn to the kitchen. Lance *lived* in the kitchen, except when he made time to come out and terrorize the guests, so I figured he'd be in there."

"His father's temperament, the no-good SOB," sniped Maria.

"I didn't have a plan. I had no idea what I was going to say or do. I was operating on fear and adrenaline, but when I saw him on the stairs, I didn't stop to think. I just…pushed."

I thought about my frantic sprint through the kitchen and frowned with the memory. Something didn't square. I shot my hand into the air.

Maria fired an irritated look at me. "Another question?"

"Just a teensie one."

"Make it fast."

"Caroline, your shoes had to have been wet. The lawn was soaked from all the rain that day. Why didn't I see your footprints on the kitchen floor? Because if they were there, I would have to've been blind to miss them."

"I wasn't brought up in a barn," she defended. "I wiped my feet on the mudroom floor mat."

"A girl who's built like a beanpole now has the strength to push my big strapping boy down a flight of stairs?" Maria flung her arm toward Caroline's torso. "What? With arms like sticks?"

"I used my foot."

Elmo redirected the barrel of his gun. "Youse want me to shoot her foot off, Ma?"

"Look at her shoe," jeered Vinnie. "What size is it—5? 6? How'd a foot that small take out someone the size of Anthony?"

"Soccer," said Caroline. "Compliments of the Federal Government and Title IX."

Seemingly satisfied, Maria leaned back in her chair and nodded to Elmo. "All right. You can kill her now."

Spencer leaped out of his chair with his hands up. "Please don't shoot but—"

BANG! Vinnie squeezed off a shot that lodged somewhere in Spencer's vicinity.

Screams. Shouts. Shrieks.

"Jesus, Mary, and Joseph," wailed Nana as she leaned forward to eye a gaping hole in the upholstery. "He killed my armrest."

"Something's happening!" yelled Spencer, ducking behind a chair. "Listen! It's happening right now!"

"Is he talking about the gunshot?" asked Margi. "Because I'm pretty sure we all heard that."

And that's when we began to hear faint rumbling sounds, like an approaching thunderstorm. Only the sounds weren't coming from above.

They were coming from below.

"Omigod!" cried Margi. "It's the dragon!"

The rumbling grew louder, as if the earth had suffered a deadly wound and was rupturing like a breached levee. The floor vibrated. Dishware rattled. A vase wobbled off the mantel and crashed to the floor.

"We're all going to die!" howled Helen.

Vinnie charged toward the bank of windows in the dining room. "I can't see nothin'! The glass is all crudded up on the outside."

"Then open a damned window!" ordered Maria.

He looked left and right, shrugging helplessly before driving the butt of his gun through a pane of glass. Peeking through the hole, he let out a terrified yelp. "It's crumblin', Ma! The whole cliff's giving way!"

I launched myself out of my seat. "*RUN!*"

They popped up en masse and started to stampede toward the front door, dragging their spinners with them.

"Leave your suitcases," I cried. "Save yourselves!"

"What am I supposed to do, Ma?" Elmo waved his gun toward the stampeding crowd. "They're getting away. I don't got enough bullets to shoot 'em all!"

Dick Teig rammed his spinner full force into Elmo's legs, sending him flat on his rump.

"You won't need that anymore, young man," said Tilly, raising her walking stick and arcing it downward in a mighty wallop across Elmo's wrist. The gun flew from his hand, skidding along the floor where Wally snatched it up.

Gee. That worked out well. "Change of plan!" I yelled in a major flipflop. "Take your suitcases and run like hell!"

Osmond raced toward the exit, face-planting on the floor when his pants dropped to his shoes. Alice paused to help him up, falling backward over George, who was struggling on his back like an upended turtle, entangled in his own pant legs.

Oh, God. I peeled them off the floor and shooed them toward the door.

Jackie grabbed my shoulders in an all-out panic. "What about my cake?"

"Forget your cake!"

"But the timer's about to—"

The floor began vibrating with earthquake ferocity.

"I'll leave it."

"Grab Maria!"

"With pleasure."

As the gang practically climbed over each others' backs in their rush toward the front door, Jackie hoisted Maria out of her chair. "Hi there. My name's Jackie. I'm a six-foot transsexual who believes that people who abuse their second amendment rights should have a brain-eating amoeba shoved up their nostrils. So I'm warning you, don't give me any lip."

I glanced toward the dining room. No Vinnie. Where was Vinnie?

Heart thundering, pulse racing, I rushed toward the foyer, wheeling around at the last minute to retrieve Osmond's suitcase with its cache of cell phones from the dining table. I ran out the front door and into the parking lot to the deafening roar of two hundred feet of cliff collapsing into the sea, devouring the bluff to within spitting distance of the inn. We stood with mouths hanging open as a plume of debris shot into the air, creating a smothering brown cloud that muddied the sun and the sky—but not the sight of Vinnie pressing his gun to Helen's head.

Five feet away, Wally had his weapon pressed against Elmo's earlobe. "Let Mrs. Teig go," he ordered Vinnie.

"Let Elmo go first."

"*You* go first."

"No, *you* go first."

"Be strong, Helen," encouraged her husband. "Someone'll save you." He looked around desperately. "Anyone seen Marion?"

"Mexican stand-off!" whooped Dick Stolee.

Better a Mexican stand-off than circular firing squad.

"It's over, Vinnie," warned Wally. "Drop your weapon."

"Youse drop yours."

"You first."

"No, *youse* first."

One thing was becoming crystal clear about this stand-off: they could both use a good dialogue coach.

"I swear I'll waste her," threatened Vinnie.

"Then I'll waste *him*," lied Wally.

"Ma!" whimpered Elmo. "Youse gotta do somethin', Ma."

"Don't whine to me about someone wanting to blow your stupid head off. The loony I'm with wants to shove a worm up my nose!"

The debris cloud drifted overhead and began to settle over us like coal-blackened smog. I swept my arms through the grit, trying to clear a path, but it enveloped us like a fog bank, masking sound and movement and breath.

I couldn't see a foot in front of me. Voices grew muffled. Coughing. Spitting. More coughing. "Don't anyone move," I called into the darkness. "Stay right where you are until the dust settles. And hold your pants up!"

I heard a sudden *oooffff*, followed by a scream and a muted *whomp*.

"What's going on?" I cried. "What's happening? Geez, some-body say something."

The debris cloud dissipated as quickly as it had appeared. Wally still held a dirt-covered Elmo captive, but Vinnie was spread-eagled on the ground with his face pressed to the parking lot pavement. Nana stood over him, saturated in dirt, looking like a half-smoked cigar as she leveled his gun at his left foot.

"I never shot no firearm before, but you so much as wiggle them ears of yours, I might have to give it a try."

"Aim for his brain," shouted Dick Teig, showing no mercy as he wrapped his arm around a sobbing Helen.

Nana frowned. "I thought I was."

As we crowded around our captives, Alice assessed the situation with a charitable heart. "Do you think you should be magnanimous and give him at least one chance before you shoot him, Marion? You could follow the example he set when he fired that warning shot into Dick's suitcase. Considering the circumstances, it was quite a thoughtful gesture."

"I wasn't aiming for the suitcase," snarled Vinnie. "I was aimin' for his head!"

TWENTY

"You should have pursued a career in law enforcement, Mrs. Miceli." Constable Tredinnick nodded toward the three members of the Cacciatore family who were squirming on the lawn by the spa, trussed up in blue-and-white crime scene tape like horror film mummies. "Very creative way to shackle the blighters."

"We thought about restraining them with belts but the guys were tired of having their pants fall down, so we went with the crime scene tape instead."

After freeing Osmond's suitcase from its web of belts and putting Margi in charge of returning everyone's cell phone, I'd called 999 to report a trifecta of incidents: the landslide, the end of a hostage crisis, and the capture of three dangerous criminals. Tredinnick had arrived just minutes ahead of a fleet of emergency vehicles whose personnel split their time between administering to the guests and evaluating the situation with the landslide.

The constable cast a troubled look about the debris-strewn mess in the parking lot. "I'm afraid Enyon's going to be gutted when he sees what's occurred in his absence. But at least he'll know what happened to Lance and why. You've done my work for me, Mrs. Miceli. I'm feeling like something of a numpty."

"It wasn't me—it was the Cacciatores. They forced a confession out of Caroline with their threats…and their guns."

An official in a hard hat and neon vest motioned to Tredinnick as he emerged from around the corner of the inn. "We'll be needing to designate this area off-limits," he announced as he joined us. "The whole bleedin' bluff could collapse straightaway, taking the inn with it, so I suggest you load up your vehicles and get these blokes out of here."

I stared at the official, dumbstruck. "Leave? But…but can we at least run back inside and get the rest of our stuff? The bloggers need their computers. I need my clothes. My tour director needs the guests' medical history forms and our travel docu—"

"No one goes back inside."

"But—"

"No one." He departed with a stern warning. "Step lively before we start accumulating casualties, Constable."

Omigodomigodomigod. This was a disaster. Everyone would be furious. No computers. No clothing. No footwear. No lodging. *Omigod.* No lodging?

On a brighter note, at least everyone had their cell phone back.

As Tredinnick escorted me across the parking lot, he slowed his steps, as if giving himself time to collect his thoughts. "You probably don't need to hear any more bad news right now, Mrs. Miceli, but I think you should know. The police in Exeter tracked down the woman who matched Ms. Zwerg's description, and…I'm afraid it wasn't her."

"It wasn't Bernice? But...but..." A vibrating lump formed in my throat. Tears sprang to my eyes. "We can't leave without her. I mean...we can't. Have you considered a search party? Or a silver alert? Do you have those over here? Or bloodhounds? My agency will absolutely foot the bill. Have you checked the villages outside Exeter? Or Lyme Regis? Maybe she's there already. Not a lot of women fit Bernice's description. She has to be here someplace. Doesn't she?" I gave him a pleading look as I dashed a tear from my cheek. "You have to find her, Constable. You just have to."

"We'll keep looking, Mrs. Miceli. I just want you to be prepared should we discover something you might not be expecting."

He led me to his squad car, where Caroline sat hunched in the back seat, her clothing and hair hemorrhaging grime like Pig-Pen hemorrhages dirt. He opened the front door for me. "Whatever is said about the situation here today, Mrs. Miceli, I commend your skill in disarming the Cacciatores without causing a single bullet to be spent."

"Disarming people is my grandmother's specialty, not mine," I sniffled as I slid onto the front seat.

"Your grandmother?"

"Tae kwon do. She has a black belt."

Caroline leaned forward in her seat. "The police will understand why I did it, won't they, Emily? They can't throw me in jail, can they? They have to know how terrified I was. They have to know I had no other choice. It was self-defense. You can see it was self-defense, can't you?"

Tredinnick leaned in, his gaze on Caroline. "Would you care to hear the results of the postmortem on Ms. Holloway, Ms. Good-friend? She died from traumatic brain injury, the likely scenario

280

being she was injured outside the hot tub and her body dumped into the water to make her death look like a drowning. But I suspect you'll be able to provide more details for me at the nick." He gave his head a disgusted shake. "How does such a right proper lady involve herself in the murder of two people?"

"I didn't kill two people." Caroline recoiled visibly. "I only killed one!"

A commotion erupted in the parking lot as Nana and company gathered in front of the squad car, clambering over each other to focus their cell phones on the tower of flames that had burst through the inn's thatched roof and was spiraling upward with the force of a raging inferno.

The inn was on fire.

"YouTube's gonna love this," whooped Dick Teig.

Jackie pivoted toward me, hands on hips, eyes narrowed, brows arched, mouthing words with such deliberate slowness, I could actually read her lips.

"I told you I needed to check my cake."

· · · · · · · · · ·

With the help of Constable Tredinnick, we found alternative lodging for everyone in two different B&Bs in Port Jacob, with its impossibly steep hills and bone-breaking cobblestones, settling everyone into their new digs before eight o'clock that night. And thanks to the gang's neurotic compulsion about keeping their belongings safe, everyone except Osmond escaped with fully packed luggage. The bloggers, Jackie, Wally, and I lost everything, but even though we didn't have a change of clothing, toothbrush, or underwear, we still had the critical documents we were carrying in our neck wallets. I encouraged Jackie and the bloggers to go out tomorrow and buy whatever essentials they might need with the knowledge that they'd receive full reimbursement for their purchases from Destinations Travel.

We might not have a stellar travel record, but we had really good insurance.

The bloggers were especially hobbled after their computers went up in smoke, but they located an internet café on a nearby street so they figured they could post their blogs in other internet outlets along the way without much hassle. I appreciated their being so flexible and felt more than a twinge of conscience about my thinking them capable of murder. But the niggling question still remained. If Caroline hadn't killed Heather, who had? And even though the bloggers might not have killed Lance, did that necessarily exonerate them from the thievery that had taken place? They could still be part of a criminal burglary ring despite their denials to Constable Tredinnick that they knew each other back in the states. But how could I prove they were lying?

And then there was the continuing worry with Bernice.

I knew it would feed her ego to know that every police force in Cornwall, Devon, Somerset, and Dorset was trying to track her down, but what if something really horrible had happened? What if she wasn't planning to surprise us in Lyme Regis? What if she'd been hit by a car and was lying dead in a gutter or a culvert? What would I say to the gang? What would I say to her family?

"Are you up for hitting the hardware store before we hit the sack?" asked Jackie as she peered out our bedroom window. Our B&B was located at the top of High Street, directly opposite Kneebone Hardware and Museum, so we had convenient access to all the local shops. "At least we can buy a couple of toothbrushes and some floss before we go to bed tonight. I refuse to invite the beginnings of tooth decay into my mouth simply because I've had a lousy day. The lights are on, so the store's still open."

We'd been so anxious to shower when we'd checked in that we hadn't obsessed about not having a set of clean clothes to change into, but Wally had come to the rescue when he appeared at our door with an armful of elastic-waist slacks and sweatshirts. "Your grandmother figured you'd need something that wasn't dirt encrusted, so she asked the group for clothing donations. Hope you can find something that fits."

Zoning out on the bed in a floral sweatshirt and swishy wind pants, I tried to recall what my Escort's Manual said in the section entitled *Paradise Lost: When Luggage Goes Missing.* I was pretty sure it advised the efficient tour escort to assemble care packets for the affected guests, rather like the ones hotels give out to guests whose bags have been lost in transit. A small gesture of goodwill might go a long way with the bloggers, but let's face it: I had a lot to make up for.

I swung my legs over the bed and stood up. "Okay, Jack. Let's do it."

We headed out the door—me in my outdated hand-me-downs and Jackie in high-water pants and a sweatshirt cluttered with bird decals and really big rhinestones. She glanced down at the bare skin exposed between her pant hem and ankles and grimaced. "How is it that I always seem to be traveling with midgets?"

Kathryn Crabbe emerged from the room at the end of the hall, off-balance and limping. She clutched the wall for support even before taking two steps.

"Are you okay, Kathryn?" I called.

"I was just on my way down to see you. I needed a break from beating the dust out of my streetclothes." She tightened the belt on the terrycloth robe that the B&B provided as an amenity to all its guests. "I can't go out, Emily. I can't try to maneuver over those cobblestones again. Not with these legs." She leaned over to rub her knees. "They're so stiff, I doubt I can walk down the hall. What am I going to do? I need clothes. Toiletries. But I'm as good as an invalid right now."

I took her arm. "Well, first thing we need to do is get you back in your room and seated so you don't fall down."

With Jackie on one arm and me on the other, she shuffled back to an armchair and sat down. "It's not so bad when I have support. Maybe what I need is a cane like Tilly's. Only until the stiffness goes away." She leaned back in her chair, the epitome of hopelessness. "If that's even doable."

"But it is." I offered her a reassuring smile. "Which do you prefer? A walking stick, a cane, or a wheeled rollator? Because I can have one here for you in a matter of minutes."

"How?"

"Tour escorts are very clever people, Kathryn. We have our ways." It also helped that the region's one-stop shopping place for ambulatory assistance devices was located across the street.

"Maybe a couple of walking sticks. They might help me blend in better with the locals."

Kathryn Crabbe wanting to blend in? I didn't see that coming.

"Okay. Walking sticks it is. Stay right where you are until we get back."

Her voice stopped us at the door. "You embarrass me with your kindness, Emily, because I don't deserve it."

I turned around to face her, temporarily speechless.

"I've been rude and inflexible and demanding…and I'm sorry. You'd think I'd be old enough to know better, wouldn't you? Apparently people who nurture oversized egos are rather slow learners."

She stared down at the hands she'd folded in her lap. "I used to be a nice person. I really did. But something happened along the roadway of my life and I turned into an old, dry, bitter stick. I should have tried to make your job easier rather than harder. I shouldn't have been so horrid to Heather. Her only sin was her taste in literature and her passion for pop culture, but I couldn't let it go. I felt offended by her very existence. I shouldn't have been so bullheaded about the fob-seal. It was hers, not mine. I've acted like a spoiled brat to everyone. I've shamed myself with my bad behavior, and I ask you to forgive me, Emily…if you can. I'm truly sorry that my participation in your tour has contributed to its ruin."

I flashed an indulgent smile. If she was asking for a second chance, she'd asked the right person. I'd lost track of how many second chances I'd been given to conduct the perfect tour—the one where there was no body count. "Say no more, Kathryn. Apology accepted. But I disagree with you on one issue. It'll take more than two unfortunate deaths, a missing person, a landslide, and a hotel fire to completely ruin our tour."

But we were really pushing the envelope.

· · · · · · · · ·

"Wow," Jackie whispered as we stepped out onto the cobbled sidewalk. Streetlights flickered on overhead, illuminating the twilight, while the fluorescent tubing that framed Kneebone's storefront windows brightened the shadows, spilling light onto the walkway and street. "Talk about throwing yourself on your sword. Do you think she meant it?"

"I'd like to think she did. Why? Don't you?"

"I dunno. Honestly, Em, I've always thought you are what you wear, but I'm stepping out in public for the first time in my life in apparel that I shall charitably describe as grandmother-wear, so I don't know who I am or what I think anymore. This outfit is really messing with my brain."

A redhead with long straight hair and heavy bangs sashayed up the hill and paused near the display window of the hardware store to take a long drag on a cigarette. With smoke jetting from her nose and mouth like exhaust from a muffler, she looked up and down the street as if she were waiting for someone.

"If I were you, Jack, I wouldn't be so quick to look a gift horse in the mouth, especially since Nana was thoughtful enough to—"

"Hey *you*!" Jackie yelled to the girl in an indignant voice.

Oh, no. Was she about to hop up on her soapbox and lecture the girl about the dangers of smoking? Yup. That's what the evening was missing—a treatise on the deleterious effects of chain-smoking on a woman's complexion. "Cool it, Jack. You're not the tobacco police. If she wants to light up, that's up to—"

Muttering a string of scathing epithets, she pounded across the cobblestones like a racehorse out of the starting gate, high-kicking and arms pumping, heading straight for the girl.

"Jack!"

The girl froze in place—paralyzed, no doubt, by the sight of a six-foot transsexual in high-water pants and rhinestones charging at her. Her cigarette fell from her lips as she opened her mouth to scream, but Jack tackled her to the ground before she could utter a peep.

"*Jack!* What are you doing? Stop it!"

I charged across the street, grabbing Jackie's shoulder as she pinned down the redhead. "Let her go! What's wrong with you?"

"She's wearing my wig!" With a burst of female outrage, Jackie reached down and ripped the wig off the girl's head, brandishing it in the air in the same way Jason might have brandished the Golden Fleece. "How did you get my wig?"

Omigod. This was Jackie's wig? Wow. It looked like something Cher might wear. I wondered how she'd feel about lending it out.

"It's not your wig. It's mine!"

"It was in *my* dresser drawer. How did it get from my drawer to your head?"

The girl kicked upward, struggling to free herself. "Get off me, you bleedin' Amazon!"

I glanced at their tangled limbs, my mouth falling open when I realized what else the girl was wearing. "My shoes! You're wearing my canary yellow ankle-tie flats. You…you stole my shoes!"

"I did not! I didn't steal nuthin'. Jory gave 'em to me."

Treeve Kneebone threw open the door of his hardware store, one hand on his walker, his voice booming out at us. "Wot's going on out here?"

"Jory?" I asked the girl as I threw a questioning look at Treeve. "You mean Jory Kneebone? Treeve's son?"

"Yeah, Jory Kneebone. He's me boyfriend."

TWENTY-ONE

"YOU NEED TO LOCK her up," demanded Jory Kneebone's girl-friend, Daisy. She stabbed a finger at Jackie. "Nutters like her shouldn't be allowed on the street. She's bleedin' barmy!"

Constable Tredinnick had hauled all of us off to the station house and seated us on opposite sides of a long wooden table—Daisy, Jory, and Treeve on one side; Jackie and I on the other—and then he'd pressed the record button on his outdated tape recorder.

"You know what makes *me* barmy?" Jackie shot back, eyes ablaze, spittle flying. "People who steal my stuff and treat it like their own!"

"Not another word out of either one of you," cautioned Tredinnick. He dragged a chair to the narrow end of the table and sat down, fingers tapping impatiently on the pitted wood. He trained a narrow look at Jory. "All right, young man, what are you on about?"

Jory swiped at the fringe of stick-straight bangs that drooped over his eyes. "It was Pops's idea. He made me do it."

Treeve yanked his knitted cap down over his eyebrows and groaned. I guess he'd expected his kid to withstand questioning for a little longer than half a nanosecond.

"What else did you nick besides the wig and the shoes?"

"Cash." Jory smiled proudly. "Splashed out in the cash department, I did. Twice."

"You *stole* the presents you gave me?" squealed Daisy, smacking him roundly upside his head. "That seals it, you bleedin' tosser. We're finished."

Jackie raised a finger. "Not to change the subject, but have you read the latest medical reports on concussions?"

"It was you?" I exploded, meeting Jory's unrepentant gaze. "You're the one who stole August's and Caroline's money? Here I was blaming my own tour guests for the thievery! Accusing innocent people. Concocting wild theories. Casting aspersions on their integrity! And all the time it was you?" I was sure I'd be even more angry when I got over being so embarrassed.

I'd been *sooo* wrong.

Again.

He grinned. "Well, it wasn't Pops. He uses a bloody walker. How would he get through the tunnels?"

"Tunnels?" questioned Tredinnick. "What tunnels?"

"The ones wot the smugglers used," Treeve spoke up. "The whole cliff is carved out like an ant farm. Where do you think the smugglers stashed their booty so it wouldn't be found? How do you think they carried it from the beach to the bluff without being seen? Through that sliver of cave at the base of the cliff, then up through the tunnels."

"Smugglers?" I gave him a squinty look. "Where do smugglers fit in? I thought the inn was the past hangout of highwaymen?"

"True, true." Treeve nodded. "The smugglers arrived on the scene after the highwaymen. Turned out to be a much more lucrative occupation."

"So you're suggesting that there's a whole network of tunnels beneath the Stand and Deliver Inn?" asked Jackie.

"I'm not *suggesting*," said Treeve. "I'm telling you for a fact. The tunnels were already part of the landscape, so when we decided to convert the farm to an inn, I says to meself, *Treeve, you old sod, why not update the things? Make 'em more accessible. Easier to use.* Jory did the work himself."

"Did I have a choice?" Jory scowled at his father. "Pops didn't want anyone to know wot we were doing, so he couldn't contract the work out. There was no one to give it a crack but me."

"Whoa," I said, making a T with my hands for a timeout. "You're the person who converted the farm to an inn? Not Enyon and Lance? You were the original owner?"

Treeve nodded. "Me…and me family before me."

"And no one thought to mention that?" I fixed Tredinnick with a frustrated look. "Not even after guests started dying and valuables went missing?"

Tredinnick shrugged. "How would former ownership of the inn have been pertinent to the case?"

"Well, it might have allowed us to put two and two together." I leaned forward on the table, giving Treeve the stinkeye. "So how did it work? Did the tunnels give you access to every room?"

"Sure did. Through a trapdoor in the closet floor. All me boy had to do was wait for a guest to vacate the room and the place was his to explore at his leisure."

"I couldn't do nothing until low tide though," Jory explained. "No place to land me boat at high tide. The beach gets flooded."

"How did you know when the rooms were vacant?" pressed Tredinnick.

Jory snickered. "I ran a pret-tee slick operation, Constable. I installed surveillance equipment just about everywhere."

Jackie sprang out of her seat like a giant jack-in-the-box. "You put surveillance cameras in our rooms?"

"'Course I put them in your rooms. I wouldn't be able to tell if you was in or out otherwise, now would I?"

I wrestled her back into her seat. She clenched her teeth. "You watched us undress?"

Jory looked affronted by the question. "No! I closed up shop before anything got X-rated. I'm not a freakin' perv."

I did a quick mental inventory of our room, unable to visualize any type of photographic equipment. "Where did you hide the cameras?"

"Stuck 'em in the teddies we left in the rooms for the new owners. Hid 'em in plain sight in the little glass eyes. Pops said it was a stroke of genius."

Jackie made a gagging sound. "That is so disgusting."

"Bugger that," argued Jory. "I ran a very posh operation. Outfitted quite a nice observation room under the spa with all me equipment, I did, so when you blokes headed to the dining room, I was ready to pop over to the inn and do me diddlin'."

"Nick their property, you mean," corrected Tredinnick. "You should be ashamed of yourself. And you!" He fired a contemptuous look at Treeve. "From respectable pig farmer and store owner to two-bit thief. Whatever happened to you, Treeve Kneebone?"

"I'll tell you wot happened," huffed Treeve as he hammered his fist on the table. "Austerity happened. The harder we work, the more the government takes away. I'm fed up!"

"Austerity hit all of us," reasoned Tredinnick, "but we didn't all resort to thievery."

"If it was good enough for me forebears, it's good enough for me," spat Treeve.

I stared across the table at him. "What are you talking about?" I searched the faces in the room for assistance. "Am I the only one who doesn't know what he's talking about?"

"I was sick of farming," boomed Treeve. "Too unpredictable. Long hours. Little return. And the pigs stunk. So, says I to meself, *Treeve, use wot little savings you've got to convert the place. Open an inn. The hospitality industry has to be easier than pig farming, and it's bound to smell better. Give it a throw.* So we got rid of the pigs and began remodeling the house and installing the spa, but when we were about halfway through, me nerves got wobbly. I'd be dealing with whingey guests and temperamental cooks and cleaning staff who might not show up, and it seemed like way too much work. So, says I to meself, *Treeve, if you sell the place, that doesn't mean you can't profit from it. Make a few adjustments to the tunnel system and bam! You'll be able to earn money the old-fashioned way: by stealing from unsuspecting strangers. Just like Sixteen String Jack used to do.*"

"Let me guess," I said as awareness dawned. "You're related to Sixteen String Jack? The infamous highwayman?"

"I am, and proud of it. I figured if he could make a living nickin' from the rich, why couldn't I? I should be quite good at it, shouldn't I? I mean, thievery's in me blood."

Jackie flashed a perky smile. "My ancestors cooked for English kings. I have haute cuisine in mine."

I raised my finger in the air. "Question: so if you sold the inn with the intention of living off the valuables you stole from the guests, why did you buy a hardware store?"

"I needed someplace to set up me museum now, didn't I? Besides, the price was spot on, and after I moved off the farm there seemed to be too many hours in the day, so I got bored with all me leisure. The life of a pensioner isn't all it's cracked up to be. Minding a store and tending me museum seemed a good way to occupy me time."

Tredinnick switched his attention to Jory. "If you set a room up for yourself under the spa, I'm thinking you might be involved in something that could be weighing pretty heavily on you about now. Tell me what happened to Ms. Holloway. It'll come out eventually. No sense postponing the inevitable."

Color drained from Jory's face, leaving his cheeks pasty white and his lips grayer than ash. "I didn't kill her," he choked out. "It was an accident. She was standing by the towels when I sneaked up through the trapdoor in the dressing room to make an adjustment on one of me surveillance cameras. I wouldn't have gone up if I'd seen her, but she was just outside me camera range. When she saw me, she screamed really loud and started running for the door. I didn't even try to chase her. All I could think was, 'Bugger me. What a cock-up. Pops is gonna kill me.' But she never made it to the door. She slipped on that wet spot on the floor, where the tub is leaking, and went down like a sack of rocks. Smashed her head up real bad." He pressed his palm against his forehead to simulate the injury. "She never got up again. I knew she was dead. I couldn't find a pulse, and her head was lying in a pool of blood."

"So that's your story?" asked Tredinnick. "She died in your presence but you didn't kill her?"

"No, I didn't kill her! I'm a thief, not a murderer. But I was afraid that if I left her on the floor like she was, you might start sniffing around me and Pops, trying to blame us for the faulty installation of the spa and such. So I decided to dump her body in the spa so you'd think she'd drowned. I mopped the blood off the floor with all the guest towels, and then I carried 'em back down to me room to get 'em out of sight and heaved 'em over the side of the boat on me way back to Port Jacob."

"You realize you've made things far worse for yourself with your intended coverup?" prodded Tredinnick.

"Wot's it matter? I'm done in anyway." He trained a damning look at his father. "And it's all your fault."

"Is not."

"Is so!"

"I suppose the two of you heard what happened at the Stand and Deliver a bit ago?" Tredinnick interrupted.

Jory swatted his hair out of his eyes again. "I haven't heard a thing these past couple of hours—except for Daisy's screams of ecstasy." His mouth slanted into a cocky grin. "Gave her a little taste of Port Jacob's finest, I did."

She smacked his ear with the back of her hand. "Port Jacob's finest bony arse, you mean. Bleedin' wanker. We are *so* finished."

"One of me customers said there was something dodgy happening on the coastal path, but he didn't say wot," said Treeve.

"A landslip," Tredinnick informed him. "The bluff collapsed into the sea to within a few meters of the inn, and the rest of it could go at any time."

Jory's grin vanished, replaced by contorted lips, wild eyes, and a strangulated sound that he hocked up from his lungs. "Bollocks!" He clamped his hands on his head. "Bollocks! Bollocks! Bollocks! You gotta get that woman outta there! She's in the room under the spa. If the whole bluff goes, she's gonna go with it!"

"What woman?" urged Tredinnick.

"The one with the bad perm and sandpaper voice."

I sprang out of my chair. "YOU'VE GOT BERNICE?"

"I didn't want her! But she walked into her room while I was looking through her odds and sods, so I had to do something with her. She saw me face. She could identify me! So I stuck a gag in her mouth, got rid of her cell phone—"

"You stashed it in her nightstand rather than steal it?" I interrupted. "What kind of thief leaves the electronic equipment behind?"

"Her phone was a bleedin' Android! I have me standards to uphold. So I dragged her into the tunnel with me and trussed her up so she couldn't escape."

Jackie gasped dramatically, hand splayed on her chest. "Just like *The Phantom of the Opera*. I wanted to audition for the part of Christine during my stint on Broadway, but I had the wrong plumbing back then."

Jory eyed her curiously. "Wot?"

She fluttered her fingers in dismissal. "Never mind."

"Bernice didn't run away?" I fisted my hands on the table, my gaze drilling into Jory. "You were holding her captive in your tunnel the whole time Constable Tredinnick and the rest of the country were looking for her?"

"Not the tunnel. Me surveillance *room*. It's a bit more high-class than the tunnel."

"Oh my God. You left an elderly woman bound and gagged and…and starving to death in your surveillance room for two whole days? What kind of monster are you?"

"I didn't starve her! At least, not up until today I didn't. I haven't been back since that girl died this morning. But I fed her while I was there. She particularly enjoyed the bourbon cream biscuits and the dark chocolate digestives."

"*You* stole my biscuits?" shrieked Jackie. "It wasn't Emily who ate her way through all my goodies?"

I gasped at the insinuation. "You thought *I* was a biscuit thief? Me? The person with the Catholic school background and active fear of Hell? How could you think I'd even be capable of doing anything that sneaky?"

"Because all my snacks disappeared. What else was I supposed to think? That the Keebler elves issued a recall? And *you*." She slatted her eyes at Jory. "You couldn't grab some cookies off the shelf in your own store? You preferred to steal mine? You little bottom-feeder. I want a refund. Right now!"

Jory ignored her outburst. "I warned your Bernice if she screamed for help while I was feeding her that I'd bop her a good one on her head. Would you believe she had the nerve to tell me that if she got a concussion as a result, she'd sue me? She's apparently read all the online medical reports so she knows her onions."

"Did you hurt her?"

"No! She's an old lady. I don't go around hurting old ladies, but I was tempted. When I pulled her gag out, she never shut up—going on about how she used to be a magazine model and how she's the reigning champion in some old pensioners' race and how she could actually look much younger but she can't order a special beauty cream from New Guinea anymore because of some moronic witch doctor. The woman never talks about anything but herself."

Jackie blinked her confusion. "What's wrong with that?"

"Don't you think she should have been polite enough to ask me something about meself? Like what me name was or where I lived or why I'd turned to a life of crime? No. She wasn't interested. She even wanted me to remove her shoes so I could admire how pretty her feet were as a result of her bunion surgery. She's...she's a bloomin' nutter! Although, in all fairness, her sandals were very nice."

Tredinnick jerked his thumb in the Kneebones' direction. "On your feet, gentlemen. I'm locking you up until I get back."

"What about me?" asked Daisy.

"Go home. And tell your parents I'll be stopping by to talk to them and you tomorrow."

Looking relieved to be escaping jail time, Daisy made a quick search of her pocketbook, retrieving something from the very bottom and slamming it down on the table in front of her. "Me ex-boyfriend probably nicked this, too, so I'm giving it back. I don't even know what it is, but he thought it was crackin'." She snorted with disgust. "Plug-ugly is more like it."

Trumpet-shaped and lavender-colored, it was mounted on a gold base with a ring through which a neck chain could be looped. "That's Heather's fob-seal," I cried.

"Well, she can have it back, but I don't know why she'd want it." Daisy held the seal up so we could see the curlicued initials on its underside. "See here? It looks like it's been scratched by a clowder of cats."

Tredinnick's voice oozed revulsion as he glared at Jory. "You nicked this from the dead woman's neck wallet after you saw her die?"

He had the decency to look slightly shame-faced. "It was hanging right there on a wall hook. Wot'd you expect me to do, ignore it? Wot kind of thief would do that?"

"You're bent as a nine-bob note," spat Tredinnick. "A bleedin' disgrace."

"Oh, yeah?" he railed as Tredinnick marched him and his father off to their cell. "Well, I'll tell you wot the real disgrace is, Detective Constable Tredinnick. It's those guests at the inn—the ones with the Iowa tags on their suitcases. No thief worth his salt could make two bob off 'em. Did they have cash lyin' around? No. Expensive jewelry? No. Pricey watches? No. They packed duff. Seedcorn hats, windsuits, and a weird hose and mask that I didn't want to touch because it looked like some pensioner's sex toy. It's not right, I tell ya. Honest thieves deserve a better selection of goods to nick."

"Brilliant," Daisy called out after them. "You bring me back a cheesy geegaw and leave the sex toy behind? Wanker!"

· · · · · · · · · · ·

Tredinnick communicated Bernice's whereabouts to the firemen who'd remained at the scene of the inn fire, so her rescue got underway immediately. Against his better judgment he allowed Jackie and me to ride back to the inn with him, so we were able to receive updates over his police radio while the rescue was in progress.

"Elderly woman bound and gagged on army cot," announced a voice amid a background of static.

"Air quality deteriorating."

"Physical status undetermined, but victim appears responsive."

Bzzzt. Bzzzt. Bzzzt.

"Removing gag."

Zzzzt...kreeeee... bzzzzt.

"Who are you calling elderly?" yelled Bernice in a voice that was even more scratchy than normal. "That's called age discrimination where I come from. What's your badge number, you moron? Just in case I decide to sue."

"Oh my God," I sobbed, tears welling in my eyes. "She's okay!"

For safety purposes we weren't allowed access to the parking lot, so Tredinnick parked his cruiser at the entrance to the driveway, where a host of rubberneckers had gathered to watch the dual spectacle of collapsing cliff and hotel conflagration. As we hurried down the drive on foot, the ambulance left the parking lot and sped toward us, slowing when Tredinnick flagged it down with his flashlight.

"You have room for another passenger?" he asked the driver.

"Hop in, Constable."

"Not me," he corrected. "Her. The woman you're transporting is on her tour. Can she ride along with you to hospital?"

"Front seat then. They're treating her in back."

When we arrived at the hospital, I caught only a glimpse of Bernice before they whisked her away. After watching long minutes tick by on the clock in the ER waiting room, I made a polite inquiry at the desk and discovered to my delight that Enyon was recovering from his appendicitis at this very hospital, so I made an unscheduled detour to his room to see how he was faring.

He looked up as I crept into his room, looking so forlorn and downtrodden that I realized there was no way I could compound his grief by sharing the disastrous news about his inn with him. "Hi there, stranger," I said as I clasped his hand. "You're looking pretty spry for a man fresh out of surgery."

"Your flattery falls on deaf ears, I'm afraid. I look a fright. I'm glad Lance isn't here to see me." His bottom lip quivered ever so slightly before he forced a half smile. "Appendicitis. Men my age don't have appendicitis. They suffer manly afflictions like heart attacks and cerebral hemorrhages. It's a bit embarrassing."

"Look at it this way," I teased. "You'll be left with a lovely scar to show off. It doesn't get more manly than that."

He sighed. "I suppose." He squeezed my hand. "Emily, dear, whatever are you doing here at this time of night? Are visiting hours still in effect?"

"Don't know. I didn't ask. I'm here with one of my tour guests actually, so while I wait on her, I wanted to poke my head in the door to say hello."

He nodded, his eyes registering somber resignation. "I do believe that tour guests are one of the downsides of the hospitality industry that no one ever talks about. They're obviously a dreadful burden. Falling ill. Having to be taken to hospital. Whinging about the food. Whinging about the accommodations. Whinging about broken pipes. Is there never an end to it?"

"She's here simply as a precaution."

He squeezed my hand harder. "Please accept my apologies for leaving you and Mr. Peppers to your own devices while our erstwhile constable raked me over the coals."

"I'm so sorry, Enyon. The whole process must have been terrible for you."

He lifted his shoulders in a nonchalant shrug, his voice taking on a faraway tone. "To be honest, I rather liked being in the nick. It was tidy in a Spartan kind of way, and quiet, and so much less chaotic than the inn, even with all the psychological tests they subjected me to. They served me three delicious meals a day plus afternoon tea, let me watch whatever shows I wanted on their expanded cable service, and Bess was there to cheer me up whenever I found myself slipping into melancholia. Unlike Lance, Bess isn't given to raising her voice, so that was quite refreshing. I even offered the good constable a few decorating hints—mostly about furniture arrangement and lighting, but the whole place could benefit from a new coat of paint. Sexy neutrals with bold accents would be quite splendid, but I doubt Treeve is *au courant* enough to keep the colors I'm thinking of in stock."

"Yeah. I don't think paint was one of his top priorities."

He sniffled pathetically. "Can I tell you something in confidence, Emily?"

"Of course you can."

"I hate owning an inn," he wailed, his features collapsing upon themselves in misery, tears glazing his eyes. "Have you heard of medical doctors completing their residencies, only to discover they don't like sick people? It happens in the hospitality industry, too. I hate being a B&B host. I bought an inn, but surprise, surprise: I hate tourists…the…the whingey, wretched, odious *sods*."

He dissolved into a blubbering torrent of tears. I stuffed a tissue into his hand.

"I agreed to the B&B for Lance, you know," he sobbed as he dabbed his eyes. "But now that he's gone, I'm left with a bleedin' white elephant to manage on my own." He gazed up at me, red-eyed and weepy. "What am I going to do? I don't want to go back there, Emily. I'd rather go back to the nick." He sniffed thoughtfully. "Do you think I should commit an actual crime so they could incarcerate me on a permanent basis?"

"No! But the situation at the inn has changed a bit since you left, so—"

"I'd bite off my arm to sell it," he reflected as he extended his palm to receive another tissue. "But the process takes so long. And I'd be snookered if no offers came along. Honestly, I wish someone would just take a match to it. At least the aftermath would leave me swimming in insurance money."

I brightened. "A lot of insurance money?"

He dabbed the corner of his eye. His expression grew wistful. "Enough to see me through the rest of my life. Plonker that he was, Lance believed in insuring property to the gills and then some."

"So...just out of curiosity, what would you do if you suddenly came into a financial windfall?"

"Do? Why, I'd..." A trace of a smile lifted the corners of his mouth. "I'd buy a cottage in the Lake District—a stone cottage with a large garden and little hothouse, and I'd go into the florist business. I've realized too late that I'd much rather spend my time with flowers than with tourists." He blinked away tears as he regarded me oddly. "Why are you smiling?"

"Because you're not going to believe what I have to tell you. Do you mind if I pull up a chair? This could take awhile."

After causing Enyon's spirits to soar deliriously by filling him in on the catastrophe at the inn, I offered hugs and goodbyes and returned to the ER to be told that Bernice had yet to be moved. I watched the clock in the waiting room tick off a couple of hours before I was cleared to proceed to her room, where I watched another few hours tick by. Bernice, for her part, was unaware of the clock in her room because she was sound asleep with an IV drip in her arm, monitoring devices attached to her chest, and an oxygen mask over her face.

Despite all that, however, she looked serene.

I envied her serenity. But even more than that, I envied her bed.

At some point during my vigil I must have fallen asleep in the chair because I was startled awake by a chorus of familiar voices.

"Was you really kidnapped and held hostage in a tunnel?" Nana asked a now-conscious Bernice.

Margi clasped her hands beneath her chin. "That's so romantic."

"Very reminiscent of a Daphne du Maurier novel," commented Tilly.

"That police fella thought you might have wandered off the cliff when you went missing," said Dick Teig. "But just so's you know, the edge of the cliff is a lot closer to the inn now, so if you get a mind to do that, you won't have so far to walk."

"Except that the inn isn't there anymore," lamented Alice.

"The shell's still standin'," clarified Nana. "It's the insides what got torched. And it's all on account of them Cacciatore folks what was holdin' us at gunpoint. It's a shame you missed it, Bernice, but bein' in a tunnel sounds like it was a lot more excitin'."

"Did you see how wide her eyes just got?" hooted Dick Teig, motioning toward her face.

"Looks like she wants to say something," said George.

"Too bad she's wearing that oxygen mask," observed Osmond. "You suppose she really needs it?"

303

"No touching the oxygen mask!" I warned as I popped out of my chair.

Lucille regarded her from the foot of the bed. "Since you're only able to speak with your eyes, Bernice, this might be a good time for you to process the really bad news with the least possible strain to your voice. Your cell phone is toast. You lost it in the fire."

"You wanna see the fire?" enthused Dick Teig.

Whipping out their phones, they began flipping through screens.

"Hold it!" My voice rang through the room with surprising authority. "C'mon, guys. You arrive at the hospital to visit Bernice and two minutes into the visit you're already grabbing your phones? What happened to comradery? To simple conversation? What happened to sentiments like 'We're glad you survived that horrifying experience and you're not injured, Bernice. We missed you when you were gone, Bernice. Is there anything we can do for you, Bernice?'"

"Maybe you didn't notice," Helen Teig said to me in an undertone. "She can't talk."

"It's on account of the oxygen mask, dear." Nana cocked her head to study the contraption better. "I never seen one that big before."

"I bet it's leftover from World War I," offered Margi.

"You're missing the point," I chided. "You don't need your cell phones at a time like this. Talk to her. Tell her what happened to you while she was missing. Remember how engaged you were with each other when you had your phones packed away and what a good time you had? Remember how nostalgic you got for the pre-cell phone days, when you actually spent time talking to each other? Do you really want to go back to the same old routine of having your noses stuck in your phones all the time and not giving a flip about what's happening around you?"

Shoe scuffing. Shoulder slumping. Gaze lowering.

Uff-da. Had I finally succeeded in getting through to them?

"So what do you say about putting your phones away and entertaining Bernice with a few personal stories that can't be found on the internet?"

They exchanged long, guilt-ridden glances with each other before Dick Teig looked at me and announced rather emphatically, "Nah." He held up his phone for Bernice's perusal. "Some fire, huh? I've already got twenty-three hits on YouTube. And that's only since last night."

"I've got twenty-six," boasted Dick Stolee.

"I titled mine *The Towering Inferno,*" said Osmond, "and my hits have already passed the century mark."

"Wasn't that the title of a movie?" asked Lucille.

"It certainly was," said Margi. "No wonder Osmond has so many hits. People think they're gonna see an old Steve McQueen flick."

"Osmond plagiarized a movie?" quipped Helen. "If he gets arrested for copyright infringement, who's gonna conduct our polls?"

Their voices rose to a crescendo as they fought to show Bernice their fire footage, arguing over whose clip would go viral first. Amid the chaos I heard the digital chime of my own cell phone, so I headed for the relative quiet of the corridor as I dug it out of my shoulder bag.

"Etienne? Is the retreat over? Did you get to meet the Pope? I've missed you so much. Please tell me you'll arrive in Lyme Regis when you're supposed to. I can't wait to see you."

"I love you, bella. Yes, I'm scheduled to arrive on time." A pause. "You sound a little breathless. Is anything wrong?"

"Wrong?" I hugged my phone to my ear as if, in doing so, I might allow his voice to wrap around me in a warm embrace. "What could possibly be wrong?"

THE END

© Photo Express

ABOUT THE AUTHOR

After experiencing disastrous vacations on three continents, Maddy Hunter decided to combine her love of humor, travel, and storytelling to fictionalize her misadventures. Inspired by her feisty aunt and by memories of her Irish grandmother, she created the nationally bestselling, Agatha Award–nominated Passport to Peril mystery series, where quirky seniors from Iowa get to relive everything that went wrong on Maddy's holiday. *Say No Moor* is the eleventh book in the series. Maddy lives in Madison, Wisconsin, with her husband and a head full of imaginary characters who keep asking, "Are we there yet?"

Please visit her website at www.maddyhunter.com or become a follower on her Maddy Hunter Facebook Fan Page.

Following is an exerpt from book 12
in the Passport to Peril series,

CATCH ME IF YUKON

"THAR SHE BLOWS!" SHOUTED Dick Teig in an effort to channel the spirit of Melville's infamous Captain Ahab.

Gliding through the waves in slow motion, plagued by flocks of screeching gulls, the humpback spewed a column of spray into the air to the excited ooohs and ahhhs of the hundred-plus guests aboard the tour boat *Kenai Adventurer.*

"Oh, wow," Dick enthused as he stood mesmerized at the starboard rail where the rest of us were shoehorned together, gawking into the water below, angling our cell phones left and right to avoid shooting video of each others' heads.

"This footage is going straight to YouTube," hooted Dick Stolee, who, as the group's tallest member, enjoyed the luxury of having the best unobstructed view. "You wanna bet this baby's going viral? The likes are gonna pile up faster than pancakes at a church breakfast."

"Didn't no one tell you?" my grandmother asked from farther down the rail. "We're not doin' YouTube no more. We found a new website what links to real global news agencies with real bylines, so we're sendin' our stuff there instead."

"We decided that for folks who've been doing this as long as we have, it was time to leave the ranks of YouTube behind and graduate to a more professional platform," explained George Farkas.

Nana nodded. "It's our best chance to join the big leagues before we die."

"How come nobody told me?" complained Dick as the whale arched its back and with a muted *whoooosh* sluiced downward into the ocean's depths, its fluked tail rising out of the water in an aquatic salute that made it appear more like a member of a synchronized swim team than a mammal whose massive bulk tipped the scales at a modest forty tons.

"We took a vote on it," ninety-something-year-old Osmond Chelsvig recalled. "At the gluten-free luncheon at the senior center last week. Weren't you there?"

"He was in the little boys' room," droned Dick's wife, Grace. "He's never going to get the timing of that water pill down right."

"I can't see a doggone thing," bellyached Bernice Zwerg in her ex-smoker's rasp from somewhere behind us. "Time for you rail hogs to stop being so selfish. Get out of the way. I can't see through you. I left my x-ray vision back on the bus."

I cranked my head around to find her standing behind Dick Stolee, where the only thing she had a breathtaking view of was the back of his jacket. Shuffling backward, I grasped her arm and dragged her through the horde of onlookers to position her in front of me. "How's that?"

She peered over the rail. "Where's Moby Dick?"

"Submerged."

"So how long do I have to stand here before he flashes us again?"

"Don't know. I don't think whales run on timers."

I'm Emily Andrew-Miceli, who with my former Swiss police inspector husband, Etienne, own and operate Destinations Travel out of Windsor City, Iowa. We cater to a subset of seniors who've marked "world travel" as the first item on their bucket lists, and we're proud to have a stable of twelve regulars from Windsor City who keep the agency in the black: eight fairly normal adults, one chronic complainer, two Dicks, and my eighth-grade-educated, computer savvy, lottery winning, martial arts–trained grandmother, Marion Sippel.

Filling up the remaining seats on our twelve-day Alaskan odyssey are seven Windsor City locals who are the founding members of a Norwegian-only book club that boasts the jaw-dropping distinction of having been in existence for over forty years. Their reading list isn't limited to Norwegian books, but club hopefuls have to verify their authentic Norwegian ancestry to join. Three of our regular guests—Lucille Rasmussen, Helen Teig, and Grace Stolee—have belonged to the group for a couple of decades, so it was on their recommendation that the other club members decided to sign up for our tour.

The girls must have forgotten to mention the unfortunate number of deaths we've experienced on our previous excursions.

Memory loss among the senior set does have its benefits.

Our boat was hovering close to the rock-ribbed shore of Aialik Bay in the Kenai Fjords National Park, a long inlet flanked by a spine of jagged mountains, towering evergreens that seemed to sprout up from the bed-rock, and distant peaks frosted with snow. The sky was cobalt blue, without a trace of a cloud. The sun was so blindingly bright that I needed to squint behind my sunglasses to avoid burning my retinas from the reflections off the water, which made picture-taking a challenge since I couldn't see what was on my display screen. I could be taking breathtaking close-ups of Dick Teig's thumb for all I knew.

"Humpbacks can swim up to twenty-five miles an hour if they get the urge," our captain announced in a subdued voice over the loudspeaker. I guess he didn't want to startle the eighty-thousand-pound behemoth that was lurking somewhere beneath our boat. "But most of the time they keep it between eight and ten, which is what I commonly refer to as cruising speed."

"I wonder how fast Moby Dick was swimming when he bit off Captain Ahab's leg?" pondered Helen Teig.

Bernice choked on a guffaw as she glanced at Helen. "You do realize Moby Dick wasn't real, right?"

"Moby Dick wasn't a humpback," offered Tilly Hovick in her former professor's voice. "He was a sperm whale. So you really can't compare."

"I wonder what kind of whale swallowed Geppetto?" asked Margi Swanson as she squirted out a stream of hand sanitizer to create a small germ-free zone on the rail.

"Probably the same kind that swallowed Jonah," theorized Lucille Rasmussen. "The kind that spits you back out."

"Sounds like some kind of involuntary gag reflex to me," mused Helen.

Bernice shook her head. "Morons."

The captain's voice broke out over the loudspeaker again. "Looks like a pod making its way toward us. Six or seven humpbacks. Starboard quarter." Then, in an obvious tease, "Y'all can swim, right?"

"Are we on the correct side?" asked Alice Tjarks as she visored her hands over her eyes to scan the water.

"We're on the right side," George spoke up.

"But what if the right side is the wrong side?" panicked Dick Stolee.

"Then we'll miss everything," fretted Dick Teig. "C'mon, guys. Other side of the boat!"

"But this is the right side," I objected as they stampeded across the deck to the opposite side, deserting their plum positions at the rail.

One of the advantages of living in a landlocked state is that residents aren't forced to learn unnecessary terms like starboard and port.

I switched my phone to video and aimed it in the general direction of the humpbacks as they glided together in their own version of a maritime flash mob, geysering water through their blowholes before slithering downward in their languid balletic dives.

"Hey, Emily, did you hear about the whale watching boat that sank in calm seas off the coast of Juneau last year?" asked book clubber Thor Thorsen as he bulldozed into the space relinquished by the gang. His camera whirred frenetically as he squeezed off a number of shots using a telephoto lens that was as long as my arm. "All the passengers got rescued, but the boat apparently went down like a rock. Don't know if they ever figured out what caused it to sink, but it makes you wonder if these tour boat companies sometimes underestimate the marine life around here."

My stomach bubbled disagreeably at his comment. Like I needed to hear that.

Thor Thorsen was an impressive physical speciman. Tall and broad-shouldered, with permanently ruddy cheeks and blond hair that was only slightly threaded with gray, his face was more intriguing than it was handsome, his wide-spaced eyes and flattened features making him look as if he had never recovered from an untimely collision with a closed door. He owned a luxury car dealership in town, but he'd recently turned the managerial duties over to his son so he could devote more time to retirement travel and his newfound hobbies, which appeared to be wildlife photography and promoting heartburn.

"Humpbacks aren't usually known for their destructive tendencies," countered Grover Kristiansen as he slid closer to me, his voice both tentative and monotone. A small-boned man attired in fatigue-green polar fleece and a wide-brimmed hat with a chin cord, he looked more like an aging Boy Scout than a former sales manager for a small business. "In fact, near Monterey, California, a group of whale watchers witnessed a pair of humpbacks trying to rescue a baby gray whale from a pod of orcas, and gray whales don't even belong to the same genus."

"Is that right?" Thor muttered with disinterest as he squeezed off a dozen more shots.

"There's also documentation that humpbacks have rescued Antarctic seals that were under attack from orcas," Grover continued with rising enthusiasm, "and seals aren't even the same species! Scientists think the whales display a higher order of thinking and feeling, just like the great apes, elephants, and humans. And that's because humpbacks have specialized spindle cells in their brains that—"

"Yeah, yeah," Thor cut him off. "You can keep talking, but I've stopped listening. Tell you anything?"

Grover stiffened at the slight but refused to be cowed. "It verifies that you have a very short attention span. You should work on that, Thor. Maybe it'll help you recommend an actual novel to the book club rather than selected articles from *Reader's Digest*."

"Two more pods headed our way on the port side," announced the captain. "This is kind of unprecedented, so we're going to idle right here for awhile longer so you can soak it up."

"This guy better know what he's doing," grumbled Thor as he quickly abandoned the rail to charge across the deck, followed by Grover, who chased behind him like a puppy. Which is when I noticed the woman standing beside the deck's orange life buoy station, eyes wide, a terrified expression on her little moon face.

"Mom?" I was trying to suppress the fact that my parents were accompanying us on this tour, but I had good reason. Mom's overprotective attitude in dealing with Nana was so over the top that I usually wore myself out running interference between them, which negatively affected my duties to the other guests. It was not the most efficient business model.

Mom waved stiffly as I walked the few steps to join her.

"Are you sure you want to stand this far back, Mom? You can't see anything."

"Of course I can see things, Em." She bobbed her head toward the shoreline. "Trees. Rocks. Water. The backs of passengers' heads."

"Have you seen the whales?"

"Oh, I imagine everyone on the boat has seen the whales."

I narrowed my eyes. "You haven't gotten close to the rail to see them, have you?"

"No, but don't concern yourself with me. I'm having a wonderful time."

In the daily routine of life, Mom usually chose martyrdom over simple fixes. I used to think her preference had something to do with her being Catholic and reading *The Giant Book of Saints* one too many times as a child. But I've come to realize that it's probably a genetic defect that originated with Nana's MacCool forebears, who always went out of their way to sacrifice their lives to avenge whatever minor slight had ruffled their kilts that day.

She switched her attention to the life buoy ring beside her. "I know you're not familiar with maritime devices, Emily, but would you have any idea how a person would go about detaching this thing if the boat started to sink?"

"The boat isn't going to sink, Mom. The tour company wouldn't still be in business if the whales went rogue and destroyed their boats on a regular basis."

"Of course not." She studied the orange ring with an analytical eye. "It's probably too small to fit around your grandmother anyway." She glanced left and right before lowering her voice to a whisper. "I don't know what she's been eating lately, but if she doesn't stop, all her elastic waistbands are going to need extenders. So—" she resumed her normal volume, "a life jacket would be much better. At least they're adjustable. Maybe the crew can spare a couple."

In addition to being obsessively preoccupied with Nana, Mom was obsessively preoccupied with order. Her idea of Nirvana was to be hired as a member of a FEMA team that was tasked with re-alphabetizing the canned goods and magazine sections of grocery stores after major earthquakes or, even better, very large book repositories such as the Library of Congress.

"I honestly don't think you need to take any extra precautions today, Mom. We're on a roll." I swept my hand skyward. "Glorious weather. Calm seas. Trust me, there's no way we're going to sink." Given my rather lengthy track record of being wrong about almost everything, I hated to speak in absolutes, but this time I knew I was right.

I hoped.

I checked my watch. "They should be serving lunch pretty soon, Mom. You wanna head down to the galley and find a seat before it gets too crowded?"

She trailed her fingers over the life preserver slowly, affectionately, as if it were a tiny ball of fur named Cottontail. "Will you promise that if something happens to me, you'll stop by the house to visit your father at least twice a week so he can practice talking to another human being? I'm afraid he might forget how otherwise. And watch your grandmother's diet. She has a nasty habit of bingeing on maraschino cherries."

"Mom, you're on vacation. This is supposed to be fun. So stop with the Grim Reaper references, will you? You're not facing imminent death."

"Of course I'm not." She flashed a perky smile. "Really, Emily, I can hardly contain myself. I'm absolutely having the time of my life. I don't think I've had this much fun since I color coded your father's sock drawer."

Which must have been a real knee-slapper considering the only socks Dad owned were black.

Leaving Mom to stand guard over the ship's most accessible life-saving apparatus, I went in search of Etienne to enlist his assistance in helping me round up the group for lunch. The advertised meal consisted of turkey wraps, chips, and fresh fruit, but for an additional twenty bucks we could order a platter of Alaskan king crab legs, complete with stainless-steel lobster cracker, moist towelettes, and bandages.

Unfortunately, my guys are spectacularly bad when it comes to wrestling with seafood that looks like the creature from the *Predator* movie. Removing husks from ears of sweet corn? Yes. Dissecting the legs of spiny crustaceans? Not so much.

Fear of shellfish is another consequence of being landlocked.

Not seeing Etienne at the port rail among the impenetrable wall of whale watchers, I poked my head inside the nearby observation cabin, with its indoor seating and huge viewing windows, to find the room deserted. That left only the main deck galley and bow to search.

Circling around the rows of passenger chairs that were bolted down mid-deck, I noticed Thor Thorsen's wife, Florence, sitting by herself, bundled up in a hoodie and tinkering with her cell phone. As physically unremarkable as Thor was impressive, she reminded me of everyone's favorite pair of slippers: plain, devoid of decoration, and a bit frayed around the edges, but blessed with the ability to soothe the sorest of feet. She was schlepping a jumble of camera lens cases that were skewed across the width of her chest, but she was so entangled in straps and nylon webbing that I hoped she didn't get snagged on some out-of-the-way hook and accidentally strangle herself.

She waved when she saw me. "Are you looking for Etienne?"

"Have you seen him?"

"You bet. Goldie was starting to feel a little queasy, so he and Margi escorted her down to the galley a few minutes ago. This is her first time on the ocean, and if she felt as bad as she looked, I bet it'll be her last. I would've taken her myself, but I didn't want to leave Thor high and dry without his equipment."

Florence was always looking to help someone. She'd received numerous citations from practically every organization in Windsor City for her leadership and outstanding community service, and had founded her own chapter of the Daughters of Norway, which many of my regulars belonged to. Word around town was that Thor often took advantage of her generous spirit, but if today was any example, she seemed perfectly content sitting by herself, lugging all his photographic equipment, while he enjoyed the sights.

I eyed the straps and cases hugging her body. "Is that stuff heavy?"

"Heavy, no. Cumbersome, yes."

I was tempted to ask why big, broad-shouldered Thor couldn't carry his own camera equipment, but I figured that was none of my business. "Have you seen the whales yet?"

She shook her head. "Doesn't look like anyone at the rail is too keen on giving up their spot, so I'll wait and see Thor's photos when we get back home. It'll be just like being there."

Yeah, why go through the hassle of paying a lot of money to see something firsthand when you could wait until it was over and see it vicariously from the comfort of your own sofa?

She waved her cell phone at me, her face a question mark. "I know the boat is equipped with satellite internet, but do you think it's working? I mean, I sent a couple of text messages to Lorraine Iversen back home and I thought they went through, but I haven't heard back from her yet, which is really unusual because she's as compulsive as I am about answering texts immediately."

"She's probably juggling a million medical issues at the moment, so I wouldn't worry too much. She got a lot dumped on her plate in the last few days." Lorraine's mother had broken her hip the day before our flight, so she'd had to cancel her reservation, leaving her husband, Ennis, to make the trip without her. "Give her time. Hospitals aren't known for having the best cell service. Too much concrete and steel."

"You're probably right. But still." She frowned at her phone. "It's just so unlike her. I mean, she's my best friend. I'd like to know what's happening so I can give her a little emotional support."

"Talk to Ennis. He might have an update that'll help ease your mind."

She nodded. "Sure. I…I just can't shake the feeling that something terrible—" Leaving the thought unfinished, she turned her cell phone off and stuffed it into the pocket of her hoodie. "Shutting the thing off might help, right? Sometimes I think it'd be better for everyone's peace of mind if the cell phone went the way of the dinosaur."

Closing her eyes, she inhaled a deep breath, then let it out slowly, as if she were in the cool-down stage of an exercise program. "There." She opened her eyes and forced a smile. "I feel better already."

But she didn't look better.

She looked as if she were carrying the weight of the world on her narrow shoulders…and the strain was about to crush her.

WWW.MIDNIGHTINKBOOKS.COM

From the gritty streets of New York City to sacred tombs in the Middle East, it's always midnight somewhere. Join us online at any hour for fresh new voices in mystery fiction.

At midnightinkbooks.com you'll also find our author blog, new and upcoming books, events, book club questions, excerpts, mystery resources, and more.

MIDNIGHT
INK

MIDNIGHT INK ORDERING INFORMATION

 ### Order Online:
- Visit our website www.midnightinkbooks.com, select your books, and order them on our secure server.

 ### Order by Phone:
- Call toll-free within the U.S. and Canada at 1-888-NITE-INK (1-888-648-3465)
- We accept VISA, MasterCard, American Express and Discover

 ### Order by Mail:
Send the full price of your order (MN residents add 6.875% sales tax) in U.S. funds, plus postage & handling to:

> Midnight Ink
> 2143 Wooddale Drive
> Woodbury, MN 55125-2989

Postage & Handling:

Standard (U.S. & Canada). If your order is:
> $30.00 and under, add $4.00
> $30.01 and over, FREE STANDARD SHIPPING

International Orders:
> $16.00 for one book plus $3.00 for each additional book

Orders are processed within 12 business days. Please allow for normal shipping time.
Postage and handling rates subject to change.

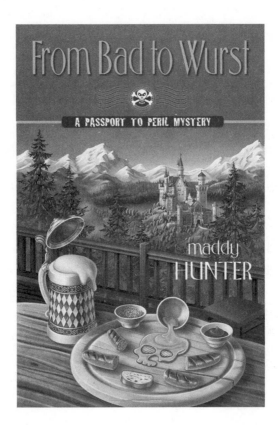

From Bad to Wurst

A PASSPORT TO PERIL MYSTERY

maddy HUNTER

FROM BAD TO WURST
Maddy Hunter

It's Oktoberfest and the globetrotting Iowa seniors are sharing their Sounds of Music adventure with several oompah bands whose dream of performing in a famous German beer hall is about to be realized. But when a deadly relic from wartime Munich rains disaster on the group, their dreams are shattered—until an unlikely guest offers them new hope.

The tour hits a sour note when tragedy strikes a guest who knew the musicians' most guarded secrets. Was the death an unfortunate accident or something more sinister? As the group travels from the beer tents of Munich to the fairytale castle of Mad King Ludwig, Emily strives to restore harmony. But with the situation escalating out of control, could the gang be looking at a terrible end to their German interlude?

978-0-7387-4034-8 $14.99

Fleur de Lies

A PASSPORT TO PERIL MYSTERY

maddy HUNTER

Fleur de Lies
Maddy Hunter

When intrepid travel agency owner Emily Andrew-Miceli takes her band of tech-savvy seniors to France, they say bonjour by cruising down the Seine River. Along for the ride are a colorful cast of cruise-goers, including four sales reps who are the creme de la creme of the cosmetic industry and a group of morticians looking for a little joie de vivre as they sort out business conflicts.

But once a guest is found dead along Normandy's famed Alabaster coast, Emily bids adieu to the hopes of a fatality-free trip. Was it a mishap? Or was murder the entree du jour? Traveling from the medieval alleyways of Rouen to Monet's famous water lily garden, Emily must untangle a web of lies that began a half century ago on the very eve of the D-Day invasion.

978-0-7387-3798-0 $14.99

Bonnie of Evidence

A PASSPORT TO PERIL MYSTERY

maddy HUNTER

BONNIE OF EVIDENCE
Maddy Hunter

Emily Andrew-Miceli, travel escort extraordinaire, and her husband, Etienne, are leading a merry band of globetrotting seniors on a tour of Scotland's Highland and islands. In addition to the usual haggis tasting and kilt shopping activities, Emily has organized a high-tech scavenger hunt—her own version of the Highland games that soon turns into all-out clan warfare. When one feuding team member is found dead, Etienne—a former police detective—suspects an allergic reaction. But upon discovering that the victim's underhanded tactics may have accidentally unleashed an ancient curse, Emily realizes she'll need to have a truly brave heart to survive this ill-fated fling.

978-0-7387-2705-9 $14.99